big brother

also by lionel shriver

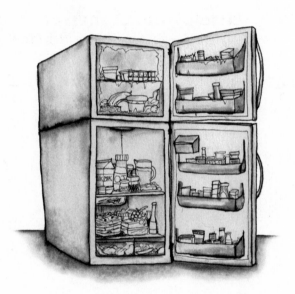

big

a novel

brother

lionel
shriver

HARPER

www.harpercollins.com

HarperCollins books may be purchased for educational, business, or sales promotional use. For information, please e-mail the Special Markets Department at SPsales@harpercollins.com.

FIRST EDITION

Designed by William Ruoto

Illustrations by Dana Mendelson

Library of Congress Cataloging-in-Publication Data has been applied for.

ISBN: 978-0-06-145857-6

13 14 15 16 17 OV/RRD 10 9 8 7 6 5 4 3 2 1

To Greg—who was unfailingly, improbably glad for anything good that ever happened to me, and in the face of whose drastic, fantastic, astonishing life any fiction pales.

The dieting industry is the only profitable business in the world with a 98 percent failure rate.

—eatingdisorderfoundation.org

I: Up

chapter one

I have to wonder whether any of the true highlights of my fortysome years have had to do with food. I don't mean celebratory dinners, good fellowship; I mean salivation, mastication, and peristalsis. Oddly, for something I do every day, I can't remember many meals in detail, while it is far easier for me to call up favorite movies, faithful friendships, graduations. It follows, then, that film, affinity, and education are more important to me than stuffing my face. Well done, me, you say. But were I honestly to total the time I have lavished on menu planning, grocery shopping, prep and cooking, table setting, and kitchen cleanup for meal upon meal, food, one way or another, has dwarfed my fondness for *Places in the Heart* to an incidental footnote; ditto my fondness for any human being, even those whom I profess to love. I have spent less time thinking about my husband than thinking about lunch. Throw in the time I have also spent ruing indulgence in lemon meringue pies, vowing to skip breakfast tomorrow, and opening the refrigerator/stopping myself from dispatching the leftover pumpkin custard/then shutting it firmly again, and I seem to have concerned myself with little else but food.

So why, if, by inference, eating has been so embarrassingly central for me, can I not remember an eidetic sequence of stellar meals?

Like most people, I recall childhood favorites most vividly, and like most kids I liked plain things: toast, baking-powder biscuits, saltines. My palate broadened in adulthood, but my character did not. I am white rice. I have always existed to set off more exciting fare. I was a foil as a girl. I am a foil now.

I doubt this mitigates my discomfiture much, but I have some small excuse for having overemphasized the mechanical matter of sustenance. For eleven years, I ran a catering business. You would think, then, that I could at least recall individual victories at Breadbasket, Inc. Well, not exactly. Aside from academics at the university, who are more adventurous, Iowans are conservative eaters, and I can certainly summon a monotonous assembly line of carrot cake, lasagna, and sour-cream cornbread. But the only dishes that I recollect in high relief are the disasters—the Indian rosewater pudding thickened with rice flour that turned into a stringy, viscous vat suitable for affixing wallpaper. The rest—the salmon steaks rolled around somethingorother, the stir-fries of thisandthat with an accent of whathaveyou—it's all a blur.

Patience; I am rounding on something. I propose: food is by nature elusive. More concept than substance, food is the *idea* of satisfaction, far more powerful than satisfaction itself, which is why diet can exert the sway of religion or political zealotry. Not irresistible tastiness but the very failure of food to reward is what drives us to eat more of it. The most sumptuous experience of ingestion is in-between: remembering the last bite and looking forward to the next one. The actual eating part almost doesn't happen. This near-total inability to deliver is what makes the pleasures of the table so tantalizing, and also so dangerous.

Petty? I'm not so sure. We are animals; far more than the ancillary matter of sex, the drive to eat motivates nearly all of human endeavor. Having conspicuously triumphed in the competition for resources, the fleshiest among us are therefore towering biological success stories. But ask any herd of overpopulating deer: nature punishes success. Our instinctive saving for a rainy day, our burying of acorns in the safest and most private of hiding places for the long winter, however prudent in its way, however expressive of Darwinian guile, is killing my country. That is why I cast doubt on whether the pantry, as a subject, is paltry. True, I sometimes wonder just how much I care about my country. But I care about my brother.

A ny story about a sibling goes far back indeed, but for our purposes the chapter of my brother's life that most deserves scrutiny began, aptly, at lunch. It must have been a weekend, since I hadn't already left for my manufacturing headquarters.

As usual in that era, my husband Fletcher had come upstairs on the early side. He'd been getting up at five a.m., so by noon he was famished. A self-employed cabinetmaker who crafted lovely but unaffordable one-of-a-kind furniture, he commuted all the way to our basement, and could arise whenever he liked. The crack-of-dawn nonsense was for show. Fletcher liked the implied rigor, the façade of yet more hardness, fierceness, discipline, and self-denial.

I found the up-and-at-'em maddening. Back then, I hadn't the wisdom to welcome discord on such a minor scale, since Fletcher's alarm-clock setting would soon be the least of our problems. But that's true of all *before* pictures, which appear serene only in retrospect. At the time, my irritation at the self-righteousness with which he swept from bed was real enough. The man went to sleep at nine p.m. He got eight hours of shut-eye like a normal person. Where was the self-denial?

As with so many of my husband's bullying eccentricities, I refused to get with the program and had begun to sleep in. I was my own boss, too, and I detested early mornings. Queasy first light recalled weak filtered coffee scalded on a hot plate. Turning in at nine would have made me feel like a child, shuttled to my room while the grown-ups had fun. Only the folks having fun, all too much of it, would have been Tanner and Cody, teenagers not about to adopt their father's faux farming hours.

Thus, having just cleared off my own toast and coffee dishes, I wasn't hungry for lunch—although, following the phone call of an hour earlier, my appetite had gone off for other reasons. I can't remember what we were eating, but it was probably brown rice and broccoli. With a few uninteresting variations, in those days it was always brown rice and broccoli.

At first, we didn't talk. When we'd met seven years before, our comfort with mutual silence had been captivating. One of the things that had once put me off about marriage was the prospect of ceaseless chat. Fletcher felt the same way, although his silence had a different texture than mine: thicker, more concentrated—churning and opaque. This gave his quiet a richness, which dovetailed nicely with my cooler, smoother calm. My silence made a whimsical humming sound, even if I didn't actually hum; in culinary terms, it resembled a light cold soup. Darker and more brooding, Fletcher's was more of a red wine sauce. He *wrestled* with problems, while I simply solved them. Solitary creatures, we never contrived conversation for the sake of it. We were well suited.

Yet this midday, the hush was of dread and delay. Its texture was that of sludge, like my disastrous rosewater pudding. I rehearsed my introductory sentence several times before announcing aloud, "Slack Muncie called this morning."

"Who's Mack Muncie?" asked Fletcher distractedly.

"Slack. A saxophonist. From New York. I've met him several times. Well regarded, I think—but like most of that crowd, has trouble making ends meet. Obliged to accept wedding and restaurant gigs, where everyone talks over the music." All of this qualified as the very "making conversation" I claimed to avoid.

Fletcher looked up warily. "How do you know him?"

"He's one of Edison's oldest friends. A real stalwart."

"In that case," said Fletcher, "he must be very patient."

"Edison's been staying with him."

"I thought your brother had an apartment. Over his jazz club." Fletcher imbued "his jazz club" with skepticism. He didn't believe Edison ever ran his own jazz club.

"Not anymore. Slack didn't want to get into it, but there's some—story."

"Oh, there's sure to be a *story*. It just won't be true."

"Edison exaggerates sometimes. That's not the same as being a liar."

"Right. And the color 'pearl' isn't the same as 'ivory.'"

"With Edison," I said, "you have to learn how to *translate*."

"So he's mooching off friends. How's this for *translation*:

your brother's homeless." Fletcher habitually called Edison "your brother." To my ear that decoded, "your problem."

"Sort of," I said.

"And broke."

"Edison has been through thin patches before. Between tours."

"So because of some mysterious, complicated story—like not paying the rent—you brother has lost his apartment, and now he's couch surfing."

"Yes," I said, squirming. "Although he seems to be running out of couches."

"Why did this *Slack* person call, and not your brother himself?"

"Well, I think Slack has been incredibly generous, though his apartment is small. A one-bedroom, where he also has to practice."

"Honey. Spit it out. Say whatever it is that you don't want to tell me."

I intently chased a floret, too undercooked to fork. "He said there isn't enough room. For the two of them. Most of their other colleagues are already doubled up, or married with kids, and—Edison doesn't have anywhere else to go."

"Anywhere else but *where?*"

"We have a guest room now," I pleaded. "Nobody ever uses it, besides Solstice every two years. And, you know—he's my *brother.*"

A contained man, Fletcher seldom looked visibly irked. "You say that like playing a trump."

"It means something."

"Something but not everything. Why couldn't he stay with Travis? Or Solstice?"

"My father is impossible and over seventy. By the time my sister was born, Edison was nearly out of the house. He and Solstice barely know each other."

"You have other responsibilities. To Tanner, to Cody, to me. Even"—a loaded pause—"to Baby Moronic. You can't make a decision like this by fiat."

"Slack sounded at his wit's end. I had to say something."

"What you had to say," said Fletcher levelly, "was, 'I'm sorry, but I have to ask my husband.'"

"Maybe I knew what you'd say."

"And what was that?"

I smiled, a little. "Something like, 'Over my dead body.'"

He smiled, a little. "Got that right."

"I realize it didn't go that well. The last visit."

"No. It didn't."

"You seemed to get on the wrong side of each other."

"There was no 'seeming.' We did."

"If it were just anybody, I wouldn't ask. But it isn't. It would mean so much to me if you tried a little harder."

"Got nothing to do with trying. You like someone, or you don't. If you're 'trying,' you don't."

"You can give folks a break. You do that with other people." I took a moment to reflect that in Fletcher's case this wasn't always true. He could be harsh.

"Are you telling me that throughout this negotiation you never talked to your brother directly? So his friend is trying to offload the guy behind his back."

"Maybe Edison's embarrassed. He wouldn't like asking favors of his little sister."

"Little sister! You're forty years old."

An only child, Fletcher didn't understand about siblings—how set that differential is. "Sweetheart, I'll still be Edison's *little sister* when I'm ninety-five."

Fletcher soaked the rice pan in the sink. "You've got some money now, right? Though I'm never too clear on how much." (No, he wouldn't have been clear. I was secretive.) "So send him a check. Enough for a deposit on some dump and a couple of months' rent. Problem solved."

"Buy him off. Bribe him to stay away from us."

"Well, he wouldn't have much of a life here. You can't say Iowa has a 'jazz scene.'"

"There are venues in Iowa City."

"Pass-the-hat gigs for a handful of cheapo students aren't going to suit Mr. Important International Jazz Pianist."

"But according to Slack, Edison isn't—'in the best form.' He says Edison needs—'someone to take care of him.' He thinks my brother's confidence has taken a knock."

"Best news I've heard all day."

"My business is doing well," I said quietly. "That should be good for something. For being generous." *The way I've been generous with you*, I almost added, *and with kids who are now my children too*, but I didn't want to rub it in.

"But you're also volunteering the rest of this family's generosity."

"I realize that."

Fletcher leaned on either side of the sink. "I'm sorry if I seem unfeeling. Whether or not the guy gets on my nerves, he's your brother, and you must find it upsetting, his being down on his luck."

"Yes, very," I said gratefully. "He's always been the hot shot.

Being strapped, straining his friends' hospitality—it feels wrong. Like the universe has turned on its head." I wasn't about to tell Fletcher, but Edison and Slack must have fallen out, since the saxophonist's urgency had been laced with what I could only call, well—disgust.

"But even if we did decide to take him in," said Fletcher, "*and we haven't*—the visit couldn't be open-ended."

"It can't be conditional, either." If I was going to think that way, and I preferred not to, I had amassed, as of the previous couple of years, most of the power in our household. I disliked having power, and in ordinary circumstances rather hoped that if I never exercised this baffling clout it would go away. For once, however, the novel agency was useful. "Saying, 'only for three days,'" I said, "or 'only for a week.' That doesn't sound gracious, but as if we can only stand his company for a limited period of time."

"Isn't that the truth?" Fletcher said curtly, leaving the dishes to me. "I'm going for a ride."

O f course he was going for a ride. He rode his bicycle for hours almost every day—or *one of* his bicycles, since he had four, competing with unsold coffee tables for limited space in a basement that had looked so cavernous when we moved in. Neither of us ever mentioned it, but I'd bought him those bikes. Technically, we pooled our resources. But when one party contributes the contents of an eyedropper and the other Lake Michigan, "pooling" doesn't seem the right word, quite.

Ever since my husband had started cycling obsessively, I wouldn't go near my own ten-speed clunker, by then gathering dust with deflated tires. The neglect was of my choosing, but didn't feel that way. It was as if he'd stolen my bike. Were I ever to have dragged the thing upstairs, greased the chain, and wended down the road, slowly and not very far, he'd have made fun of me. I preferred to skip it.

Every time Fletcher went for a ride I got annoyed. How could he stand the boredom? He'd come home some afternoons in a state of brisk satisfaction that his time had improved, usually by a few seconds. Churning the same route through the cornfields to the river a smidgeon faster was of no earthly consequence to anyone. He was forty-six, and soon the computer on his handlebars would simply track his disappointment in himself. I didn't like to think that I begrudged him something all his own, but he had the furniture making, which was private enough. He used those rides to shut me out.

I felt so guilty about this annoyance that I went to lengths to disguise it, forcing myself to *suggest* he go for a ride in order, say, to get out of his system some frustration with Tanner, "since it makes you feel so much better." But a too-lilting falsetto gave my falsity away. Most confounding: he *liked* that the cycling annoyed me.

Clearly, I was a bad wife. Aerobic jaunts would lengthen his life. After Cleo, his ex, went so bizarrely off the deep end, Fletcher had grown ever more consumed with control, and as obsessions went the cycling was harmless. Between exercise and his stringent diet, my husband had lost the tiny roll at his middle for which my own mashed potatoes and muffins had been to blame. Yet I'd cherished that little roll, which had softened him in a larger sense. By soliciting forgiveness, the gentle excess had seemed also to dispense it.

I required that forgiveness in some quantity. During the previous three years I must have put on about twenty pounds (I was loath to stand on a scale and confront an exact number). When running Breadbasket I'd been pretty thin. In the catering trade, food has a way of becoming repulsive; a vat of cream cheese is indistinguishable from a batch of plaster. But in my subsequent endeavor, the Mexicans on my staff were forever bringing trays of tamales and enchiladas into work. I'd cooked on my feet; now I sat in my office. Thus I'd come to squander an appalling proportion of my mental time on empty vows to cut down to one meal a day, or on fruitless self-castigation over a second stuffed pepper at lunch. Surely on some unconscious, high-frequency level other people could hear the squeal of this humiliating hamster wheel in my head, a piercing shrill that emitted from every other woman I passed in the aisles of Hy-Vee.

It wasn't fair, but I blamed Fletcher for those twenty pounds. I may have been a quiet sort who hugged the sidelines, but that didn't mean I was a pushover. I was the kind of person at whom you could finger-wag and tut-tut-tut, who wouldn't talk back, who would submit to all manner of browbeating while seeming to take it all in like a good little camper, and you'd walk away and think, *There, that's put her straight*, and then I'd sift off and blithely do whatever you'd just told me not to.

That defiant streak had backfired when I started noshing pointedly between meals on whatever entire food group Fletcher had recently disavowed. (The repudiation of cheese was deadly. The day after that announcement, I returned from the supermarket with half a wheel of Brie.) His spurning of the very dishes that had entranced him during our courtship and early marriage—banana cream pie, homemade deep-dish pizza—hurt my feelings. I shouldn't have conflated love and food, but that's a mistake women have made for centuries, so why should I be any different? I missed cooking, too, which I found therapeutic. Hence I still baked an occasional coconut layer cake, which Fletcher would boycott, and even the kids would avoid as their father glowered nearby. Well, someone had to eat that cake. Fatally, I felt sorry for it.

We had at least evolved a ritual compromise. From each contraband confection, I cut a one-bite *amuse-bouche*, arranging it with a dab of whipped cream, a garnish of mint, and a couple of pristine fresh raspberries on a large china dessert plate with a sparkling silver fork. This I would leave in the middle of our prep island, the way kids put out cookies for Santa, then make myself scarce. Fletcher would never take the bait while I was watching; still, it meant more to me than I can say that these illicit samplers of what he now deemed "toxic" vanished within the hour.

Strictly speaking, as a nutritional Nazi my husband had grown more attractive, but I'd been attracted to him before. Besides, a pointiness was now more pronounced. He had a high forehead and long oval face; shorn to a prickly furze to minimize the balding, his head was bullet-shaped. His long, strong nose in profile looked like a checkmark, and the wire-rimmed glasses added a professorial sharpness. Some strict, censorious quality had entered the triangular geometry of his wide shoulders and newly narrow waist, so that simply being in his physical presence made me feel chided.

As I collected our dishes, it bothered me that Fletcher hadn't stayed to tidy the kitchen, which wasn't like him. Commonly we dispatched cleanup with the interlocking fluidity of synchronized swimmers. We were at our best working side by side—neither of us understood or relished "leisure" time—and my fondest memories were of just this sort of cleanup on a grand scale. When we first started dating, on nights I'd catered a big buffet Fletcher would install Tanner and Cody in sleeping bags on my living room floor, so he could help with the kitchen. (When I first saw him shake his hands at the sink—thrusting fingers downward *splat-splat*, a small, instinctive motion that ensures you don't dribble water all over the floor on the way to drying your hands on the dishtowel—I knew this was the man I would marry.) Swabbing counters, sealing leftovers, and rinsing massive mixing bowls, he never complained; he never had to be told what to do. He only took breaks to sidle behind me as I removed another set of warm tumblers from the dishwasher and kiss my neck. Believe it or not, those cleanups in spattered aprons were romantic, better than champagne and candlelight.

Such memories in mind, I could hardly begrudge sudsing the broccoli steamer after lunch for two. I reviewed our conversation. It could have gone worse. Fletcher might himself have announced "over my dead body"; I'd slyly said it for him. I'd never asked outright, "Is it okay if my brother stays in our house for a while?" He'd never said yes or no.

Our house. Of course, it was our house.

Having rented most of my life, I still hadn't shaken the impression that this address on Solomon Drive belonged to someone else; I kept the place fanatically neat as if the real owners might walk in any time unannounced. The house was larger than we required; the kitchen's plenitude of cabinets invited the purchase of pasta- and bread-making machines that we'd use once. Deserving of the contemptuous tag *McMansion*, our new home had been an overreaction to the cramp of Fletcher's tract rental, one of those "temporary" resorts men seek post-divorce, from which unless a new woman puts her foot down they never move. I'd been flushed with awe that I could suddenly afford to buy a house, in cash no less, and in some ways I bought it simply because I could.

Also, I'd wanted to find Fletcher a workspace. Furniture was his passion, so I bought his passion for him. Naïve in the ways of money, I couldn't have known beforehand how much he would resent me for it.

Earlier in our marriage, Fletcher had worked for an agricultural company that made genetically modified seed. I'd been keen to enable him to quit because he wasn't a natural salesman—not from environmentalist aversion to fiddling with nature, or political outrage that corporate America wanted to patent what was once literally for the picking. I didn't hold many opinions. I didn't see the point of them. If I opposed the production of non-germinating disease-resistant corn, it would still be sold. I considered most convictions entertainment, their cultivation a vanity, which is why I rarely read the newspaper. My knowing about an assassination in Lebanon wouldn't bring the victim to life, and given that news primarily aggravated one's sense of helplessness I was surprised it was so widely heeded. Refusal to forge views for social consumption made me dull, but I loved being dull. Being of no earthly interest to anyone had been a lifelong goal.

In kind, this brick neocolonial had no character. It was newly built, its maple floors unscarred. I adored its unstoried blankness. The sockets were solidly wired, and everything worked. I'd never courted character on my own account, save in the sense of being disinclined to shoplift or cheat on my husband; Edison was the one who sought the designation "a real character," and he could have it. I gloried in anonymity and by then violently resented that the glare of an uninvited public spotlight had turned me into someone in particular for other people. (For pity's sake, you'd think after purposefully burying myself in the very middle of the country the least I could expect was to be inconspicuous.) I had enough history, and with the lone exception of Edison himself my instinct regarding the past was to draw the shade.

The big, lobotomized house formed the perfect neutral backdrop against which Fletcher's furniture could stand out. At this point my husband's handiwork had replaced most of the department-store appurtenances of our original combined households. (This joining of domestic forces was the first time in my life that someone had helped me move. With ferocious efficiency, Fletcher could carton a room in an afternoon, which has to be even more romantic than prizing the fiddly scraps from the food processor.) So lithe were his creations that whenever I walked into the living room the furniture seemed to have been grazing on throw rugs moments before. Its back corners curled like stag horns, bowed legs prancing on pared feet, the couch was weighted down with pillows, without which the skittish creature might have cantered out the door.

Though Fletcher liked to think he was improving, my favorite piece was one of his first. We called it the Boomerang. Its red leather cushion was oval. The rail forming the contiguous arms and back slooped high on the right, then arced down on the left, until the far end of the left-hand arm almost touched the floor. The chair looked as if it had been hurled. The slats supporting the great rising back line were also curved—laminated Macassar ebony, rosewood, and maple that he'd soaked for a week to bow. The Boomerang was a talisman of sorts. Most people who've refined a skill may cling to such a touchstone: early proof they've got the goods. The object to which they can always refer when a current effort is foundering: *See? If you can do that, you can do anything.* I'd no equivalent myself, because I didn't care about product. I liked process. Be it a marmalade cake or the absurd merchandise I sold then, output was chaff to me the instant of completion. I found finishing projects perfectly awful.

After scrubbing the beige film from the rice pan, I peered out the front window. It had started to rain, but that never drove my intrepid husband home. Safe in my solitude, I crept upstairs to my home office and booked a plane ticket between LaGuardia and Cedar Rapids, choosing an arbitrary return date that we could always change. I wrote a check for five hundred dollars with "incidentals" scrawled in the lower-left-hand corner. Enclosing the check and e-ticket printout, I addressed a FedEx mailer to Edison Appaloosa, care of the address Slack had dictated that morning, and booked a pickup on my account.

My having bought this house with the proceeds of my offbeat business two years before might have meant that I had the "right" to install my brother in its guest room without permission. But pulling fiscal rank struck me as vulgar and undemocratic. There were three Feuerbachs in that house, and only one Halfdanarson.

What called me to run roughshod over Fletcher's opposition was something else. I was not, as a rule, held hostage to family. At some point I would make the disagreeable discovery of how deep a tie I retained to my father, but not until he died; meantime, I was free to find him unbearable. My sister Solstice was sufficiently my junior that I could almost be her aunt, and it was only at her insistence that she visited me in Iowa every other summer. (She grew up in the fractured remains of a nutty, failed family, on which she'd long tried to impose a more appealing cliché. So she was the only one who bought presents, sent cards, and paid visits whose perfect regularity suggested a discipline.) My lovely mother Magnolia had died when I was thirteen. Both sets of grandparents had passed. A loner until Fletcher, I'd borne none of my own children.

Edison was my family, the sole blood relative whom I clearly and cleanly loved. This one attachment distilled all the loyalty that most people dilute across a larger clan into a devotion with the intensity of tamarind. It was Edison from whom I first learned loyalty; it was therefore Edison from whom all other loyalties flowed, and the beneficiaries of this very capacity to cling fiercely were Fletcher and our kids. I may have been ambivalent about the past we shared, but only Edison and I shared it. In truth, I hadn't hesitated for a heartbeat when Slack Muncie called that morning. Fletcher was right: it was a trump. Edison was my brother, and we could really have ended the discussion then and there.

chapter two

I'm picking your uncle up at the airport at five." The pecans on my pie smelled nicely toasted, and I pulled it from the oven. "Be sure and join us for dinner."

"Step-uncle," Tanner corrected, standing at the counter getting toast crumbs on the floor. "Right next door to total stranger in my book. Sorry. Got plans."

"Change them," I said. "I wasn't asking. You and Cody will be at dinner, period. Seven o'clock, if the plane's on time." I'd always felt shaky about exerting authority over my stepchildren, even shakier now that Tanner was seventeen, and when you don't feel confident of authority you do not have it. If he did as I said, he would obey out of pity. "When you have a houseguest," I added, laying on the parental shtick even thicker, "you may not have to be around for all the other meals, but you do on the first night."

"Is that so?"

I wasn't sure what I'd said was true. "I mean, I'd really appreciate your being here."

"So you *are* asking."

"Pleading."

"That's different." He wiped butter from his mouth with his sleeve. "The guy was here once before, right?"

"A little over four years ago. Do you remember him?"

"Got a dim recollection of some blowhard. Kept yakking about bands nobody's ever heard of. Couldn't remember my fucking name."

The characterization stung. "Edison has a son somewhere, but his ex got full custody when the boy was a baby. So your uncle doesn't have much experience talking to kids—"

"Got the impression the problem was the way he talked to *adults*. He was boring the shit out of everybody."

"He's a very talented man who's led a very interesting life— much more interesting than mine. This is a rare opportunity to get to know him." I was speaking to a brick wall.

I hadn't quite cracked my stepson. Tanner had a blithe sense of entitlement, a certainty that he was destined for an undefined brand of greatness. Though already a month into his senior year of high school, he had yet to evince the slightest interest in the college education for which I was expressly saving the proceeds from my business. He wanted to write, but he didn't like to read. That summer the boy had announced that he'd decided to be- come a screenwriter as if doing Ridley Scott a personal favor. I'd wanted to shake the kid; had he any *idea* the poor odds of breaking into Hollywood even as a runner? Uncertain whether my impulse was kind or cruel, I'd held my tongue. I had pointed out that his grammar, punctuation, and spelling were atrocious, but Tanner imagined that word processing took care of all that silly prose-style folderol. Anyway, he'd said, for screenwriting you had to know how people *really talked*, for which a grasp of proper grammar was only an impediment. Okay, I'd thought begrudgingly, one point for Tanner. Throughout his adolescence, Fletcher and I had praised the boy's every poem, extolled the creativity of his half-page short stories. Parents are supposed to. But, to my horror, Tanner had believed us.

Tall, pale, and unmuscled, the boy had that undernourished look that girls so often fall for. His dark hair was painstakingly disheveled. The clashing layers of his clothing showed like peeled-back layers of old wallpaper: a checked sweatshirt over dangling striped shirttails, parted to reveal the elastic of plaid boxers rising above his slumped, unbelted jeans. Most of his friends stopped by in the same state of harlequin half-undress. Tanner carried himself with his hips canted forward, and he'd recently developed a disconcerting habit of touching himself while he talked—smoothing palms down his hips, or up his rib cage to his flat chest. He may have been chronically unimpressed, but that skepticism did not extend to himself, and I was amazed how readily his peers and teachers alike took his superficial assurance at face value.

I had to watch myself with Tanner. When I noted that "girls" would fall for his looks, I should have clarified: at his age, I'd have been one of those girls. It's not that I was tempted to be flirtatious with him; after all, I could still discern traces of the wary, closed-down ten-year-old I first inherited, who had to be coaxed into the open like a cat from under a bed. Nevertheless, I recognized my teenage stepson as just the sort of poised, hip, self-convinced young man with whom I was besotted in high school, where I'd huddled the halls praying above all to be left alone. (My classmates at Verdugo Hills were more than happy to oblige. Unlike Edison, I continued to go by "Halfdanarson," the surname with which I was born; I never let on that I was Travis Appaloosa's kid.) What I had to watch with Tanner, then, was resistance. It was tempting to parade before myself how as a grown woman I no longer fell for such a huckster, and I didn't want to indulge a too-ferocious, slightly vicious determination to see through him.

Viewed from the impunity of marriage, the penchant for un-requited passion that persisted through my early thirties had paid off. The likes of Tanner might not have known I was alive, but if you never spoke to the young man he would never reveal his disillusioning enthusiasm for the Bee Gees. Having nursed my loves in private, I had kept them inviolate, and was now spared looking back at a string of deranged entrancements with morti-fied incredulity. Marathon devotion had developed my emotional endurance, in contrast to Tanner's sprints with three or four girl-friends a year. I feared that my stepson wasn't learning to love women but to harbor contempt for the women who loved him.

"Glop that much jam on your toast," Fletcher grunted en route to a glass of water, "might as well be eating cake."

"Whole wheat!" said Tanner. "And he still won't give it a rest."

I'm sorry, but I don't eat daaaaaaaaairy! Our thirteen-year-old, Cody, had abandoned her piano practice to tug the pull-string doll propped on the dining area's middle shelf in case her father needed razzing. The doll was a first effort from four years before, and then a mere whimsy of a Christmas present. I'd sewn it from scratch on the heels of Fletcher's sudden health kick. The crafts project had doubled as therapy, embodying my struggle to keep a sense of humor about the fact that he would no longer come near my celebrated manicotti.

The stuffed ragamuffin wore a miniature version of Fletcher's standard black fleece, to which I'd glued his signature dandruff of sawdust. The doll had stovepipe black jeans, and other than a few teasing threads that spiked upright it was bald. The calf-high leather boots were constructed from the tongues of a fatigued pair of the life-size kind and soled with a retread strip that had fallen off a truck on Highway E36. I'd fashioned the wire-rim glasses out of aluminum paperclips and stitched a permanent scowl of disapproval into the forehead. One hand clutched a chisel (really a jeweler's screwdriver), the other a square of foam rubber that I'd had to explain was tofu. The fabric was starting to fray, but it had become a matter of professional importance that the mechanism inside was still going strong.

Shoes off the rail, Tanner! The Boomerang took me three months!

Since I'd involved my best friend Oliver Allbless in the joke from the beginning, it was his voice I'd recorded, and he'd proven adept at mincing his tones into the huffy and judgmental. The electronic device buried in the torso included twenty edicts and exclamations. Little had I known that my mischievous little handicraft would soon become a monster.

The Fletcher doll was an instant hit with our kids, to whom the mocking recordings of their father's oppressive decrees helped to endear their stepmother. Taking the teasing good-naturedly, Fletcher had been touched by the scale of my effort, down to engaging Oliver to design an updated digital technology. (Not much better than rubber bands, the governor belts that drove the plastic records and turntables inside the old Chatty Cathys from the 1960s had been prone to snap—which is why few of these collector's items still functioned.) Dinner guests never wearied of pulling the string. The following year, Solstice had *begged* me to fashion a similar caricature of her new boyfriend, whose incessant repetition of faddish expressions like "Good to go!" and "That's my bad!" was driving her crazy. I'd been reluctant. I was still running Breadbasket. To work the same magic, the doll would have had to capture the boyfriend's build and dressing habits. Sensing my hesitation, Solstice offered to pay. I cited a price high enough to put my sister off, but she attached photographs and a list of pet phrases to an email the very same day.

Word of mouth no longer depends on gabbing over a picket fence, and with the aid of the Internet the customized pull-string doll business went viral. By that year's end, I had folded Bread-basket, and Baby Monotonous—though thanks to Fletcher's goading misnomer some locals believed *Baby Moronic* was my company's real name—had headquarters outside New Holland and a full-time workforce. The formula was irresistible: ridicule paired with affection. And while expensive to make, the dolls were far more expensive to buy. Besides, they'd not have been so popular if they were cheap. Costing about the combined price of a KitchenAid mixer and a top-of-the-line Dyson, a Baby Mo-notonous doll had become a status item, one by popular accord more rewarding than the average vacuum cleaner.

Aptly for the last father-son interchange, the third time Cody pulled the doll's string it declared with exalted sanctimony, *I want DRY toast! I want DRY toast!*

Both kids fell about laughing.

"I'd like to know why that thing never stops being funny," said Fletcher.

"Doesn't matter why," said Tanner, struggling to stand up straight. "They're always funny, they only get funnier, and that's why Pandora is rich."

"We're not rich," I said. Leaving aside my stepson's inflated assessment of our family's circumstances, *rich* was a word for other people, and generally for those one doesn't like. "We're only *doing okay*. And be sure not to say anything like that around your uncle." I corrected with an eye roll, "Step-uncle."

"Why not?" asked Tanner.

"It's impolite to talk about money. And your uncle Edison seems to have fallen on tough times. You don't want to rub it in."

Tanner looked at his stepmother sideways. "You don't want him to tap you."

"I didn't say that."

"Didn't have to." Tanner may have overestimated his literary gifts. But he was pretty smart.

D riving to Cedar Rapids Airport, I wondered how four years could have passed, the longest Edison and I had been apart. We had talked on the phone—though more than once his number had been suddenly out of service. He was constantly shifting digs, and often away on tours of Europe, South America, or Japan. It was up to me to track him down by calling other musicians like Slack. Exasperation that my older brother didn't keep up his end of our relationship was pointless. He always sounded happy to hear my voice, and that's all that mattered to me.

In the flurry of ordering bolts of fabric and bales of cotton stuffing, maybe it was little wonder I hadn't seen Edison. While establishing my headquarters, hiring actors for the recordings, taking on yet more staff to handle orders and ensure that the portly doll with the hard hat that demanded, "Where's my grub?" went to Lansing, Michigan, and not to Idaho, it had been tricky to remain attentive to Fletcher, Tanner, and Cody, or even to fit in phone calls to family farther afield. Although one call three years back had sounded fractionally off-key. My product had just begun to capture the popular imagination, and I was still excited; why, my pull-string dolls were apparently all the rage among the upper crust in my brother's own city, having just been the subject of *New York* magazine's lead story, "Monotonous Manhattan"—with inset scripts of Donald Trump and Mayor Bloomberg dolls. But the tone with which Edison congratulated me on my appearance on that cover had disinclined me to dial again soon. All the words were in the right place, and the slight sneering or testiness might have been in my head; you could never quite trust the phone.

Since then, for me Monotonous had become too successful—meaning, all that remained was for the enterprise to become less so. Only a tipping point awaited, beyond which orders would decline. It wasn't a "problem" with which I expected others to sympathize, but recently I'd been suffering from an insidious lassitude that derived from having everything—more than, really—I had ever wanted. On the personal side, I had found Fletcher Feuerbach, to others tightly wound, but warmer and funnier behind closed doors than most suspected. (Stripped, he was a surprisingly handsome man, and he had once said the same of me: we were "stealth attractive.") I'd had none of my own children, but my adoptive ones were still speaking to me, which was more than could be said of the average teenager one had borne; I'd skipped the bawling-baby stage of childrearing, and gotten in on the best part. On the career side, I had never been ambitious, and suddenly I headed a thriving business of the most improbable sort: one with a sense of humor. I'd made just enough money that the prospect of making a little more left me cold.

Wise high-flyers kept this battle with the baffling flatness of success discreetly to themselves. Picture how bitterly hordes of the frustrated, disappointed, and dispossessed would greet any complaint about being too satisfied and too wealthy. Be that as it may, it really isn't a very nice sensation to not want anything. Thwarted hopes are no picnic, but desire itself is energizing. I had always been a hard worker, and this damnable repleteness was enervating. Without a doubt, there was only one solution to my growing torpidity, my Thanksgiving-dinner stupor writ large:

I needed a new project.

Brown with elegiac hints of yellow, cornfields drying for the October harvest slipped past my window. Overland electrical cables scalloped rhythmically by on creosoted poles, while globular water tanks on narrow stems glowed in autumnal sun like giant incandescent lightbulbs. The pastoral effect was blighted by big-box stores and strip malls—Kum & Go, Dollar General, Home Depot, and the recent explosion of Mexican restaurants, while as ever the Super 8 bannered in garish black and gold plastic: GO HAWKEYES, SUPPORT OUR TEAM! Yet on pristine stretches the countryside expressed the timeless groundedness and solidity that had captivated me as a child on visits to my paternal grand-parents: white clapboard, potato crops, the odd horse. Whatever foofaraw was roiling the rest of the country always seemed far away.

Since then, Iowa had changed. A wave of illegal immigrants had arrived to work in the pork-processing plants. State politics had grown a febrile right-wing fringe. Most family farms of the sort my grandparents tilled had long ago been sold or rented to agribusiness, so that numerous farmhouses, barns, and outbuildings along this route had collapsed. The crop already subsidized to the hilt, more than half of that corn would be converted to ethanol—netting still more lucrative federal subsidies and so slathering a whole second layer of corruption on a grain once a byword for wholesomeness and a hokey sense of humor. The subdued isolation that was soothing to me was soporific to modern young people, for whom the anonymity in which I wallowed was swallowing. Just like my father in his youth, my stepson was frantic to get out.

By contrast, Fletcher was born in Muscatine, and his never having moved from his home state didn't signal a lack of imagination; rather, a contented acceptance and even a certain profundity. "Iowa is somewhere," he said once, "and that's as much as anywhere can claim." The modesty of the Midwest, its secure, unpretentious self-knowledge, its useful growth of crops that people ate as opposed to the provision of elusive "services," appealed to us both.

Nearing the airport, I looked forward to having Edison around again—finally, company with *appetite*. My brother had been imbued with all the verve, the flair, the savoir faire that I lacked. Tall, fit, and flamboyant, he'd inherited our father's Jeff Bridges good looks without also assuming the oiliness that had always contaminated Travis. Edison's younger features were fine, almost delicate, and last I'd seen him the somewhat broader lines of his face at forty still hadn't buried the high cheekbones. He kept his dirty-blond hair just long enough to flare into an unruly corona around his crown. The manic keyboard of a smile glinted with a hint of wickedness, the predatory voracity of a big cat. In my early teens, my misfit friends were always smitten with my brother. He had an energy, an eagerness, a rapacity; even into adulthood, he never hugged me without lifting me off the floor. Edison was bound to breathe some life into that vast blank house on Solomon Drive, a residence that, since the advent of Fletcher's mad cycling and cheerless diet, had erred on the grim side.

For I was a homebody. I hated travel, and gladly let my brother act as my alter ego, catching red-eyes while I slept. I recoiled from attention; from childhood, Edison could never get enough of it. Aside from the obvious competition with our father, I was mystified why my brother wanted so badly for other people to know who he was. I could see coveting recognition for his talent, but that wasn't what made him tick. Ever since I could remember, he'd wanted to be famous.

Why would you want to sell millions of people on the illusion that they knew you, when they didn't? I adored the fortification of proper strangers, whose blithe disinterest constituted a form of protection, a soft, oblivious aspic of apathy in which I could hide, like a square of fruit cocktail in strawberry Jell-O. How raw and exposing instead to be surrounded by strangers who want something from you, who believe they not only know but own you. I couldn't imagine why you'd want droves of nit-pickers to comment on your change of hairstyle, to regard everything from your peculiar furniture to the cellulite in your thighs as their business. For me, nothing was more precious than the ability to walk down the street unrecognized, or to take a seat in a restaurant and be left in peace.

But then, the joys of obscurity were my own discovery. Like everyone else in L.A., I was raised to regard being a nobody as a death. It may have been easier for me to reject that proposition because from the age of eight I grew up with celebrity at ready hand—or celebrity by association, the worst kind: unearned, cheap.

I found being admired myself unpleasant, and far preferred looking up to someone else. While I'd looked up to numerous teachers as a child, that comfortable hierarchy—in which the weaker party isn't humiliated by the submission—is decreasingly on offer in adulthood. Grown-ups are more likely to despise than adulate their bosses, and in my own self-employment I could only despise or adulate myself. Long gone were the days American electorates looked up to a president like JFK; we were more apt to look askance at politicians. Celebrities splashed across magazines excited less adoration than envy; in an era of the famous-for-being-famous, the assumption ran that with the right PR rep this talentless no-account with all the goodies could be you. I used to look up to my father, and the fact that I did no longer pained me more than I admitted. I loved Fletcher's graceful, sinuous furniture, but I didn't look *up* to him. In fact, maybe if you look *up* to your spouse there's something wrong.

I looked up to Edison. I knew little about jazz, but anyone who tripped out that many complicated notes without creating sheer cacophony was accomplished. I was never sure the level of recognition Edison had achieved in his rarified circles, but he had played with musicians whom folks in the know seemed to recognize, and I'd memorized their names in order to rattle off an impressive list to skeptics like Fletcher: Stan Getz, Joe Henderson, Jeff Ballard, Kurt Rosenwinkel, Paul Motian, Evan Parker, and even, once, Harry Connick, Jr. Edison Appaloosa was listed on dozens of CDs, a complete set of which enjoyed pride of place beside our stereo—even if we didn't play them much, since none of us was big on jazz. I was in awe of his travels, his far-flung col-

leagues, his fearless public performances, and his sexy ex-wife—
the vast canvas on which he'd painted his life. He may often have
made me feel mousey, tongue-tied, not quite myself. I didn't mind
so long as someone in our family was dashing and flashy, gunning
a harvester through the hay of the daily grind. Fine, he smoked
too much, and kept insensible hours. Fletcher and I were up to our
eyeballs in sensible, and a splash of anarchy was overdue.

Still, I pulled into short-term parking with a pang of mis-
giving. Edison himself wasn't the beanpole he'd been as a track
star in high school, and though he hadn't kept up with the running he'd always been one of those men (they simply don't make
women like this) whose naturally athletic build sustained all
manner of drinking and sloth. My brother was sure to ride me
mercilessly for looking so shopping-mall and middle-aged.

Cedar Rapids Airport was small and user-friendly, its beige
décor a picture frame for whatever more colorful passengers de-
planed there. At the end of September, baggage claim was deserted, and I was relieved to have arrived before Edison's flight
landed. If people divide into those who worry about having to
wait and those who worry about keeping others waiting, I fell
firmly into the second camp.

Soon the connecting flight from Detroit was posted on Car-
ousel 3, and I texted Fletcher that the plane was on time. While
passengers threaded from the arrivals hall and clumped around
the belt, I loitered from a step back. In front of me, a lanky man
in neat khaki slacks—with a tennis racket slung over a shoulder
and the remnants of a summer tan—was conversing with a slender brunette. The young woman must have saved her apple from
the in-flight snack; she polished it against her cashmere sweater
as if the fruit would grant three wishes.

"I can't believe they gave him a middle seat," said the tennis player.

"I was grateful when you offered to switch," said the woman. "I was totally smashed against the window. But letting him have the aisle didn't help you much."

"They should really charge double, and leave the next seat empty."

"But can you picture the ruckus, if on top of having to put your hemorrhoid cream in a clear plastic bag you had to stand on a scale? There'd be an insurrection."

"Yeah, not socially practical. But I lost my armrest, and the guy was half in my lap. And you saw how hard it was for the attendant to get the cart past him."

"What gets me," the woman grumbled as luggage emerged on the belt, "is we all get the same baggage allowances. Our friend in aisle seventeen was packing a quarter ton in carry-on. I swear, next time they try to charge me extra because one pair of shoes has pushed me over twenty-six pounds, I'm going to offer to eat them."

The man chuckled. Meanwhile, no sign of Edison. I hoped he hadn't missed the plane.

"I gather they've had to recalculate the number of 'average' passengers older planes can take," said the man. "But you're right: normal people are subsidizing—"

"What 'normal people'?" the woman muttered. "Look around you."

Searching again for Edison, I scanned their fellow passengers, to whose geometry I'd become so inured that at first I missed the snotty woman's inference. Earlier generations built on acute angles, today's Americans were constructed with perpendiculars, and the posteriors lining the baggage belt were uniformly square. Given the perplexing popularity of "low rise" jeans, tight waistbands crossed the hips at their widest point and bit under the gut, which the odd short-cut top exposed in all its convex glory. I avoided the unfortunate fashion, but with those twenty extra pounds I didn't stand out from the crowd myself. So I felt personally insulted when the sportsman muttered to his companion, "Welcome to Iowa."

"Oh, that's mine." The woman slipped her Granny Smith, now very shiny, into her handbag before leaning close to her acquaintance. "By the way, on the plane with that guy, what I really couldn't stand? Was the *smell*."

I was relieved the woman's suitcase had arrived, since the pariah whom she and her seatmate had so cruelly disparaged must have been the very large gentleman whom two flight attendants were rolling into baggage claim in an extra-wide wheelchair. A curious glance in the heavy passenger's direction pierced me with a sympathy so searing I might have been shot. Looking at that man was like falling into a hole, and I had to look away because it was rude to stare, and even ruder to cry.

chapter three

Y o, don't recognize your own brother?"

Wheeling to the familiar voice at my shoulder was like striding through a sliding door and smacking flat into plate glass. The smile I'd prepared in welcome crumpled. The muscles around my mouth stiffened and began to twitch.

" . . . *Edison?*" I peered into the round face, its features stretched as if painted on a balloon. Searching the brown eyes, nearly black now so hooded, I think I was trying *not* to recognize him. The longish hair was lank, too dull. But the keyboard grin was unmistakable—if sulfurous from tobacco, and tinged with a hint of melancholy along with the old mischief. "Sorry, but I didn't see you."

"Find that hard to believe." Somewhere under all that fat was my brother's sense of humor. "Don't I get a hug?"

"Of course!" My hands nowhere near met on his curved back, the form soft and warm, but foreign. This time when he embraced me, he didn't lift me off the floor. Once we disengaged and I met his gaze, my chin rose only slightly. Edison had once been three inches taller than I, but he was no more. It was now less physically natural to look *up* to my brother.

"Do you—did you not need that wheelchair, then?"

"Nah, that was just the airline being impatient. Don't walk fast as I used to." Edison—or the creature that had swallowed Edison—heaved toward the baggage belt. "But I thought you didn't see me."

"It's been over four years. I guess it took me a minute. Please, let me take that." He allowed me to shoulder his battered brown bag. Visiting my brother in New York, I'd trailed after his ground-eating galumph, nervous of getting left behind in a strange city as he threaded nimbly through slower pedestrians without colliding with lit cigarettes. Yet walking with him toward the airport exit, I was obliged to employ the step-close, step-close of a bride down the aisle.

"So how was your flight?" Dull, but my mind was spinning. Edison had stirred a range of emotions in me over the years: awe, humility, frustration (he never shut up). But I had never felt sorry for my brother, and the pity was horrible.

"Plane could take off," he grunted. "Even with me on it. That what you mean?"

"I didn't mean anything."

"Then don't say anything."

I'm not supposed to say anything. I was already climbing the steep learning curve of an alien modern etiquette. Edison could crack wise at his own expense, and had he shown up in a form bearing some passable resemblance to the brother I remembered he most certainly would have hounded me about my hips. But when your brother shows up at the airport weighing hundreds more pounds than when last you met, you don't say anything.

We finally reached the exit. I said, casually, why don't I bring the car around, though I was parked only a hundred yards away. A middle-aged woman with smartly cut auburn hair who'd been loitering by the information booth had followed us outside— confirming my suspicion that Edison and I were being stared at.

"Sorry to bother you," said the stranger. "But are you by any chance Pandora Halfdanarson?"

For many a younger sibling with an older brother looking on, being solicited for an autograph, or whatever this woman wanted, would be a fantasy come true. But not today, and I came close to denying I was any such person just to get away. On the other hand, explaining to Edison why I'd lied would make a bigger mess, so I said yes.

"I thought so!" said the woman. "I recognized your face from the profile in *Vanity Fair*. Well, I just had to tell you: my husband gave me a Baby Monotonous doll for our anniversary. I don't know if you remember it—well, of course not, you must make so many—but it's wearing a stiff suit and snooty hat, and the TV remote is stitched in one hand. It says things like, *George! You know you're supposed to cut down on salt!* And *George! You know I can't bear that shirt!* And *George! You know you don't understand Middle Eastern politics!* Or sometimes it preens, *I went to Bryn Maaaaaaaawr!* I was offended at first, but then I just had to laugh. I'd no idea I was so critical and controlling! That doll helped save my marriage. So I wanted to thank you."

Don't get me wrong: I'm usually very nice to satisfied customers. I might not enjoy being recognized in public as much as some people would—as much as Edison would—but I don't take any la-di-da status for granted. The main thing that rattles me about such encounters is the embarrassment: this woman recognized me and I didn't recognize her, which didn't seem right. So usually I'd have been warm and chatty and grateful, but not today. I shook off the fan mumbling, "Well, I'm very happy for you, then," and pivoted to the crosswalk.

"Is it true?" the woman cried at my back. "You're Travis Appaloosa's daughter?"

Annoyed, since I'd not told that to *Vanity Fair* and the journalist dug it up anyway, I declined to answer. Edison boomed behind me, "Got that ass-backwards, lady. Travis Appaloosa is Pandora Halfdanarson's father. Which is *eating the fucker hollow.*"

Fortunately, when I drove up to the curb she'd cleared off. Hefting his bag into the back, I said, "Sorry about that woman. Honestly, that hardly ever happens."

"Price of fame, babe!" His tone was opaque.

It took some doing to get the front passenger seat of our Camry to go back to its last notch. Climbing inside, Edison braced one hand on the door; I worried whether the hinges could take the stress. I'd have helped him myself, but I didn't think he could lean on me without us both collapsing. He lowered himself into the bucket seat with the delicacy of a giant crane maneuvering haulage from a container ship. When he dropped the last few inches, the chassis tilted to the right. His knees jammed the glove compartment, and I had to give his door an extra oomph to get it shut. Those heavy hips were good for something.

I had trouble releasing the parking brake, with Edison's thigh pressed against it, and getting the gearshift out of park was hampered by the spill of his forearm. I was desperate to call Fletcher and warn him, though advance notice that the brother-in-law who had shown up at the airport looked thrice the size of the brother-in-law he'd once hosted would have been useless. As

I pulled from the lot, my phone rang, and I recognized the caller. After our curbside encounter with that Baby Monotonous fan, this was the last thing we needed, and I didn't answer.

Edison rustled into the pockets of his black leather jacket—the hip kind with lapels, though this one would have required the benevolence of half a cow. I recognized it as a replacement of the calf-length leather trench coat that he'd worn for years, with a tie-belt, soft as the skin of an eggplant, always worn with the collar raised. He'd looked so cool in it, so Mafioso mysterious and—sleek. I wondered what happened to the original, out of nostalgia, but also because whether Edison had kept his smaller clothes might be a key to how he saw his future. This wider, unfitted jacket had more the texture of plastic, and none of the fine styling of his old trademark. I'd no idea where one got such clothes; I'd never seen apparel that size in Kohl's, or even at Target.

He withdrew what looked like a mashed Cinnabon, the white frosting drooling over its waxed paper. I did not say, *You know, that strikes me as the last thing you need.* I did not say, *You know, I read once that those buns clock in at 900 calories apiece.* I did not say, *You know, we're going to be eating dinner in less than an hour.* In all, everything I did not say would have nicely filled out the entire recording of one of my pull-string dolls.

Yet even the innocuous question I put instead sounded loaded: "So what have you been up to?" As if it weren't obvious.

"Few CDs," he said through frosting. "Mostly New York gigs, and a lot of the scene has moved to Brooklyn. Hooked up with this guitarist Charlie Hunter who's really starting to headline. Some killing up-and-comers: John Hebert, John O'Gallagher, Ben Monder, Bill McHenry. Really hit it off with Michael Brecker at a hang at the 55 Bar last year, and it's a damned shame he just died of leukemia. Man, between the two of us, we could have done Birdland standing room only. Regular thing in Nyack—restaurant, which is a drag, though with so many venues closing we all gotta take what we can get. Maine Jazz Camp for bread, but also 'cause your brother got a few promising *protégés*, believe it or not. Working on my own tunes, of course. Long tour of Spain and Portugal coming up in December. Maybe London Jazz Festival next fall. Some interest from Brazil, though that's not nailed. Money's not good enough. Cat in Rio's working on it."

I was accustomed to Edison's catalogue of names that meant nothing to me. Eyes on the road, I could almost hear my brother as he'd always sounded: brash, slick, sure of himself; whatever the disappointments of the present, something lucrative and high profile lay just around the corner. I thought: He'd never sounded fat over the phone.

"Talk to Travis lately?" asked Edison.

Travis Appaloosa sounds made up—since it was. "Dad," né Hugh Halfdanarson, had assumed his barmy stage name when I was six and Edison nine, too late to sound anything but artificial. So we always called him Travis, with an implicit elbow in the ribs, a get-a-load-of-this. Yet during my childhood and adolescence *Travis Appaloosa* had lilted with the tuneful familiarity of Bill Bixby, Danny Bonaduce, and Barbara Billingsley. Maybe any sequence of syllables that rings out across the nation every Wednesday at nine simply cannot sound ridiculous. From 1974 to 1982, Travis Appaloosa was part of the landscape, just as Hugh Halfdanarson had always hoped.

"About a month ago," I said. "He's obsessed with his website. Have you seen it? There's a quiz on *Joint Custody* trivia. A 'Where Are They Now?' tab that updates you on whatever drugs Tiffany Kite is currently shooting up—"

"Or which ten-year-old boys Sinclair Vanpelt is shtupping—"

"Though you'd be surprised, Floy Newport is mayor of San Diego."

"The underestimated one. They're the ones who sneak up from behind. The devious little fuckers who plot behind your back. Who use the fact that nobody pays any attention to them to bide their time, and then make their move when you least expect it."

Edison's tone was playful but needling. Of the three kids in our father's supposedly cutting-edge one-hour drama, Floy Newport was the closest I had to a doppelgänger, although—oddly, since Edison of all people should know the difference—he was confusing Floy the actress with Maple Fields, the character she played. On *Joint Custody*, Maple was the middle one, sandwiched between prodigies, eternally unnoticed and not especially good at anything. Whereas Edison had reviled the character he most resembled in the show, Caleb Fields, as much as the vain pretty boy Sinclair Vanpelt who played him, I'd identified with Maple Fields completely.

"On that website," I said. "Believe it or not, Travis has also listed out the plots of every single episode. In order. Several paragraphs apiece."

"Talk about time on your hands."

"Too bad we didn't video that woman back at the airport for him. 'Travis Appaloosa' meant something to her. That's a dying breed."

"She was about forty-five? The right age. Probably watched every season. It's a whole cohort, Panda Bear. They're not that old, and they're not all dead yet."

"Only a few names from the shows you grew up with stick in your head," I said. "As a rule, Travis's isn't one of them."

"You'd be surprised. You don't use his surname. I still get asked about the geeze more often than you'd think."

In point of fact, I had gone by Pandora Appaloosa for a while in college. A little lost, I imagined that if other people thought they knew who I was, then I would know, too. But before long, the very query I was courting—"Any relation to Travis?"—began to seem not only like cheating but counterproductive. My classmates at Reed would only want to hear about my dad the TV star; in contemporary terms, I had reduced myself to a hyperlink to someone else's Wikipedia page. So I reverted to Halfdanarson when I moved to Iowa. In recent years even fans of retro TV were unlikely to recognize my father's pseudonym, which disuse was returning to the goofiness that had first sent my mother into peels of laughter. But I was mostly glad of having resumed the ungainly Swedish singsong my father had shed because Halfdanarson was my *real name*.

I'd usually have savored ragging on our father with Edison, that ritual touching base with our sick, stupid history. I rarely discussed my childhood with Fletcher. I hadn't even let on that my father had been a television actor in a wildly successful show until months into our relationship, and when I finally let it slip I was relieved to learn that Fletcher hadn't watched *Joint Custody* when it was on in prime time. Yet no matter how firmly I'd emphasized that my offbeat upbringing in Tujunga Hills was an arbitrary footnote in a life otherwise ordinary by design, Fletcher always took reference to the program as a pulling of rank, and I avoided the subject. Only with Edison, then, could I access a past that, however loath I was to depend on it for a sense of importance, I was reluctant to jettison completely. It was my past, whatever it meant, the only one I had.

I grew up with a set of parallels that expressed varying degrees of distortion and caricature. I didn't only have a father named Hugh Halfdanarson, but one who doubled ludicrously as Travis Appaloosa, who played another father named Emory Fields, a fake dad who was a far more successful paterfamilias than the self-absorbed monomaniac I saw only occasionally at home. I wasn't simply Pandora Halfdanarson, but could choose to be Pandora Appaloosa if I wished, and on Wednesday nights for eight years I recognized an idealized version of myself in Maple Fields, a sweeter and more altruistic little girl than I who was always trying to get her parents back together. In turn, Maple Fields was played by one of those rare child actors who wasn't unendurable, either on-screen or off-, even if Floy Newport was probably not her real name either. I idolized her and sometimes thought they should have kept filming the show and canceled our real family. So you can see how my fashioning mocking duplicates for a living might have seemed almost inevitable. After all, my favorite episode of *Night Gallery* was "The Doll."

This time driving back to New Holland our traditional sharing of notes—first and foremost, on whatever crackpot strategy Travis had recently devised to restore himself as the apple of the public eye—felt diversionary and dishonest. As we continued to discuss the latest on Joy Markle and Tiffany Kite, I could get with the program only so long as I trained my gaze on I-80. Side glances at the unaccountable mass in the passenger seat broke the spell, and it would suddenly seem a bit rich for Edison in this condition to be deriding anyone else for having failed to live up to youthful promise. For that dizzying sorrow on glimpsing the *large gentleman* in an airport wheelchair had only intensified, and I'd no idea how I would make it through the whole evening to come without falling apart.

chapter four

C alling, "We're ho-ome!" in the hallway, I tinged the announcement by descending into a minor key, a note of warning that my family would fail to pick up on. Here I'd hoped to present Tanner with a member of his extended family whom he could plausibly "look up to," but with my brother's spine compacted two inches Tanner was already too tall. Nothing about being obese diminished Edison's accomplishments, but I had a feeling that wasn't the way Tanner would see things.

When Edison trailed me to the kitchen, Fletcher's face mirrored what my own must have looked like when I turned to my brother's voice at the airport: that flat smack against plate glass, the shock of having your expectations so thoroughly thwarted. My husband is not an impolite person, but when he looked up from the stove he said absolutely nothing and forgot to close his mouth. Time stretched. He was dying to look at me, but cutting away would have seemed unwelcoming. "Hey," he said feebly.

"Hey, bro, good to see you, man!" Edison clapped Fletcher's shoulder and attempted that double handshake up the elbow, but my husband was too dazed to do it right, and they settled on a pat of an embrace. Edison might not have precisely enjoyed this brand of encounter, but he must have had frequent enough experience with meeting someone who'd last seen him at about 165 to have learned to take a compensatory satisfaction in other people's transparent hypocrisy. They couldn't say anything, and whatever they said instead was so extravagantly and obviously at odds with what was going through their heads that the disparity must have stirred a sour internal smile.

"Tanner?" I led Edison over to where my stepson slouched at the table, taking in the scene while dawdling at his laptop. I could already read in the twist of his mouth the ruthless description of our new houseguest that he'd post on Facebook. "You remember your uncle Edison?"

"Not really," said Tanner warily.

"Hell, kid, you've really shot up," said Edison, extending his hand. "Can't say I'd recognize you on the street, Tan." Nobody called Tanner "Tan."

Tanner continued to slouch, so when he extended his arm to limply shake Edison's hand it was from as far away as possible. "Can't say I'd recognize you, either, Ed." Nobody called Edison "Ed."

"So you're seventeen? Figure my son Carson's about your age," Edison supposed.

Tanner exclaimed, "You don't even *know*?"

That's when Cody filtered into the doorway. With fair flyaway hair and a diffident manner, she was a shy girl, as I had been. Responding to her natural modesty and diligence, I'd tried for years not to show her any partiality over her more arrogant brother. Although no prodigy at the piano, the girl had a precocious sensitivity that would either be the making of her or would doom her for life as an easy mark. This was one of those moments in which she distinguished herself, for her instincts were pitch perfect. Cody took a mere instant to assess the situation, after which she ran to my brother crying, "Hi, Uncle Edison!" and gave him an unreserved hug.

He hugged her back, hard. I wondered how many times recently anyone had held him like that—with joy, with affection, with no trace of distaste. I wished I'd hugged him that way myself.

"So what's cookin'?" asked Edison, hovering by the stove.

"Ratatouille and shrimp with polenta," said Fletcher.

"I'm afraid the shrimp are only the frozen supermarket kind," I said. "It's the landlocked Midwest, and Fletcher decides the only animal protein he'll eat is seafood."

"No prob—smells great!" Edison helped himself to a large nearby jar of peanuts and asked for a beer. I poured him a lager and followed him anxiously to the table. Fletcher had made the dining set, and the chairs all had finely curved arms—between which my brother was not going to fit.

"I'm sure you're worn out after your trip," I said hastily, "but you may not be—comfortable in these chairs." I did a rapid inventory: the living room was furnished with Fletcher's rigid normal-size-person creations. But one broken-down recliner in the master bedroom was leftover from the days I lived alone; I'd refused to part with an ugly chair so sumptuous for curling up to read. My husband's confabulations of oak, cedar, and ash were more sensuous for the eye than the ass.

I tried to be offhand about it. Turning off the ratatouille, Fletcher was stoic, Cody eager to help. Once upstairs, my husband and I finally met each other's eyes. Desperate to talk to him for hours, I could only shake my head in dismay.

"Mom," Cody whispered as we knelt on one side of the recliner and Fletcher took the other. "What happened to Uncle Edison?"

"I don't know, sweetie."

"Is he sick?"

"According to the latest thinking on the subject"—we heaved to a stand—"yes." Though I was personally unsure how labeling obesity an "illness" got anyone anywhere.

"Does he eat too much?"

"I think so."

"Why doesn't he stop?"

"That's a good question." We paused at the top of the stairs.

"He makes me sad," said my stepdaughter.

"Me, too." I kept my voice steady for her sake. "Very, very sad."

I was determined not to make a big deal out of this project, but the recliner was heavy, and in order to get it around the turn at the landing we had to tilt the chair on its side. A certain amount of huffing and Fletcher's barked directions must have leaked to the kitchen. When we lugged in the recliner, Edison was holding forth to Tanner while leaning on the prep island. I felt bad about making him stand so long, which he must have found tiring. The peanuts were finished.

"I'm not dissing Wynton Marsalis," Edison was opining. "He's brought in some bread, if nothing else. But the trouble with Wynton is he feeds this whole nostalgia thing, like jazz is over, you hear what I'm sayin'? Like it's in a museum, under glass. Nothing wrong with keeping the standards alive, so long as you don't turn the whole field into one big snoring PBS doc. 'Cause it's still evolving, dig? I mean, you got a certain amount of lost free crap, which the public hates, and drives what few folks do listen to jazz even further into the ass of the past. Cats who blow all freaky don't appreciate that even Ornette riffed on an underlying *structure*. But other Post-Bop cats out there are *killing*. Even some of Miles's contemporaries are still playing, still innovating: Sonny, Wayne . . ."

"Talk about 'ass of the past,'" said Tanner, focused on his keyboard. "What's with all the 'cat' and 'man' and 'dig'? That shit must have been pretty moldy by the time you were a kid."

"Yo, every profession got its *patois*," said Edison.

"It's true, they really do talk like that," I said, after we'd set the recliner down in the kitchen to rest. "I've visited your uncle several times in New York, and all the other jazz musicians talk the same way. Time warp. It's hilarious."

When Edison withdrew his cigarettes, I urged him to the patio. We didn't allow smoking in the house.

"Jesus, it's like he's trying to sound like a jazz musician," Tanner grumbled once Edison had shambled outside. "Like some stereotype of a jazz musician that wouldn't wash in a biopic because it's trite. You're not going to tell me, Pando, that he grew up *speaking jive*."

"Just because you learn something in adulthood doesn't mean it's fake," I snapped. "You could be a little more gracious. Like, give us a hand, because I think we're going to have to move the table."

Lodging the chair at the head of the table was an operation, since the recliner wouldn't fit in front of the step up to the living room without our moving the table a foot toward the patio door—which meant Tanner had to push his own chair right up against the glass. Reseated but cramped, he looked put out, doubly so when he had to get up again to let Edison inside. As my brother sank with obvious relief into the crazed leather cushion, I caught Fletcher appraising the room critically. He was house-proud. Now the room was off-center, and the dirty maroon eyesore hardly set off his dining table.

"Hey, Pando, I almost forgot," said Tanner, typing with the very urgency I had dreaded. "Some photographer called while you were gone, about a re-sked of the *Bloomberg Businessweek* shoot. Wish you'd pick up your damn iPhone. Taking a handwritten message on a pad is like carving on the wall of a cave."

"Oh, God, not another photo shoot," I said before I realized how that sounded. "I hate them," I continued, *them* making it worse, since the very plurality was the problem. "I can't stand having to decide what to wear, and it doesn't even matter since I always look hideous," *always* continuing to dig my grave. Since it was true enough, in my haste to say something more self-deprecating still to cover for the embarrassing fact of the shoot itself, I almost added, but pulled up short just in time, that lately all I could think when I saw pictures of myself in the media was that I looked fat.

"They don't always come out so bad," said Tanner. "The *New York* magazine cover, where they added a pull-string on your back? That one was a kick."

"Little cheesy, though," Edison proclaimed from his new throne, and drained the last of his beer. "That rag's gone to shit. One step from *Entertainment Weekly*." It shouldn't have taken me so long to realize that Edison might have regarded that cover as an invasion of sorts. New York was his patch.

"*You* ever been in *New York* magazine?" Tanner charged my brother.

"Nah. I'm more the *Downbeat* type."

As I retrieved napkins at his side, Tanner muttered, "Look more like the *beat down* type to me." I hoped Edison hadn't heard him.

I should have been glad that Tanner stuck up for me, but I didn't want the responsibility of being the one he looked up to. Baby Monotonous had come to me flukishly. I hadn't planned the venture or even wanted it, much less worked hard for it until it landed in my lap. I believed I set a bad example.

"Well, we should all enjoy this making of hay while the sun shines," I said, laying plates. "Baby Monotonous dolls are a fad. Fads don't last. Like pet rocks—a perfectly ridiculous gift item that you kids are too young to remember. They lasted about five minutes. In that five minutes, someone made a bundle. But if he wasn't smart, he'd have been left with whole warehouses full of stones in stupid little boxes. I've been very lucky, and you should all be prepared for that luck to run out. Orders are already starting to level off, and I wouldn't be surprised to see those dolls start cropping up on eBay by the hundred." Orders hadn't leveled off.

"We're never putting Dad's doll on eBay!" said Cody.

"Pando, what's with trashing your own company all the time?" said Tanner. "Someone finally gets a business off the ground in this family, and all you can do is apologize."

"Thanks a lot, Tanner," said Fletcher at the stove.

"Basement full of furniture says this house got only one *going concern*," said Tanner.

"Nobody buys quality anymore."

"Thanks a lot, Fletcher," I said.

It was a pale facsimile of family banter—the fast-paced, rollicking back-and-forth to which our foursome had indeed risen on occasion, but which I generally located only on television. I'd grown up in such proximity to scripted family follies that you'd think I could have done a better job of faking it. But ever since I'd walked in with Edison in tow our interchanges had been forced.

For once when I told the kids to wash their hands before dinner, there were no groans; with a thick glance between them that I recognized from my own childhood, they scooted off, both spurning the nearest bathroom for the one upstairs. After a lag, I followed. I wasn't sure how I wanted to admonish them—probably with something bland and pointless about trying to be nice. When I arrived outside the door, they weren't even bothering with the pretense of running water.

"Then, like, he drops some peanuts," Tanner was saying in a harsh whisper, "and stoops to pick them up, right? Except he loses his balance, 'cause that whale gut throws him forward, and he ends up on his hands and knees! I'm not kiddin', Code, the son of a bitch couldn't get off the floor! So I had to help drag his ass upright, and I thought we was both goin' down! Even his hand is huge. And sweaty."

"He is kinda gross," said Cody. "Like when he bends down, and his shirt's too small so it hikes up and you can see his crack with little black hairs in it, and these huge butt-blobs bulge over his belt."

"Guy could do his own retro TV show, just like Grampa's: *My Three Chins*," said Tanner. "And he's got a bigger rack than Pando."

"If I looked like that, I'd just wanna die. His ankles are bigger around than your *thighs*. Hey, you think Mom knew he'd turned into such a load?"

"I kinda doubt it. But notice how she keeps pretending how everything's all normal? Like, nobody's supposed to mention that 'Uncle Edison' barely fits through the fucking door."

I'd heard enough. Clearing my throat, I walked in. "Get it out of your system *now*. Just because someone's overweight doesn't mean he has no feelings." Yet when I closed the door behind us, the atmosphere remained conspiratorial.

"But how long's this guy gonna hang around?" said Tanner. "In twenty-four hours he could bust the whole place up. What if he sits on the john and it cracks to pieces?"

"I don't know how long he'll stay," I said quietly. "But while he's here, I want you to imagine what it might be like if you two grow up, and then you, Tanner, visit your sister and her family, and maybe you've had a hard time, and maybe you've been hitting the Häagen-Dazs. Wouldn't you want your sister to still treat you like the same person? Wouldn't you feel hurt if her family made fun of you?"

"Tanner will never get fat!" said Cody. "He's got to watch his *figure* so he can keep pawing all over his *girl*friends."

I shot back, "That's what I thought about *my* brother."

That sobered them up. As we walked back downstairs, Cody dragged on my hand. "I'm sorry," she whispered. "What I said, I didn't mean it." She was close to tears. I assured her with a squeeze that I knew she hadn't. Prone to self-recrimination, Cody was all too capable of tossing sleeplessly that night, berating herself for having been mean about her uncle even out of his earshot. I'd only ever seen her try to be nasty to impress Tanner, and she was lousy at it. At school, she perennially befriended the social dregs out of compassion, pulling her own mid-level status down several notches in the process.

We sat down to dinner. Fletcher passed his shrimp dish, in a tangy tomato, zucchini, and eggplant sauce over bars of baked polenta. As a special concession, he allowed the rest of us to spike it with Parmesan. The guest, Edison helped himself first, after which our largest rectangular baking pan was half empty. I took a tiny serving to ensure enough remained for everyone else, and Cody did likewise—unless the totem of excess at the end of the table was putting her off her feed. Me, I still had an appetite, but couldn't meet my brother's eyes; simply looking at him felt unkind. So I stole glances when he was occupied with his food, terrified he'd catch me staring—at the rolls of his neck, the gapes between straining buttons on his shirt, the tight, bulging fingers that recalled bratwurst in the skillet just before the skin splits.

I announced that Cody was studying the piano, and she said she "sucked," but that she'd be grateful if Edison would give her a few lessons. He acted game—"Sure, kid, no problemo"—but his tone was surprisingly cool, considering that he'd usually jump at the chance to show off. I encouraged Fletcher to show my brother what he was working on in the basement later, though Edison couldn't come up with anything to ask about cabinetry besides, "What's the latest project?" (another coffee table) and "What materials?" (though Fletcher was doing some striking work with bleached cow bones, his terse reply was "walnut"). There's nothing more leaden than this sort of exchange, and awareness that Edison didn't care about the answers to his lame questions made Fletcher protective and closed.

Yet Edison grew more animated when I pressed Tanner to tell his step-uncle about his interest in becoming a screenwriter.

"The feature film industry is a total crapshoot," Edison advised, rearing back in the recliner. "Half the time when after years of frustration the project's finally lined up with casting, crew, everything, some douche pulls the money. Most Hollywood screenwriters just do rewrites of other people's rewrites, and never see a script shot. You should think about TV, man. They get shit out the door. Travis, our dad—I guess you're sort of related, right? Wouldn't count on a guy who sells Pocket Fisherman on Nick at Nite to provide you a lot of contacts. But he may still know people who know people, and that's the way it's done. Me, I got friends out there who went into the industry, including one guy at HBO. Be glad to put you in touch."

If I could have gotten away with it, I'd have been pulling the ridge of a flattened hand across my throat. Tanner's expectations were already unrealistic. I didn't want him encouraged.

"Thanks," Tanner grunted skeptically.

"Tanner's met his step-grampa," I said. "A cautionary tale."

"What's that mean?"

"An unpleasant story that should keep you from making the same mistake."

"What's so *cautionary* about my grampa being a TV star?" I noted that in this instance Tanner had dropped the "step."

"*Was* a TV star," I said. "He spends most of his time opening used-car lots and doing Rotary Club lunches—"

"Lecturing on *environmentalism*, believe it or not," said Edison with a laugh. "Chump never recycled a Coke can in his life."

"—or," I went on, "printing truckloads of anniversary T-shirts, when Travis Appaloosa is the only man on God's earth who knows or cares when the first episode of *Joint Custody* aired on NBC. TV Land used to occasionally have him on in the graveyard slot, but he burned that bridge by badgering the channel to run *Joint Custody* marathons the way they do with *Twilight Zone* and *Andy Griffith*. Last time I talked to him he'd gotten a fire under him about putting together a reunion show like *The Brady Bunch* did—only the child actors Travis worked with grew up to be wasters, bar one, and the mayor of San Diego has better things to do. Cautionary. I'll say."

I knew I'd been going on, but someone had to counter the deadly proffering of Edison's helping hand. I was loath for our kids to feel exceptional for the wrong reasons, and so to fall prey to the same unjustified sense of importance from which I'd suffered as a kid. While superficially self-effacing, my keeping my parentage under wraps at school may have been even more corrupting than Edison's bannering of his father's identity at every opportunity. I'd still smugly carried around the fact that my father was *Travis Appaloosa* like a secret charm, an amulet to ward off evil, when really it was no better than a pet rock.

Even more averse than I to playing up my Burbank connection, Fletcher changed the subject—turning to the one topic sure to fill out the rest of the meal: *all that jazz*.

"Hey, I've played with some heavy cats, dig?" Having scraped out the remains of the polenta, Edison upended the bowl of Parmesan on top. Tanner and Cody locked eyes, which bulged in unison. "Stan Getz hired me for three years—paid better than Miles, believe it or not. But just my luck the really iconic recordings haven't been the gigs I've been on. So nobody remembers that, yeah, Edison Appaloosa played with Joe Henderson—

because I wasn't on *Lush Life*. Paul Motian, too—and it's hardly my fault the guy has pretty much stopped playing with pianists. And, man, I could shoot myself over the fact that nobody, *nobody* thought to record that jam session with Harry Connick, Jr., at the Village Gate in 1991. *Harry Connick!* Rare for him to sing in those days. Crack pianist himself, and said I had 'the touch.' Okay, he wasn't big yet. But Jesus fucking Christ, I could have been everywhere."

I didn't enjoy the thought: *He sounds like Travis.* It bothered me that my brother was still trotting out the same list of musicians that I'd learned years before to impress aficionados. It was a list, apparently, that Edison recited to himself.

"Thing that really gets me in New York these days," he went on, Parmesan pasted in the corners of his mouth, "is this obsession with 'tradition.' Some of the younger cats, they sound like fuddy-duddies. Studying all these chords and intervals like those mindless fucks in madrassas memorizing the Koran. Ornette, Trane, Bird—they were iconoclasts! They weren't about following the rules, but tearing them up! Personally I blame jazz education. Sonny, Dizzy, Elvin—they didn't get any degrees. But these good doobies coming out of Berklee and the New School—they're so fucking respectful. And *serious.* It's perverse, man. Like getting a Ph.D. in how to be a dropout."

We didn't usually have wine with dinner, but tonight was an occasion. Edison had opened the second bottle—which made Fletcher's jaw clench—helping to explain why my brother was dropping consonants, slurring vowels, and adopting a drawling cadence like the honorary African-American he considered himself to be. Most of the founding fathers of jazz were black, and Edison claimed being a white guy was a disadvantage in the field, especially in Europe, where "real" jazz musicians had to look the part.

" . . . See, what Wynton's done by bringing in Jazz at Lincoln Center is cast the genre as elitist. As *high* culture, *high* art. *Elitist*, can you believe it? A form that came straight outta whites-only water fountains? But that's the drill now, man. Middle-aged boomers hit the Blue Note when they're too out of it to keep up with hip-hop and figure they need to ditch pop for something more sophisticated. It's a pose, man . . ."

As my mind wandered, I considered the script for an Edison doll:

I'd have been famous, man, if only I was black!

I've played with some heavy cats.

Jazz prodigy my ass! Sinclair Vanpelt couldn't play "Chopsticks."

Yeah, as a matter of fact, Travis Appaloosa *is* my dad.

I can't *believe* no one recorded the Harry Connick jam.

Yo, pass the cheese.

Well, that last line would be a recent addition. I collected the plates, while Edison heaved from the maroon recliner—again—to head to the patio to smoke. So Tanner had once more to get up, push his chair in, and maneuver out of the way. It was chilly for the end of September, and each lumbering departure and reentry lowered the temperature by five degrees. The central heating couldn't keep up, and Cody had to slip upstairs to get us both sweaters. I was reconciled that Tanner and Cody had to negotiate a world in which people smoked. Given that my brother was not only chronically short of breath but also himself a *heavy cat*, the kids probably wouldn't view him as a role model. But Fletcher tensed every time we went through all this brouhaha for an un-filtered Camel. He didn't want anyone smoking around the kids.

I unveiled my pecan pie. Fletcher wouldn't have any, but it used to be my brother's favorite dessert as a boy. If glutinous with corn syrup, the pie was already baked; besides, look at him: what difference did it make? Although I guessed that's what he routinely told himself.

"Edison, you want ice cream with this?" I called plaintively. But I knew the answer.

I lay on my back in bed while Fletcher folded his clothes, which without the maroon recliner he had to stack on his dresser. Finally I said, "I had no idea."

After slipping between the sheets, Fletcher, too, lay in a wide-eyed stupor. We seemed to be experiencing a domestic post-traumatic stress, as if recovering from an improvised explosive device planted at our dining table.

"I'm starving," said Fletcher.

A bit later he said, "I rode fifty miles today."

I let him get it out of his system. After another couple of minutes he said, "That polenta dish was huge. I thought we'd have scads left over."

I sighed. "You should have had some pie. Before Edison finished it off." I nestled my head on his chest. For once his build seemed not a reprimand, but a marvel.

"What *happened* to him?"

I let Fletcher's question dangle. It would take me months to formulate any kind of an answer.

"I'm sorry," said Fletcher, stroking my hair. "I'm so very, very sorry."

I was grateful that he opted for sympathy over judgment. Sympathy for whom? For his wife, first of all. For Edison as well, obviously. But maybe—in a situation I'd unwittingly gotten us into and had myself contrived as horrifyingly open-ended—for everybody.

chapter five

I shuffled downstairs the following morning, a Sunday, to find Edison in the kitchen, which Fletcher and I had swabbed down laboriously the night before and was once more a melee of mixing bowls.

"Morning, Panda Bear! Thought I'd earn my keep. Breakfast on the house." He'd fired up our cast-iron griddle, above which he dribbled batter from a dramatic height. Once the batch began to sizzle, he pulled a cookie sheet from the oven that was towering with pancakes—chocolate chip, I would discover.

I usually had a piece of toast.

"Thanks, Edison, that's very—generous."

Tanner was not yet up, and Fletcher had fled to the basement. So I sat down next to Cody, who was parked before a stack of five. Thus far she had carved a single wedge from the top pancake and placed it on the plate rim. In a show of politeness, she cut a doll-size bite from the wedge and chewed elaborately. As well as pancake fixings—jams and sour cream—there was also a bowl of scrambled eggs, getting cold, and large enough to have decimated both cartons. If I wanted toast, that was on offer as well—piled and pre-buttered. I nibbled on a triangle. It oozed.

"Wow," I said faintly as my own stack arrived—layered with more butter and drenched in maple syrup. Resourcefully, my brother had finished the open bottle and located our backup in the pantry. "Is there any coffee?"

"Coming up!" He poured me an inky mug-full.

I slipped up and looked in the fridge. I took my coffee with milk. The empty plastic gallon sat on the counter.

"Whatcha looking for?" Edison had already adopted a proprietary attitude toward our kitchen.

"The half-and-half." Of which ordinarily I took a tiny splash on top of the milk, but straight would do for now.

"Sorry about that," said Edison. "Needed some coffee myself, to power through the flapjacks. There wasn't much left, and I killed it."

I'd opened a fresh pint the previous morning. "Never mind, then. I'll take it black." I returned to the pancakes I didn't want, fighting a burst of petulance. All I did want was my usual white coffee, and not this bleeding-ulcer-in-a-cup. I told myself he was trying to be nice, but it didn't feel nice.

"Think I should take a stack down to Fletch?"

"No, he wouldn't touch them. Not with the white flour, and especially not with chocolate chips." My tone was a little clipped.

"I could make another batch with buckwheat and walnuts, no prob. We'd just have to get more milk."

"No, *please* don't make any more pancakes!"

Edison's ladle froze; I might as well have slapped him. The rebuke rang in my ears, and I flushed with remorse. My brother had just gotten here and there had to be something terribly wrong for him to be looking like this and I wanted him to feel welcome and loved, which was the only way he would ever get a hold of himself.

I took my coffee to the stove and put an arm around his shoulders. It shocked me that it took a small but detectable over-coming of revulsion to touch my own sibling. "All I meant was— you should knock off all this work and join us for breakfast. I just had a bite, and the pancakes are terrific."

The touch more than the verbal reassurance made the difference. "Vanilla flavoring," he advised. "And you have to really watch these suckers, or the chocolate burns." He insisted on finishing the batter, at which point Tanner emerged as well.

"Jesus fuck! This is fantastic!" Reviling his father's preachy nutritional guidelines, Tanner exulted in white flour and chocolate for breakfast. Six pancakes would disappear down that scrawny gullet no harm done, and my stepson's enthusiasm helped to turn the emotional tide. Edison basked in Tanner's praise for his breakfast. I may have had more than I wanted, but that was a small sacrifice to make my brother feel appreciated, and Cody finally consumed half a pancake. Why, it seemed we'd have a garrulous, boisterous time together so long as we all kept eating.

At eleven a.m., aside from yet another kitchen cleanup, the day yawned. "So, Edison," I ventured, "have you thought about what you'd like to do while you're here?"

"Go cow-watching?"

"We don't look at cows!" said Cody.

"Yeah, believe it or not the Midwest has electricity now," said Tanner. "They're even talking about bringing in something called 'broadband' so you can make contact with civilization right through the air—though I think that's a wild rumor myself."

"Tanner's right," I said. "There's plenty to do in Iowa, you East Coast snob." That said, I'd never been keen on activities for their own sake. I preferred work to play—a temperament I'd recognized on meeting Fletcher Feuerbach. I'd been catering a July Fourth cookout for Monsanto when a quirky, taciturn seed salesman fled the corporate chitchat to mind the grill. He helped clear and pack up, leaving me in no doubt that tying off trash bags and arranging leftover deviled eggs in plastic containers was his idea of a good time. Little wonder I brought him home, where he washed every single serving platter before he kissed me. For both of us, work *was* play.

"You can always practice," I added. "Cody doesn't monopolize the piano more than an hour a day."

"Whoa, busman's holiday!"

It wasn't the response I'd expected. "I could show you Baby Monotonous."

"Cool," said Edison noncommittally, stabbing his gooey stack. "But I been working my ass off. Gigs, sessions, practice; until recently, booking the club. Keeping current with the scene, burning the candle at both ends. I'm pretty whacked. Don't mind doing jack for a while. I was just glad a gap in my schedule made it possible to fit in a visit. Catch up, get reacquainted. Finally get to know these kids a little."

Edison's hectic version of his life jarred with Slack's forewarning that my brother seemed dispirited, but I now interpreted that caution as concerning Edison's girth. Besides, I was accustomed to finding my brother's life opaque. I had no idea how one went about arranging a European tour. I didn't know anything about all those names he threw around, Dizzy and Sonny and Elvin, and I'd learned the hard way not to ask "Who's this?"

when Edison played a track; he always took my head off because I could never remember whether "Trane" played the saxophone or the trumpet. Aside from courteously listening to his own recordings—once—before sliding their cases into the section of our music collection that gathered dust, I didn't listen to jazz, and I didn't fathom who did go to those clubs when the pianist wasn't their brother.

"What's your schedule?" I asked. "I mean, coming up."

"This tour of Spain and Portugal. Three solid weeks on the road. Takes more out of me than it used to. Haven't taken a sabbatical since I hit New York in 1980. Truth is, Iowa could be the ticket—if that's okay with you. Somewhere I got a legit excuse to beg off more gigs in the Village: a fifteen-hundred-mile commute. Recharge the batteries. Smell the coffee."

With lots and lots of half-and-half.

"Now, when's the Spain and Portugal tour again?" I asked neutrally.

"Early December." His answer was muffled with pancake.

That was in just over two months. If I was understanding Edison's concept of a *sabbatical* correctly, and he intended to stay with us until heading off on this tour, that would make for an awfully long "visit," but it was also not an ellipsis. We just had to go the distance without everyone in this family gaining fifty pounds.

"You're not maintaining an apartment at the moment, I gather." I was diffident. "So where's all your stuff? Your piano?"

"In storage." This answer, too, was thick with chocolate chip. "I got your classic cash-flow crisis, dig? Royalties from Steeple-Chase in the pipeline. And plenty work on the horizon, of course. So I, uh." He wiped maple syrup from his mouth. "You know. Appreciated the little loaner."

"Oh, no problem!" That had been hard for him to say. "And if you need . . ."

"Well, yeah, now that you mention it—a little, you know, pocket change . . ."

"Sure, just tell me . . ." The kids were on their computers, but they were listening. I didn't want to embarrass him. "Later today."

However happy to slip him whatever he needed to tide him over, I'd never been in the parental position of giving my older brother an allowance. Edison had always been the big spender. On my visits to New York he'd never let me pay for anything, putting me on the guest list for his own performances and inveigling me into dives with cover charges for free because he was known, flashing C-notes at waiters and taxi drivers. Now the one with means, I felt a loss that must have been mutual. He'd liked his being the big spender. He'd liked his being my protector. So had I.

Yet what bothered me while scrubbing burnt drips of batter from the stove wasn't giving Edison a "loan." So far, no one, not even my impolitic stepson, had addressed my brother's dimensions head-on. I myself had not once alluded to Edison's weight to his face, and as a consequence felt slightly insane. That is, I pick him up at the airport and he is so—he is so FAT that I look straight at him and don't recognize my own brother, and now we're all acting as if this is totally ordinary. The decorousness, the conversational looking the other way, made me feel a fraud and a liar, and the diplomacy felt complicit. Now in order to have a convivial morning together I'd eaten a breakfast five times more filling than usual, and Tanner's and my gorging had provided cover for Edison's eating far more. That cliché *not mentioning the elephant in the room* was taking on a literal cast.

chapter six

Edison was touchy about any suggestion that he got the idea of playing jazz piano from Caleb Fields. Me, I could never remember whether my brother started studying piano with a storied black old-timer in South Central (*not* Melrose—our driver kept Jack Washington's hairy address a secret from our parents, and so did I) before or after the first season of *Joint Custody* aired. Travis had always believed that Edison was competing with a television character, and was still riding his firstborn for aping the ambitions of a contrivance—though the imputation was rich, since our father's fictional children had always seemed more real to Travis himself than his actual kids.

Travis called the series a "cult show," but if so the cult comprised exactly one person. In truth, *Joint Custody* was not one of those iconic programs like *Star Trek* that go on to distribute generous residuals. That woman at the airport, for example: she wouldn't have been a "fan" of *Joint Custody*. She'd simply watched it. I wasn't sentimental about most of the junk we'd parked in front of, either, although I was abashed to admit that I could still hum the theme song for *Love, American Style* and that I continued to nurse a nostalgic crush on the late Bob Crane.

Calling the concept "groundbreaking" gave the show too much credit, but the producers did do their homework. Take a look at its forerunners. *The Rifleman*: a widowed rancher struggles to bring up a boy with a Tourettesian impulse to cry "Paw!" at every opportunity. *Family Affair*: a widower raises two insufferable brats with the help of a stuffy, charmless English butler. *My Three Sons*: a widowed aeronautical engineer with three boys finally remarries after ten seasons—wedding yet another hapless victim of spousal mortality. *Flipper*: the performances of a widowed father and two sons are all overshadowed by a bottlenose dolphin. *The Andy Griffith Show*: widowed, single-parent sheriff convinces even most North Carolinians that there really is a town called Mayberry. *The Beverly Hillbillies*: widowed hick makes a bundle on *bubbling crude . . . oil, that is . . . black gold!* *Bonanza*: a patriarch in Nevada ranches with three grown sons born to three different mothers, all of whom are dead. *The Brady Bunch*: a widower and (it is blithely presumed) widow with three kids apiece know *it's much more than a hunch!* that the subsequent family show will live eternally in syndication, to Travis's particular disgust. *The Courtship of Eddie's Father*: a querulous little boy matchmakes for his widowed dad, whose being called "Mister Eddie's Father" by the Japanese housekeeper the scriptwriters believed would continue to seem beguiling even after being repeated eight hundred times.

Extraterrestrials who picked up the airwaves emanating from the United States in the sixties and early seventies would have concluded that our species was much like salmon, and once the females had borne their young nature had no use for them and they promptly expired. On the other hand, once you threw in the widowed women who spearheaded *The Lucy Show*, *Petticoat Junction*, *The Big Valley*, *The Partridge Family*, *Julia*, and *The Doris Day Show*, the married males weren't exactly thriving, either.

So the producers of *Joint Custody* were on a crusade. Nearly half the marriages in America were ending in divorce, and the failure to reflect this fact on television was hypocritical. (In *The Brady Bunch* pilot the mother Carol was divorced, but the network vetoed the idea; subsequent scripts never referred to how her marriage ended. The audience opted wholesale for the industry's default setting. Only one competing program ever had an excuse: *Eight Is Enough*, in which a newspaper columnist with eight kids loses his wife after four episodes. The actress who played the wife really and truly died after four episodes.) Worse, claimed the producers, this misportrayal did a disservice to the legions of kids whose parents had split and who deserved to watch programs that wrestled with problems arising in fractured families like their own. This is old hat now, when TV series are cramming as many gays, transvestites, half siblings, and third marriages as they can wedge into half an hour, but it was radical for 1974. Alas, convincing my father that his becoming a network TV star was doing the nation a public service did not benefit his character, and it made him proprietary. When *One Day at a Time* came along, in which actress Bonnie Franklin is unashamedly divorced, he was resentful and accused the producers of having stolen the idea. So much for his championing of social realism.

In retrospect, *Joint Custody* did form a cultural conduit between the doe-eyed sixties and the bottom-line eighties. The premise ran that the mother, Mimi (played by Joy Markle), has had enough of the hippy thing—leaving her idealistic husband, Emory Fields, reverting to her maiden name of Barnes, and going establishment with a family law practice in Portland (the show opened with a few pans of the Fremont Bridge, but it was shot in Burbank). Stuck in the past, Emory is an eco-warrior who lives in a cabin of his own construction in the Cascades, with no running water or electricity and only an outhouse; he grows organic vegetables that die. The role may seem farsightedly right-on in terms of more recent obsessions with conservation and climate change, but the scripts weren't really sympathetic with Emory's insistence on doing everything the hard way. Mimi despairs in one episode that his exclusive emphasis on not using up resources and not polluting the environment encouraged the children to believe that "the most they could hope to aspire to was to be harmless."

But in the main the program is about the three kids negotiating the tricky terrain of parents who hate each other, as well as the logistical travails of shuttling between households, given the eponymous legal arrangements. Mimi is authoritarian, less concerned for her kids' creative expression than for their career prospects. Emory espouses countercultural fulfillment, and his permissiveness often gets his kids into trouble. That might have all worked okay, except two of the three children just *had* to be prodigies.

Oh, that's only one of the reasons we hated those two so much. Still, fictional aptitude is cheap, like athletic prowess from steroids. A scriptwriter can stuff a few token foreign phrases into the dialogue, and voilà: his character is fluent in eight languages. Sinclair Vanpelt played a precocious jazz pianist without mastering one minor seventh. As for why jazz, in 1974 every kid wanted to be a rock star, and the pilot's development team wanted Caleb Fields to take the road less traveled. But between Caleb Fields having been conceived as super-hip and the genre itself being still halfway happening in the early 1970s, Edison may have gotten a distorted impression of jazz as a logical route to seeing your name in lights. Maybe that explained the bitterness of his diatribes about how marginalized the form had grown, and about what a farcical shard of market share he and his colleagues commanded—"most of which is Norah Jones."

Fourteen in the first season, Caleb is the rebel of the three, who carries on a whole parallel life as a *hep cat* in dark clubs in Old Town and the Pearl District, where he has to keep his status as a minor on the QT. The oldest has no patience with either parent, and adolescent viewers identified with his driving ambition to leave them both in the dust. He wears a porkpie hat and black turtleneck, and it's a running issue in the show that he's started to smoke. As for Sinclair himself, he had a lanky build that resembled Edison's own—at least back in the day—and the two of them were good-looking in a similar vein. Sinclair's hair was brown, Edison's dirty blond, but both mops tended to tendril, and one similarity my brother would be hard-pressed to deny: he'd styled his longish hair, which went electric in humid weather, just like Caleb Fields's for his entire life.

Otherwise Sinclair was a supercilious snob who chummed smarmily with our father whenever Edison and I were around during rehearsals, marginalizing us into mere extras. I have one clear memory of Sinclair's registering the fact that Travis-slash-Emory had an actual son near his age. Edison and I were loitering in the studio wings because our family was supposed to attend an NBC picnic in Griffith Park after the taping. Between takes, Edison took it upon himself to demonstrate to Sinclair how to play properly with crossed hands—at which point my brother confirmed, yes, he *did* know what he was talking about: lo, real-life son was now studying real-life jazz piano. "God," Sinclair exclaimed, "that is—*too droll!*" The actor's doubled-over laughter would secure Edison's enmity forever after. But neither Sinclair's arch condescension nor his affected world-weariness would help him much once the show was canceled and he failed to be cast again in any other major role. (He scored one guest appearance on *Family*, but being conspicuously gay didn't convert to an advantage until the mid-1990s, by which time he was dissolute-looking and half bald.)

Teensy, the youngest, is only four in the first season, and she's a *math* whiz. I guess it's pretty impressive that an actor so young could rattle off all those numbers idiot-savant style, since the scriptwriters were persnickety about her human-calculator answers to multidigit equations being correct. But it would be surprising if Tiffany Kite herself had finally mastered the multiplication table by the time the show wrapped up eight years later. She had black ringlets and the soulful brown eyes of a refugee. To my personal consternation, as Tiffany grew older she only got prettier and so, of course, became more of a princess. In the show, Teensy is a perky genius but still a little girl, and they got a whole episode out of her phobic avoidance of her father's outhouse: in Emory's custody, Teensy refuses to go to the bathroom, and on her daughter's return Mimi has to dose the poor kid with laxatives every time.

Then there's Maple, the only three-dimensional character on the program—the kid always conveying messages between her warring parents and editing the content along the way ("Did your father *really* say that?" "Did your mother *really* say that?"). Since the middle child alone is not bequeathed magical powers, she's actually likable. Sandwiched between two attention-grabbers with a high wow factor, Maple has no heaven-sent gift as a shorthand personality and no idea what she wants to be when she grows up. Accordingly, I've sometimes heard contemporaries thumbnail a conscientious, decent, but undistinguished woman who is roundly ignored and sometimes taken advantage of as: "You know, she's a Maple Fields." Both on and off camera, Floy Newport was unassumingly attractive in that way that L.A. always overlooks. Maple Fields was the one character in *Joint Custody* whom Edison almost never mentioned.

I still felt conflicted about our father's program. Naturally Edison and I had made a lifelong sport of ridiculing the show, but external ridicule was another matter. Pressured by Tanner and Cody, I'd broken down a couple of years earlier and ordered all eight seasons on DVD. Accustomed to the slicker fare of HBO, you forget how crude, obvious, and hammy television used to be, as well as technically rinky-dink; I naturally remembered the sets as sets, but they looked like sets to Tanner and Cody as well, who couldn't believe the show was so "lame." I was discomfited. I tried to laugh with them, but I couldn't, and before we'd finished the first season I put the DVDs away.

At least for me it had been a revelation to see Travis, since it's always a revelation to see images of your parents younger than you are now. Suddenly all the surety and authority you've accorded them falls away, and these glimpses of outsize icons as ordinary lost people with no road map, no special access to the truth or to justice or to anything, really—well, such epiphanies are tender and sweet and frightening all at the same time. I even softened briefly, thinking maybe Edison and I had been too hard on Travis. It was hardly an outrage that he kidded himself about how handsome he still was or exaggerated his own importance like most people. Another revelation: while our father prided himself on his sophistication, it was clearly his wholesome farm-stock presence to which the casting director had taken a shine; Travis Appaloosa played it, but Hugh Halfdanarson had gotten the part. In fact, Travis had originally auditioned for *Apple's Way*, in which a father quits the L.A. rat race for his hometown in Iowa, only to find the transition from slick to hick traumatic. But Travis didn't have the fish-out-of-water quality they were looking for. In Iowa, as far as the producers were concerned, Travis fit right in.

The one aspect of our father's show that I still admired was its representation of the way siblings live in a separate world from their parents, who for kids function as mere walk-ons. *Joint Custody* captures the intense, hothouse collusion between siblings, while Mimi and Emory are played for fools. Often ashamed of tugging the children's loyalties in opposite directions, the parents fail to grasp their kids' salvation: the children's uppermost loyalty is to each other.

To the degree he intuited the ferocity of mutual clinging that got Edison and me through our childhoods intact, my husband resented it. I didn't think he should have resented it on our marriage's account; when Edison first arrived on Solomon Drive, I was still of the view that being a devoted sister made no implicit incursions into my devotions as a wife. But as an only child, Fletcher should have envied this intimacy on his own account. If you don't have a sibling to keep the sides drawn, you're stuck lumped in with your minders, an alliance that makes you a traitor, your own tattletale, with the schizoid psyche of a double agent. Edison and I did rat each other out from time to time, but these were isolated strategic sorties in the complex politics of the playroom about which our parents knew nothing. We used our mom and dad as weapons in the far more central relationship to one another. Certainly with Tanner and Cody I tried never to forget: children know your secrets. You do not know theirs.

Ironically, given the show's ostensible edginess, when I was thirteen our own family took a turn toward the network cliché of times past. I came home from school to find, of all people, Joy Markle waiting to receive me. In retrospect, Travis's selection of his costar to break the news—with the physical implication that now the fake mother had replaced the real one—was in poor taste.

When she wasn't playing Mimi, Joy's metallic blond hair was no longer bunned in a metaphor for strictness that must have made her scalp hurt. I suppose she was pretty, though not beautiful, a lack she tried to make up for when playing herself—and like so many of the people I grew up around, Joy Markle did *play* herself—with an undercurrent of sluttiness, exposing the lace of her bras well before the practice was fashionable. That afternoon she wore a low-cut dress, an unfortunate scarlet—which signifies and rhymes with *harlot*—and when she stooped to talk to me I knew there was something wrong. I wasn't that much shorter than she was, and this impulse to kneel in order to you-poor-dear could only have been in the service of melodrama.

Travis was at the hospital, playing his own part to the hilt, though he wasn't unaffected. To the contrary, and it must be an unnerving experience to gesture toward emotion professionally

for years on end only to be mugged by the raggedy, artless inelo-
quence of the real thing.

Edison and I harbored conflicting versions, because my
brother thought of himself as savvy, while I thought of myself
as gullible. So Edison maintained that he'd known for years that
Travis and Joy were having an affair, while I maintained that neither of us realized until Travis started seeing her openly after our
mother's death. (They didn't last. Many an affair topples without
anyone to cheat on, like a three-legged stool whose supports are
reduced to two. They needed my sweet, credulous mother from
Ohio for their otherwise too-predictable showbiz shenanigans to
be any fun. Yet Travis and Joy's subsequent falling-out added a
bona fide acrimony to their portrayals of Emory and Mimi, making the last two seasons the best of the series.) There was only
one reason I cared whether Edison had known all along about
our father's philandering: if so, I couldn't bear the idea that he
hadn't told *me*.

Raised in Oberlin, our delicately comely mother hailed from
a solid, formerly industrial family of some standing; her father
edited the local paper for decades. When she met Hugh at a re-
gional horse show in Dubuque, I doubt she took seriously his
aspirations to act, assuming he'd soon put the pipedream aside to
tend his parents' farm. After all, a life of pies cooling in windows
and relief about long-awaited rainfall would have suited her well.
My mother has long been a touchstone of authenticity for me,
and my migration to the Midwest was an homage to her of sorts.

Yet at parties in L.A., she was at a loss how to dress, and
confided to me once that she waited out many a drunken gathering in a locked bathroom, while other revelers tiddled on the
door and finally went away. Detesting her husband's pompous,

self-promoting new friends, Magnolia Halfdanarson privately wept every time *Joint Custody* was renewed for another season. (She only went by "Appaloosa" in public, to humor our father; her checkbooks were printed with the name of the man she thought she had married.) So she may have been depressed, and in that case the condition had worsened after Solstice was born three years earlier. But I'd only had the one; how was I to know whether a mother sleeping whole afternoons was normal? Likewise I couldn't be expected to differentiate between depressed as in has-a-serotonin-deficit and depressed as in for-good-reason. If the question was whether she knew Travis was cheating on her, the answer was probably yes, if only because the answer to that question is almost always yes.

Edison had come to glory in having a mother who killed herself, which told well in New York jazz clubs. Remember—he's the one who went by look-at-me Appaloosa, which even for those never brainwashed to accord it legitimacy every Wednesday at nine was still bound to raise eyebrows as no convincing family surname but a breed of horse. Not looking to differentiate myself with a sleeve-tug bio, I never thought her death was suicide. Though obviously devastated to have lost her so young, I didn't regard having a mother die of natural causes as a narrative letdown, much less as a personal insult.

She was standing at the intersection of Foothill Boulevard and Woodland Avenue, and she stepped off the curb. That is the whole story, though as it happened a UPS delivery truck barreled past a fraction of a second later.

Edison would have it that our mother sighted the truck and gave herself up to its bumper on purpose, a lateral variation on hurling oneself off a bridge. Magnolia despaired of her husband's betrayal, ergo the loss of our bashful, winsome mother in our teens was Travis's fault. This simple, durable construction had long bulwarked my brother's preconceived opinion: that Travis was an asshole.

If I held few opinions, I did cling to a handful—like the view that facts are not the same as beliefs, and that most people get them confused. When your mother dies, you want the loss to mean something, reprieving grief from its purest, most intolerable form, in which there is only loss, with no compensation, no takeaway. Driven by this craving if not for a moral then at least for an accusation as a kind of mortality kewpie doll, even commonly honest people will reconfigure the mangle of the truth into a form that has pizzazz. By contrast, here is what *I* reconstructed:

Hundreds if not thousands of times per day we make small rudimentary decisions while thinking about something else. When I ascended our front porch steps, I was never thinking, "Raise your right leg; establish firm footing, lift left heel and push off." No, I was probably wrestling with whether I could sneak a little sour cream into our evening's casserole without Fletcher noticing. I'm no neurologist, but there must be a watchful part of the brain that carries out routine tasks and frees the rest of your head to ponder the telltale pastel effects of dairy products.

If so, the watchful part is not perfect. I've experienced it enough times myself: those instants when the overseer blinks out like a flawed digital recording. When the bit that allows the rest of your mind to be distracted itself gets distracted.

My mother stepped off a curb. She was a good mother in a traditional sense, and had inculcated in her children the importance of looking both ways. This time she didn't.

You could say that left me with pure and therefore intolerable loss. But I did derive something from Magnolia's fate. One afternoon in my mid-twenties, I was cycling along a deserted two-lane street in New Holland, and I ran smack into a parked car. Picking myself up and examining the crumpled bike frame, I thought of my mother. What I took from her moment of inattention was incredulous gratitude: that I did not plow my bike into parked cars all the time. That for decades I had been devising recipes for salsa, guiltily dreading Solstice's impending visits, or contriving phrases for my husband's pull-string doll, all the while making incalculably numerous, crucial negotiations of this perilous world, and I still hadn't died.

That was enough for me. But so minor a matter as thankfulness for the competent multitasking of the human brain 99.9 percent of the time would never be enough for Edison, for whom plot had always to be writ large. Perhaps this seems a stretch, but for me it was all of a piece: his appetite for Cinnabons and suicide alike, his insistence on building his life along such drastic lines that thinking big had manifested itself in his proportions. If my brother's weight was symptomatic of something wrong, then it also emblemized a vanity. He wasn't the type to submit to slings and arrows with a bit of a paunch. In the same style in which he'd schemed to succeed, so also would he fail: on a grand scale.

chapter seven

O ver the next ten days I offered to show Edison Baby Monotonous several times, but he always begged off to check out some jazz interview online. In the end I rather insisted. If *Vanity Fair* and *Forbes* were interested in my business, my own brother might express some small curiosity about what I did for a living.

Edison had been sleeping late, so I arranged to drop back by the house mid-afternoon and ferry him to the premises. Aside from the preparation of meals—a large enough issue to defer for the moment—I wasn't sure what my brother got up to while I was at work. I think he spent a fair bit of time on the Web, the great time-killer that had replaced conspicuously passive television with its seductive illusion of productivity—although Fletcher said that down in the basement he could hear the yammer of the TV, too, for hours on end. What Fletcher did *not* hear, unless Cody was practicing "Bridge Over Troubled Water," was the piano.

Perhaps I overemphasized the value of keeping busy and might have learned to relax more, but I did find it disturbing how, especially with the assistance of media gizmos, it was possible for time and time and more time to pass in the process of doing absolutely nothing. I liked to imagine that I was incapable of doing nothing for whole afternoons myself, but maybe what disturbed me was that I *was* capable of it. I feared this was a knack one could get the hang of rather readily, and it was therefore now lurking in my house, waiting for me to pick it up like a winter flu.

When I returned to Solomon Drive to escort Edison to my headquarters around four p.m., I found him faced off with Fletcher in the kitchen, surrounded by groceries on every counter. Edison's face was red. He was huffing, hands held out from his jeans, quick-draw. Fletcher stood rigidly opposite, his expression steely. If this was a duel, my husband was the sheriff, my brother the outlaw.

"Edison," I said. "You ready to go?"

"Better believe it," he said gruffly, eyes narrowed.

I surveyed the counters, mounded with corn chips, pork rinds, canned beef chili, croissants, soda, double-cream sandwich cookies, pizza rolls, frozen french fries, and coffee cakes. I was sure to hear about it in the car, though from picking out the items that needed refrigerating—three packs of butter, smoked mozzarella, and two *quarts* of half-and-half—I could infer the gist.

"Mind if we take your pickup?" I asked Fletcher, keen to scram. I didn't want to take sides. "I think Edison's more comfortable in it."

"Go ahead. He's already used it to truck half the poison in Hy-Vee into our house."

Edison snatched the pork rinds, grabbed his jacket, and hunched out the door. After he'd clambered into the passenger seat, he spooled out the seatbelt to its maximum extension, while I took two feet of slack out of the driver's belt. He bunched his arms and tripled his chin into his clavicle. Scowling, he squeezed his eyes to slits. His inmost self was balled into a dense pellet in the middle of a wide berth of shielding flab; I sensed he could not make himself small enough, nor could his defensive perimeter ever be sufficiently ample to make him feel at a safe length from hostile forces. As if to demonstrate that for pure protection he could not get fatter fast enough, by the time I'd backed from the drive he'd opened the pork rinds and was stuffing them through the taut portal of his pursed lips, chewing snacks the texture of spray insulation foam in a spirit of reprisal. I wondered if he was aware that the object of his retaliation was himself.

We didn't say anything until he finished the bag.

"Don't take this personally," he grunted, crushing the cellophane. "But your husband is a prick."

"What did he say?"

"I'm not gonna repeat it."

I pictured my husband picking his words with care. That was what made his rare invectives so stinging: he didn't lose his temper. I knew how long the perfectly chosen slight could last— like being called a *mousy dishrag* at Verdugo Hills High, when my muttering back, "That's a mixed metaphor," had branded me only more conclusively as a twit.

"You had an altercation, I presume," I said. "Over the groceries."

"I was being *helpful*. Trying to pull my weight."

I waited for his embarrassment over his choice of expression to dissipate. "You know he has strong feelings about food."

"Who doesn't? Nobody's making the guy eat my groceries."

"I suspect," I said delicately, "the issue was the kids?"

"They're teenagers. Stock nothing but chickpea kibble, and they'll hang at Mickie D's. Christ, Fletch wasn't a food fascist last time I was here. What happened?"

"Well . . . our kitchen used to be crammed with leftovers from Breadbasket—poppy-seed tray cakes or big Ziplocs of potato salad, which we'd either have to eat or throw away. Something of a trap, when you're from the waste-not-want-not school."

"And your cooking is the shit," said Edison.

"Thanks. Though that's a trap, too."

"Lotta pitfalls for potato salad."

"Yes, you have to ask yourself if there was ever a time people just ate something and got on with it. Every time I open the refrigerator I feel like I'm staring into a library of self-help books with air-conditioning. Anyway—when Fletcher realized the leftovers were having the predictable effect, he sort of freaked. You have to understand: his first wife got heavily into crystal meth. That's why he got custody of Tanner and Cody. She first started snorting crystal to lose weight. But soon she was leaving the kids unattended, disappearing for days. Lost several teeth . . . Got all these sores she'd pick at, and they'd get infected . . . Then when she came down off a tear, all she'd do was sleep. The whole spiral—it was pretty traumatic. Left Fletcher with a control thing."

"You don't get that way in an afternoon. That guy," Edison grumbled, "has always had a 'control thing.'"

"His nature errs in that direction," I conceded. "In any case, when he resolved to drop a few pounds, this obsession with fitness and nutrition snowballed. Meanwhile, Tanner never lets his friends forget that his *real* mother is a drug addict. Just like you always bragging about how Mother killed herself. It makes him seem darker and more complicated."

"Man, this isn't the Iowa where we visited the Grumps."

"No, it's grown a pretty vile underbelly," I said—though you'd never know that from the innocent vista out the window. In plowed-under cornfields, tufts of dried husk fluffed the clods. Feedlots snuffled with wholesome cows. Photogenic silos poked the flat horizon. "Iowa's developed a massive crystal meth problem."

"Mexicans," Edison supposed.

"Only at first. You can get all the ingredients at Walmart, except some sort of ammonia that's used on farms as fertilizer. So now it's homegrown, along with tomatoes and green peppers. Which is worse. The local stuff is purer. The ice from Mexico—"

Edison chuckled. "*Ice!* Don't think of my kid sister in the Midwest as hip to user lingo."

"In this state, grannies on Medicare are *hip to user lingo.* Farmers take meth to stay awake, like when they have to pull all-nighters bringing in crops. So do truckers. They call it 'high-speed chicken feed.' And because it burns up all this energy, around here meth is a housewife problem. A diet drug."

"*Maybe* I can see why having an ex who became a meth head would make you more conservative," said Edison, folding his arms again. "But that cat's got no reason to be abusive toward *me.*"

However brutally, Fletcher must at last have referred directly to the subject I'd avoided since Edison's arrival. I was tired of feeling like a coward. I'd thought my tact was kind, but maybe I'd simply been trying to make life easier for myself.

"Listen . . ." I trained my gaze on the road. "We haven't

talked about it. But I couldn't help but notice . . . since the last time I saw you . . . you're a little heavier."

Edison slapped his knee and hooted. "'Oh, Mr. Quasimodo, I *couldn't help but notice* you're *a little* stooped over.' 'Excuse me, Mr. Werewolf, I *couldn't help but notice* you're *a little* hairy.' I guess you've finally 'noticed' the Empire State Building is *a little* tall, the sun is *slightly* bright, and the Earth is a *smidgeon* on the round side."

I laughed, too, if only in relief. "Okay, okay! I didn't know how to bring it up."

"How about, 'Whoa, bro, you sure are fat!' Think I don't know I'm fat? They make mirrors in New York, you know."

"All right." I braced back from the steering wheel. "When I first laid eyes on you at the airport, I was floored. I'm still floored. I don't understand how you could have put on so much weight in just a few years."

"Try it sometime. It's not that hard."

He was right. Add four Cinnabons per day to a calorie-neutral diet, and you could gain 365 pounds in a single year. "But . . ." I asked feebly, "why?"

"Duh! I like to eat!"

"Well, everybody does."

"So it's no big mystery, is it? Everybody includes me, and I like to eat a lot."

I sighed. I didn't want to get his back up. "Would you *like* to lose weight?"

"Sure, if I could push a button."

"What does that mean?"

"That I would *like* ten million dollars. I would *like* a beautiful wife—again, I might add. I would *like* world peace."

"How much you weigh is within your control."

"That's what you think."

"Yes. That is what I think."

"You gained a few pounds yourself. You *like* to drop those, too?"

"Yes, as a matter of fact."

"So why don't you? Or why haven't you?"

I frowned. "I'm not sure. Ever since Fletcher became such a goody-goody, it's seemed almost like my job to be the one who's bad. My coming home from the supermarket with a box of cookies has provided a release valve. If we only stocked edamame, you're right: we'd lose the kids to Burger King for good."

"Pretty complicated for learning to skip lunch, babe."

"Well, maybe it is complicated."

"So for me it's even more complicated, dig?" He was getting hostile. "You can't even lose thirty pounds, and I'm supposed to lose—I don't know how many."

"I don't need to lose *thirty* pounds, thank you. More like twenty, at the most."

"Don't worry, if this is a contest, you get the gold star."

"It's not a contest. But we could both agree not to make things worse. That's a start, isn't it? The way you're eating lately, you're only getting heavier."

"There's the one little problem of my not giving a shit."

That was, of course, not one problem, but the problem.

A s I parked in front of Monotonous, Edison said, "Huh. This all yours? Pretty big."

It wasn't much better than a warehouse, with offices on one

end—but it was my warehouse. My idea, my employees: my project.

"I couldn't have anticipated it at first," I explained as Edison heaved from the cab, "but one of the keys to this product taking off has been the way it excites competition. Not between companies, but between my customers. Who's got the wittiest doll. Or the crudest. We've had more than one order for a male Monotonous that does nothing but burp, snort, sneeze, hawk, and spit. That has hiccups and a hacking cough. One customer wanted it to stink when it farted, but that was technically beyond us."

The short walk to reception, with Edison, was not short. "Then there are the pornographic ones," I said. "I had to decide whether to accept the orders at first, but there were so many . . . If a wife wants to give her husband a doll that barks, 'Suck my dick, bitch!' why should I care?"

I introduced Edison to Carlotta, our receptionist, whom I'd alerted about my brother coming by for a tour. I had not warned her about anything else, and was glad she took the lack of obvious family resemblance in stride. "It's a real pleasure to make your acquaintance," she said, pumping his hand warmly. "Your sister here's the best boss a body could hope for. And I'm not just saying that to wheedle for a raise."

I brought him into the big open area, which hummed with two dozen sewing machines. The walls were stacked with hundreds of fabrics, while one corner mounded with clear plastic bags of cotton stuffing. "All the dolls are custom jobs, but we have standardized a little," I said, raising my voice over the machines and leading him to the piles of unclothed dolls with no hair or facial features. "Over here, you can see we've got three basic body types in both sexes: thin, average, and portly. Three fabric colors seems to cover the racial bases. These we mass-produce. Angela also churns out denim and leather jackets, though we often add a distinguishing detail—embroidery, a political button. It's the personalized touches that people like."

"So—what, they send you a photograph."

"Sometimes we work from one jpeg; other customers send five or six. And a list of expressions. We recommend a minimum of ten. We'll do up to twenty, but the poetry—honestly, it is a form of poetry—seems to work better with fewer."

Edison frowned. "This is shit the cat in the photo says all the time. In real life."

Clearly, my brother had neither read my interviews nor looked at my website. I wondered if I felt hurt. I marveled that I didn't seem to. Instead I felt an increment sorrier for Edison. If I felt any sorrier for Edison, I would faint.

"That's right," I said. "We all repeat ourselves, but certain signature phrases become a form of branding. Most people aren't aware of what they say all the time unless it's called to their attention. The repetitions are telling. Our dolls are expensive. But as a substitute for therapy, they're dirt cheap."

I introduced Edison to my staff. I was proud of my workforce. A business with an inbuilt sense of humor gave rise to a natural joviality, and as long as orders weren't piling up we had a good time. They were nice people, so my impulse to protect my brother from my employees was disconcerting; my first introductions were tainted with a challenging demeanor, like, *So? What are you looking at?* that made my workers glance to the floor. Some of them may have read correctly in my hard stare, *You're not so skinny yourself, you know.* I was dismayed that my brother's size seemed to be all that people saw. I wanted to object, *But his mind is not fat, his soul is not fat, his past is not fat, and his piano playing isn't fat, either.*

But I wasn't giving my employees enough credit. You have to provide Iowans good reason to be unkind, and if anything a conspicuous weakness for pork rinds made my nightclubbing East Coast brother seem more down-home.

"Don't you believe that guff this lady spouts about Monotonous going down the tubes any minute," said Brad, the weedy guy who inserted the recording mechanisms. "This biz is going like gangbusters. Gonna be one distant day when people in this country run out of folks they wanna make fun of."

I explained that Edison was a jazz pianist in New York City.

"You mean, like—*doo-doo-doo-REEE-do-REE-do-do-do-dum-dum-DEEDLE-DEEDLE-dum-do-dum* . . . ?" Brad's screeching recital was comically cacophonous.

Edison laughed. "More like, *dit. Du-dit. Du-dooo-doodly-do* . . ." He completed an impromptu ska line with a catchy swing beat, and everyone clapped.

"Lord, that stuff's right over my head!" cried Angela, tugging the arms of a miniature denim jacket right-side out. "Afraid you're more in the land of Barry Manilow, honey. Now, it's a shame you've missed the corn. But while you're out here, make your sister lay in some good country-style ribs. And head over to the Herbert Hoover Presidential Museum—it's a real treat."

"Right after we visit the monument to Enron." Since Angela didn't pick up, Edison swallowed any more cracks about this state memorializing an Iowa native still a byword in the rest of the nation for catastrophe and incompetence. When he bantered genially about what kind of a whip his kid sister cracked, I demonstrated: time to get back to work.

"We contract out for the electronics," I explained once we'd retired to my office. "But we do the audio. At first I had customers send their own recordings of the subjects—who around here we call 'vics,' like in cop shows—so the dolls could speak in the vic's actual voice. But we got complaints that, even if the vic said, 'Big diff, baby, big diff!' fifty times a day, it was the dickens to get it on tape. Also, skulking around after spouses with secret digital recorders in their pockets made people feel creepy. So we hire actors, and I think the satire is more successful hyped up in a different voice—and it softens the ribbing somehow. Matching the right actor to the script is part of the art. Among other things, I'm a casting director."

"You gotta admit, as manufacturing goes," said Edison, lowering into my office armchair, "this operation's pretty out."

"I know it's nuts," I said easily. "Still, people make stupider products."

"Like what?"

"Whole factories in China do nothing but produce ghastly, hideous, pointless toys for American kids, who break them after playing with them once. I make attractive toys for adults out of natural materials that become treasured members of the family. And these dolls aren't only a way for people to tell each other what drives them crazy. They're also a way to show they love each other."

"How you figure that? Seems to me what you'd buy when you were fucking dark on somebody, man."

"It's surprisingly difficult to nail people verbally. Some customers take months studying the subject and taking notes. That intensity of attention is a compliment. And for us at Monotonous, it's been a mini psych course. You should see some of these phrase lists." I rifled the papers on my desk. "They're tiny character studies. Like this one. Louisa's working up his costume, and calls him 'Dr. Doom.'" I handed Edison the printed-out photo of a gangly guy with wild red hair, his hands despairing midair, along with its accompanying script:

> We're not going to make it.
> All I do all day is *RUN, run, RUN, run, RUN, run, RUN, run, RUN!*
> Don't ask *me*.
> This is impossible.
> I don't have any time.
> It's a *disaster*!
> I have too much to do.
> It's not going to happen.
> *Fugetaboutit.*
> We'd never find a parking place.
> That won't work.
> I bet it's sold out already.
> Can't do it!
> What are we *doin'*?
> I give up!

"Real life of the party," said Edison.

"Chronic paralysis and defeatism. Revealing, no? Or this one's fun." In the photo, a short, plump young woman in a spangled spandex skirt was raising a glass to the camera; one of my staff was bound to have fun with all that jewelry. The phrases in the commissioning email read:

I don't have *that* many credit cards.

Over the next year, that's only fifty cents a day!

No problem, we can take out another home equity loan.

This house is worth a fortune!

I'm not *telling* you how much it cost.

But that bag was half price!

All you care about is *money*.

We only have a *cash flow crisis*.

I owe it to myself to have a *few nice things*.

[Meekly] I guess I went over my texting limit.

I'm not having this conversation unless you use a civil tone
of voice!

"We've had more than one of those. This one's more subtle."
I handed over a photo of an elderly woman in a severe brown
dress who looked both self-righteous and aggrieved. Probably an
in-law or grandparent, prone to deferring:

Oh, I'll have whatever flavor of ice cream no one else wants.

Don't turn down the air-conditioning on *my* account; I can
always wear my coat.

Don't mind me, it's what the *children* would like to do that
matters.

No, no, if Betsy wants to watch *American Idol*, I can always
read.

Let Doug take the folding chair. I can sit in the dirt.

You'll do no such thing! Why, they say there's nothing better for your back than a rock-hard mattress.

If everyone else wants the window open, who am I to say
closed? It's a democratic country.

I'm perfectly happy with plain tap water.

Oh, you all go on without me! I'd just be in the way.

You have the last waffle, dear. I can always have gruel.

"This bitch is a bummer, man," said Edison, surprised to find my enterprise more engaging than the average toy factory.

"We call her the 'L'il Ole Me' doll. Now, theoretically the 'bummer' doesn't realize she's passive-aggressive. Still, if that lady has a shred of self-awareness, next time she'll ask for strawberry ice cream, period. Because that's what she *wants* and she can have what she *wants* if she asks for it directly.

"Oh, and this one came in this morning. It's my latest favorite." The photo showed a fit, overbearing wiseass wearing a "Biff's Bail Bondsman" bowling shirt and hefting an axe. It was easy to imagine him lambasting:

Get a grip.

Suck it up.

Stop your whining.

Hop to!

That excuse would never wash in the *army.*

[Sung, to Cat Stevens tune] *Oh, baby, baby, it's a hard world!*

Nobody *cares,* capiche?

Hang tough, bud.

On yer bike!

Give it a rest.

Don't be such a *pussy.*

Shut your pie hole.

Keep a lid on it.

Yeah, tell me another one.

I do a hundred push-ups every morning, kid—you could
do *five*.

I grinned. "How'd you like that asshole for your dad?"

"Yeah, well, we got our own asshole."

"We should really make a Monotonous of Travis."

"Get the impression I couldn't afford it."

"Gratis. You have connections. *'Back in the seventies'* "—I assumed our father's gruff, overaggressive masculinity—" *'television
actors got no respect!'* "

"But this is an upmarket product. Toys for the rich."

"Not exclusively. Besides, when you play at Irradiated—"

"Iridium."

"That place had a thirty-dollar cover for one set. Two-drink
minimum. You serve a wealthy clientele yourself."

Somewhere in that billboard of a face, I detected a wince.
Edison reflexively rooted a chocolate bar from a jacket I wished
didn't have such voluminous pockets.

"Why do you think that's going to make you feel any better?"

Edison raised his eyebrows warily. "Chocolate makes most
people feel better. And what makes you think I need to 'feel better' anyhow, sister?"

The air went prickly whenever anyone went near Edison's
food. "I was only thinking we'll be eating dinner soon. Maybe
you should save your appetite."

"Got appetite to spare," he said as if raising a gun.

I backed off. Ever since obesity had become a social issue on
top of a personal one, big people must have encountered the con-

viction that what they ate was everyone else's business. In truth that chocolate bar did feel intensely like my business, but only because he was my brother. Whenever he ate rich or sweet things around me I got agitated, no less so than if he'd carved himself with a razor blade in plain view.

As we ambled to the car, Edison still had caramel in his mouth, and when he said something I didn't understand him. He swallowed. "Pretty *impressive*," he repeated with irritation, stopping to look me in the eye. "I mean—this company of yours. It wasn't real to me. Like, I understood the catering bag. I thought that was cool because it was a fucking lot of work, if nothing else. But this Monotonous thing. It's a bigger deal. Don't take this wrong, but I'd never have thought you had it in you. Like, organizationally even. This factory is whack, man. But it's a big achievement, and I'm"—his voice quavered as he put a chocolate-stained hand on my shoulder—"I'm real proud of you."

That had been difficult for him to get out, and I admired him for saying it anyway, so when I rejoined, "I'm proud of you, too," that's what I meant.

chapter eight

C ody adored her uncle. She continued to express the easy physical affection that had come so naturally when she instantly intuited how often he must have been subjected to ridicule and avoidance. Though never a kid person, Edison was a sucker for my stepdaughter. Only her regular entreaties finally moved him to come near the piano, about which if I didn't know better I'd have said he was phobic.

Cody was still working on "Bridge Over Troubled Water," having discovered the LP in my ragged collection and ordered a Simon and Garfunkel songbook online. Thanks to Edison's coaching, she was learning to play against the song's overwrought sentimentality.

"Don't milk it," my brother would advise over her shoulder. "Be cool."

"Why don't *you* show me, then?" she insisted one evening.

I dithered setting the table to keep a curious eye on their exchange. I couldn't understand why my brother hadn't been playing. In my late twenties when a neighbor was giving it away for the price of removal, I'd secured that secondhand Yamaha upright for Edison in the first place, since he refused to visit me in Iowa unless he could practice. Hence one of the points of friction between Fletcher and Edison on that seminal visit had been piano morning, noon, and night. Fletcher got sick of it. So I'd never have expected the opposite problem: that Edison wouldn't touch the keys.

"*Please*," Cody implored. "You stayed with us when I was little, and you played all the time. You were great!"

"Huh," said Edison. "You remember that, babe?"

"It's one of the main reasons I decided to take piano. You inspired me." (I wasn't sure this was true.) She threw her arms around her uncle's ratty black cardigan the size of an afghan. "*Please, please!*"

He rested his hands on her shoulders before removing them quickly, as if afraid he might be arrested. "Okay, then."

They traded places, and the bench creaked. The eerie disproportion between player and piano put me in mind of Schroeder, banging out Beethoven on a toy.

He played the first verse straight. There was a funny hesitation in his playing—a delay while he found the chords. But by the time he hit the refrain he was striking the keys with more surety. I'd seldom heard him play a familiar tune without—well, I know this makes me sound ignorant, but to my ear?—without messing it up. In wonderment, I stopped folding the napkin before the battered maroon armchair. I'd always found that song a bit much; the recorded version was hyped with yearning strings. But Edison's rendition was calm and wistful. It was beautiful. I felt a pang. Only when he played a regular song in a regular way did I realize how very fine a pianist he was.

Maybe it was his beginning the tune without embellishment or departure that enabled him to bring me along, but this time, when he started another verse and the chords began to bend, I didn't fight the changes in my head, but heard the logic of the progression, in which the tune was recognizable, yet— better. He kept taking the chords into a more dissonant range until the song lost all semblance of the bathos that contaminated the cloying track I grew up with. Just when I started to resist, when the song was in danger of getting clamorous, the original melody lost, he brought it back, and played a final refrain straight again—sweet, mournful, no violins. I guess that was the first time I thought maybe the song, at its core, was pretty good, too.

Cody burst into applause, and I joined her.

"Now, why don't you do that more often?" I asked softly.

Edison shot me a dense look. "You got all night?" Then the legs of the bench shrieked on the wooden floor, and no amount of Cody's cajoling would get him to return.

With that one recollection I wouldn't want to imply that matters in our household were harmonious. Dinners were a battlefield. Ever since being blinded by the light in the aisles of Hy-Vee, Fletcher had prepared most of our evening meals (an invasion of my territory that really shouldn't have rankled so, given the trouble he saved me). Following Edison's arrival, my husband's fare had grown only more viciously nutritious. We were drowning in bulgur and quinoa. But he couldn't stop Edison from adding butter to the grains, or burying his tempeh in pepper jack; my brother was a guest, and a grown-up.

Then there were the other evenings, when Edison cooked. He made chili by the vat, and boasted his lasagna—three pans of it—used five kinds of cheese. Even with Edison's industrial forklifting of these quantities at dinner, the leftovers were overwhelming, and the freezer began to bulge with plastic containers and foil-wrapped squares. On nights Edison concocted Fletcher's version of traif, my husband would prepare his own separate meal, baking an unadorned fillet of defrosted pollock in the toaster oven and squeezing his pot of short-grain brown rice onto the one burner Edison hadn't co-opted. Fletcher's refusal even to taste what Edison had spent all day preparing infuriated my brother. Also, Fletcher perching at the end of the table with his special little fish and his special little rice made him seem prissy and aloof.

I acted grateful for Edison's massive meals, which made my brother feel less of a parasite. Yet cooking made his life all the more about food. Skillets of simmering ground beef allowed for plenty of snitching, and the volume of his dishes slyly dwarfed the chef's ample portions at table. It was our kitchen, and he was only able to install the ingredients thanks to the cash I slipped him and the loan of Fletcher's pickup. In providing the venue and materials, I was complicit. Though avoiding our bathroom scale as consistently as Edison avoided the piano, I'd surely put on two or three more pounds myself.

My brother's generosity extended to making the kitchen look like Chechnya, but not to cleaning it up. Thus I spent the end of those evenings scrubbing pots and wiping counters, while Edison picked crusts from a moussaka whose fried eggplant had absorbed an entire quart of extra-virgin olive oil. With Fletcher retired to bed, we'd open a bottle of wine and stay up late, recalling especially egregious examples of Travis's desperate bids to wrest "has-been" into the present tense.

"Ever consider reverting to Halfdanarson?" I asked one night, propping a foot on the dining table and tipping my chair back. "The associations with Appaloosa are getting embarrassing."

" '*Edison Halfdanarson*' would never fit on a poster. 'Sides, kiddo, I made my rep with Appaloosa. Stuck with it."

"Mother thought it was hilarious when you took Travis's hokey surname. She thought you'd grow out of it."

"I grew into it. Appaloosa attracts attention. Halfdanarson—no offense, sis—sounds like a clod. A nobody."

"Not anymore," I said sharply. With any allusion to Baby Monotonous the air curdled, so I returned to our stock fodder. "Remember the episode when Mimi was trying to manipulate the kids into taking her maiden name? Saying stuff like, 'Maple *Barnes*—has a ring to it' and talking up her 'estimable' lineage. One of the better shows. Funny—think they picked those surnames to mean something? *Barns* are civilized, manmade structures, and *fields* are part of nature, like Emory's environmental thing, but *barns* and *fields* still go together, as if Emory and Mimi were meant for each other after all . . ."

Edison snorted. "You give those guys *way* too much credit. Ever notice how you're always sticking up for that series?"

I laughed. "Maybe I don't want to believe it was totally appalling."

"But you watch a few lately? In real life?"

"Unfortunately, yes. It hasn't aged well. Still—we never missed one, did we? Every Wednesday night—we'd go through that game of pretending to forget or having something else to do, but we always ended up in front of the set at nine. I kind of liked it when I was younger, and Travis watched it with us, too."

"That was the tip-off, man. When he stopped. That's when he started up with Joy Markle."

"Maybe it's hard to blame him. Mother always had a headache. I don't think she saw more than a handful of episodes. He must have felt, you know, snubbed."

"Hell, she hated it. She hated the show and what being a TV star did to Travis. She hated L.A. She hated all the phonies Travis swelled around with. Her life, what she wanted, you know, the singing thing, just got—run over."

"Her death may have been a metaphor at that," I said wistfully. "Still, you ever wonder whether we rag on Travis mostly because he's alive? I mean, Mother died before we could look at her critically, from an adult perspective. That protects her."

Edison grunted. "Guess it's possible that if she were around today she'd drive us nuts. And that one record she made, *Magnolia Blossoms*, the vanity job? I swiped the last copy from Travis. Doubt she coulda made it as a pro. Voice was too fragile."

"*She* was too fragile. But she did sing with an unusual purity. I used to love it when she didn't think anyone was home and she'd light into 'I Am a Poor Wayfaring Stranger' beside the pool. It was even better when you accompanied her—all those Cole Porter tunes you two worked up, like 'Ev'ry Time We Say Goodbye'? That's how I always picture her, standing behind you at the keyboard and singing '*I di-ie a little.*' She'd have been thrilled you made it as a pianist. If she could see you now . . ." I looked away.

He wasn't offended. "Hey, you still remember the words? To the theme song?"

"Gosh, I haven't tested myself for years."

"*Now, Emory Fields is a right-on dad,*" Edison began, his voice deep and robust. I should have warned him to keep it down, since it was two a.m., but when I joined in I was too curious about whether I could still summon the lyrics.

Maybe people with a more Christian upbringing never forget the words to "Oh, Come All Ye Faithful." Others are able to light into "Margaret, are you grieving / Over Goldengrove unleaving" decades after memorizing the Gerard Manley Hopkins to get an A in English. I'm not sure if they mean anything— these permanent scorings into our skulls, like engravings on a tombstone. In any event, it turned out that one such carving in my head would be the last memory to erode in a nursing home. Indeed, if I ever fail to recall the theme song to *Joint Custody* in full, you can turn out the lights:

Now, Emory Fields is a right-on dad,
But his cool hippie shtick's gettin' older.
That flower power doesn't heat his pad,
And his homemade shack's gettin' colder.
The pit latrine doesn't seem so rad;
With no indoor john, his lady smolders.

Refrain:

Joi-oi-nt Custody!
Fra-a-ctured family!
Mom hates Dad and Dad hates Mom—
That ain't what they cooed when you were little.
They keep on sayin' it's not your fault
But here's the mystery riddle:
You never did think it was your fault.
But still you're caught squeezed in the middle.

So Mimi packed, took her maiden name,
Passed the bar, and moved back into the city.
Uptight, upright, she's a grown-up dame,
But one side of this split is quite a pity.
The only thing Emory wouldn't let her claim:
One plain nice girl, two gifted kiddies.

[Refrain]

Though Teensy Fields's a mathematical whiz,
One-plus-one don't make two in this equation.
Getting Mom and Dad together is sister Maple's biz,
But they won't respond to her persuasion.
Hipper than a hippie, Caleb's keen to play jazz,
Leave the parents to their petty confrontations.

[Refrain]

Whose side are you on?
Whose side are you on?
Whose side are you on?
MINE!

The tune was a little drippy, if still the sort of melody that, once wormed into your head, tyrannizes the rest of your day. But the refrain had a hard-rock bash-bash that didn't lend itself to the under-breath delivery appropriate for the hour. On the show, too, that last add-on finale had been shouted over a wild drum track, "*MINE!*" consonant with a shimmering cymbal crash, which I'd duplicated by reaching with a wooden spoon to clang a stainless-steel mixing bowl in the dish drainer.

"I swear," I wheezed, doubled over laughing, "that *'one plain nice girl, two gifted kiddies'* line traumatized me for years—"

I clapped my mouth shut, took my foot off the dining table, and brought the handcrafted front chair legs to the floor. Edison straightened in the recliner and rearranged his cardigan as my husband marched to the sink for a glass of water. For a minute nobody said anything, though Fletcher shot a pointed look at the empty wine bottle. "Are you," he said measuredly to me, "ever coming to bed?"

"Of course," I said. "I didn't realize how late it was. Sorry."

What would appear my transgression was that we had been loud and woken my husband, which was inconsiderate. He'd be up in three hours, though he didn't have to be up in three hours, so that wasn't what I felt bad about. When Fletcher loomed in the doorway in his robe, I was inevitably reminded of the way Travis's entrance into our Tujunga Hills kitchen had pooped the party when we were kids, and we'd fiddle with homework or mutely load the dishwasher, waiting for our father to go away. So my real treachery was replicating that old social geometry. Fletcher and I were the ones who were supposed to *hang*. My husband and I should have stopped talking when my brother walked in.

T o the extent that I was looking forward to Edison's departure for his tour of Portugal and Spain at the end of November, it was overwhelmingly because of this *Joint Custody*–esque "caught squeezed in the middle" business. When I came home from Monotonous, did I loiter in the kitchen with Edison, or head to the basement to say hello to Fletcher? If I did the latter, my husband would keep feeding a piece of timber into his deafening table saw while wearing plastic goggles sufficiently hazed with sawdust that I couldn't have any idea what was going on behind them. I'd wait for the operation to be completed before I waved, but rarely earned more than a nod before he started cutting another piece. What was the use? I'd go back upstairs. If Fletcher did emerge later to make dinner that night, Edison would be yammering on the sidelines from his maroon throne, usually telling jazz stories. ("Jarrett is such a prima donna," Edison might opine, "that he'll stop the performance if anyone in the audience so much as *coughs*. I ain't kidding—during winter concerts they actually hand out free *cough drops* to the whole crowd before the precious maestro deigns to touch the keys. Or he'll lead the audience in a 'group cough' to get it out of their system. Give me a break!" It wasn't subtle: Edison was fiercely jealous of Keith Jarrett, one of my brother's few contemporaries of whom the rest of us had actually heard.) I could have tolerated Edison's garrulousness if it weren't for the fact that he never said anything. I mean anything with honest emotional content. He loved to spout information, and he wasn't a bad raconteur. But Edison could talk all day, at the end of which no one knew him any better than before.

Worse, I could feel Edison driving Fletcher insane. My husband's rage was so palpable to me that I was terrified that my brother as well could pick up its dog-whistle shriek. Yet as Edison sucked all the conversational air from the room, Fletcher grew outwardly only grimmer and quieter. Tight-lipped by nature, my husband couldn't become more so without ceasing to speak altogether. Which is pretty much what he did. Our silent communion had morphed into not talking to each other, period.

In addition to being my technical consultant at Baby Monotonous, Oliver Allbless was my confidant. It was to him I poured out my unalloyed disgust with Fletcher's fanatical cycling, my perplexity over why the rigidity of my husband's diet should be driving us apart when after all it was only food, my indignation over being misquoted in profiles since no one else wanted to hear me complain about appearing in national magazines, and my less politic opinions of my stepson's ridiculous ambition to become a screenwriter. A nice-looking man, lanky and mild of manner, Oliver and I had a history, one whose importance I had played down to Fletcher, who intuited it anyway. So in the main I tried to keep them apart, while putting them in the same room just often enough to flaunt: *See? I have nothing to hide.* Oliver was deferential in Fletcher's presence, bowing to the alpha male in such a textbook show of submission that we might have been featuring in *Wild Kingdom.* He would ask to see Fletcher's latest furniture, and carry on neutral conversations with me about ethanol's dubious energy efficiency, never letting on that he was privy to anything more intimate in my life than my perspective on agricultural policy. Since Edison's arrival I'd skipped this awkward exercise, in dread of being torn not two ways but three. Yet at length I did arrange for my best friend to join us for dinner. I wanted him to meet Edison, if only so we could talk about him once my brother went home.

I'd prepared Oliver for my brother's transformation, and when they shook hands my friend covered his incredulity more skillfully than most. At dinner, he admired Fletcher's barley and mushroom salad, though as Tanner muttered at my elbow, "God, it even tastes beige."

"You know, your namesake, Somebody Fletcher," Edison told my husband informatively, "started a cult in the early 1900s. Called himself 'The Great Masticator.' Everybody went ape-shit for 'fletcherizing.' All about *chewing*, every bite, between thirty-two and *forty-five* times. You even had to chew, like, orange juice. Cat turned eating into such a drag, bet you two woulda got along like a house on fire."

Curving the conversation from my brother's less-than-appreciative response to Fletcher's cooking, Oliver inquired about Edison's jazz career, the response predictably extensive. Edison asked nothing about Oliver in return. Keeping a backseat, I felt conflicted. I wanted to feel proud of my brother; I also wanted Edison to behave as piggishly as possible, the better to demonstrate to Oliver what we'd been putting up with.

"So, Tanner," said Oliver, a master of social evenhandedness. "What colleges do you plan to apply to?"

Tanner glanced warily at his father. "Like, none, if you want to know the truth. I'm not into college."

"Not yet," said Fletcher tightly. "None of them's admitted you."

"Know what, quote, 'higher education' is about, don't you?" Hitherto, Edison's ratta-tat-tat conversation had been powered by an edgy irritation that I'd learned to recognize as petulance over Fletcher's dreary cuisine. Now that I'd unveiled my ricotta pie—lighter than cheesecake, though with anything half the calories my brother would eat twice as much of it—Edison relaxed and grew more expansive. "Know what a diploma is really about? It's a little piece of paper says you followed the rules. Says you're a good doobie, and you'll do what folks expect you to. Degrees are all about jumping hoops and fulfilling an arbitrary set of requirements, and it don't matter what those requirements are, only that you ticked the boxes. It's a rehearsal for nine-to-fiving your life away. Employers want that piece of paper to be sure you'll drag your sorry ass into an open-plan office day after pointless day, and no matter how futile or flagrantly idiotic the order is, you'll *do what you're told*."

"How would you know, bud?" said Fletcher. "You never went to college."

"Sure, that's what they want you to think," said Edison coolly, his hand twitching into the pocket of his cardigan; he was weighing the merits of finishing his diatribe versus escaping for a cigarette. "Oh, college must be some behind-closed-doors secret initiation that I can't understand till I get there, like the Masai taking pubescent boys into the bush. Big surprise, bro: they cut your dick off."

"In some fields it is important to master a body of information," said Oliver.

"The information is available, man, if you want to go get it. The degree's just about *appearing* to have mastered the information, know what I'm sayin'?"

"I'm not sure I want to drive across a bridge designed by someone who learned mechanical engineering off the Internet," said Oliver. "What I learned at U of I—"

"Tan here don't want to build bridges, do you?"

"Not especially," said Tanner. (For the motorists of the future I was relieved.)

"What good's college gonna do a television scriptwriter?" Edison had converted Tanner's ambition to TV for him. "Believe it or not, my dad went to *agricultural* school. Think that helped get him the lead in *Joint Custody*? Instead of taking calculus, Tanner is literally better off *watching TV*. Putting his feet up with a laptop and drafting a pilot. And you should listen to this cat—he got some killin' ideas, too. Same as my biz. Sax player walks into the Vanguard, they don't care if you went to Berkeley-with-a-Y or Berklee-with-an-E. All they wanna know is can you blow."

"Without a B.A.," said Fletcher, "I'd never have gotten that job with Monsanto."

"Yeah, well," said Edison, "I rest my case."

"He's right, Dad," said Tanner. "I don't want to sell seed corn."

"It's not all about what you *want*," said Fletcher. "I may not have liked that job much, but I supported my family. We had food and a roof, and I wasn't a burden on my parents or my neighbors or the state. That's what it's about, not following your 'dream.'"

"Well, in that case we should all save a lot of trouble and I can just fucking kill myself right now," Tanner grumbled.

"Set your sights that low, mere survival's exactly what you're gonna get," said Edison. "Look at my little sister—I mean, my really little sister. Went to UCLA, studying I don't even remember what. Now she's a publicist. What a life. All day promoting *other people's* accomplishments. But Solstice has 'food and a roof'! Christ, man, I don't know how that girl could be related to me."

"You don't know her," I said. "She's actually pretty nice."

"God help me, Panda Bear, if anyone ever says, 'Edison Appaloosa is actually pretty nice.'"

"No danger of that," Fletcher muttered.

"Only interesting thing about that woman is her stupid name," said Edison. "Didn't grow up in the same family. *Joint Custody* was over, and everything got all ordinary."

"Mom," Cody piped up. "Where did you go to college?"

"Reed," I said. "I'm a 'Reedie.'"

Edison chuckled. "Because it was in *Portland*. Wanted to jump into the other side of the screen."

I blushed. "There may have been a power-of-suggestion factor. Portland had acquired a pleasantly familiar feeling. But the school was small, and out of the way, and at least back then easy to get into."

"What did you major in?" asked Cody.

"English."

"What's the point in studying the one language you already speak?" said Tanner.

"In those days, lots of people majored in English when they weren't sure what they wanted to do," I said. "That or psychology, but I'd already earned a G.E.D. in lunacy at home. Getting a degree in English gave me time to think. That's what you could use, Tanner, if you don't mind my saying so."

"Perfect example," said Edison. "Four years reading a bunch of crap she totally forgot a long time ago, and look: she runs a catering business, and then makes *pull-string dolls*. What was the point? Fuck college."

"College isn't only about who follows the rules. It's bigger and cruder than that," said Oliver carefully. "It's a sorting mechanism; it weeds out the losers. There are exceptions—Edison, you're obviously one of them—and you tend to hear from those exceptions, because they're in a position to be heard. But so many people get an education now that *not* having one means more than ever. It's like joining the slave class, Tanner. It's marking yourself as lost."

"Know what *else* marks you as the 'slave class'?" Tanner mumbled to his sister. He'd jerked his head in his step-uncle's direction.

Uncomfortably, Tanner was right. The country now sported an alarmingly large underclass—large in every sense.

T he dessert course had been served with one predictable abstention. So before sliding the ricotta pie back in the fridge, I sheered a one-bite sliver onto a clean plate, then garnished it with a segment of nectarine and the usual sprig of mint. The confection had turned out well—close-grained, moist, and not too sweet, with a hint of lemon zest and a crisp, tender short-crust of which my grandmother would have been proud. Per tradition, I left this marital *amuse-bouche* conspicuously on an empty counter, its fork turned tantalizingly for the right-handed. I helped Fletcher with the kitchen until we were down to drying, then spent more than long enough upstairs saying goodnight to the kids to allow for a single, surreptitious mouthful of contraband.

But when I came back down, the kitchen was sparkling—with the sole exception of one plate, one fork, and one bite of ricotta pie, for which one of the diners this evening had no appetite: garbage, in other words, which I scraped mournfully into the trash.

Hoping to get better acquainted with my brother, Oliver had lingered with me and Edison after Fletcher went to bed. When I slipped into our bedroom around midnight, Fletcher was lying on his back, eyes open. Undressing in the dark—a regular habit since putting on weight—I apologized for waking him.

"You didn't," he said. "How would I get to sleep, with that racket?"

Edison's computer was plugged into our stereo, then pumping out "Bird," or someone else with a snappy handle I was supposed to know. "I could ask him to turn it down. Although it gives us cover. To talk."

"What would we talk about?" said Fletcher. "Duke Ellington?"

I slid under the comforter. "How about—how exciting it is you got that new commission. With those great reviews on your website, word about your work must really be starting to travel—"

"Can it, Pandora. It's only two matching end tables, the guy wants them pretty boring, and after materials I won't clear two hundred bucks. You're trying too hard."

"It's just I feel like I've hardly seen you in ages."

"Wonder why that would be."

"It's temporary."

"I can't believe we have another month of this."

"I'm sorry."

"You're not that sorry. All the in-jokes about *Joint Custody*. The chummy digs at your dad and Joy Whatserface. The ritual haggle about what really happened to your mother. You're having a ball. Jesus, I should move out and you two can get married."

It was the most he'd said in days. "That's crazy," I said lamely.

"I know you think of this 'visit'—although I doubt that's what it's called when it goes on for two months—as some sort of good deed. But what *good* are you doing him? Giving him the run of the kitchen, so he can get even fatter?"

"I can't say, 'No, Edison, you can't have another cookie.' I'm not his mother."

"And he doesn't do anything. Jesus, I bike just to get away. There's a miasma in the house. Of sloth. Of laziness. Of malaise. But what's going to be any different for the guy on the other end of this? He's got a huge problem, and when he leaves here it's only going to be *bigger*."

"I've been hoping being around family cheers him up. Something about his not playing the piano—it's weird. Maybe for you it's a reprieve, but there's something wrong. I wonder if he's depressed."

"If I were that big a load, I'd be depressed, too."

That was the chicken-and-egg question I'd not been able to parse. Was Edison fat because he was depressed, or depressed because he was fat?

"He really thrives on how nice Cody is to him," I said. "I don't think most people are very nice. I've seen it, when we're out and about. The looks. As if he's—doing something to them, as if he's an affront. The worst is in the supermarket. With the mounded cart. I feel like I'm surrounded by a giant eye roll."

"Sure, he's all too happy to feed off Cody's goodwill. She's a sweetheart. But he's using her up. And what does she get out of this?"

"Piano lessons? And practice at compassion. Which maybe she could teach you sometime."

"Are you kidding? I do nothing but bite my tongue. Besides, what Cody's really practicing is *pity*. Which isn't doing your brother any favors either."

"But when her friends are over, she always sticks up for him, and won't let them call him names, even behind his back. That takes guts." I made another fruitless effort to bridge the distance. "Your daughter's pretty remarkable."

"And what about Tanner?" I wasn't sure if Fletcher was angry at Edison or at me, and he may not have known himself. "All your brother's talk about being a big cheese in New York and coming from a celebrity L.A. family—he makes fun of your dad, but he plays the Appaloosa card for all it's worth. So Tanner thinks he can waltz into California and start writing episodes of—whatever." Fletcher didn't watch much television. "That kid has to get real! Even if he doesn't go to college, he could at least learn to make something. Nobody in this country knows how to sink a nail anymore. They're all dependent on the tradesmen their kids are taught not to become. In the next few decades, the handful of guys who can patch a roof will write their own tickets. But no. Everybody has to be an *artist*."

"You're an artist."

"I still make things people can sit on. They just happen to look good. Tanner could do a lot worse than apprentice himself in our basement. Instead he thinks he can float out of this house into la-la land, where in truth he'll be pimped out to perverts on some street corner. Your *brother* is shoring up the boy's illusions."

"Edison is trying to get Tanner to like him. But Tanner disdains Edison, and doesn't try very hard to disguise it, either."

"Tanner disdains everybody. He can still be influenced. It's just a pose."

I was of two minds about whether to encourage Tanner to follow his "dream." Was a mother's role to preserve his hopes, or to confront him with the practicalities of survival on a planet with seven billion people who all wanted to be famous? Other than urge him to go to college—if nothing else, as delay, giving him time to grow up safely, with a meal plan, in a dormitory—hitherto I had restrained myself from being, as Edison would say, *dark* on his screenwriting ambitions. I'd entertained dubious futures as a teenager myself. Surely I'd have resented any pragmatist who observed that half the girls in my middle school also wanted to be vets, that competition for places in veterinary schools was surprisingly stiff, that if I felt faint during inoculations I didn't have the stomach, that all I really wanted was a pet. Once closer to Tanner's age, I wouldn't have appreciated being admonished by a balloon-busting grown-up that very few candidates were admitted to NASA and that the majority of those who were never made it to outer space; I'd have despised any adult shrewd enough to discern that my brief infatuation with becoming an astronaut was merely a metaphor for a desperation to get as far away as possible from other people.

Yet like Fletcher I also despaired that Edison had been promoting Tanner's familial links to fame. This pervasive craving to be recognized as special amounted to an abdication of power, an outsourcing of your core responsibilities. I spurned the fawning of strangers, but I did feel special to myself. I had found that "feeling special" was a private experience, and no one else's projected fascination could substitute for quiet absorption in your own life.

"Tanner's bombarded with celebrity every time he boots up his computer," I said.

"This is different. With your nut-job dad's TV thing, your brother *claiming* to be a world-renowned piano player, and you—

you and Baby Moronic on the cover of magazines. It all gives him the wrong idea. He thinks everything is easy."

"Just four more weeks." I finally put a hand on his thigh. We hadn't had sex since Edison's plane landed. One more thing on hold; I shivered with sorrow. I'd have hated to be the houseguest whom my hosts were frantic to send packing.

I didn't tell Fletcher, but I'd noticed the systematic disappearance of foodstuffs, like whole pounds of dried apricots and Brazil nuts, which I made sure to discreetly replace. Fletcher wouldn't miss the cheese, but I still found it alarming that a brick of Swiss could be unopened one day and gone the next. Weird things vanished, too: a pint of tahini, a bottle of toasted wheat germ, a jar of sour cherry preserves. I could always buy more groceries, so I was mostly perturbed by the haunting image of their consumption. The tahini, for example: it was oily but tended to settle, and the heavy, dry bottom layer would stick in one's throat. It pained me how pleasureless it could only have been to binge on wheat germ.

There was a weekday window of opportunity for the mouse to play while the *cats* were away—when I was at Monotonous, Fletcher was cycling, and the kids were at school. Yet one afternoon I'd been feeling under the weather and knocked off work early. I'm surprised he didn't hear me come in, but then my brother was occupied. For a moment I stood in the kitchen doorway and watched. Our wooden prep island was littered with bottles. The sides of the depleted Karo were glistening. I recognized an ancient Christmas present that had slid to the back of the pantry: pecans and hazelnuts candied in a thick brown goo.

That jar was empty and drooling, too. The honey was out. Bizarrely, a bottle of Indian lime pickle. Cranberry sauce. And this was all in addition to our confectioner's sugar, which Edison was spooning straight from the box.

He looked up. Some people might have seen the comic side. Syrup from earlier in the pillage glued the white powder to his chin in an homage to Santa Claus. The sugar talcumed his hair, aging the tufts at his temples ten years. It snowed over the cuffs and roll collar of his ubiquitous black cardigan. It dusted the toes of his broad, snub-toed black shoes and a three-foot radius of terra-cotta floor tiles. Moistened white paste mucked rabidly inside his mouth, which he had opened to emit whatever far-fetched explanation might substitute for the self-evident. The nausea I'd been fighting took a turn for the worse.

I fought a cowardly urge to flee. Instead I began rinsing jars for recycling. I lowered my eyes while he swallowed hard, wiped his face with a dishtowel, and closed the box—neatly folding the inside waxed-paper bag and inserting the cardboard tab into the opposite slot with precision. We were way beyond his making up some little story about deciding to bake a cake, and I was relieved he didn't try.

"You know," I said quietly, "it would have been less upsetting to have interrupted you snorting cocaine."

"Sorry about the mess," he said, brushing his sweater gray. "I got hungry."

"No, you didn't. You got something, and I don't know what it's called, but it's not called hungry."

I must have sounded angry, but by the time I'd rinsed the third jar I left the hot water running and hung my head in the steam. "What . . . ?" I said. "What . . . ?" I kept shaking my head, until whatever had been bothering my stomach earlier that day rose in a great bolus—not vomit but a sob, which must have been trying to get out for the last month. Edison came around and embraced me from behind, pressing his cheek against my back, while my eyes drizzled into the sink. Later I'd decide that the olive Burberry I'd been wearing when I came home would have to be dry-cleaned. Across the shoulders, down the lapels, and all over the sleeves, the coat would be ashed in the impotent consolation of confectioner's-sugar handprints.

chapter nine

It sounds unkind. But aside from Cody, we were all eyeing with desperation the red-letter day of November 29th, the date of my brother's return flight to New York. In our defense, having a guest of any size for two whole months is trying for most people. Making conversation was exhausting. Between my brother's running commentary and his iTunes hooked up to our stereo, Fletcher had trouble concentrating. He worked in expensive, often imported woods; if he was calculating an order, a piece an inch too short could be disastrous. Our laundry burden had increased; three of Edison's voluminous outfits filled out a washer load. Mornings, we were *constantly* out of half-and-half, when we were stocking the stuff by the half-gallon.

My brother was not a physically careful person, which had for weeks expressed itself in a series of small damages that still added up to a sustained sense of violation. He experimented with my stovetop milk steamer and left it on high to run dry; he melted the rubber gasket and blew out the safety valve. He used a metal spatula on my favorite nonstick sauté pan. He broke one of the finely etched wineglasses I'd inherited from our paternal grandparents. Boiling water for pasta, he placed a Revere Ware pot off center on the burner, and flames licked up the side to overheat the handle; the kitchen reeked for hours of melted plastic. Alas, in the advancing season he'd taken on building fires in the fireplace, but employing the same quantity that typified everything he put his hand to, devastating our supply of kindling and burning black spots with rolling coals into our hearthside Persian carpet.

Edison continued to keep unsociable hours, so when I awoke I tiptoed downstairs and refrained from listening to the radio while I made my toast, lest I disturb our slumbering houseguest overhead. On the other hand, I preferred these mornings to the ones after Edison had found tackling the stairs too much of a drain and slept in his clothes in the maroon recliner—obliging the whole family to church-mouse through breakfast and make do with juice or tea, because running the coffee grinder would wake him up. And Edison had sleep apnea. However grating his heavy snore, the long silences during which he stopped breathing altogether disturbed us more. The loud snorts with which these deathly respites concluded were startling, but still a relief.

Given a taint invading the ground floor, I doubted he always smoked out on the patio when the rest of the family was out or abed, especially now that into November it was getting cold. Whenever he did amble out the sliding door and back in again, he dropped the temperature not five degrees but ten.

As if he regarded himself as currently on the road and therefore in the care of hotel staff, my brother's contribution to keeping the house clean was to get in the way of the vacuum cleaner.

We'd kept our décor minimal, the better to feature Fletcher's woodwork, but lately it featured Edison's dirty dishes, broken-down slippers, and splayed copies of *Downbeat* instead. Fletcher was a neat man with a spare aesthetic; the first thing he did on emerging from the basement or returning from a bike ride was collect this detritus, lips pressed into an em dash. Despite the regular admonitions of the Fletcher doll, my brother routinely forgot that my husband's furniture was oiled, not varnished, and cups on the rosewood coffee table would leave rings without a coaster. Since the collateral damage of my brother's Midwestern sabbatical was, by the transitive property, all my fault, I would skulk in my husband's wake with a stick of Land O'Lakes to vanquish the circles with rubbed-in butter—the while wondering, if I had learned this trick from our mother, why my brother had not. Whenever Edison showered in the upstairs bathroom, the mat got soaked, along with the floor, and anyone walking in soon after would muddy the tiles with footprints. The guest room was a nest of soiled clothes I had regularly to harvest myself. Now cratered down the middle like a half-dug grave, the mattress would have to be replaced.

I hadn't concerned myself with the arbitrary, dart-in-a-calendar spirit in which Edison had chosen his return date when we'd changed his airline reservation in October. Presumably once back in New York he was expecting to stay with colleagues for a day or two, perhaps Slack Muncie now that his friend had enjoyed a breather, before heading off with a band to Barcelona. A lack of specificity about his many other bookings through the spring caused me an unease whose scrutiny I avoided. According to Edison, he'd be making enough money off the tour of Spain and Portugal to put down a deposit on a new apartment and haul his things out of storage. (I'd proposed to augment his earnings, too, if that would help him land his own place again, although there was an ugly side to this offer—more than a suggestion that I would pay my brother to not come back here.) That had been the concept all along, right? That this stay in New Holland would see him through a professional dry patch. Presto, he could return from his European tour with cash in pocket, ready to reestablish himself in the Big Apple and attend to his busy schedule. It had all made sense on paper until I laid eyes on him. But I felt I'd done my bit, you see. I thought my whole family had more than done its bit.

Only in retrospect do I appreciate that this "doing your bit" is a deadly misapprehension of the nature of familial ties. Better understanding them now, I find blood relationships rather frightening. What is wonderful about kinship is also what is horrible about it: there is no line in the sand, no natural limit to what these people can reasonably expect of you. When I moved to Iowa and stayed for two solid years with the Grumps, I was often apologetic about not yet having found a job and apartment. My grandmother (unwittingly paving my exit by teaching me to cook) used to pat my hand warmly and say, "Why, the very definition of *family*, dear, is the folks who will always take you in." I'd found her paraphrase of Robert Frost comforting at the time, but during this long fraternal visit that aphorism had come back to bite me. Ergo, what Edison could "reasonably" expect of me was potentially infinite.

I now recognize that responsibility, once assumed, cannot be readily repudiated—not without doing so much damage in the process of its abdication that you might better have never assumed the responsibility in the first place. Whether or not I realized it when I first sent that plane ticket and five-hundred-dollar check, I had taken Edison on. All however many hundred pounds of him. This contract had no end date of November 29th if you studied the fine print. There are instances when pet owners are overwhelmed and leave dogs they didn't realize would be so much trouble at the ASPCA; foster parents have second thoughts, and return unruly charges to the state. But flesh-and-blood family works in only one direction.

A AAANNN!" Or I'm not sure how you'd spell it, a wordless exclamation of torment at a volume I may never before have heard my contained husband reach. Certainly the comic-book "argh!" would not do justice to the sound.

I dropped the pan I was scrubbing in the sink and rushed to the living room just as Edison slipped out to the patio for a smoke. I was terrified Fletcher had hurt himself. "Are you all right?"

My husband was standing with a sketchpad and whiffling. He didn't seem to be bleeding, but the reedy wheeze in his throat would from anyone else be a scream. He was reared back, as if from the grisly specter of fresh roadkill. I turned to what Fletcher could not bear looking at: the Boomerang.

It was, yes, only subtly out of kilter. Three of the supporting back slats no longer swept upwards in the even curves of a rib cage, but suffered from interruptions, where they poked the wrong way. The arc of the swooping top rail, which formed the whole flung, soaring sweep of the piece, also jerked at a sudden angle, from which a splinter frayed. In a material as uncompromising as wood, subtly out of kilter was the same as—well, completely fucked.

"Oh, no," I said softly, kneeling to the chair. I examined the slats—fractured unevenly, being laminated, and save for a few shreds cracked all the way through. The top piece was splintered along a good six inches of rail.

With that instinctive ear for sorrow, Cody had slipped downstairs and joined me.

"Not the Boomerang!" As she rested a cheek on its red leather seat, we looked at each other with shared dread. "Dad, I'm so sorry. I love this chair. It's, like, a member of the family. All my friends think it's awesome!"

Fletcher was not to be bought off with compliments. "I *told* him not to sit in it. I told him not to sit on any of these pieces. They are designed for normal people. Normal, halfway disciplined, halfway intelligent people."

It was news to me that Fletcher had banned my brother from his furniture. I had batted away my own misgivings, choosing to trust the robust construction of my husband's wares—a faith that spared me the mortification of telling Edison that he couldn't sit where the rest of us did because he was too fat.

"But you can fix it, can't you, Daddy? We can send the Boomerang to the hospital to get well!" Cody was mature for thirteen, and the childishness was a ploy.

"Are you sure that's what happened?" I asked wearily.

"Did I sleepwalk into the living room with an axe? Have the kids been practicing their baseball swings indoors? They don't play baseball. You didn't have anything to do with this," he directed to Cody, "*did* you?"

Her eyes panicked: on the spur of the moment she was having a hard time concocting a plausible scenario whereby it was all her fault. "I don't know. I did sit in it yesterday. Doing my homework. My laptop is . . . sort of heavy . . ."

"What, in this house," said Fletcher, "aside from my frail daughter's *six-pound* laptop, is 'sort of heavy'?"

"I guess that is the most logical explanation," I said glumly.

"That son of a bitch didn't even have the integrity to tell me! He left it propped together, the slats pulled to, the railing pressed back into place. So I sit down, and whoa! After all these years, think that chair can't bear *my* weight?"

"Edison! Could you come in here, please?" I'd not shouted loudly enough for him to hear on the patio unless he was keeping an ear cocked for this very summons. The door slid and clicked, and it took too long for Edison to waddle into the room.

"Yo, whussup, man?" His expression was blankly pleasant.

Still kneeling, I stroked the injured slats, as one might reassure a pet about to be put down. "This chair is broken. Did you have anything to do with it?"

"Hell, no, course not. Don't know anything about it."

I sighed. Never having mothered a small child, I'd no idea how you dealt with stonewalling denial in the face of incontrovertible evidence to the contrary. "It would really be better if you confessed."

"Confessed what? I didn't do anything! Still, that's a real shame. That chair is *out*, man. But you can repair it, right? Like, superglue it or something. And your man here. He's like, a genius in that basement, know what I'm sayin'?"

"You don't repair high-end custom furniture with *superglue*," said Fletcher.

Tanner had trailed downstairs, and the added audience of his checking out the drama from the doorway only made everything worse.

"Hey, be glad to help if I can," said Edison cheerfully. "Run out tomorrow and get the repair stuff—whatever it is. Just say the word."

" 'The word'—or words"—Fletcher looked Edison in the eye, and my brother took a step backwards—"are *I'm sorry. I'm sorry I'm such a fat fuck*—"

"Sweetie," I implored, "I know you're upset—"

"I'm sorry I'm such a lard-bucket loser that I've got nothing to do all day but plop my enormous ass in furniture I was EXPRESSLY forbidden from sitting in. I'm sorry I'm so completely full of shit—"

"Dad, don't!" Cody wrapped her arms around her father's waist. "Please just shut up, please!"

Fletcher shook her off. *"That I pretend to be an internationally famous jazz musician, when I'm really some broke, homeless, self-indulgent food junkie leeching off my sucker of a sister and ruining her whole family's life. I'm sorry my head is fat, my thighs are fat, my fingers and my toes are fat, and even my dick is fat, though my gut is so fat that I haven't actually laid eyes on my dick for the last two years. That's why, when I destroy an irreplaceable, priceless object, I leave it delicately propped together for somebody else to find, because I'm not enough of a MAN to admit I broke it."*

As a strategy, the diatribe backfired. When Edison turned white and hustled blindly past us out the front door, not even grabbing his coat when it was below freezing, Cody abandoned her father and rushed after him.

"Sweetheart, it's a beautiful chair, but it's still a chair," I said. "Which you can't make whole no matter how viciously you berate my brother. Don't you *ever* do that again."

I drew on my own coat, threw Cody's and Edison's over my arm, and set off to catch up with them. At that size, he wouldn't have gotten far.

T hat guy fucking hates me." Edison was hulking down Solomon Drive, his forward-canted bearing recalling the urgency with which as a taller, slender man he had strode the streets
of Manhattan in his smashing leather trench coat. Yet this evening's velocity was as much side-to-side as straight ahead. Cody
clutched one hand, which made it difficult for me to walk on his
other side; Edison alone consumed the width of the sidewalk.

"Fletcher doesn't hate you." The rebuttal was reflexive,
though I didn't know what you called it if not hatred when you
wished so passionately that someone simply wasn't there.

"I think you're wonderful, Uncle Edison!"

"*Please* put these on, it's cold," I implored. We'd bought
Edison's coat at Kohl's on one of our more successful outings
together, but he ignored the big down jacket that took as much
room in my arms as a sleeping bag. Cody spurned her coat, too—
either out of solidarity with her uncle or because she couldn't bear
to relinquish his hand.

"Look, man, it's too bad about the chair"—he still wasn't
owning up precisely—"but that don't give him the right to dis
my career, man. You got the CDs, right? Far as that cat's concerned, I'm making them up. He should try Googling my name,
man. Check out my Wikipedia page, man. I don't appreciate being talked to like some down-and-out zero, man." The fast and
furious "man"s punctuated his speech like a case of hiccups.

I took advantage of a grassy verge to draw alongside. "He
lost his temper. That one chair is—I know it's 'just' a chair, but
especially when it's something you've made yourself you can love

an object. To Fletcher, breaking that chair is worse than breaking his arm. The Boomerang is a ward, a responsibility. He feels
like he wasn't looking out for it. I wouldn't compare a chair to a
child, but he was still—bereaved. When people get upset, they
say things they don't mean."

"Sometimes they lose their rag and say *exactly* what they
mean." Chin buried in his neck, Edison scowled at the sidewalk. The streetlight scored dramatic shadows in the folds of
his face, and a halo around his head as the light caught the frizz
of his curls gave him a saintly, martyred cast. "He doesn't give
you much credit, either, Panda Bear. Whole company, nationally
distributed product? Cat acts like you go off every day to a quilt-
ing bee."

"Fletcher's furniture business isn't doing that well," I said.
"He works really hard, but people around here won't pay what
his stuff is worth when they can get ready-made dining sets from
Target for three hundred bucks. You know what it's like when
you've hit a rough patch. It makes you—ungenerous." I was tiring of this ritual: explaining Fletcher to Edison, and Edison to
Fletcher. It didn't work.

"My staying here has obviously got uncool," said Edison, "if
I'm 'ruining your whole family's life.' I should move up the plane
reservation. Get out of your hair."

"You're not in our hair!" said Cody. "And you promised to
help me with 'April Come She Will.'"

We were coming up on more trees, which would push me
back behind him; I stepped ahead, turned around, and stopped
them both. Handing off her coat to Cody's free hand, I draped
the broad down jacket around my brother's rounded shoulders,
hoping that he remembered our companionable afternoon shop-

ping for it. Only with the streetlight shining directly into them could I now see how constricted his pupils were, how the tiny muscles around his eyes had a twitchy tremble. "It's my house too, and I want you to stay," I said. "Because I love you."

People hear that all the time from family, but the impact of this simple, standard avowal on my brother at that moment was both deeply moving and alarming. Releasing Cody's hand so she could shiver into her coat, he embraced me in a grateful cocoon of flesh and feathers that made me feel warm and safe, my brother briefly restored as my protector, but also a little smothered. I was the middle child, the stepmother, until recently the mere caterer of other people's grand occasions. Well before sharing a rare center stage in my long-in-coming marriage, I'd grown accustomed to feeling ancillary—a bit off to the side, an afterthought. This was my first intimation of what it might feel like to be too important.

E ventually Cody and I cajoled Edison back to the house. He didn't have anywhere else to go.

By our return, the Boomerang had been banded with yellow packing tape from a wood shipment that suggested a crime scene. Fletcher was buried in the basement. When I tried to coax him upstairs, he only acceded to talk things out when I observed that a standoff wasn't fair to me.

Banishing Cody and Tanner to their rooms so no one could play to the gallery, I sat the antagonists down at the dining table, where Edison sank into the maroon recliner and Fletcher sat stiffly at the opposite end. Having already worked on my brother during our dark, frigid walk home, I got him to concede it was "barely possible" that in "a moment of distraction" he'd sat in the Boomerang, and that maybe he had "the dimmest memory" of a little cracking sound that "he hadn't paid attention to at the time"—in which hypothetical case he was sorry, an apology sufficiently hedged to save a little face. Loath to let my brother off the hook with anything short of a groveling mea culpa and still grieving for the talisman of his talents, Fletcher expressed his skepticism of this half-confession with the regular hollow *pock* of flossing his teeth, hurling bits of Swiss chard two feet across the table.

"Fletcher, would you please do that later?" I asked.

With a glare, he propped his elbows on the table and stretched the ligature wound on opposite forefingers into a six-inch garrote. "You have any idea what that one piece means to me—that piece in particular?"

"The very fact that Edison was afraid to tell you about the damage," I interceded, "assuming, of course, he did sit there by mistake—suggests he does know how much it means to you." I wasn't sure about this reasoning, which imputed greater powers of empathy to liars, but it sounded good at the time. I raised my eyebrows at Fletcher, to indicate it was his turn. Maybe I'd have done all right with toddlers after all.

He lowered the floss. "I'm sorry I called you fat." I inferred this was all he planned to concede.

"Look, man, I know I'm fat." Finally Edison addressed himself to Fletcher directly. "But the way you say it, it's like I'm scum. It's not a description but a verdict. Like I'm an abomination, the source of all evil and corruption in the universe. I eat too much, but I ain't murdered anybody. I ain't no pedophile. I didn't even filch your wallet, man."

"What is this?" said Fletcher sourly. " 'Fat pride'?"

"I'm not proud of myself, or I am, but not for my weight. Still, when I polish off a doughnut, that's not doing anything to *you*."

Fletcher took this in. I honestly believe he did experience Edison's overeating as a form of assault. "You're killing yourself, you know."

"If so, that's my business."

"I'm not so sure. I had a wife start committing suicide by degrees, and it definitely felt like my business."

"Then maybe it's lucky we're not married."

"You're putting your sister in a lot of pain, and I am married to her."

"That's between me and Pandora. She got something to say to me, she can say it."

"It's a compliment, you know," said Fletcher. "That she cares. But you make my wife cry, and I don't like it."

I 'm the one who suffered the injury, and you're mad at me."

"He hurt a thing," I said in bed that night. "You hurt his feelings. You'd never have let fly like that if he were missing a leg, or had a deformity."

"He deformed himself. Fat isn't a 'disability.' I may have apologized, but maybe a short, sharp shock is what he needs."

"Nobody needs cruelty."

"Your look-the-other-way routine doesn't drop his weight an ounce."

"But Edison's right on one point," I said. "You act as if you're on a moral crusade. His weight makes him a social pariah. It reduces the likelihood he'll remarry. It has grave implications for his health. But it isn't *evil*. Just like all that exercise of yours has nothing to do with being good. I know you think it does. It makes you feel good, and feel good *about yourself*, and superior to people who slob around all day. But it's mostly a waste of time that doesn't do anything for anybody else but you."

"This is too much. Your brother eats us out of house and home and smashes up the furniture, and who gets raked over the coals? Me. For selfishly *cycling* too much. How about, 'Thank you for putting up with my pain-in-the-ass brother for two solid months'? How about, 'I'm so sorry he destroyed one of the best pieces you ever made'?"

"I *am* sorry . . . Do you think it's repairable?"

"The slats, maybe. Re-creating that upper hoop from a single piece of wood is another matter. I'm not sure I've got the heart. You do something once as an act of love. You do it all over again as an act of drudgery."

"Well, either fix it or cannibalize it for other work, but in any case drag it to the basement. Right now it's like we have a dead body in the living room. It's accusatory."

"What's wrong with *that*? You keep acting as if your brother's the victim, the poor fat guy. But *he* is victimizing *us*."

"Maybe he's not a victim, but he is a soft target. Pick on someone your own size."

"You're such a sap. Ever ask yourself whether you'd put up with half the shit that guy pulls if he weren't obese?"

"Two more weeks," I said. "For me. Please let's get through the home stretch without doing any more damage."

"It's your brother who's doing the damage." A darkness of tone implied that he wasn't only talking about the chair.

Lying side by side, we weren't touching. I wanted to reach for his hand. Everything would be all right if only we made physical contact. Yet each time I commanded my hand to move, I saw Fletcher's hateful grimace in the living room, and Edison's expression as well—so stricken that my husband might have swung at his jaw with a plank. The few inches of cold cotton yawned between us like an Arctic ice sheet.

Sleep being out of the question, at length I asked quietly, "What about *your* 'look-the-other-way routine'?"

"Are you kidding? I'm the only one in this house who ever uses the F-word."

"That's what I mean. You think Edison is wearing on his sleeve how weak he is—how lazy, how indulgent. So what must you think of me?"

Fletcher faced me on his side; the sheer relief of his hand on my cheek made me dizzy. "Honey. What are you talking about?"

"What we never talk about." As I closed my arms more tightly around my middle, I realized that I lay in bed this way routinely, hands clasped around opposite rolls at my waist. "I'm not the same size I was when we got married, and you know it."

"God, sweetheart, your brother—there's no comparison!"

"See? You *have* noticed."

"Maybe, a little, but so what? Women your age almost always fill out a little. I don't care! You're still as beautiful to me as the day we met." He smoothed the hair from my eyes, but I turned my face to the wall.

"That's just what you think you're supposed to say." I was determined not to cry. "I feel like a cow. None of my old clothes fit anymore. And meanwhile, you're so strict about your diet that now you won't even eat those miniscule taster plates I leave you—"

"Hey, hey! I *love* those little cheats. I just can't stand looking like a hypocrite when your brother's around. Which I'm sorry to say he always is."

"But you bike all the time, and you're skinnier than you've ever been—"

"That's about me. Like you said—about what makes *me* feel better, about my*self.* It has nothing to do with you."

"It makes you feel better than me. After all, if what you said to Edison is anything to go by, I disgust you."

"No, no, no!" Fletcher turned my face toward him. "I admire the dickens out of you! Running a profitable start-up? Still managing to be a great mother to kids who aren't even biologically yours? Jesus, putting up with me, and my farce of a furniture business? What's a couple pounds next to that?"

"It's more than a couple of pounds," I mumbled. "But if you're ashamed of me I don't blame you, because I feel ashamed of myself, too. Sometimes I think I eat to punish myself. For eating. Don't say anything—I know that makes no sense. And now with my brother here, with his *issues*, and the huge meals he makes, and then to turn up my nose at his cooking would seem mean, and like siding with you in a way that's ganging up on him . . . Well, it's worse than ever. Which makes you hold me even more in contempt, and think I'm just, completely— gross."

Fletcher kissed my neck. "You are still," he whispered, "*stealth attractive*. In this bedroom? Nothing 'stealthy' about it, either. No lousy burrito is ever going to change the fact that I love you and you're my wife."

Limp with despair, I allowed my husband to run his hands adoringly over all the parts of my body I despised—the thighs that puckered in harsh light, the stomach that once ski-sloped from my rib cage but these days bulged even when I lay on my back, the breasts that I used to wish were larger and now I hated for being larger since the only reason I sported proper knockers was that I was overweight. But if I had come to loathe my own anatomy, then Fletcher Feuerbach would love it for me, so in gratitude I returned his affections and slept soundly in his arms that night. Maybe the greatest favor a spouse can tender is to overlook what you can't.

M y forty-first birthday arrived later that week, and the kids arranged to do to me what I did by profession to other people every day. Unsurprisingly, the laughter gets a little strained when the joke's on you.

Edison cooked, I don't remember what, though we can be sure it was *filling*. I remember ruing on that birthday that an occasion of any sort put consumption at the center. Gatherings were tagged by whatever you might put in your mouth: let's have *coffee*, get together for a *drink*, do *dinner* some night. The very chronology of the day was marked off with ingestion—*breakfast* time, *lunch*time, *supper*time—which was why one seldom arranged social get-togethers at eleven in the morning, or three in the afternoon.

After the meal, my booty: Fletcher had carved me an ergonomic kitchen stool that kept my back aligned, and I tried not to take it as an insult that he thought I had bad posture. Edison's present of cheeses and summer sausage was a nice gesture, yet I wished he'd been able to think of a gift that didn't involve food. Cody played me a rendition of "Bridge Over Troubled Water" that showcased her growing ability to improvise, the performance setting the stage for my main present from Tanner and Cody, who had teamed up this year.

My stepchildren had commissioned a Pandora doll from my own company. I still have it. In preference to the skinny model, they'd selected the mid-range build, which at headquarters we chose for vics who were distinctly chubby. The doll has short, crazy yellow yarn hair and an expression of optimistic goodwill that seems faintly imbecilic. It's clad in a Baby Monotonous sweatshirt, with our logo stitched on the breast. I pulled the string at the back, occasioning much raucous laughing and clapping each time:

I'm too humble and meek to drop names, but my dad is *totally* famous.

Joi-oi-nt Custody! Fra-a-ctured family!

Travis is a *cautionary tale.*

It's in this week's *Forbes* magazine, but don't worry—any day now my company's going to fold.

Oh, no! Not *another* photo shoot!

I'm not rich; I'm just *doing okay.*

My nationally successful product is a silly passing fad.

I love my kids, and that's why I want them to be absolute nobodies.

I'm an entrepreneur who writes my own ticket, but I expect everyone else to go to community college and sell seed corn.

I may have become a household name, but all I ever *really* wanted is to be ignored.

He ain't heavy—he's my bro-o-ther!

When I arrived at that last line, belted out to the tune of the Hollies' hit, Cody biffed her brother and objected, "You *promised* you'd leave that one out!"

"Don't worry about it, kid," said Edison. "I think it's a riot."

If Edison could be that good-humored, I could take the ribbing in stride too, and I thought that publicly I managed to seem charmed. I was indeed touched that they'd gone to so much trouble, though privately I was chagrined. What was modesty to me was false modesty to everyone else.

Even my pretense of taking my own medicine with brio was later held up to the cold light of day and found wanting. Fletcher corralled us into a standing group photo, and I still have that picture, too. Edison takes up half the shot, with Cody and Tanner squeezed around me. I'm clutching my new look-alike, but my grip on the doll is anything but fond. I might have been trying to strangle it.

chapter ten

Whenever I encounter a picture of myself, the first thing I assess is my weight. I am attached to particular photographs not because they memorialize a signal occasion, but because they depict me as thin. I could probably arrange my every photo in a precise order of preference that would perfectly correspond to a continuum of my size. The most beloved are those from the Breadbasket years, when I was gaunt, which makes me look sexless and insignificant. I don't care. Being underweight might not be fetching, but it still strikes me as a badge of nobility—yes, I realize how ludicrous this sounds—and I envy my previous incarnation's appearance of enjoying a little leeway. I scoffed at Fletcher's association of physique with vice and virtue, but I bought into the same equivalence myself.

So Tanner and Cody imagined that I was hiding (or failing to hide) my vanity when I shied from photo spreads. But I couldn't bear to look at pictures of myself from the previous three years precisely out of vanity, and that's why I didn't order extra copies of *New York* magazine or even obtain one hard copy of the *Forbes* piece: I looked *fat*.

All right, I'm ashamed of this. I don't know if this heightened concern for size was done to me or is something I have done to myself. What I do know: (1) I am not the only one who appraises their photographs with exactly the same eye; (2) the folks who also "weigh up" pictures of themselves are not all women.

Confronting a photograph of oneself is always a fraught business, for one's own image doesn't merely evoke the trivial fretting of "I had no idea my nose was so big." This sounds idiotic, but every time I encounter a picture of myself I am shocked to have been *seen*. I do not, under ordinary circumstances, feel seen. When I walk down the street, my experience is of looking. Manifest to myself in the ethereal privacy of my head, I grow alarmed when presented with evidence of my public body. This is quite a different matter from whatever dissatisfaction I may harbor over the heft of my ass. It is more a matter of having an ass, any ass, that other people can ogle, criticize, or grasp, and being staggered that to others this formation, whatever its shape, has something to do with me. Every once in a while I can connect a droll set of my facial muscles with the real, in-head experience of finding something funny and keeping the source of this amusement to myself. But in the main I fail utterly to recognize myself, the me of me, in my photographs. I do not identify with the cropped, once naturally blond head of hair with a tendency to frizz; when I have again neglected to color the roots for three solid months, the camera chastises, but I know that walking around with gray down the center part feels exactly the same as when the gray is covered. I'm not convinced that my elemental self even *has* hair. I do not identify with my short fingers; my relationship to my hands is to what they do, and digital stubbiness has never impaired their competent folding of buttermilk biscuit dough. I do not feel like someone with a neck lately on the thick side, with its implications of low sophistication and loutishness; I grew up in L.A., for heaven's sake. About all I truly recognize in my photos is my clothes—and I will greet the image of a quilted jacket from 1989 with the joy of meeting a long-lost friend. The fact that my clothing has been visually available to other people I do not find upsetting. The body is another matter. It is mine; I have found it useful; but it is an avatar.

Given that most people presumably contend with just this rattling disconnect between who they are to themselves and *what* they are to others, it's perplexing why we're still roundly obsessed with appearance. Having verified on our own accounts the feeble link between the *who* and the *what*, you'd think that from the age of three we'd have learned to look straight through the avatar as we do through a pane of glass. On the other hand, I sometimes suspected that my female employees who were lavishing fifty dollars per week from their modest salaries on makeup had mastered a secret that eluded me most of the time and only intruded when I looked at snapshots: like it or not, you are a *what* to other people. You may not recognize your heavy thighs, your cornflower eyes, but they do, and competent interface with the rest of the world involves manipulating that irrelevant, arbitrary, not-you image to the maximum extent. Ergo, if the makeup's application was skillful, that fifty bucks could not have been better spent.

Which brings us back to weight. Ever since Edison gave me cause to, I've made a study of this: the hierarchy of apprehensions when laying eyes on another person. Once a form emerges from the distance that is clearly a human and not a lamppost, we now log (1) gender, (2) size. This order of recognitions may be universal in my part of the world, though I do not believe "size" has always been number two. Yet these days I am apt to register that a figure is slight or fat even before I pick up a nanosecond later that they are white, Hispanic, or black. Especially when the subject in question is on the large side, many of us probably detect "on the large side" even before determining large person of which sex. Accordingly, in eyewitness testimonies to the police, "slim," "average-build," "heavyset," or some more refined variation thereof features without fail. In fiction, authors who do not immediately identify roughly how much a character weighs are not doing their jobs, and walk-on thumbnails in short stories invariably begin something like, "Allison, a tall, skinny girl with freckles" or, "Bob was an affable, gregarious man whose enjoyment of imported British ales was beginning to announce itself in his waistline . . ."

This is important if only because each of those three weight categories we used at Baby Monotonous attaches to a constellation of character traits—a set of stock qualities that, with no other information to go on, we impute to size. Mind, there is no neutrality in this game. As in countries like Australia, where participation in elections is a legal obligation, being one weight or another is a kind of voting that doesn't allow for abstentions. You are three-dimensional, and you have to weigh something.

Begin with "average"—like most middle positions, considered the dullest and least worthy of comment. Yet even "average" in this morass of preconceptions has grown complicated. Here in Iowa, anyway, we are no longer in accord on what dimensions qualify as standard. Granted, lofty health authorities have sought to impose the "body-mass index," thus providing a numerical definition of the normal—although I'm stymied by how the formula of "weight divided by height squared" invented by some Belgian in the early 1800s has suddenly become so fashionable two centuries later.

In Westdale Mall in Cedar Rapids, the norm is another story. My fellow citizens are so consistently broad of backside, round of shoulder, stout of leg, and plump of bicep that we might all be trooping across a canvas by Fernando Botero. Like cubism, futurism, or art deco, giantism has become a recognizable style in which the bulk of the population is drafted. Strolling public promenades, I am often struck by a powerful collusion, one in which during the years leading up to Edison's arrival I had participated to the hilt. I would think: these people are nearly all heavier than I am, so I'm not overweight. Size is relative. If everyone is fat, no one is fat.

Despite the Midwest's sneaky, steady expansion of what constitutes average contours, we still blithely assume that every one of these so-called normal people would desperately like to be thinner. It's taken as a given that Mr. and Ms. Average are dissatisfied with their weights, avoidant of mirrors, inclined to take their dress or jean size as a personal indictment, and sufficiently anxious about getting on a scale in the presence of others to put off doctors' appointments for months on end. It stands to reason, then, that these days even mid-range mass in America's heartland conveys a disposition to shame, frustration, and disappointment—if also a constitutional inclination to cut other people slack.

But what, or rather who, is the skinny? By conceit, the rail-thin are harsh, joyless, and critical. They suffer from the same chronic dissatisfaction as average-size people, but on top of applying a ruthless ruler to themselves they are reliably dissatisfied with *you*. Their proclivity for self-control inexorably bleeds into controlling everyone else as well. They don't know how to have a good time, and don't hesitate to poop your party, too. Scrawnies are superior, haughty, and elitist. Vain, self-centered, and cold. Picky. Stingy and withholding. Aloof. Uptight. Judgmental and condescending. Brittle, not only in appearance but in demeanor and bearing. Dishonest (likely to decline the offer of dessert because of feeling "far too full"), and insincere ("You look terrific!"). Nasty, although usually behind your back. Fearful, not only of food but also of people who eat it, as if libertinism might be contagious—thus prone to an unconscious apartheid, instinctively partial to the company of their own withered kind. Rigid—God forbid you should invite one of these paragons for a drink when *it's time to go running*.

One small subsection of the skeletal manages to get credit for an intellectual absorption in higher things than lunch or a scatterbrained tendency to skip meals out of forgetfulness, but they are *all men*. There lives not a slender Western woman about whom it is presumed at first meeting that she is too involved in her work to remember to eat.

Stick figures imagine they inspire envy, when in fact they excite dislike. Incredibly, the self-starved never appear capable of taking any pleasure in the very vessel for which they've sacrificed. So get this: despite the correlation of emaciation with smugness, they seem always to wish they were *even thinner*.

Lastly, the well and truly fat. I think we long ago put to rest their reputation for jollity. Misery, more like it. Melancholy, perhaps. Helplessness. Self-indulgence and self-deceit. Defensiveness. Resignation to the present; fatalism about the future.

Self-hatred and self-reproach. Shyness. Self-pity, albeit richly deserved; a persecution complex, although ought it be called a "complex" when you're genuinely persecuted? A self-deprecating sense of humor. Humility. As a consequence of having all too often been on the pointy end of malice, kindness. An enfolding warmth. Generosity. Born of self-evident frailty, cheerful acceptance of whatever might also be wrong with you. A longing to be left in peace, and a preference for staying home. Gentleness. Harmlessness. Languor. Frankness. Ribaldry. A down-to-earth nature, and a lack of pretension.

Now, these are stereotypes, and exceptions amid real people of every size are legion. Moreover, I've been as brainwashed as the next woman into accepting the prescribed dimensions of a fetching figure. Nevertheless, when I look at the lists of attributes we instinctively ascribe to the very thin and the very fat, I would rather be fat.

M y disquisition on photographs may have seemed a departure from our story. It wasn't.

In the few days leading up to Edison's flight back east, I'd been pressing him to decide how he wanted to mark his departure. Cody, I emphasized, would be heartbroken, and I would miss him terribly, too. On this last point, I was sincere.

Admittedly, for weeks I had been impatient to see the back of my brother, indulging in frequent fantasies about a return to regular life. I had repeatedly rehearsed arising at my leisure to switch on a kitchen radio that was already tuned to WSUI—as opposed to KCCK, the only station in Iowa that plays nothing but contemporary *jazz*. I would catch the beginning of *Morning Edition* with no concern for waking anyone with sleep apnea in an armchair. Gloriously, I would drizzle my coffee with two tablespoons of half-and-half from a nearly full pint container that would last through the rest of the month. I cherished the vision of coming home from Baby Monotonous and saying absolutely nothing. I pictured dinners with my family when alternating chefs weren't at war, and we weren't faced with either a nauseously mammoth feast or savagely drab, ascetic fare as penance for the night before; in short, I pictured Fletcher preparing his signature polenta, but remembering the Parmesan cheese. I looked forward to having frequent sex with my husband again, after which I would drop blissfully to sleep, rather than staring at the ceiling for an hour after yet another terse, furious wrangle over whatever Edison had most recently broken.

For I may have been torn over whether Edison's overeating was a sign of depression, but there was no question that his overeating was depressing *me*. I couldn't wait to escape the nagging sense that I should be doing something about my brother's weight, while at once feeling at a loss as to what that might be. Removed from his bad influence, I would lose what was now *at least* twenty pounds. I would drag out my bicycle, Fletcher's condescension be damned. I would send Edison newsy emails while he was on the road in Europe—updates on Cody's progress through Simon and Garfunkel's catalogue, or Tanner's blessed reconsideration (well, I said this was fantasy) of a foolhardy career path. I yearned for the halcyon day when Edison Appaloosa would not be my problem.

Yet I knew full well beforehand that the moment I waved goodbye at security—washing my hands of my brother and returning smartly to what passed in America for a happy family and a pile of new orders at Baby Monotonous—I would feel hollow and morose. Tortured by that sagging, empty maroon recliner. Sheepish about having resumed our eclectic musical diet of R.E.M., Coldplay, Shawn Colvin, and Pearl Jam, only to find that these previously beloved pop classics now sounded facile. Perplexed over why I had not consciously enjoyed what I had mostly dismissed as background noise, when I was obviously developing a taste for jazz despite myself. Saddened that despite a rare, sustained exposure to my brother's expertise I still couldn't distinguish John Coltrane from Sonny Rollins. Self-flagellating about the fact that, though I'd sometimes put on one of Edison's own CDs while he was here in a theater of interest, I had never listened attentively to a single one. Mortified that I had failed to get my brother to talk about his broken marriage or his estranged son. Dismayed that I had never come to any understanding of what had driven him to get so big. Crestfallen that I'd had a once-in-a-lifetime chance to truly get to know my only brother as an adult, and I'd squandered most of his visit on waiting for him to leave.

So when I said I'd miss him, I meant I would miss what we had not experienced, and I don't know what that's called: nostalgia for what didn't happen. I knew that when he left I would feel dreadful, and in that sense during his final few days in our house I did savor his company, which at least reprieved me, however briefly, from my own remorse.

It was the Saturday before Edison's Tuesday flight, and we'd just finished one of my brother's overkill brunches: french toast. Making an effort to be sociable on Edison's last weekend,

Fletcher (*I want DRY toast! I want DRY toast!*) had joined us with his unbuttered whole wheat. Tanner and Cody left to meet friends at the mall. Somewhere between noon and one p.m., the phone rang.

Travis.

My brother talked to our father about once a year and had thus filled me in as to what Travis really thought of Baby Monotonous—rather, "your sister's toy company." For his no-account, plain, below-the-parapet second-born to have made a name for herself with "doll babies" was apparently a leading source of his trademark consternation. My father's affront was one of the few bankable benefits I reaped from my peculiar product's popularity. In a word, revenge. While ours was one of those many families in which it was hard to pinpoint what exactly we kids might crave revenge *for*, this sense of deserving compensation for a big, ineffable, nameless atrocity persisted nonetheless. Yet I knew I was being small-minded. Travis was pathetic. Triumphing over the guy in his seventies was therefore itself pathetic, and way, way too late.

As a rule I talked to Travis more like once a month, since these dutiful daughterly calls made me feel less like a heel for otherwise dumping a delusional monomaniac on Solstice merely because she lived nearby. (But, hey. Her choice.) My father asked rarely about my affairs, and even then in a cursory manner ("How's tricks, Pandarama?"). Then we could get on with the important business of Travis's non-life now that even companies who produced the most mortifying products had dropped his endorsement (Ab-Sure, which made medical trusses, was the last to go).

Thus far Edison and I had twice placed joint calls to our father, during which I had barely gotten a word in edgewise. These three-way conversations had been quite a contest, since it was a hard call whether Edison or Travis was more of a windbag. First Travis would fume that nowadays TV stars raked in nearly as much moolah as the Hollywood kind, when he'd earned "chump change"—our father's backhanded fashion of informing us that he had already spent most of aforesaid chump change, so no, we would not be inheriting any money to speak of. With no pretense of a segue, Edison would then reminisce about his Rio tour in 1992, listing every unknown-from-Adam band member and describing a wild impromptu jam session in a tough, dangerous favela.

Thus on hearing our father's voice when I picked up the phone that Saturday my heart sank: there goes an hour down the drain. But I did wonder at the fact that, contrary to custom, Travis had called us.

"Pandorissimo!" cried my father gaily. His benevolent embellishments of my name were meant to bestow the family nonentity with Personality for a Day. With a woebegone look, I mouthed *Travis* to Fletcher. Noticeably more genial as Edison's exodus loomed, he was sponging up the french-toast custard that had dribbled all over the kitchen floor.

"Now, listen," Travis barreled on in my ear. "Have you seen this new series *Mad Men*? Pretty noteworthy that AMC is commissioning original drama now, and I'm thinking I might be able to capitalize on some opportunities there. But everyone I run into out here can't shut up about this show. I've checked it out, and for the life of me I don't see it. Set in the early sixties, fine, hardly real 'historical' drama, in my book. All this buzz about the sets and the clothes, when I could have tricked out the whole season with a trip to Goodwill. Lotta that show's mileage is from Christina

Hendricks's bazookas. Cheap shot. And this whole man-with-a-past, not what he pretends to be. Hackneyed beyond belief. Give me *The Fugitive* any day."

"I can't say. I haven't seen this new show," I lied. "We don't watch much TV."

"That's what everybody says. Listen to folks in this town, you'd think they all lived in caves without electricity. Then in the same breath they start slobbering about *Mad Men*. It don't compute, kiddo. Now—Pandorable. That was right nice of that hunky carpenter of yours to email a pic of your birthday. Sorry about not giving you a shout on the day, but I had such a stack of fan mail to get through that I didn't manage to fit it in."

"So this is my *birthday call*?" I wasn't thinking sharply. I merely noted that, had Fletcher not sent our group snapshot, Travis would have forgotten my birthday altogether. It wouldn't have been the first time.

"Down payment on next year's, anyway. Meanwhile, your jazz *artiste* brother still camped at your place? Cooling his heels before the next *whirlwind tour*?" I said yes, he's right here. "Why not put the little man on, then?"

I handed Edison the phone and went back to the griddle.

"Yo, Trav, you just caught me," said Edison from his recliner, after licking his fingers. (So close to his departure I'd resigned myself to my role as an "enabler," and the night before I'd made a lemon-almond tart for dessert—trying to make up for my eagerness to be rid of him in the most unfortunate manner possible. Edison was dispatching the leftovers.) "Heading for the Apple on Tuesday, then on the road in Europe—"

It was not Edison's style to telescope his musical plans into a half sentence, but something down the line pulled him up short.

His face flushed. I hurried around the prep island until I could hear the sound escaping from the receiver: our father hooting.

"I don't have to listen to this," Edison said quietly, and pressed the disconnect.

"What happened?" I said. "What did he say?"

He stared straight ahead and breathed. He didn't touch the pie. Finally he looked over, but not at me. "You bastard," he said to Fletcher.

"What'd I do?" It was a replay of the feigned innocence with which Edison had denied breaking the Boomerang.

"You just *had* to email that photograph."

Fletcher wiped down the sink with, I thought, undue diligence. "Why not? Your sister's birthday. Include Travis, insofar as he cares."

"*Include Travis* in the fact that his son is now, quote, 'a human parade float.'"

"Oh, no," I said. "Oh, Edison, I'm so sorry."

Fletcher raised his hands in theatrical dismay. "Wouldn't he already know you've had a bad case of the munchies?"

"I haven't seen the guy for years. Meaning he hasn't seen me, either."

"Yeah, but." Fletcher fluttered his fingers. "The Internet . . . ?"

"That guy has never typed anything into a search field but 'Travis Appaloosa' in his life. So why would he be up to date on my *appetite*?"

Fletcher finally stopped messing with the sink. "You can't protect people from what you look like. When you're umpteen hundred pounds, it's not a secret. And it's not *my* fault that to snap a family photo I have to take three steps back to fit you in the frame."

Impatient with letting the prep island afford my husband a bulwark, Edison pulled himself up and stalked into the kitchen. My husband had riled a very large animal, and instinctively retreated. "There's the inevitable, and then there's *deliberately* shoving up in my father's face what he doesn't have to know. You realize I police my Wikipedia page *every day*? Making sure the picture they're using is still from five years ago. Ever check out my webpage? There must be a hundred shots in the gallery, and they're good ones, too. From all over the world. Same goes for my Facebook page. In not *one* of them do I weigh more than one-sixty-five."

"You can try and rewrite history if you want. But your problem is reality, and an old picture on your Wikipedia page doesn't change that."

"This is payback, isn't it? For your fucking chair."

"Sending a simple birthday photo to my father-in-law isn't 'payback'—"

"Your fucking *chair*, man! A piece of *furniture*, in exchange for my *dignity*, man—"

"You're so concerned with your dignity, then try stopping at one plate of spaghetti!"

"You have any idea what I just had to listen to?"

"Travis is a jerk. Why should you even care what he thinks?"

"He's my *father*, man! I can't help if my dad's a jerk, he's still my *father*, man! You just *humiliated* me—"

"You've humiliated yourself!"

"Stop it!" I ordered Fletcher. "Leave him alone!"

Fletcher shot me a piercing look: look whose side little sister is on.

"Fuck it." Edison waved his hand. "What's done is done,

right? You accomplished what you set out to do. Made my father's day, you'll be happy to know. Bet he'll have that photo blown up into a life-size cardboard cutout. Have it plastered all over the family Christmas letter."

"He doesn't send Christmas letters," I said.

"He will now." Edison turned, and I put a hand on his arm to stop him.

"Don't go," I said. "This is no way to leave things. With you flying back in three days—let's try to talk this out."

"Look, if you have to know? Even parade floats sometimes have to take a dump."

The stairs creaked; it was apparently worth the extra effort to use the upstairs bathroom, putting a full story between him and Fletcher.

"Did you?" I asked, keeping my voice low. "Did you send that picture to Travis on purpose, to make sure he knew Edison's gotten so big?"

"Come on, Travis was bound to find out sooner or later."

"He didn't have to find out from you. Just like he wasn't going to find out from me. Talking to Travis, and *even to Solstice*, I've never made the faintest allusion to Edison's having changed. I've also kept it to myself that he has money problems. I've said he's between apartments, so we took advantage of the gap to catch up. Period. Don't you know anything about families?"

"Plenty," he said coldly. "You're forgetting I have one."

"*We* have a family, thank you. I meant siblings. You don't *tell*. Not on your brother, and not on your brother-in-law, either."

For a few minutes we furiously cleaned the kitchen, and I was annoyed when we finished, leaving nothing to vent myself upon. In desperation, I attacked the smears around the cabinet handles, while Fletcher loitered helplessly, at a disadvantage with nothing to do.

"The problem is what the guy looks like," said Fletcher, "not that Travis knows. Why do you always stick up for your brother and never for me? 'Forsaking all others,' remember?"

"I have forsaken all other romantic attachments, but as for the rest of the world, it's not that simple."

"It's simple, all right. You've gone back to the old team. The same childhood buddies who clung to each other to defeat the big bad fake children on TV. But you're a sidekick, you know. *Little sister.* A tag-along. He's helping himself to your house, your family, your apparently *infinite* patience, and your money. What do you get out of it?"

The question stopped me cold, and I don't know what I'd have said if we hadn't been interrupted by a great bellow from upstairs—a cry of despondency so deep that it sounded like less a response to a single calamity than a lament over a whole life.

I told Fletcher to stay put. Once I'd hurried upstairs, Edison's howl had subsided to a more sustainable wailing, reminiscent of the uninhibited bereavement in news reports from the Middle East. The bathroom door was shut. Water was leaking from underneath. An enlarging pool on the hallway floorboards was streaming toward the stairs. I failed to avoid stepping in it as I rapped on the door. "Edison, are you okay? What's happened? What's all this water?"

More wailing. He didn't sound able to talk.

I tried the doorknob. "I don't want to invade your privacy, but you've got to unlock the door. Whatever's wrong, let me help you. We're developing a lake out here."

After a pause, the bolt retracted. When I opened the door, I was treated to one of those revelations people lately call "too much information": it seems my brother had not evacuated his bowels in quite some time.

The toilet was brimming. Floating on a skim of waste water, turds were scattered all over the floor—under the sink, beside the shower stall, against the wall of the tub, and dammed at the door, so two balls escaped before I closed it behind me. Having pulled up his pants just enough to save us from more embarrassment, Edison was slumped on the edge of the tub, sobbing in his hands. The scene might have been funny. It wasn't.

Brisk efficiency was the ticket—the bright, blithe, unbothered spirit in which our mother had changed our sheets when we wet the bed. It is a female knack, this contending with effluents quickly and in good cheer, thus minimizing disgrace down to the routine untidiness of a dropped napkin.

So I plunged the toilet—something of a job; a fair bit of both shit and paper had plugged it up. After snapping on rubber gloves, I whisked up wandering turds and popped them in the bowl, flushing at intervals. It's surprising how when you *act* unfazed, you *feel* unfazed; you'd think that, as habitually as I picked up socks, I went about collecting lumps of excrement on a daily basis. I got a couple of old towels to soak up the water on the floor, retrieved the two brown escapees, and dried the hall. By the time the horror had subsided like the end of *The Sorcerer's Apprentice*, Edison's wailing had diminished to an erratic sob.

I turned my back and suggested he fasten his fly. Peeling off the rubber gloves, I joined him on the rim of the tub and put an arm around his shoulders. "When I was a kid, that was my deepest fear. It must be every kid's deepest fear. Whenever I flushed after a 'number two,' I'd look at the bowl in terror. The water would rise at first. I was always convinced it would keep rising."

"Fletch is right," Edison blubbered; I doubt I'd seen my brother cry since he was twelve. "All I do is humiliate myself."

I squeezed his shoulder. "By the time you're on the road in Portugal, this will have foreshortened into a hilarious little story that we'll laugh about on the phone."

"There is no Portugal."

"Well, that'll be news to the folks who live in Lisbon." I'd been assuming a lightness of tone that was hard to drop.

"There is no tour."

"Ah." I let this sink in. I must have known, deep down, that there was no tour. "So if you fly back to New York on Tuesday—do you have anywhere to live?"

"No."

"Then where have you been planning to go?"

"I don't know."

"What about all those gigs—in the spring?"

A flick of his head said it all.

"But why did you feel you had to invent all this stuff?"

"I could hardly show up in Cedar Rapids and say, 'Hi, it's your big brother, I've come to stay for the rest of my life,' now could I?"

"Whatever's gone wrong . . . The eating to compensate, or forget, or hide, or whatever you're doing . . . You can't go on like this."

"Maybe I don't want to."

I'd have liked him to have meant that he didn't want to keep eating himself to death. But the alternative interpretation was more likely: that his steady overconsumption was purposive—a slow-motion suicide-by-pie.

chapter eleven

I allowed Fletcher to believe that the cries of anguish upstairs on Saturday afternoon were solely the result of his having emailed that jpeg to Travis—which protected my brother's pride and further chastened my husband. By then I was accustomed to controlling the flow of information, a nice way of saying that I had grown chronically dishonest with everyone.

Fortunately, our master bedroom had an en suite bath, so Fletcher didn't use the kids' bathroom down the hall, the one that Edison shared. The next day Tanner sniffed out a turd I had missed—puddled in that dark, hard-to-mop area behind the toilet. Fortunately, too, when he cried, "Oh, *gross!*" that Sunday afternoon, Fletcher was off on a manic cycle ride. No longer faking myself into a strong stomach for Edison's benefit, I confess that sweeping the partially melted excrement into a dustpan was revolting, and I immediately exiled both brush and pan to our outdoor trash can.

When Tanner pushed me to explain how a lump of shit

could possibly have gotten on the floor, I said I didn't know. Edison probably got the blame by default. Perhaps that shouldn't have mattered, now that he'd be gone in two days, but I was no longer sure I could bear to shove him onto that plane—with no home to return to, friends whose goodwill might still be strained, and no European tour to make him feel important. I feared his return flight would effectively touch down on Houston Street, where Edison and I had once tucked into sandwiches at Katz's Delicatessen that bulged with twelve ounces of pastrami apiece. Yet I had not told anyone else that Edison's packed itinerary was bogus, not even Fletcher. Well—especially not Fletcher. Not that he would care. But he would care that I cared.

That same afternoon I had also to field a call from Solstice, to whom Travis had forwarded the incriminating jpeg. (For that matter, he'd probably sent it gleefully to his entire contact book.) Atypically, my sister didn't solicit any newsy updates about our kids and cut to the chase. "He's been there for two months. How could you not have told me?"

"Told you what?" I said flatly.

"That's what I mean. That's what gets me. That pretend innocence. You can seem so open and confiding, and then it turns out you don't tell me anything."

"There's not much to tell," I said.

"Oh, yeah? Edison's turned into a beach ball and he's obviously developed some kind of huge problem, but you don't even *mention* it, though we've talked at least a couple of times since he moved in with you. It's just so classic! Anything going on, and it's a little secret between you two. You were always like that, a tight, closed, hostile *unit*, and you never included me in anything—"

"How could we? Edison left home when you were *four years old.*"

"After he left, you two were always having whispery phone calls with your bedroom door locked. Think I couldn't hear you? And then you started meeting up, in New York. Hitting the town, living the high life. Nobody ever invited *me* to New York!"

"That first trip was the summer before I went to college. You were still a little kid."

"I practically grew up an only child! And then he visits you in Iowa for months. Know how many times I've scribbled an invitation on my Christmas card to come stay with us in L.A.? He never even emails, 'No, thanks.' The last one was returned to sender. Not knowing my own brother's address—"

"Half the time *I* don't have Edison's address—"

"You have it now," Solstice jeered. "It's your address. And who knows, if you'd have shared with me about Edison's troubles, maybe I'd have been able to help—"

"How? By shipping him a StairMaster? I'm sorry if I didn't regale you with descriptions, but he deserves his privacy, and I didn't think it was considerate to broadcast the fact that he's got a weight problem—"

"A 'weight problem' is an understatement! He obviously needs people to reach out. I'm his sister too, Pandora. But I don't know how I'm ever going to be a real sister to Edison if you keep running interference and coming between us."

One more time I swallowed: *Edison may have loomed mythically large in your childhood, if only as an absence. But he's oblivious to you, my dear. For decades I've been protecting you from your brother's indifference.* Instead I said curtly, "Your relationship to Edison is not my responsibility. If you want to 'reach out,' nobody's stopping you." I hung up with the certainty that she would initiate no contact with our brother of any kind. She was afraid of him.

My sister's having being born so much prettier than I had always seemed ample compensation for a little loneliness growing up. Though Solstice was the sole beneficiary of Travis's late-life discovery of real children, her well-adjusted façade was a poor cover for grievance, which would burst the banks of her contrived niceness at the slightest pretext. Constantly feeling cheated, she could only have mustered this searing sense of deprivation if she had no idea what she'd been left out of, for there was little to envy about the *Joint Custody* era. I didn't feel close to her, and she made me feel hunted. For years she'd sent ensnaring care packages of weird and conspicuously useless presents in acknowledgment of no occasion whatsoever: a knitted rooster too loosely woven to use as an oven mitt, a set of porcelain chopstick cradles, a fragile handheld fan so lacy that it wouldn't have generated a breeze even if any of us had been dainty enough to use one. Superstitious about throwing the knickknacks away, I was forever rifling a kitchen drawer and coming across, say, a velvet change purse with a hole in it. This cascade of uninvited benevolence did, however, accomplish its purpose. I was too busy to send trinkets in return, so the totems planted all over our house created a cumulative sensation of beholdenness and ingratitude.

Now, how bitterly comical: two months' worth of spattered pancake batter, coffee rings on rosewood, and cigarette butts all over the patio were straining my marriage to the breaking point, and Solstice was *jealous*. From all sides, I was castigated for being too chummy with a brother whom, I had lately ascertained, I hardly knew.

On Monday night, we took Edison out for his farewell dinner at Benson's, the closest New Holland has to chic. We ate on the early side, since my brother had to pack after dinner. The evening got off to an unpleasant start, since we were seated in a cove near the kitchen. "Excuse me," Cody said loudly, "but we'd rather sit over there." When the waiter mumbled about the middle table being reserved, she wouldn't let it go. "The one next to it would also do just fine. There's hardly anybody here. We don't want to sit off in the corner." She leveled the guy with an unrelenting stare, and he was helpless to resist a thirteen-year-old girl. Once we were reseated, with a great to-do about finding a larger chair for Edison that chagrinned Tanner, Cody was still furious. "You know why he put us there, don't you?"

"That was dead sweet of you, kid," said Edison. "But I'm used to it."

"I'm not ashamed of you, Uncle Edison."

"Cool," said my brother, adding wanly, "but that's not the same as being proud of me, is it?"

Cody looked flustered. "I didn't mean—!"

"I knew what you meant, babe. And I'm touched, really. But I shouldn't be putting you in this position, dig? You're a kid. Hard enough to stick up for yourself."

"You should have pulled rank, Pando," said Tanner. "Local celeb, you could demand to sit anywhere you want. Jesus, you never use it for anything!"

"That's 'cause my sister's got class, man."

Edison's demeanor was subdued. He didn't go on any riffs

about Charlie Parker, and since his arrival I'd never seen him eat so little at a meal—sawing small, unenthusiastic bites from his prime rib, most of which we'd doggie-bag, and he barely touched his wine. It was as if he'd been putting a number over on us for all these weeks, and the energy required to keep it up had run out a single day too soon. Keen to spare him a reprise of his fanciful plans, I consumed much of the dinner with diversionary tales of new orders at Baby Monotonous, but the spirit of the evening was so forlorn that I didn't make anybody laugh and my imitations of a germ freak's dialogue went over flat. Maybe the dismal dinner was a tribute at that. Edison was leaving, and we—or most of us—were sad.

When we got back home it was only nine. Edison excused himself to pack. As my husband got ready for bed, I lay on the spread, my chest heavy.

"I know you've *grown accustomed to his face*," said Fletcher between *pocks* of dental floss. "But you have to admit it'll be a relief."

"Yes," I said. "But the relief makes me feel guilty."

"It shouldn't. You—we—have gone way beyond the call of duty."

"I haven't heeded the call of duty in the slightest. You're the one who's always reminding me that I haven't helped. That he's bigger than ever. "

"And you're the one always telling *me* that it's not in your power to save him."

"Maybe it has been in my power to save him. Maybe I've been a coward. Maybe it's easier to pretend to help him by lazily putting him up and running out the calendar, instead of really helping him, which would be hard."

Fletcher threw his floss in the trash. "I'm sorry your brother is fat. I'm sorry he's still fat—or 'big,' as you've started to say, as if that's any different. I'm sorry he's probably unhappy. But that's not your problem. You should be facing forward. We've got some repair work to do. This whole thing has been a big ask, and though we've had some fights we've gotten through, and I haven't, incredibly, murdered him. Let it go."

The weight on my chest felt figurative: I needed to get something off it. "On Saturday. He confessed. There is no tour of Spain and Portugal. No gigs in the spring. He has no work, and nowhere to go."

In the bathroom doorway, the hand holding the toothpaste froze. "That doesn't change anything."

"Maybe to you it doesn't."

Fletcher strode to the bed and stared me down. "You are not seriously considering asking him to stay any longer."

"I can't stand sending him back to nothing."

"Yes, you can. Or if you can't stand it, you'll have to stand something else."

"That sounds threatening."

"It was supposed to."

I sighed. I didn't want this to be happening. I fell back on platitudes. "When you get married, you don't only take on the one person, but everyone who comes with them. Their colleagues, their friends you don't like, and their families. Like I took on Tanner and Cody. Joyfully, I might add."

"I did not marry Edison Appaloosa. That said, I challenge you to find any other man who'd put up with a brother-in-law who's that much of a royal pain in the butt for two solid months. So, big picture, I've been pretty tolerant. But I'm at my absolute limit. You can't keep that guy in our house for *five seconds* past the witching hour of four o'clock tomorrow afternoon and still be married to me."

We were not a couple that wielded divorce as a commonplace weapon. We had never in our seven years together made the slightest reference to the possibility of our splitting up—though the omission may have been a sign of fragility at that. I doubted he'd planned to put his ultimatum quite so drastically, insofar as he'd planned anything. Yet Fletcher was not a man to level such a statement and take it back.

I stalled. "What do you expect me to do?"

"What I told you to at the start. Give him some money. Enough to get a hotel and then an apartment. Enough to find a job, any job. He could work at Burger King if he had to."

"What a lovely picture. Besides. If I send Edison back to New York with a wad of cash, he won't find himself an apartment with it. He'll eat it."

"You don't have to turn your back on the guy. Phone, email, be *supportive*. That's what normal families do. You're constantly telling me I don't understand about siblings, but I do know that you're not obliged to adopt them."

"Phone calls. Email. Certainly Edison *disembodied* is a great deal easier to take. How nice for me."

"You did understand what I said?"

"I did." I closed my eyes.

"And you're actually *torn*?"

"Torn up."

"Do you still love me?"

I hoped he didn't regard my pause as an insult. I was taking the time to think that I rather admired the uncompromising nature of his edict: it's him or me. There may have been a fearful center to all this nonsense about soy milk and cycling, but my husband was a strong man, a handsome man, a man-man. And he made exquisite furniture.

"Yes, I do," I said with conviction, opening my eyes again to reach for his hand. "And I love our lives together, and the children I've tried to treat as my own. But after Monotonous took off, everything went all larkish and happy-clappy. I wonder if I need difficulty. And real difficulty isn't something you go out and find, but something, or someone, that finds you. You don't get to choose it. That's part of what makes it hard."

"Lost me there, friend. What am I supposed to make of that?"

I sat up. "That you should go ahead and brush your teeth. That I'm feeling awful, that I'm dreading driving Edison to the airport tomorrow. That I'm having a nagging sensation right now, with him packing down the hall by himself, and I think I should go in and keep him company, especially if this is his last night."

"*If* it's his last night?"

"The upshot is, I don't know what I'm going to do. I really don't."

For a moment, lumbering off the bed, I had a vivid presentiment of what it felt like, physically, to be Edison, dragging along hundreds of pounds every time he walked across a room. It must have been exhausting.

I rapped on the guest room door; admitted, I closed it behind me. The room was piled with folded clothes. My brother's battered leather case open on the floor looked already full. "How are you coming?"

"You bought me too much shit," said Edison amiably.

"You can have one of our suitcases. We won't miss it." I made no move to retrieve another bag. "But Edison—where are you going to go?"

"Aw, Slack'll take me in, for a while. I drive him a little bats, but we go way back. I got plenty of friends. My *whole* life's not fantasy. So don't you worry, I'll get by. I always do, one way or another."

We were awkward with one another. There was a chair at the desk, but I continued to stand. "What about work?"

"Oh, something's bound to turn up eventually." It was the kind of hazy assurance that most relatives took at face value, so they could get off the phone and go back to sorting the laundry. It felt artificial for us to regress to that airy "keeping in touch" whereby basically you're on your own.

"I don't understand why we couldn't get you to play the piano more often," I said. "You used to visit me and play all day. I could hardly get you to leave the house."

"Complicated." Edison pushed a few more toiletries into a zipper case. "More'n we got time for. I'll get back to playing in due course. Just for now—bad associations."

"With the piano?" But he was right; we didn't have time. We had had time, of course. So I dropped it. "Hey, I bet you're a bit short. What say we stop by the bank tomorrow, and I give you a little something to see you through."

"It's embarrassing, if you wanna know the truth. But Slack's more likely to open the door with a smile if I show up with some bread."

Merely bending down to pick up a stray pack of Camels put him out of breath. I used to love the way the blond tendrils corkscrewing from his head whipped when he ranged a keyboard; on a lean, younger man, the collar-length hair had looked sexy. But now that halo of curlicues rendered his head rounder and imparted a Little Lord Fauntleroy aspect; his arms and legs short in relation to his trunk, his proportions were those of a toddler. I'd never been attracted to my brother in some untoward sense that I was aware of, but I had always relished his being attractive to others. In my girlhood, association with a sinewy, good-looking guy whose jeans rode low on narrow hips had provided me a social ace in the hole every bit as powerful as a father who was on TV.

"Listen," he said, fitting the Camels into an open carton. "I don't know how to say this. You been pretty cool. Even with this company you got going—I mean, you're the one who's happening, with all the—interviews, and photo shoots and shit, everybody wanting a piece of you . . . I know what that's like, believe it or not." For a moment he returned to his old bluster; ever since the overflowing toilet, Edison had dropped his boastfulness cold. But I *wanted* him to be boastful. "Or I knew what it was like in my twenties. I used to be a pretty heavy cat."

"I know. You're still a heavy cat."

"Very funny."

"I meant in both senses, *dig*?"

"You making fun of me?"

"I should hope so."

"Look, I was only saying—you're busy, I get it. And I know I kind of overstayed my welcome. But it's been great to have—a place to chill. And that kid Cody, she's been—she's pretty hip, man. Gonna be a heartbreaker someday. I just want to say . . ."

"You just want to say thank you. And then I say you're welcome."

"Yeah, whatever." By and large Edison didn't do gratitude, and his coming this close touched me.

"I wish I could ask you to stay a little longer. But Fletcher . . ." I wasn't sure about telling him this, but I wanted him to understand what a bind I was in. "He said if you stayed here 'five seconds' past your flight departure tomorrow he wants a divorce."

"Whoa! That cat must really hate me, man. Though what I ever did to the guy is beyond me. Don't see how anybody could get that bent out of shape over a fucking chair."

"It's not just the chair. Fletcher's an only child, and for him the brother-sister thing is suspicious. And he and I met on the late side. He missed out on a lot of my life, and all the *Joint Custody* stuff makes him feel more excluded. Maybe he thinks I have to actively choose him. Over you. To prove something. I haul you off to the airport, and then he's the only man in my life again. Or almost—he doesn't like my hanging with Oliver, either. It's the same thing. One man, one woman, that's all Fletcher understands."

Watching Edison stack jazz magazines for recycling, I flashed on my seventeen-year-old brother packing just like this, but with more vigor, dashing around, loading a backpack with cassettes that were wrapped in stacks with masking tape to travel without cracking. Dropping out before his senior year, he'd been in the process of deserting me for New York to try his hand as a jazz musician. Given his age, I'd been braced for his departure after high school. But our mother had died the year before, and I wasn't ready to lose my lone remaining ally. At least college would have entailed term breaks when he might have come back home, whereas his hitchhiking blindly across the continent threatened an indefinite exile. I remembered lingering dolefully in his room at fourteen, unsure when was the right time to give him his farewell present to remember me by—a bracelet of woven brass and copper wire that I'd soldered at summer camp—unsure whether to give it to him at all, in case it was square.

Joint Custody had been renewed for another season, and would end up running two more years, during which I'd be left defenseless before our family's script-enhanced alternative children without the aid of my older brother's shared contempt. That was the period of the show during which Mimi was suing for full custody of the younger two kids, using every confidence they'd ever shared about their father against him in court. Maple was especially caught in the middle. Having been for years assiduously "controlling information," she had to decide whether to stick to declarations of ignorance under oath. As Edison hulked about the guest room bunching socks, while down the hall my husband would be raging on his back wide awake, I recognized the pinched feeling that Floy Newport had evoked so well: wrenched between competing loyalties, destined to betray both parties, bound to please no one, including herself— although I worried if it was tawdry to understand your emotions through the aegis of a television character. See, I couldn't help but recall how bereft Maple had been in the previous season, when her older brother Caleb also decamped upon coming of age to try his hand at becoming a jazz pianist. Since Sinclair Vanpelt was still under contract, the fictional Caleb only moved to Seattle, and continued to make appearances on the show to give his racked sister Maple advice on her deposition. At seventeen, Edison Real Person had shown Sinclair-slash-Caleb how it was really done if you were serious about jazz, *man*: you moved to fucking New York.

Barely old enough to shave, Edison had left for a dangerous city where he had no place to live, an odyssey he was now repeating a second time. When Edison picked up stakes for Manhattan as a teenager, I'd envied him; I'd felt abandoned. Yet I hadn't feared for him. I'd had perfect faith that my seventeen-year-old brother would land in New York on his feet. Releasing Edison to the big bad world at forty-four was terrifying.

"Remember leaving for New York the first time?" I asked. "You seemed so manly to me then that I didn't think twice about whether you'd manage. But now I appreciate you were only Tanner's age, and I see how brave you were. You didn't know anybody there. You just swung that pack on your back and stuck out your thumb."

"Yeah, Travis thought it was a big ha-ha. Expected me to come back tail between legs within the week. That was motivating, dig? I had a lot on the line."

"I wasn't worried then. But I am now."

"What's the difference?"

I took a breath. "At seventeen, you weren't morbidly obese."

"Jesus, getting clinical on my ass."

"So far I don't think I've been clinical enough." I pulled Edison to sit beside me on the bed. "I don't have to tell you this. You're putting yourself in the way of diabetes. Stroke. High blood pressure. Heart disease. You already have sleep apnea, which is also related to your weight."

Edison looked bored.

"And that's on top of making yourself miserable, and scotching the chance that any self-respecting woman will put a hand on your knee. All my girlfriends used to have such crushes on you! This is a waste, and an atrocity, and it has to stop."

"Look, don't take this wrong, but like I said—that's my business."

"Fletcher's right, killing yourself is lots of people's business. For me to keep pretending it has nothing to do with me—it's wrong, morally wrong, if you can bear my sounding so unhip."

I had no idea what I was going to say next until I said it. Inventing the whole thing as I went along, I was filled with a sense of sacrifice, but also of power. Much like Fletcher's ultimatum the previous hour, this was a move that I could not take back:

"I want to make you a proposition. That you stay in New Holland. I will find you—I will find *us* an apartment. I will move in with you. I will take care of you, and support you financially. *But only if you lose weight.*"

Edison squinted. "How much weight?"

"*All of it.* Until you look like the photographs on your website."

"Come on, man, got any idea how long that would take?"

"I'm not sure until I do the math. Many, many months. But it would have to be radical. Not a matter of skipping a second piece of cake."

"You even know how?"

"I'll find out. I'll be your coach. I need to lose weight too. Besides, we both know 'how' really. It's not rocket science. You don't eat so goddamn much."

"But what about Fletch? Your kids?"

"The kids, I can keep in touch with. But Fletcher—won't like this," I said, making the understatement of the decade. "I'd be taking a risk."

Edison stared in silence. "*You* would do *that* for *me*?"

Both exhilarated and frightened by what I had just offered, I was tempted to say, *Actually, you'd better let me sleep on this*, though I realized I had been sleeping on exactly this for quite some time. "Yes."

"Oh, man." He shook his head, bewildered.

I stood and gripped his shoulders, looking him in the eye. "But the other question is: Would *you* do *this* for *me*?"

That was not quite the right formulation. In the fullness of time I'd regret it.

"Wow." Edison's mouth dropped, and I was glad of the wave of momentousness that crossed his face. I didn't want him to undertake this lightly. I'd rather he not undertake it at all. "You cleared this with your man?"

"He'll be a little surprised."

"He'll be motherfucking livid. You and me, in our own pad? Cat's gonna hunt me down and kill me, man."

"Luckily we don't keep guns."

"Only one thing would piss that fucker off more than my being fat." His eyes went steely. "My *not* being fat."

"There will be no cheating," I said. "It will make your leaving for New York City at seventeen without a dime or a phone number seem like a trip to the post office. Because, Edison—it will be, bar none, the hardest thing you've ever done."

II: Down

chapter one

I didn't sleep much," Edison croaked from his swirl of covers when I poked my head in his door. It was already ten a.m., and we had a great deal to organize—or I did.

"Good. If you're unsettled, you're taking this seriously. Now, get up." I wasn't accustomed to ordering my older brother around. After letting him gorge himself into ever more parlously poor health for two solid months, the while keeping my eyes timidly averted like a "mousy dishrag," the bossiness was refreshing.

Fletcher had absconded to his basement and the kids were in school, so once Edison shambled downstairs we had the kitchen to ourselves—in the middle of which he stood, lost, befuddled, turning one way and then another, at last appealing, "What do I do?"

"That's the right attitude." I had worked out the protocol while lying next to Fletcher's ramrod body, making out the dim gray outlines of the drapes as my mind raced. "For now, we are moving immediately into a motel. From there we will find an apartment. The end of food as you know it will not begin until we find permanent lodging. In the meantime you will see my doctor. This interim will also give you time to either marshal your resolve, or conclude you're not up to it."

"What if I'm not?"

I was glad he realized the commitment was so forbidding that he might not be able to make it. "Then no apartment, and it's straight to the airport."

"You'd hate me," he said morosely.

"I wouldn't hate you. I'd be disappointed in you is all."

"That's what Mother used to say. Cut me to the quick."

There was more than a whiff of the maternal about this whole project, and I would have to live with having acquired not two children but three.

"But, breakfast . . ." Edison wafted his fingers. "What's the drill?"

"I'm hoping we can find our private ground zero within the week. During which you may eat. But I want you to use this time to think about why you eat, and to reflect on the fact that every morsel you put in your mouth you'll effectively have to spit back out. That is, everything you eat from now on you will have to *uneat.* This morning, I suggest coffee and toast. You can devour the loaf and slather it with a pound of butter if you have to, so long as you contemplate the extra starvation that every bite will cost you. Which may induce . . . the dawning of restraint."

Even Edison's two slices made him self-conscious. "I wish you wouldn't watch me like that."

"Get used to it."

I fixed him with the same steady stare as he raised the half-and-half over his mug. His usual ratio was one part coffee to two parts whitener, leaving a thick, tepid milkshake that over the morning he would down at least four times. Under my hard eye, he dribbled only a couple of tablespoons and scowled at the results. "It's not the same."

"Better not be," I said. "Ever look at the calorie count of that stuff? Twenty per tablespoon. I haven't said anything, which I'm ashamed of, but you've been going through a *gallon* of half-and-half every five days." I scrawled on the kitchen phone pad. "At five thousand six hundred and seventy calories, that's nearly two pounds' worth of fat per week. So enjoy white coffee while you can. You'll have to learn to drink it black."

That meant *I'd* have to learn to drink it black. It wasn't only Edison who needed a few days to "marshal resolve." Black coffee on an empty stomach made me ill.

I scurried up to my study to book rooms at Blue Cottages, a motel with separate white clapboard huts and cobalt shutters only two blocks down the road; to begin with, I'd be virtually next door to the kids while they got used to the new state of play. My starting at noises from downstairs recalled the covert, traitorous sensation of buying Edison's plane ticket in the first place. I still hadn't talked to Fletcher.

I fetched bags from the attic, a large one for me and another for Edison's spillover. I packed in the master bedroom on tiptoe, and simply removing my toothbrush from our communal glass felt disloyal. To the naïve eye, this furtive stuffing of underwear would have looked like a wife breaking her wedding vows—vows that I had taken in great earnest. I desperately didn't want Fletcher to catch me in this sneak-thief mode, his heart stabbing with fear that I was leaving him.

Which I was. I was lying to myself. I wasn't sure if I was

leaving for a few days or for many months, but in any case this departure was a violation of contract.

I was helping Edison with his luggage—that is, taking it down for him—when the basement door slammed. Fletcher rounded from the hall and bounded up the stairs to take the suitcase from me, the spring in his step restored. However chimerical Edison's European travels, his bags were packed, and that was all that mattered. "Hey," said Fletcher, hefting the bulging brown bag effortlessly downstairs. "Thought I'd come up and say goodbye before you guys leave for the airport."

Despite my coffee's furtive dash of half-and-half, I still felt sick. "There's been a change of plans." I trailed him to the foyer, where he plunked Edison's bag. "We're not going to the airport."

Fletcher wheeled. "You do remember what I told you?"

"That if Edison stayed *here* five seconds after that plane takes off you and I were"—I couldn't say it—"going to have problems. So he won't be *here*. As for the plane, you didn't say he had to be on it."

"Pretty legalistic."

"If you're going to make ultimatums, you've got to expect I'm going to adhere to them to the letter. Anyway, I've booked us into Blue Cottages for now."

Fletcher had a good ear for pronouns. "Us."

Edison was bringing up the rear with his lighter second bag, with which he was still struggling. I let him struggle. I thought: That's another twenty calories down.

"I'm going with him. Then I'll find us an apartment. I'm going to help him lose weight."

Fletcher's eyes could have burned pinholes in paper. He stood supremely still. With exceptions, like the Boomerang debacle, his wiring was reversed. What triggered rage in most men drove Fletcher Feuerbach to extremities of composure.

"Losing weight is generally an activity one can do by oneself," he said, his enunciation precise. "In New York as well as Iowa, from what I've read."

"You're an athlete. So you should appreciate the concept of a personal trainer."

"I don't have one."

"You don't need one. Edison does. Maybe I do too, for that matter. I'd be a lot easier to live around if I dropped a few pounds myself."

"Let me get this straight." Fletcher looked between me and Edison, who had huffed to the foyer. "You're *moving in* with your brother, so you can read each other the nutritional label on the cottage cheese. How long is this hand-holding supposed to last?"

"If I catch him with a single Ho-Ho"—I shot my brother a look—"it will last as long as it takes me to drive right back home. At eighty miles an hour, running lights. But if he shows determination, and follows my instructions—my *orders*—and it seems to be working . . . Well, I can't say how long until he gets on a scale. He can't use ours; the numbers don't go that high." I no longer beat about the obesity bush.

Fletcher looked straight at Edison and employed an aggressive third person. "He can't do it."

"We'll see about that, bro," said Edison. "You don't know me well as you think."

"I know your type. Before I rescued my kids from a lying, thieving, abusive meth-head, I heard more high-flown resolutions than you've had hot suppers. It's just more self-deceiving bullshit. Put you alone in a room with a plate of french fries, and the spuds win every time. The will is a muscle. Yours is flabby as the rest of you, *bro*."

"You got no idea what I been through. My version of being tested ain't going on some jive-ass bike ride. So you want to put some money on it, man?"

"What, so you could pay off the bet with my wife's money? Think I'll pass. Wouldn't want to double up your embarrassment."

"We'll see who's embarrassed, motherfucker."

This was the first instance in which Edison had gone public with what must have still been a pretty wobbly pledge. It was a cold perspective on my own husband: Fletcher could prove a useful tool. Edison would dislike failing in front of me; he would *revile* failing in front of Fletcher. But if my husband's antagonism was beneficial for my brother, the moment was fast approaching when I should also be keeping an eye on what was good for me. Lest I sound improbably selfless, in truth I was already safeguarding my *project*. I had always been single-minded in this way, and the blinkered focus was really a form of egotism: *my* project.

"Could you give us some privacy, please?" Fletcher asked my brother with rare civility.

"Well, the one thing not up for grabs is I'm outta here. I'll be in the car." Edison marched out wheeling the lighter bag, his carriage as stiff and upright as his mass permitted. Being left alone with my husband made me strangely fearful.

"Are you also walking out on my children?" Pronouns again. With which Fletcher sometimes took his children back.

"Any apartment I even consider will be within walking distance of this house. They can visit us as much as they like." Since I didn't also mention being able to visit them, I must have known what was coming next.

Fletcher didn't get mad; he got sad. Which was worse. He was both tender and matter-of-fact. It meant something to me that the words came heavily, and there was no malevolence in his voice. "I can't promise I'll welcome you back."

However gently put, it was a right hook. "This isn't against you."

"You're leaving your husband and kids in the lurch for your fat-fuck brother. How's that not against us?"

"I'm taking some time out from one family to attend to another," I said staunchly. "Why would you punish me for that?"

"I'm not threatening to 'punish' what you'd obviously like me to see as an admirable largeness of heart. I'm not being spiteful. Really. But you do something like this, and it has consequences. For how I feel. Not any different from the physical world. Bring a hammer down on a piece of molding, it cracks in half. And not because the molding *wants* to crack in half. It's simple cause and effect. Your being willing to throw us all over for this fool's errand—it makes me feel expendable. Expendable for jack."

I liked the way my husband talked. What other people often missed in his commonly taciturn manner is that he is very thoughtful—usually in both senses of the word, if presently in only one. "It's not a fool's errand," I said weakly.

"That slob's not going to drop any weight. You've got him all worked up about some grandiose scheme, which mostly appeals to him because it means not having to *face the music* back in New York. You'll keep paying his tab, and he doesn't have to sort out his life. But the minute he can't have a cracker, it's over. *Why* is he so important to you?"

"He has to be important to somebody."

" . . . What if I forbid you?"

"Don't try that. I seem to recall skipping the 'honor and obey' part."

"I forbid you," he said limply. There was a hint of the sardonic, but he wanted to make it official.

"All right, I forbid you to forbid me. Checkmate."

"He's a sponger you're related to by accident. I'm your husband by choice. If you 'love' that loudmouth it's a kneejerk genetic thing; I'm supposed to be the real love of your life. Frankly, I'm *insulted.*"

"You're choosing to be insulted, which is perverse. Why can't you understand that I need to accomplish something more meaningful than making *doll babies*"—I used Travis's flattering term—"that torture people with what's wrong with them? That shove up in their faces how repetitious and tiresome they are, that make people seem cartoonish and ridiculous?" It came out in a rush. "Because I strongly believe that if someone doesn't do something—and I'm the only one who can—my brother is going to die."

He sighed. "Well, well, another trump card."

"I don't play it lightly. Can you imagine how I'd feel if he, you know, collapsed from a heart attack, and I'd never lifted a finger to help?"

"So this is a big preventive guilt trip. An insurance policy. To be able to tell yourself, when he collapses anyway, that you tried."

It didn't sound so great put that way, but I conceded, "That's about the sum of it."

"Then you're really going to do this." I was surprised it took him so long to circle around to the perfect fruitlessness of his appeal. He knew me.

"Yes. I don't know if he can do it. If he can't, I'll come home."

"If I want you home."

"Yes."

"And you'll risk that I won't."

"If the alternative is walking outside and telling Edison we're going to the airport after all—leaving him all alone, without a hope in hell of losing an ounce without someone to cheer him on—abandoning him to mockery and ostracism, and letting him drop dead in five years if he keeps overeating at this rate—yes."

Fletcher sagged against the banister. "That puts me in my place. On your list of priorities, my kids and I come somewhere between the toilet paper and the aluminum foil."

"Being anywhere near the toilet paper makes you pretty important." The levity fell flat.

"I already had one wife who didn't rate her obligations to her family."

"I cannot put methamphetamine addiction on a par with a crash diet."

Impasse: my willfulness versus Fletcher's incredulity. At least in his next laying down of the law I detected the glimmer of recognition that this was actually happening.

"I don't want you dropping by all the time because you forgot your hairbrush. If you're ready to come back for keeps, we can discuss that. But if you need something, ask the kids for it"—the go-between image this conjured was piquantly reminiscent of *Joint Custody*—"because I don't want a wife half in, half out. I don't want to suffer a lot of little goodbyes. I'd rather go through one big one. Come here."

Fletcher opened his arms, and we hugged hard. I didn't want to go. I didn't even enjoy Edison's company as much as my husband's, and though I had just spent ten minutes explaining I now had no idea why I was doing this. I indulged a brief, ugly hope that I'd come upon my brother dive-bombing another box of confectioner's sugar by something like Day Two, and then I could go home.

Fletcher bowed to rest his forehead against mine. "So is it up to me to tell the kids? That the pretty, considerate, tender, diligent woman I brought home seven years ago, who's a smashing cook and doesn't even happen to be a drug addict, won't be living here anymore?" A rarity, his voice cracked.

"If that's your version?" I slipped a hand around his neck. "I'd rather head them off on the way back from school. If only to assure them that the woman you brought home hasn't really gone anywhere, loves them to pieces, loves their father to pieces, and will be back."

Fletcher insisted on lugging out the other two suitcases, and packing the bags into the trunk. When we were ready to go, he leaned through the driver's window and kissed me. "You know, I didn't mean we couldn't talk."

"Thank you," I said. "That's a relief."

Edison shook his fist out his window. "Yo, I'll see you eat your words, man!" Our departure had taken on the jittery, nervous gaiety of embarking on an intrepid Arctic expedition. If we were driving exactly two blocks away, the journey stirred the same amalgam of optimism and anxiety as starting out on a poorly equipped slog of daunting distance, during which conditions were bound to turn nasty, unanticipated obstacles could prove insurmountable, and rations—this much was certain—would grow perilously sparse.

"Tell you what, brother-in-law, you make a go of this, I'll do better than eat my words," said Fletcher, coming around to

Edison's side. "What's your sister gotten you to promise? What's the target?"

"One-sixty-three. Back to what I weighed for years, or bust."

"You cross that finish line, and *I* will eat an entire chocolate cake in one sitting. That's my version of being made to eat shit. But you're a long way from one-sixty-three, pal, and I'm betting I get to stick to cauliflower."

"You're on, pal. I'd starve for years to see your pious mug plastered with fudge icing."

As we drove off, I considered the disparity: Edison was gambling with pride, Fletcher was gambling with cake, and I was gambling with my marriage.

D ropping Edison's luggage beside his bed, I announced, "I got you your own cottage, since our sharing the same room would be too weird. But that means I can't keep an eye on you. Nothing prevents you from hitting the vending-machine Doritos. Just remember what I said: any further weight you gain before the starting gun is more weight you have to lose. The Cool Ranch will cost you a whole lot more than a buck fifty."

"What about lunch?" Edison whined. "Breakfast was jive, and I'm starving."

"Get used to it. When were you last really hungry? Physically hungry?"

"I'm hungry all the time."

"The hell you are. You confuse hunger with *boredom*." I was curt; I was hungry, too. "I'll be next door. I have research to do. There's an ocean of fast food on the main drag half a mile from here, but you'll have to walk. As for walking: get used to it."

"Jesus. From Florence Nightingale to Mussolini in twenty-four hours."

"You ain't seen nothing yet. Pretty soon you'll be living with Attila the Hun."

I retired to the adjacent cottage, a small, sweet room with a pink chenille bedspread and curtains of blue dotted swiss. Despite the homey touches, any motel room has a sobering bleakness. Here it is, the cubicle asserted. Roof. Bed. Light. TV with limited channels. Toilet. Desk, with nothing on it but a flyer from the Cedar Rapids I-Max. This, aside from the food we were about to all but forswear, is everything you need, and needing this little was sort of awful.

Fortunately, I had work to do. I called Carlotta, warning that I'd be making myself scarce at Monotonous for the rest of the week, and booked Edison a checkup with our family doctor. I booted up my laptop, agreeing to a larcenous $12.95 per day for WiFi. I wasn't used to skipping lunch myself, and battled a growing petulance by heeding my instructions to Edison: *Observe*, I recited, feeling like some Sufi space case. Hunger is a surprisingly mild experience. You could hardly call it pain. So why is it so nagging, so insistent? So distracting. It would have to become the norm. It would have to become a pleasure.

My stomach yowled: Fat chance.

Unable to concentrate on the New Holland real estate listings, I slipped out to the vending machine, having fixated on those Doritos. To our mutual embarrassment, I ran into Edison. "Thought I'd get a granola bar," I claimed, digging for change, and my brother grumbled, "Guess you should make that two." On return to the computer, I discovered that the granola bar had as many calories as corn chips.

I kept an eye on the clock. Tanner and Cody both walked home, and there was an intersection at which their passages from different schools met. His friends having peeled off, every afternoon Tanner waited at the same oak tree for his sister, whose walk was a bit longer, so they could saunter the last fifteen minutes side by side.

For Tanner to have continued the tradition into his senior year of high school was impressive, surely a last vestige of his role as Cody's protector when Cleo was metamorphosing from their mother into a demanding, ill-judged pet—one of those baby alligators or pythons that eventually slither off into the sewer. When I lifted the duty of care from him, Tanner had experienced equal parts relief and resentment. His sister's unambiguous embrace of their father's second wife irked him. Though they remained a duo of sorts, readily closing ranks in outrage when Fletcher banned frozen pizza, they now led drastically different lives, which exaggerated the disparity in their ages. But Tanner interpreted any distance between him and his sister as all my fault.

Whereas Cody's memory of their real mother rapidly grew dim, Tanner had been just old enough when their father remarried to conclude expediently that, in preference to choosing between the old mother and the new one, he didn't need a mother at all. Which was why I was especially nervous of telling my stepson about my "fool's errand." If never precisely hostile, Tanner had long given me to believe that my part in his life would always be elective. This made him treacherously inconsistent—fond one moment, icy the next. I worried I was about to give him a pretext for discarding my unnecessary ass completely.

Turning onto Pine Street, I spotted Mr. Cool at the end of the block, his back resting on the oak tree, into whose bark the siblings had years before scored their initials.

"What's this?" he drawled as I pulled up to the curb. "Limousine service. It's not *that* cold." He must have cherished the final stretch with his sister; he didn't want a ride home.

I got out of the car; Cody was running late. "We need to powwow."

"Couldn't wait fifteen minutes?"

"No, it couldn't."

"Gosh, I'm all pins and needles." Unfortunately, he was in his remote, sarcastic mode.

"It's so sweet of you to wait for your sister like this. In L.A. we were driven everywhere, but otherwise it would have meant the world to me as a girl if Edison had done the same thing."

"*Edison's* in no shape to walk anybody to the end of the driveway."

"That's what I wanted to talk about," I dived in. "And maybe it's good Cody's not here yet. I'll need you to look out for your sister for a while. You know, the way you used to. I'll still be a resource, of course—"

"So you're leaving Dad," he said—matter-of-fact, with a trace of satisfaction. "Guess he brought it on himself. Least he'll be the healthiest misery guts in town."

"I'm not leaving anyone." Hastily I detailed my grand plan—adding judiciously that I wasn't at all sure it would work.

He heard me out. "So you're leaving Dad."

Rolling my eyes in exasperation, I spotted Cody across the street. She looked stricken. I never showed up in the car like this. Obviously, someone had died.

I waved, and she lumbered with a pack as big as she was to their Meeting Tree. "What's cookin'?" she asked warily.

"Monotonous isn't enough for her," said Tanner. "Pando's starting a fat farm."

"You're a lot of help." This was not the reassuring briefing I'd rehearsed. I ran through the drill again, which to my own ears sounded far-fetched, self-destructive, and delusional, this time ending, "But I am *still* your mother, I am *not* leaving either of you, and I am *not* leaving your father!"

Cody frowned; it was a lot to take in. "Is Dad clear on that?"

"Not as clear as he should be," I admitted.

"You said we could visit you guys," she said. "Why can't you visit us back?"

"Because your father finds this idea very annoying, and I'll be honest, he's pretty mad. Anyway, he thinks your uncle doesn't have the discipline to lose weight."

"Do *you*?"

I couldn't lie to her. "Maybe not. But the only way to find out is to try."

"So . . ." she said sullenly. "No more real pasta, just that clumpy soba stuff. No more sneaking fresh brownies when Dad's in the basement. It's gonna be like living in a concentration camp. Not even any more rides to swimming practice, because you're going to be keeping Uncle Edison from hitting the Eggos. However you do *that*."

"Yeah, I sure wouldn't want to get between that guy and the refrigerator," said Tanner. "Like putting yourself in the way of a buffalo in heat."

I sensed they would at least have a wonderful walk the rest of the way home at my expense.

B ack at Blue Cottages, I plunged into my online short course in losing weight. A search on "diets" produced 43 million hits. I recognized the well-publicized regimens—South Beach, Atkins, alternate day, glycemic index, Dukon, Weight Watchers, Scarsdale, and The Zone—but that was just the beginning. Cabbage diets, smoothie diets, blood-type diets, and coffee enemas. Low-fat, low-carb, low-calorie; 2-4-6-8, what diet do we appreciate. Açaí berry, chicken soup, grapefruit, and lemonade. It got crazier: there were potato chip diets, cookie diets, pizza, candy, peanut butter, and popcorn diets. Hot dog diets, red wine diets, vinegar diets, *Twinkie* diets; chocolate, ice cream, or baby food diets, and one that recommended tapeworms. I was skeptical of the "negative calorie" diet, though I thought the "air diet" might have something to recommend it, and the "cigarette diet" would at least appeal to Edison.

Navigating the Web maze was perilous, since many of these pages were commercial come-ons, planting the kind of cookies that don't have chocolate chips. What struck me about the enormous industry I'd brushed up against was that all these plans, programs, supplements, and pharmaceuticals were hawking the one product that American consumers both badly wanted and couldn't buy: that little packet of determination to stick to the program like a sachet of low-fat salad dressing. Even costly procedures like liposuction couldn't protect you from eating yourself silly once the arthroscopic puncture was healed, couldn't keep you from slurping every pound of the yellow glop surgeons pumped into a bedside pail in reverse. No highly paid nutritional consultant could *not* eat a cupcake for you. Despite the dizzying array of products packaged deceitfully as such, in truth a slim figure was not on the shelf. I had just tripped over a gravel pit of 43 million pet rocks.

After three hours of this, I felt soiled, and all I could think about was food.

"I don't think any of the methods I researched is the answer," I told Edison over our dismal supper at the Olive Garden. "They only raise the obsession to a power. So enjoy your meatloaf while you can. I think we'll have to make food go away."

"Seem to recall that's called 'dying,' man," said Edison through his dinner roll; only my glare had prevented him from larding on a third packet of butter. "What about going local? Crystal meth."

"So you can be thin with no teeth, covered in sores, and brain damaged."

"Gastric bypass?"

Keeping myself from wolfing down my baked salmon, I was trying to think deeply about the experience of eating it, and didn't respond to Edison right away. I mashed the pink flakes around my mouth, their texture sandy from overcooking, the flavor disquietingly sweet. At best, the fillet was mildly agreeable, but only when I paid fierce attention; ordinarily I didn't. That must have been when I first began to formulate my theory about the elusiveness of the edible. I had looked forward to dinner all afternoon; I might look back wistfully on this meal once anything so substantial as salmon was off the menu; but in that exact moment with the fish on my tongue it was as if I were chewing for something that wasn't there, as in childhood I'd scrambled irately through a cereal box that failed to contain its advertised prize. The more I chewed, the more bewildered I grew by how this fleeting, unseizable pleasure had so enslaved my countrymen that many of us were willing to disgrace ourselves for it; demoralize ourselves for it; demolish a host of other pleasures for it, like running and dancing and sex; *destroy this very pleasure itself* in its pursuit—for every tidbit I'd consumed since putting on weight had been contaminated with an acrid aftertaste of self-reproach; and even, in extreme cases like the one my brother was fast becoming, die for it. The mystery was oppressive.

"I don't think so," I said at last. "Gastric bypass is major surgery, and things can go horribly wrong: infection, stroke. Death, even, which is the very event you get the operation to avoid. Tying off your stomach into a change purse may keep you from eating more than a quarter cup in a sitting, but you still have to starve. The only thing surgery does is take away the decision making. But your decision making is the problem. Even with a bypass, you can cheat; eventually you can tolerate larger quantities, and then you're back where you started. Besides"—I pulled out my clincher—"they'd make you stop smoking."

"Forget it," said Edison.

"I'm sorry to quote Fletcher, but he's right: the will is a muscle. We have to touch our mental toes." I was assiduous about using the first-person plural. "And—we know you like to eat, and so do I. So the real question is: What else do you enjoy?"

Edison slumped. "Hard to admit, babe. But at this point I'm not sure there is anything else."

"Ah," I said delicately. "Then that is the heart of the matter."

I wondered if that wasn't the answer to the mystery, countrywide. It wasn't that eating was so great—it wasn't—but that nothing was great. Eating being merely okay still put it head and shoulders above everything else that was decidedly less than okay. In which case I was surrounded by millions of people incapable of deriving pleasure from anything whatsoever besides a jelly doughnut.

chapter two

D r. Corcoran had a flat, unadorned frankness that I had always liked. He delivered reliable information with a practiced neutrality. He'd treated a second-degree burn from boiling pasta water and kept it from getting infected. He'd stitched a stab wound from my careless removal of an avocado stone so neatly that I regretted the invisibility of the scar; from catering, my hands were crisscrossed in prized tribal tattoos. With that diffident blankness Corcoran cultivated, I hoped he'd be good for Edison, who didn't need to feel any more harshly judged.

However, during our joint appointment I noticed that lightning-bolt chevrons now etched the doctor's brow, suggesting that in his leisure time he forwent that blankness for a great deal of scowling. By the end of this consultation, I would be interpreting his neutrality in a different light. It was fatalism. For his practice to have bought such a sturdy, high-poundage scale, he must have seen enough wide-load patients for the investment to earn out.

"You're pre-diabetic," Corcoran delivered in a bored, of-course spirit, once Edison had dressed in the examination room and we had assumed chairs before the doctor's desk. His mono-tone was almost flip. "Your blood pressure is elevated. At a BMI of over fifty-five, your chances of getting most cancers are signifi-cantly raised. You have edema in your extremities—that's fluid retention, from poor circulation. Your lung capacity is reduced, and if you keep smoking emphysema is almost inevitable—"

"One problem at a time," I interrupted. "Is Edison in good enough health to go on a severely restrictive diet without keeling over?"

"Probably." Corcoran sounded casual. "We can bring down the blood pressure with medication. His heart's in better shape than it has any business being, though he's still a prime candidate for cardiovascular disease. What did you have in mind?"

"From what I've read, we'd eventually have to step it up to eight hundred, then twelve hundred. But to start with, between five and six hundred calories a day."

Since Edison didn't gasp, he mustn't have had any notion how little sustenance that amounted to: two-thirds of one Cinna-bon. As for Corcoran, I swear I remember him laughing. Maybe not a belly laugh, but a distinct guffaw. "That's ambitious."

"With Edison's size, there's no point in doing this if we're not ambitious," I said. "Could you tell me what he weighs?"

The doctor glanced at the patient for permission.

"It's not a state secret, man," said Edison.

"Three-eighty-six."

My brother added, "But that's including boxers."

It could have been worse. I borrowed a pad and pencil to do the following calculations: 386 − 163 = 223 pounds to lose; 223

× 3,500 calories per pound = 780,500 total calories to burn off. I ballparked that Edison would burn an average of 3,000 calories a day—more at the beginning, less at the end. So 3,000 minus, say, an average of 800 calories of consumption = a 2,200-calorie shortfall per day. And 780,500 ÷ 2,200 = 354.77.

That was days. I dreaded telling Fletcher. Even if Edison stayed improbably on the straight and narrow, we could be roommates for a year.

I opted to look for an unfurnished apartment, figuring that we'd be grateful for the task of making the place habitable. Even before the marathon began, I had grasped the special challenge of this project for me in particular. Hitherto, anything I'd taken on, from bedroom curtains to Baby Monotonous, had entailed, well, doing something. This project was about not doing something, which defied my nature. The project itself took up no time, but rather opened up grotesquely more of it—for I was sobered to consider what a big chunk of the day shopping for, preparing, consuming, and cleaning up after meals routinely colonized. The task of buying mattresses would be a mercy.

Three landlords in a row had sounded positive on the phone, only to lay eyes on Edison and inform us regretfully that the apartment had been taken. Oh, they fell all over themselves to apologize—"Gosh, I'm so, so sorry you guys made the trip! It's such a coincidence, 'cause this place has been on the market for weeks!"—which around here was the tip-off; their cadence slow and deliberate, Iowans were prone to a nasality that grew pronounced when they were plaintive. I think the owners were afraid he would break things. I wondered if there was a civil rights issue we might have pressed. Those real estate people would have been far more nervous about slamming the door in his face if Edison were black. But when I did some checking, I discovered that the Americans with Disabilities Act didn't cover the obese. Landlords refusing to rent to lard-asses was perfectly legal.

New Holland has a small population, about 16,000, but still sprawls on its edges, and keeping our search to within a half hour's walk from Solomon Drive was restrictive; I worried we'd run out of options. Driving around with Edison, I was glad for familiar landmarks that might ground my brother and make him feel at home: the decorative wooden windmill in the center of town; De Vries Bakery, which still sold S-shaped, almond-paste Dutch Letters; Norman Borlaug Park, with its entrance hoop of ungainly cutout tulips; the towering white silo on the edge of town that had always signaled the interminable four-day drive from L.A. was finally over. Yet while I'd accustomed myself to its dimensions in adulthood, Edison still found the windmill jarringly small. The bakery would soon become a torture. Even so inclined, we could no longer climb gleefully on the retired fire engine in the park, because contemporary parents had killjoyed this "death trap" of a jungle gym to the dump. Himmel's Meatpacking Plant having modernized, its roof no longer sported the signature pink plaster pig.

Nearly buried in the flotsam of chain stories that littered the whole region like the detritus of a flood, these teasing, dreamlike glimpses of childhood visits to our grandparents seemed only to unnerve my brother. Edison was fundamentally at a loss to explain to himself what he was doing here, with a look on his face every time we crossed the whole town like, *This is IT?* The wide skies and open spaces seemed to make him claustrophobic, as if he might drown in all that nothingness. Admittedly, too, early December didn't show off the area to its advantage. The fields were dirt. The skies were gray.

At last we were met at a development called Prague Porches by an affable man himself seriously overweight. Dennis Novacek had a clubby quality, and noticeably brightened on encountering a would-be renter even bigger than he was. At least fifty, he'd probably been a big man a while; his gut had shifted downward to center around his groin, and sloshed independently of his gait, lurching left when he stepped right. He recognized Edison as a confederate, so I let my brother do the schmoozing. The two of them took the same protracted time laboring up the stairs, while Novacek remarked how a single flight got your blood running but didn't tucker you out. He called our attention to the proximity of Dunkin' Donuts and an all-you-can-eat buffet a five-minute drive away. Edison didn't disabuse the owner of his assumptions, instead bonding with the landlord over their mutual enthusiasm for the "garlic-butter stuffed crust" at Pizza Hut. Again I was glad; if my brother was leery of making proclamations to strangers, he was coming to appreciate the sinister immediacy of the commitment—for the very first morning after we accepted a set of keys the party was over. Funny, the only thing that bugged me a little was his neglecting to correct Novacek's misapprehension that Edison and I were married.

The two-bedroom was more attractive inside than its generic exterior would suggest, with a big picture window overlooking some spindly oak trees that had lost most of their leaves. It sobered me that if this diet went according to plan I would see those trees bare and snow-covered, in bud and in full leaf. With everything white and clean, the apartment had an appropriate spareness, the same this-is-life-and-there's-not-much-to-it starkness of the motel. It was a wiped slate. The simple functional kitchen concealed no bottles of maple syrup in its cupboards, no boxes of confectioner's sugar. Since the premises were newly renovated, the white walls and beige carpet bore none of the stains of other people's failings. Its faintly medicinal, punitive aura recalled a rehabilitation clinic, and that's exactly what we'd turn this place into. I wrote the check.

While we waited for it to clear and for Dennis to track down my credit score, I left Edison at the motel and drove to an address on the edge of town not far from Baby Monotonous. It was an Iowan outfit called Big Presents in Small Packages, or BPSP; though they were imitating a popular national brand, I liked the idea of supporting another local business. Their website included before and after photos that should have been hard to fake. I'd checked with Dr. Corcoran, who'd supervised patients on their program and didn't dismiss them as shysters. I needed to lay in supplies immediately, although subsequent purchases I could make online. Entering the innocuous storefront with trepidation, I remembered the children's books I used to read to Cody, in which deceivingly unassuming rabbit holes or wardrobes proved portals to another world.

"Hi there, what can I do for ya?" No more than thirty but already settled into a floral-bloused middle age, the generously proportioned receptionist was not a great advertisement for her employer's products—although having railed so recently against fat discrimination I couldn't have it both ways. She led me to the array in a glassed-in case. "Now, everybody raves about the cappuccino. And there's some that swear by the banana, though, me, I think it's kinda artificial-tasting. You partial to citrus? 'Cause we got a clear line, too."

"It's not only for me, and my brother is . . . a major project," I said. "I guess it makes sense to lay in a variety, so we don't get tired of one flavor?"

The woman's involuntary laugh reminded me of Corcoran's. "Think you'll find after a real short while 'variety' don't make much difference."

"With your other customers—does it work?"

"Sure, it works—if you follow the program," she said cheerfully.

"And—do they?"

"Most folks get religion at the start. But it takes a special type to stick with it. And then there's the backsliders." She looked me in the eye with a wan half-smile. "We get plenty of repeat customers." I inferred this was not a business whose employees were paid partially in stock.

"Me, I tried everything for a while," she carried on, stacking my order. "Just made myself unhappy. My husband likes me the way I am, and these days I reckon there's no point fighting nature. Life's too short."

"My brother's life being too short," I said, "is the problem."

"Keep us posted!" she cried, raising her Big Gulp in a toast. "We can always use more testimonials for our website."

The trunk loaded, I called Fletcher from the parking lot.

"A year," he repeated.

"Probably." I wouldn't do myself any favors by playing down the figures.

"A week is a long time in politics, they say. A year is a long time in anything."

"It certainly is."

"I'd be angry, except it won't be a year. It won't even be a week."

"It doesn't help for you to pray we go belly up."

"He's going to break your heart, Pandora."

I asked after the kids, and his accounting was lifeless. Tanner had been caught skipping school. Yes, he was being punished; Fletcher didn't say how. All his answers were short. He might have been responding to a marketing survey.

Edison and I moved into Prague Porches two days later. When Dennis Novacek met us at the property with the keys, he kept offering to lease us appliances—washer, dryer, dishwasher, full entertainment center, anything he could think of, probably stuff left behind by previous tenants—addressing himself not to Edison but to me in a newly obsequious spirit. Right: he'd Googled the name on the check. Doubtless he was kicking himself that he could have demanded a higher rent. I had long since stopped taking mere recognition as a compliment. I coveted anonymity for this undertaking, and having transitioned from person to personage with our new landlord was a pain in the neck.

Our three bags made little impact on all that space. We busied ourselves with unpacking, but there was nothing to unpack into, so in each of our rooms we made piles on the carpet. The beds I'd ordered had arrived that morning, and constructing the frames consumed a couple of hours; Edison's heft was helpful for nudging them into place. Otherwise, we didn't even have a table—though there would be no meals, so no matter. The scene was reminiscent of two strapped newlyweds in a ramshackle prefab, where the couple would picnic shyly on the floor with bread, cheese, and wine—a spartan tableau on which they'd later look back fondly: look how happy we were when we had nothing. I wasn't sure it would work that way for Edison and me: look how happy we were when we ate nothing.

"There's something about this pad, man," said my brother, surveying the bleak expanse.

"What?" Though I felt it, too: a burbling terror.

"Makes it real. I guess we're not heading out to fill the fridge with brewskies."

"The refrigerator won't be strained. But think of it this way: we'll never need to clean it." One more thing *not* to do made me feel robbed.

For that evening we'd planned "The Last Supper," and—indulging the very kind of thinking we'd soon have to jettison—we spent hours debating restaurants. Finally, after I'd wiped down counters that were already clean, it was dark enough to go out. We set off in a funereal spirit for one more meal that on the far end of this project Edison would have to "uneat." I say Edison, since we'd neglected to address one uncomfortable issue: long before I, too, lost 223 pounds, the Incredible Shrinking Sister would be fencing spiders with a straight pin. But we'd have all too much time to resolve this disparity in the months to come, and for now I wanted to set off on this venture as a team.

Once we'd settled on a little bistro that at least wasn't a chain, I'd called ahead to warn that my companion would be a "large man," so could they please arrange for a widely proportioned chair. To ensure a decent table, I'd made the reservation in my company's name. Tanner was right. Having submitted to all those humiliating photo shoots should be good for something. When we arrived the staff was duly gracious, and Edison's plush wide-bodied armchair had probably been dragged from the manager's office.

I told my brother he could order whatever he wanted. The only rule for the evening was that our consumption be slow and reflective—conscious. "You bolt your food as if you're afraid someone is about to take it away," I explained. "Someone like yourself, actually. It's as if you're eating behind your own back. But tonight you have permission. Personally, I think you eat so much because you *don't* enjoy your food, not because it's so satisfying you can't stop. Since you're obviously turning to food to provide something it can't, the amount you eat is potentially infinite. It's like you're twisting the tap of the sink to fill the bathtub. So you can keep turning the sink taps on fuller and fuller, but you're never going to fill the tub."

"After the other day with that freaking toilet, you can keep your bathroom metaphors to yourself, babe," he said distractedly, studying the menu with the intensity that yeshiva students devote to the Talmud. "What do you think, the wild mushroom and goat cheese tart or the deep-fried 'onion flower'?"

Those batter-dredged whole-onion things ran to a thousand calories apiece. "*I* think you should order the cold turkey."

"Where's that . . . ?" He finally looked up. "Oh."

Through the first course and breadbasket I tried to teach him what I'd learned with my salmon fillet a few days earlier. I held up a tiny piece of walnut bread and then *fletcherized* it. "Really think about it," I commended. "About what it is. About what it isn't. About what you get out of it. And try to store up the memory for later. So you can reference the flavor. So much of eating is anticipation. Rehearsal and then memory. Theoretically you should be able to eat almost entirely in your head."

"Too deep for me, little sister." All the same, he did as I asked. Though he'd ordered a second appetizer, by the time he was through with that tart, flake by contemplated flake, he canceled the whole fried onion.

"Yo," he said as we waited for our main course—I'd asked the kitchen to drag this meal out for as long as possible. "You still ain't told me how we're gonna do this."

I drummed my fingers. "Would you agree that you have a tendency to be *extreme?*"

"Like how?"

"Well, look at you, Edison. If you're going to overeat, you don't just get a little potbelly; you turn into a human rotunda. I thought we could use that tendency to our advantage. If you have an 'on' switch, then you also have an 'off.'"

"I don't know why, kid, but you're making me nervous."

"All these menu plans on the Web, with their exacting rules and portions. They're a torture. I think it's easier, rather than making dozens of tiny, self-depriving decisions a day, to make one big decision. After which there's nothing to decide."

I laid out the parameters. Surmounting a dumb shock, Edison promised to trust me.

The Last Supper lasted nearly four hours, and we extracted every available drop of savor from that meal like wringing a dishrag dry. I shared one of my peri-peri tiger prawns, and together we dissected the crustaceans, working our knives into the little triangles of shell at the tails to prize out the last orts of shrimp inside. We exchanged portions of our entrées, slicing Edison's black-and-blue filet mignon so thin that the beef was translucent, slicking each piece with a glaze of béarnaise sauce accented with a single pink peppercorn. We cut each of my sea scallops into six wedges like tiny pies, constructing bites with a strip of chorizo, a leaf of arugula, and a languid shred of celeriac like edible haiku. During dessert, I crushed individual seeds of the raspberry clafoutis between my front teeth; the chocolate in

Edison's fudge cake seemed dark in every sense—plummeting, infinite, and wicked, though we took so long tining single black crumbs that the ice cream melted. By the end, we had polished off the bread sticks, the caponata dip, the butter packets, and the mints, and while I let Edison have most of the bottle because I didn't want to get dozy on this of all evenings, we drained the inky, subtly granular Mourvèdre-Cabernet to the last drip. Eating might not have been all it was cracked up to be but it wasn't negligible either, and I kicked myself for having blindly, blithely shoveled from my plate for most of my life as if stoking a coal furnace. I would be sucking on this memory candy for months, rolling it around in the back of my mind until it was eroded to a shard.

I am less nostalgic about the next morning.

Edison must have been hungover—he'd had a cognac with the cake—and dragged into the kitchen, where I was filling the stovetop espresso pot I'd brought from Solomon Drive. (By then having forsworn caffeine, Fletcher wouldn't miss it.) I was ratty myself, dreading black coffee on an empty stomach, but my brother was a surly ball of resentment and free-floating ill will. "There's nowhere to sit, man!"

"We'll take care of that. But meantime, without the soothing of half-and-half, we should have breakfast before coffee."

"I'd be down with that if you meant a tall stack of chocolate-chip pancakes."

"The secret to which you told me"—I held up a BPSP envelope—"was vanilla?"

"Ha-ha," Edison grumbled, slumping onto the counter.

"Man, that dinner last night was *killing*. I bet they do a mean steak-and-eggs brunch."

I'd swiped two water glasses from the motel. Into these I poured one BPSP envelope each: protein, vitamins, minerals, and electrolytes. I dissolved the powder with tap water and stirred. "Mmm, yummy!"

"Can the chirpy shit, Panda Bear." He took his first slug. "Fuck!"

I took a sip. I had to admit it was pretty thin. "Let's hope the strawberry is better."

We milled aimlessly with our beverages, gawking dispiritedly out the picture window at the oak saplings below, their fragile branches metaphors for the flimsiness of our resolve. My newfound sense of savor failed to extend to vanilla protein powder, and I downed the rest in one go. Predictably, even the two fingers of coffee with which I chased our feast-in-a-glass set off an acidic reaction. I had often skipped breakfast altogether, but this morning was different, and I felt piercingly underprivileged without any compensatory sense of accomplishment. I had not even completely skipped breakfast, and I was just as overweight as the night before. Apparently I had no lunch to look forward to, much less any dinner. My entire sense of order had been upended; my life had no protocol, no structure, and on top of that I had to deal with my grumpy, babyish, sniveling older brother.

"This feels fucking stupid, man," he mewled repeatedly, chain-smoking at a cracked-open window. "I'm fucking starving."

"You promised last night you'd trust me. You promised you would not cheat, and you understood that if you ever do cheat I will quit this project faster than you can say 'Quarter Pounder with Cheese.' You remember the rules: you may have diet soda, water—fizzy or still—and herbal tea, but only with lemon and artificial sweetener. I might lay in some sugarless mints. But other than that, four glasses of that sludge a day, period. Now, let's get out of here, I can't stand it."

I was so relieved to have rented unfurnished accommodations that I could have kissed my own hand. Something to do! And I was already reconsidering an earlier resolution, made in the heady delirium of a full stomach. Any asceticism had initially seemed apropos, and with our family history I can see how I might have wanted to renounce the source of so much neglect throughout our childhoods. Yet after only half an hour of beige carpet and vanilla protein powder I had vowed that, in addition to a couch, two armchairs, and a "dining" set in name only, we were first and foremost buying a TV.

chapter three

There's no point in glossing over it. Those first few days were awful. We felt silly. The withdrawal of food felt arbitrary and, absent any immediate results, pointless. The scale of our ambition was so daunting as to seem demented, and I feared that Fletcher was right: we'd never make it through the week. Though the meager protein shakes must have taken the edge off, I was still gnawingly, unrelentingly hungry, which put a drag on the passage of time and infused every passing moment with a gray sensation. I found myself thinking that I didn't really care about having put on "a bit of" weight; as Fletcher said, I was a woman in my forties and a little padding was only to be expected. I didn't need to attract a mate because I was already married, and here I was imperiling that very security for this unfeasible exercise.

All the same, I am a stubborn person and, as my stepchildren discerned, more prideful than I pretended; the prospect of crawling back to Solomon Drive with a bagel and cream cheese clutched in each messy fist was anathema. So I relied on hubris on the one hand, affection on the other—often reciting the long list of lethal ailments that my brother's bulk invited. Though their abstraction was problematic, the last thing that Dr. Corcoran had imparted at the door of his office had hit home. "Mr. Appaloosa," he'd said gravely. "I don't have any old, fat patients."

If the main thing that got me through day by day was Edison, only in retrospect can I infer the corollary: the main thing that got Edison through day by day was me.

Why, by the evening of the very first day my brother was in tears, which meant I'd seen him cry twice within ten days; the Gibraltar of a sibling I'd grown up with had crumbled to landfill. The furniture we'd bought that afternoon had yet to be delivered, so he puddled against the wall on the living room floor like a human beanbag chair. He'd already strained my patience, since the shopping expedition hadn't proven the welcome distraction I'd planned. He'd alternated between an unhelpful finickiness and an equally unhelpful indifference, wandering out of the store every five minutes for another cigarette. He'd perked up a little when I proposed heading to Hy-Vee, but the improved attitude was short-lived: all we needed was paper goods, cheap china, tea bags, diet soda, artificial sweetener, and sugarless mints. He never exhibited any appreciation for the fact that I was starving, too. We'd been roommates for less than twenty-four hours, and he was getting on my nerves.

For me, what made the discomfort so debilitating was the very fact that it was so low grade. Going hungry when overweight is a distinctly bourgeois form of suffering, and when no one else would feel sorry for you, it's hard to feel sorry for yourself. Edison, however, didn't share my difficulty with self-pity.

"Why can't I just have a sandwich?" he whined. "What difference does it make?"

I plunked next to him on the carpet. "One sandwich is the gateway to two. I know you're not used to being hungry. But it's not that bad. Your body is designed to use fat for fuel. It's doing what it's supposed to."

"I don't care! Look at me. I'm still a fat fuck. Now I'm a miserable fat fuck. I can't do it. I can't do it, Panda. A whole year of this, I can't do it."

"Shush . . ." I fluffed the dark blond curls from his face. "This is the hardest part. The very first day."

Giving him strength made me feel stronger, and after I'd brought him a wad of toilet paper to blow his nose I prepared us lemon-ginger tea, trying to look brisk and vigorous as I squeezed every sorry drop of flavor from those sad-ass bags. The more I focused on my brother, the less I suffered myself, and I wondered if in time the solution for Edison, too, might be to worry a little more about me.

"So now what?" Edison scowled at the proffered mug. "It's only eight o'clock, man!" The television hadn't arrived yet, either.

"Well . . ." I settled back beside him, cradling the tea as Edison had cupped his cognac the night before—which already seemed weeks ago. "We've been around each other for over two months, and you still haven't talked to me."

"Balls. I'm a fucking motormouth and you know it."

"You haven't explained what happened. For you to end up like this. There's more to it than corned beef on rye."

"What, you expect some bare-all confession?"

"Out of sheer desperation to fill time? Yes. I want to know what's made you so depressed."

"Let's see. I had a shit-hot wife who walked out. I got a son I ain't seen since he was four. I ain't got laid in years. I got no money and no work, and at the age of forty-four I'm dependent on my nationally famous sister for my allowance. Sounds pretty depressing to me."

"That *Reader's Digest* version only got us to eight-thirteen. I don't get it. I got the impression that pretty soon after you left Tujunga Hills you took Manhattan by storm."

"That may be putting it kinda strong. But I played three years with Stan Getz! I did some serious venues, man. The Vanguard, the Blue Note. I played—"

"With some heavy cats," I deadpanned. "So why aren't you still playing with heavy cats?"

"Look, it's not like I sucked. Cats change their sound. And, around when I started having trouble with Sigrid, I may have got . . . a little difficult. You know, I was a fucking star, man—"

"Like Travis," I said heavily. "That's a pretty dangerous role model you've got for yourself. Travis Professional Asshole."

"Maybe I got it from Travis at that. It didn't go down too good. I, like, walked out a few times. In the middle of gigs. When the audience wouldn't shut up, or the bass was amped too loud."

"That's what you ragged on Keith Jarrett for doing."

"Takes one to know one. But Jarrett can get away with it—"

"Which is why he makes you mad."

"I got with the program in due course, dig? Came round to the view that pulling that everything-just-so-or-I-refuse-to-play shit was unprofessional. But I'd already got a reputation. Cats got leery of playing with me, so the primo gigs stopped coming my way. And I never played with Miles! Every dude even carried the guy's horn been sitting pretty ever since. Those cats can act up much as they like, insist on silk dressing gowns and berate the audience about their cell phones—"

"But you've recorded all those CDs." I'd heard the *if I'd only played with Miles* riff before. "I know you haven't made them up, because you've sent me copies."

"Anybody can make CDs, man. Snagging a distributor, getting reviewed by Ben Ratliff—that's another bag altogether."

"Still, you kept playing."

"Yeah, but lower down the pecking order. Cornelia Street. Small's. Fat Cat. People noticed. I was going in the wrong direction. In fact, I never told you this, but . . ."

"What?" I sensed there was so much he'd never told me that, rather than killing an hour or two, we could be up all night.

Edison took a hard slug on his tepid tea in the spirit of downing a double whiskey, and I wondered if the primary point of boozing was that prop—not what was in it, but the glass. "There was this period, in the mid-nineties. *Joint Custody* had only been off the air, what, twelve, thirteen years? Plenty club hoppers grew up watching it. So for a while I tried marketing myself as 'the Real Caleb Fields.' I was actually listed in the *Voice* as Caleb Fields."

At least he sounded sheepish. "Did it work?"

He shrugged. "Brought in a few curiosity seekers. Hey, you use what you got, right? And we're, you know . . . not chopped liver. He may drive us nuts, but Travis was a network TV star. We're special, kid."

I almost didn't say it, but keeping just this sort of remark to myself was why after all these years, and two months in the same house, my brother and I still didn't know each other well. "You mean *you're* special."

When Edison looked over, the fire in his eyes wasn't from crying. "Look. I've worked motherfucking *hard*. Maybe I'm rusty right now, but you've seen it—most of my life I've practiced six or seven hours a day. I've hustled—since nobody out there walks up to you on the street and just offers you a gig because you look like a nice guy. I've listened and studied the gamut, from Jelly Roll Morton, to Monk, to Chick, to Bley. In the days before you could get every obscure recording under the sun on iTunes, I tracked down all their music, everything those cats recorded—"

"Ever catered a dinner party for seventy-five?" I deliberately refrained from playing the Baby Monotonous card. "Missing three nights of sleep in a row chopping onions and rolling out tart crusts—?"

"Don't talk about food, man. Please."

"I've worked hard, too. If that's the standard, lots of people are 'special.' And there's a big difference between feeling special and feeling privileged. Entitled."

"Maybe I am *entitled*. I got something, I'm—"

"You have *talent*, and I don't."

"Hey, kid. This isn't going anywhere."

"It's going somewhere all right, just not where you want to go."

We sat for a minute in silence.

"My life is shit. You're flying high, and I'm in three hundred eighty-six pounds of shit. Beats me why you want to make me feel even worse."

"I'm not." I softened. "We grew up thinking wrong, Edison. I've tried to get it through to Tanner and Cody, without much success, either. This whole obsession with . . . It's just, you care too much what other people think of you!"

I didn't imagine it possible for Edison to slump any lower against that baseboard, but he did. "Other people don't think about me at all, babe, not these days. You know, when I tried going by 'Caleb Fields'? Some of the audience always walked out in a huff. They thought they were coming to see Sinclair Vanpelt. Can you believe it? The little fuck who thought an arpeggio was an Italian pastry."

I laughed. "Yeah, that's pretty rich." I patted Edison's knee and got up. We'd kept "dinner" in reserve; though that morning I'd had no idea how one might look forward to protein powder, I advanced on the kitchen with gusto. "How are you feeling?" I called as I stirred.

"Light-headed. Pissy. Fat."

"At your size, by tomorrow morning you'll have already lost a pound and a half."

"And you'll be able to tell the difference?"

"A journey of a thousand miles . . ."

"Eat your homilies, sister."

"Homilies, then"—a word that sounded like something made out of cornmeal—"for dessert."

T he next morning Edison was astonished to have lasted twenty-four hours on a quartet of envelopes dissolved in water, and an entrenched petulance was contaminated with self-congratulation. Overcome with relief that we were no longer on the very first day, I had lined up tasks for our second. Yet running errands was constantly impeded by one of us having to pee. We were supposed to be drinking a minimum of four pints of liquid per day in addition to the shakes, and without food water goes right through you. Twice we had to U-turn back to our Prague Porches bathroom before we finally made it to Walmart—by which time Edison refused to budge, and stayed behind in the car.

"You never heard the expression 'Ignorance is bliss'?" joked the hefty guy behind me at checkout, nodding at my boxed, heavy-duty scale, big enough to require a platform caddy.

"Yeah, honey," the woman ahead chimed in amiably. "I'd rather not know."

"Well, there's ignorance," I allowed, "and there's self-deceit."

"Self-deceit makes life bearable," said the philosopher behind me, loading his case of Bud onto the belt. "Make 'em see too clear in the mirror, whole human race'd jump off a bridge."

I laughed. "My brother and I just started this horrific all-liquid diet. And if we don't start charting a little progress"—I patted the box—"we're definitely jumping off that bridge."

Shouldering his beer, the guy followed me outside and offered to help load the scale in the car. A farmer, I guessed, brawny enough that, if agriculture hadn't grown so mechanized, he'd have been quite a hunk. "Keep the faith, ma'am," he said, closing the trunk; he must have glimpsed Edison's mounded outline in the passenger seat. "But don't you forget—the right to lie to yourself is what makes this a free country!"

"Doesn't anyone in this place ever *shut up?*" Edison groused when he was gone. "Everywhere we go, in five seconds a new yokel is your best friend. Jesus, at least in New York total strangers don't yak your head off."

At some point I might defend Iowans' conviviality as making the most mundane transactions rich, personal, and satisfying, but now was not the time.

I called home later that afternoon and got Cody. "I don't care what Dad and Tanner say," she said quietly. "I think what you're doing is wonderful."

I put Edison on, and for once Cody did most of the talking. When he got off, he was abashed and at a loss for words. I asked what she'd said. "Teenage girls should never be given access to the fucking Internet," he grumbled. "She's been doing searches. On obesity. So it was all this 'I love you, Uncle Edison' stuff and 'Mom is giving you this big chance and if you don't take it you're gonna die.' I'd heard about all the badgering kids do when their parents smoke. Same thing. It's unbearable. It's fucking blackmail."

At six p.m. we went to see a film, and I don't remember what we saw. All I can remember is the thick fug of artificially buttered popcorn. When following the BPSP program (which we had started calling "Blip-Sup"), smell is so intense that I worried whether we could ingest some fraction of the 1,500 calories in a large bucket through our noses. Torn on whether inhaling the theater's salty infusion was a joy or a torture, I would soon conclude that, if you ever had a choice between the two, you picked joy.

That night the TV—a little 24-inch LED, though Edison had rooted for a monster 65-inch plasma—still hadn't been delivered. At least the twin recliners had arrived, so we didn't have to pick up my brother's story where we'd left off while sprawled on the floor.

During that second day, when I wasn't concocting recipes in

my head—adding cranberries to cornbread, or doctoring ground lamb patties with fennel and paprika—I'd been reflecting on what little Edison had told me so far. Professionally, he'd struggled more than he'd ever let on. I'd been self-indulgent. I wanted to revere my brother, and in the service of that reverence had for years taken his braggadocio at face value.

It had seemed lucky at the time, but his getting the big breaks when he was only twenty or so wasn't lucky at all. When things go swimmingly at that age you think it's just the beginning, because you've been instantly recognized as one of the Chosen People. I was increasingly antagonistic to this designation, not only for Edison, but for myself and my kids. No, nothing was wrong with feeling valuable in some way, if deservedly so. But Edison had always regarded himself as exceptional in a manner that was indolent and presumptuous. His character would have profited in his twenties from, say, working on the assembly line of an air-conditioner plant. I had never worked harder than when running Breadbasket, and in sweating over four gallons of tomato sauce I came to appreciate the hard work of others around me—the deliverymen, the bakers, the postal workers, most of their toil unsung. No one ever told them that they were special.

Tanner expected the same instant recognition the moment he bestowed his literary largesse on Steven Spielberg. The only cure for this ignorant arrogance is fetching lattes for a decade and staying up nights slaving over scripts you now realize no one wants to read. Only gradually do you come to appreciate that the occupation you aspire to is harder than you thought, that the supply of other young, self-anointed apples of their own eyes is inexhaustible, and that you're not as uniquely gifted as you'd thought. It's surely a fine emotional art—dousing your hollow hauteur without quenching the fire in your belly altogether—but the kids who master it come out the other side both shit-hot at their professions and bearable as human beings.

There must have been a jazz equivalent of paying the dues that my brother was now forking over in middle age, and he'd have fared better to have had the callowness beaten out of him when he was young enough to bounce back. A surprisingly large number of up-and-comers in every generation fancy themselves geniuses waiting to be discovered, and having that baseless self-regard ratified while on the penumbra of adulthood can be ruinous. I hate to say it, since I remember my school days as forlorn, and then in our teens we lost our mother, but the truth is that Edison and I grew up spoiled, basking in the glow cast by a father whom all of our classmates recognized off the set. What my brother had needed when he ventured out on his own at seventeen was a good kick in the pants, and I could connect our spoiled upbringing, and the seamless continuation of this pampering when he obtained high-profile come-hithers as a fledgling performer, to his current size.

I remembered Edison from that era, when at eighteen I visited him for the first time in New York. He had energy, and older musicians fed off his sense of discovery at the keyboard. That freshness was electric, and contagious; I could see why they all wanted to play with him. Only later would I pose the perfidious question: Had his surname opened doors? The series then airing its last few seasons, he must have raised bemused eyebrows with "Appaloosa." I wouldn't dismiss my brother's talent, but one revelation you're denied when the waters part too readily in your youth is that lots of people are talented. Even an irrelevant novelty can single out one from the pack.

In any case, it must have come as a shock when, rather than rocket further into the jazz stratosphere, by thirty he'd started to founder. (I was staggered he'd resorted to calling himself Caleb Fields, even briefly.) I'd never envied people who peak early, condemned forever more to reminisce about a stellar past they'd not been savvy enough to appreciate as parvenus. Arguably, by mid-career Edison would have been better off falling flat on his face, obliging him to make a go of something else. By his mid-forties, he couldn't imagine himself doing anything but play jazz piano, and he'd found just enough work all these years to keep him in the game. It was a trap. I'd seen the type in the entertainment world of L.A., people who get so far and no farther, seething resentfully on the margins at people who direct real Hollywood movies or act in real Broadway plays. These near misses often get just enough reward here and there that they won't give up, but their occasional small successes are in some ways worse than nothing. Failure affords release.

"So," I introduced over the day's final packet of Blip-Sup, which we had learned to sip at a contemplative pace. "When we left off, you'd become a conceited prima donna and suffered the consequences. What happened next?"

"Well, this is out of order . . . Just promise you won't freak out."

"On five hundred and eighty calories a day, I don't have the energy to freak out."

"Sigrid. When she was pregnant. Like, eight months. Anyway, she walked into one of my rehearsals, and I was high."

"On what?"

"I don't mean pot, which would make for a piss-poor story. The real thing."

"You took *heroin?*"

"You promised you wouldn't freak out! And I don't mean I was a junkie. Takes an average of *ten years* to get *physically* addicted to that shit, which out here in *Iowa* nobody would realize."

"We have one of the worst meth problems in the country, so don't pull rank."

"Anyway, big deal, I tried it. You know why Bird was so great, don't you? He was high. So you have to try getting high to understand the music. He could play that out because he didn't give a shit. You want me to 'not care so much what other people think of me'? Score me some smack."

"You can't imagine I'm going to buy the idea that taking heroin is an obligation of your profession, like practicing scales."

"Yeah, well, Sigrid didn't buy that, either. I'd already pushed it being . . . you know, not always what you'd call considerate. With the kid on the way, the smack was the last straw. She turned heel that afternoon and packed her bags."

"Did you keep taking it?"

"Nah. It was a little *too* good, if you know what I'm sayin'. Made me nervous. You think I got no discipline—"

"I never said that, Fletcher did. And look at you: two days on eight envelopes of guck."

"It was a short flirtation, few months max. Never touched it again. For Sigrid, it was too late. I made one big appeal after Carson was born, but I made the mistake of getting wasted on JD first. 'Cause I was nervous. Not the best way to present my case. She wasn't impressed."

"Did you . . . did you drink a lot?"

"For a while. But I pulled up short from that, too. Can't play too good plastered. Got sloppy."

"I'm just getting the impression that it's always been something."

"Please don't say I got an 'addictive personality.'"

"I didn't. You did."

"A large pepperoni pizza, in the scale of things, seemed the least bad option. I could still play the fucking piano."

"But when did you stop buying slices and order the whole pie? More to the point, why? When you visited us four years ago, you were trim as ever."

Edison rubbed his face. "It's hard to get the chronology right. The last time I came to see you, I may not have been playing at the top—like, maybe I hadn't got into the Vanguard in ten years. But that's mainly because the owner never forgave me for walking offstage when some bozos by the bar kept blathering through the whole first set. I was totally within my rights, too, and if it had been Jarrett? She'd have backed up the musicians, and tossed those bridge-and-tunnel rubes out on their ear."

"Edison. You were going to explain why you started to overeat."

"I'm tryin', man, I'm tryin'! But I gotta set the table, if you know what I'm sayin'. Point is, I still had connections, still had a rep. Lotta cats, even younger cats, were *grateful* to play with me. But you got any idea what a place like Cornelia *pays*? Like, on a weekend, maybe a hundred bucks. That's before dinner and cab fare. The Jazz Gallery pays *zilch*. Clubs like Barbès in Brooklyn, I'm lucky to walk out with forty. I was playing every sorry gig I could get my hands on, but I was slipping behind, man. Coming up short on the rent. Once I got three months in arrears, if I didn't do something I was gonna get evicted. So I didn't see no other way out, man. I just didn't see no other way out." Edison was shaking his head with his chin in his hand. I gave him time.

"So," he resumed. "I sold the fucking piano."

"Oh, no!" Edison's Schimmel was the first major purchase he'd made with the proceeds of those more lucrative early years, and it was his most prized possession. At under six feet, the piano wasn't quite a grand, but it had tyrannized his every relocation. "I thought you said it was in storage."

"I did *store* it, didn't I? In somebody else's house."

"What was it worth?"

"More than I got for it," he said bitterly. "I swear the day they hauled that sweet instrument outta my place was worse than the day Sigrid walked. And the *timing* was sorta dark. See, once the movers left, I shuffled off to get me some ciggies. And what's on the newsstand, fresh that day? *New York* magazine. My own sister grinning from the cover. A little more *rounded* than I remembered, so it took me a second."

"You should be glad I could stand to drop a pound or two," I said coldly, "or you wouldn't have any company on this diet."

"Touchy, touchy! I call myself a fat motherfucker, you can handle *rounded*."

I *was* touchy—and irritable. I envied Edison his cigarettes, the distraction, the occupation of his hands. Sugarless mints didn't do the trick. Uncut by passing the macaroni, pure talk was draining. At least the literal draining of herbal tea and diet soda meant I had to keep heading for the bathroom. I now looked forward to peeing: it was something to do.

"I asked you what set off this food bender," I said on return, "and you keep talking about something else."

"No, I'm *not* talking about something else. That day—I'm selling my piano to stay alive, which is cannibalism, man—it's like gnawing your own arm to keep from starving. At the very same time my kid sister's rolling in it, some kind of industrial—magnate! Talk about rubbing it in! Well, far as I can pinpoint it, that's where it started. I beelined to a joint on the corner that served a mean rack of ribs. Corn muffins, mashed potatoes. Soon as I polished off that first rack, I ordered another one. Then I had the mud cake. Think I had two of those, too. It just seemed—like I deserved it, like a good feed was the least I could ask. I don't even remember feeling full."

"I don't get it. What did an article about pull-string dolls have to do with you?"

"You can't be that stupid. You obviously find it incredibly satisfying, so go ahead. Enjoy. One of us should get something out of it, and it ain't gonna be me."

I squinted. "You're not blaming me for your getting fat, are you?"

Edison rolled his eyes. "It's not about you, it's about me in *relation* to you, dig?"

Okay, I didn't want to play innocent to the point of seeming an idiot. Siblings did use each other as yardsticks. Yet I'd never begrudged Edison his accomplishments, which I'd so venerated that for years I'd turned a willful blind eye to the fact that he'd been struggling. If I'd ever preened about running my own catering business, it was only to impress him. I was dumbfounded why having been born three years later would make so much difference. "I wasn't trying to *beat* you."

"Well, you did. If you beat me without trying, that's even worse."

"What good has it done me? Travis hates me. And keeps pretending I'm nothing but a housewife. You hate me, from the sound of it—"

"Gimme a break! Maybe I wouldn't get much of a kick out of making dolls. But to say hitting the big time all over these magazines as a nationally celebrated *entrepreneur*, and making I don't know how much bread in the process, to say that hasn't done you 'any good'—well, babe, that's just ridiculous. Travis hating you—in the way that you mean—well, I want Travis to hate *me* like that. It's a compliment, that level of resentment. You make him mad. I make him laugh."

"If you really want to impress Travis—or make him 'resent' you, which I guess is the next best thing—then you lose that weight."

"Oh, for fuck's sake, anybody can go on a *diet.*"

"No, anybody can't. It's the one thing most people can't do. Haven't the last couple of days been hard? They've been hard for me. I can't stand it. All I can think about is food."

"Being slimmer of the year," he said, "ain't what I ever wanted to be famous for."

"Maybe nobody dreams of growing up to be formerly fat. But they sure don't dream of growing up to be fat. If only because— when you walk down the street, it's all people see. You big as a house, but in any meaningful way you're invisible."

"Maybe I like it that way."

"That makes a lot of sense. Jazz pianist with ambitions to international renown seeks above all to pass by unnoticed."

"It does make sense, if you understand me at all." Edison lit another cigarette. I was starting to regret letting him smoke in the apartment, which already stank, and his consumption had skyrocketed. But yanking his last crutch would have seemed like abuse of the disabled.

" . . . You didn't buy it, did you." It wasn't really a question.

"Buy what?" He knew perfectly well.

"*New York* magazine. Your own sister on the cover, and you grabbed your Camels and walked away."

"It was five bucks!"

"You wouldn't have bought it if it was ten cents." The jibe had a dolorous cast. "But back to the piano. I don't understand why before selling the Schimmel you didn't come to me."

"You have no idea. You're so used to being the middle kid in our family that you can't get your head around what it might be like to be me."

"If I were in dire straights I wouldn't hesitate to come to you, if I thought you could spare the money."

"Exactly."

"I don't understand."

"No, you don't."

"This is all some . . . birth-order nonsense?"

"Call it whatever cliché you want. I'm your big brother. That means *you* go buy *New York* magazine with *me* on it. That *you* come to *me* for cash, and you can have it, too. That I don't end up a charity case living on my kid sister's dime."

Interestingly, whatever reservations Edison once had about tapping my resources had evaporated. That was obvious when he'd lobbied for the 65-inch plasma flat screen the day before. Like those of most people who'd made a go of an enterprise, my profits were finite—money is always finite—and a large proportion of the gravy had been poured back into the business. But something sinister happens whenever people plop you into the category of the wealthy. It's as if your money, by conceit inexhaustible, isn't real, so your generosity isn't real, either.

"Besides," said Edison. "I only realized you could have

helped me out after I'd already sold the Schimmel and then saw that cover story. That catering bag was barely in the black. From what you'd said on the phone about this 'Baby Moronic' biz—"

"*Monotonous.*"

"It sounded whack. I thought you were out of your freakin' tree. So when a tenor player mentioned he'd bought one for his wife's birthday, I didn't make the connection."

"That's because whenever I tell you what's up with me, your mind wanders. I've always been able to hear it. Your grunts and uh-huhs are in all the wrong places."

"Don't take this wrong, but that catering trip . . . You moved to *Iowa* . . . Then you married some closemouthed seed salesman turned carpenter I got nothing in common with . . . The only reason I got to find that riveting is you're my sister."

"That's not enough?"

"Sure it is. Sort of. But we live in totally different worlds, man. I'm up jamming till the wee-smalls in Manhattan, and you're rustling around in all this—corn."

If I'd long aspired to be dull, I had apparently achieved my goal. So what was my problem? Well, I had a headache. I felt weak. I couldn't keep a grip on the reason I was subjecting myself to this deprivation. I missed my husband, and Edison wasn't the only one who could be bored by a sibling. I couldn't stay focused on what I was doing in this bland, underfurnished apartment, and I suspected this mutual vagueness of mind was why Edison and I seemed incapable of getting his story to flow in a comprehensible fashion. I bore down.

"Back to the main agenda," I said. "The Schimmel must have been worth thousands. That would have bought you some time."

"It bought me something," Edison muttered.

"Meaning?"

He covered his face with his hands. "I ate it, man. I ate my piano."

"Oh, *Edison*." I sounded like our mother.

"I'm on the town, I'm not warming up a two-sixty-nine can of soup, am I? That's when things started to get heavy. Or I did. And restaurant food is pricey."

"I just . . ." I threw up my hands. "I'm dumbfounded! You were a high school track star!"

"You could understand if you made an effort. Yeah, I used to look pretty good. Then I didn't. That's the point. Once I got sort of fat, one more baby-back didn't matter. See, when you look sharp, you got something to protect—an investment to preserve, a power to keep. But when you're already big, there's nothing to lose from being bigger. Now, going wide didn't help me professionally, I admit. Especially for the younger cats, this middle-aged fat guy fucked up their image. So suddenly I'd notice in the *Voice* that bands I been playing with for five years are listing with a different piano player. Which made me eat more. 'Cause it passed the time. 'Cause I was hungry. 'Cause I was pissed off.

"So I'd do a wedding, and . . . There was one in particular, on Long Island. It turns out the band wasn't supposed to eat the buffet. We were meant to get a plate, in the kitchen, like, you know, the Negroes. Nobody said so, *per se*. So I took a chance, and between sets I hit the spread. It was good grub, too, shrimp and lobster and roast beef, so maybe I piled it on kind of high. A *little* high. Then we all got an earful when we were packing up, and the *happy couple* took two hundred bucks out of our pay, a shortfall the band passed on to me. Two hundred bucks! And it was a quintet, so five ways that was only three hundred per *before* my bad-boy deduction, leaving me with a lousy C-note. No way I ate two hundred bucks' worth of their damned food. But one look at me, and everyone assumed I ate the whole roast pig. Like the head-shaking tut-tuts I get in restaurants—when I'm sitting there eating a regular turkey club like everyone else? I can hear the other guys at the lunch counter thinking: *These porkers always complaining about glandular problems, but whenever you see them in public they're up to their nuts in onion rings . . .*

"Anyway, after that wedding fiasco, my rep took another hit, and cats started warning me before asking me on a gig: 'Don't know if you're interested, 'cause we don't get dinner on this one,' or 'You're not allowed to touch the food.' Fucking insulting. Wasn't like I couldn't go five minutes without a cheeseburger.

"You getting the picture, Panda Bear? Money got super tight. Cats who should've been thanking their lucky stars to be associated with someone with my résumé are starting to avoid me. I'm getting fat—yeah, of course I *noticed*—and that was a drag, too. That's the thing: getting fat makes you fatter. The weight itself is such a bummer that it drives you right into the arms of a lamb shawarma. Too many shawarmas translate into fewer gigs, more chowing down to forget my troubles, even fewer gigs. It's, whaddya call it, a *feedback loop*, know what I'm saying? Meanwhile, the Schimmel may have paid off the arrears, but after I ate through the rest of that dough I was back where I started. Couldn't keep the apartment, even in Williamsburg. Which is getting pretty full of itself, actually, but never mind.

"So I put everything in storage. Slack helped, rented a van. Thousands of CDs. Cartons of sheet music. Whole library of jazz biographies. Had a box set of twelve Miles LPs, *Chronicle*—all the recordings he did with Prestige. Limited edition, numbered, only ten thousand pressed. Gorgeous, all brown and soft, with heavy sleeves. Bio, photos, liner notes on each set. Shoulda sold it when I had the chance, but I couldn't bring myself, man. I just couldn't part with it."

He sounded so morose, I had to ask. "But your stuff is still in storage, right?"

Edison stared out the window to the lights of the Burger King glimmering through the trees. "Fell behind on those payments, too. Went back to Box My Pad last spring, thought I'd try to strike a deal for back rent. They'd already auctioned my unit. Unless the lucky bidder was a jazz fiend, he'd have hauled most of my shit to the dump. Dozens of framed posters from gigs, some in German, French, Japanese. My sound system. My vinyl—including Mother's *Magnolia Blossoms*, I'm afraid. All my photographs, aside from the few I'd uploaded to my website. Clothes, not that I could wear most of them anymore."

"So that's what happened to your leather trench coat," I said softly.

"Keep seeing that Miles box set on some mildewed mattress. Rained on. LPs cracked in half. And all those CDs. Mine's a pretty old laptop, small memory by current standards. I'd only transferred a fraction of that music to the computer."

"You lost *everything*?"

Edison spread his hands. "What you see is what I got."

I don't think of myself as a hopeless materialist, but this revelation hit me hard. It's sometimes so difficult to be sure of what and who we are, our sense of ourselves is so precarious, so tentative—and these physical totems are guide wires. Edison's posters had been emblems he could touch, sure verification that every European tour had not been in his head. Having accompanied him to many a music emporium in New York, I knew how rigorously he'd worked to compile that rarefied CD library now either cluttering some disappointed scavenger's rank basement or scattered to seagulls. That was our family's last copy of *Magnolia Blossoms*. And I mourned that coat.

"So that's when you started sleeping on your friends' couches?"

"No. Gotta understand, yeah, some of the cats made themselves scarce. But a hard core of my friends would do anything for me, man. Word went out I was having trouble keeping a crib, and they found me a place. That club in Red Hook—"

"Three Bars in Four-Four." (At 44 Visitation Place—a haunting address I remembered.) "The one you managed."

"Well, not exactly. I never, like, managed it, though I can see how, over the phone, you might have, you know—got that impression."

"Yes. I got that impression."

"There was a room over the club. See, Three Bars is a real seat-of-the-pants operation, can't afford a cleaning service, and the whole idea of the hang was they'd stay open ultra late—by which time the staff was dying to go home. So the deal was, I'd clean the place after closing, and in exchange I could stay in that room on the second floor for free. Of course, it wasn't up to code, not much better than a closet with an electrical socket. Only one window, covered in spiderwebs. But I didn't need much, and I could use the club john to wash up. During the day when Three Bars was shut I could practice on the house piano, and being right upstairs meant I also became, like, the house keyboard player. Slack and the other cats would come by after their own gigs, since by then just about everybody'd moved to Brooklyn. It was a cool place, really smoking. Still is, far as I know. Honest, for a while there things weren't so bad."

"So why don't you still live there? Hardly sounds opulent, but you could play."

"Yeah, well. Three Bars sells food, right? Not just burgers, but fish, a chicken salad with mango and cashews and shit. Good home fries . . ."

I didn't like where this was headed. Edison wouldn't look at me.

"So they noticed stuff disappearing," he continued reluctantly. "From the kitchen."

"Oh, Edison," I said, again with that maternal color. "It sounds as if your friends really went out on a limb for you. Just a little self-control . . ."

"Yeah, yeah, I heard that from several parties, thank you. But it's not easy for me to get around lately, and sweeping wore me out. Bringing in all those glasses to the dishwasher, I was already in the kitchen. No fridge upstairs, and I'd been warned against storing even dry goods, because of rats. So by six in the morning I was famished, and nothing in Red Hook was open yet. I always put everything back, plastic covers sealed up. And that chicken salad was killing."

"It sure killed something."

"Yeah. My last chance."

I clinked my cappuccino shake glass against his. "Your next-to-last chance," I said, and we downed the dregs.

chapter four

Having let it hulk oppressively in its box by the door, we finally unpacked the scale on Day Four. Eschewing the measly drama of a digital readout, I'd chosen the old-fashioned kind with a wide white face and red needle. We dragged our sentinel beside the picture window, where it stood at attention against the wall, its big round head keeping stern watch as I patted out every last grain from the day's third set of envelopes. We'd already formed fierce opinions about the flavors. Edison liked the butterscotch; I was rounding on the view that only the vanilla could go the distance.

It was time for our first weigh-in. I decided not to down my shake beforehand; why add eight more ounces to what could be a grim reckoning? In the future, we'd always need to measure our progress at the same time of day, since one's weight can vary a good five pounds over twenty-four hours, and I didn't want us to get disheartened after living all day on Blip-Sup—a shorthand that had already metamorphosed to "Upchuck"—only to weigh in even fatter. By now, Edison badly needed some demonstrable achievement to hold on to. Given his size, we couldn't really see any difference after four days of starvation, so I could begin to understand how nefariously that process worked in reverse. You eat a whole cheesecake and look in the mirror and big deal: nothing's changed.

For my part, I'd started this experiment with no baseline. In the frenzy and chronic nausea of the Breadbasket years, I'd scrawnied down to 117: a lifetime accolade. For most of my life I'd circled around 130, which at 5'7" put my BMI at an irreproachable 20.4, and that's how I thought of myself: *I weighed 130*. Yet ever since I'd grown determined to show Fletcher that he couldn't push me around with a head of broccoli, I had given the scale in our bathroom wide berth.

An especially contemporary form of cowardice. My compatriots may have connived to amplify what constituted normal proportions, our dress sizes deflating as wildly as university grades were bloating in the other direction. (I'd just seen on CNN that Levi's planned to bring in the buttock sizes *slight*, *demi*, and *bold*, while considering yet a fourth, *supreme curve*. How easily I could picture the hilarity at that sales meeting.) But had we therefore ushered in an era of absolution in relation to the waistline? Hardly: the weigh-in was now subject to the most ruthless of interpretations. I believed—and could not understand why I believed this, since I didn't believe it—that the number on that dial was a verdict on my very character. It appraised whether I was strong, whether I was self-possessed, whether I was someone anyone else would conceivably wish to be. Because I'd been dodging my confessor in the master bath at home, the scale in Prague Porches would also put an exact numerical value on my tendency to what my farmer friend at Walmart claimed "makes life bearable": self-deceit.

So Edison and I faced our arbiter with the foreboding of having been sent to the principal's office. Manfully, I volunteered to go first. I slipped off my shoes. I pulled off my sweater. I removed the change from my pockets, and even took out the comb. Presenting myself like a human sacrifice, I stepped onto the platform. The red needle swept gracefully, inexorably up: 168.

My cheeks flamed. I stepped back off the scale as if it were physically hot. My head told me that there was no earthly reason to take that number to heart. If temporarily in absentia, I was a decent mother. At least with Edison, I was a devoted sister; if Fletcher would only let me, I was still a devoted wife. I'd now run two businesses, the second a resounding success. These were the aspects of my life that mattered. Furthermore, I was already doing something about this situation, and the higher my weight to start with the longer I'd be able to accompany Edison on his grueling mission. Yet none of this reasonable, rational reassurance moderated by an iota my burning sense of shame.

"Wow," I said, flustered. "That was a shock."

"Maybe now you got some appreciation for what it's like to clock in at three-eighty-six."

"It's just a number." A number that meant I'd gained twice as much weight in the last few years as I'd thought. "Now, hit the deck."

Edison removed his shoes and stepped up to the plate with his eyes closed. "You read it, babe. If those sorry-ass shakes are all for squat, break it to me gentle."

"Three-seventy-seven! Edison, in only four days you've lost nine pounds!"

"Not too shabby, right?"

"Shabby? This is fantastic! Those stupid Upchucks work!" After Edison had ambled off the stage of his star turn, I clasped his hands and jumped up and down. "We should celebrate! . . . And I don't know how." Indeed, our abstinence eliminated all the traditional means of marking an occasion. We couldn't pop champagne or book a table. Wanly, I restirred our shakes, and we toasted with the grainy, watery elixir of our salvation.

We did manage some sense of festivity that night, plugging Edison's computer into our new sound system and dancing around the living room with his iTunes set on "party shuffle"—a term I welcomed, since we needed every hint of revelry we could scrounge. To say that my brother "boogied" might have been pushing it, but I did, while he jigged around the room inscribing sardonic Middle Eastern hand movements like a belly dancer. With one denied, other senses as well as smell were growing more acute; besides, my ear for jazz had grown unwittingly better educated during my brother's crash course on Solomon Drive. Rather than clash in a jangle of discordant riffs—which I'd pictured as rusted garden furniture and incomplete board games crammed in a jumbled garage—the music sounded more tuneful and orderly. When we played the who's-this game I could at last identify Charlie Parker.

Yet what I most remember is suddenly coming up short. "Edison. Stop a second. I don't know about you. But *I don't feel hungry.*"

Edison contemplated his midsection. "Huh. You're right, babe. I don't, either."

"Do you have a funny taste in your mouth?"

"Now that you mention it—like an animal crawled in there and died."

"It's ketosis! I've read about it, but I didn't really believe it!"

Thereupon, that night officially became our Ketosis Party: the magic moment when our bodies gave up on ever seeing take-out again and resigned themselves to eating in.

B ut our project was going so well! Edison became far less begrudging, and admitted to having more energy than when he was pigging out, even if he refused to grant that the giddy highs of ketosis could quite compare to heroin. It was Edison and Pandora against the world, just like when we were kids. On walkabouts—exercise that also killed time—we shared a mounting superiority to our brethren still groveling in the gutter of earthly delights, lifting our heads at an imperial tilt down gauntlets of fast food. We sampled salty lung-fulls of french fries with the discerning noses of perfumers, able to tease out palm oil versus beef tallow, to detect the tang of ketchup or mellow of mayonnaise. Yet gliding past KFC was like window shopping without our wallets, and we were never tempted. We were invincible, like superheroes; we had special powers. Though I'd imagined myself little concerned with status, living on four slender envelopes of protein powder per day while everyone around me wallowed in buckets of extra-crispy was my most consuming experience of aristocracy. This *rising above* sensation grew especially intense over Christmas, when in Hy-Vee we would waltz obliviously past pre-basted turkeys and mincemeat pies to haughtily assemble our prissy purchases of paper towels and pink packets of aspartame.

We both had black days, of course—days I prefer not to recall. I'm not sure what triggered them, but certain mornings I'd wake with *oh, no, not this again*, groping for my clothes in a mi-asma of misanthropy. Everything I laid eyes on was infuriating: the cold wet teabags on the counter; the knocked-over recycling bag, its spilled bottles of diet soda drooling on the linoleum; the toothpaste Edison had let crust around the bathroom sink and the skid marks he never brushed from the toilet; my fat, indolent brother most of all, especially if he made the smallest remark that sounded *cheerful*. Since I couldn't abandon my business during the whole Christmas rush, I'd gone back to work, and employees for whom I'd thought I harbored great affection inspired nothing but hatred. When they came to me for advice on a commission, I'd snap that this was only a glorified toy company and nothing we did mattered so they could at least make a few trifling deci-sions on their own. I would look up at the clock in disbelieving *outrage* that only ten minutes had passed.

At Prague Porches those evenings, everything on TV seemed moronic, and I'd fix tea I didn't want and slosh most of it down the sink. Usually inclined to find the repetitive rhythms of daily life becalming as a lullaby, I have never been so bored. And I mean aggressively bored, maliciously bored, as if my boredom weren't merely an affliction but a weapon, and when I turned it on Edison with a glowering, sooty-eyed glare I could have been aiming a bazooka. I was bored with his droning on about musi-cians nobody in their right minds ever listened to anymore. I was bored with his whining about his terrible life when most of what had gone wrong in it was his own damn fault. And the tunes from his computer would sound demented—manic, screeching, fingernail-on-a-blackboard. He learned not to take the dyspep-sia personally, since Edison had his own version: lumping in his recliner, utterly inert for hours, falling in and out of a rancorous half sleep. Those black days, they lasted for lifetimes, and once the storm passed the restoration of a gliding serenity and smug supremacy over all the little people and their little food problems felt all the more victorious.

That's why what happened the first week of January seemed so inexplicable. We had hit our stride. I'd already left him alone for whole workdays, from which I'd return to find Edison parked placidly in front of *30 Minute Meals*, sipping a Diet Coke. I did remark once, "Do you think that's the best program to be watching?" and he said blithely, "Food porn. Least you didn't walk in on me jerking off." I thought it was harmless.

As well as enjoying several buoyant visits from Cody, I had stayed in regular phone contact with my family, and Fletcher's conversation had been so cryptic and chilly that when he proposed a little face time I leapt at the chance. I told Edison I was meeting Fletcher at our favorite coffee shop downtown after work, and my brother's reaction was odd: "What are you seeing *him* for?"

"He's my husband, dummy. A better question is what am I living with *you* for."

Perhaps a bit pointedly—this is the new me who walks everywhere—I arrived at Java Joint on foot, though with New Holland's paucity of sidewalks that meant teetering around icy puddles on verges and recoiling from rattling semis. Just as pointedly, Fletcher arrived by bike, wrapped in Lycra, for which it was too cold. I waited as he locked up and unclipped his lights. We hugged, awkwardly, and hustled inside. "You know, when the weather improves, I might like my bike back," I said.

"Well, sure," he said, thrown off guard.

We nestled opposite in a booth, while Fletcher warmed his

hands around his neck. He ordered a glass of soy milk and a lactose-free whole-wheat banana muffin, which in the old days would have contrasted sanctimoniously with my usual pastry here—a crumb Danish with cheese—but which took on a more indulgent hue beside my lone cup of black tea. "You want some?" he offered.

"No, thank you." Declining food was effortless. It had nothing to do with me.

"This thing's enormous." Hunched over the muffin, he shoveled a clump with embarrassment. I was familiar with this phenomenon. When I joined my employees at lunch just to be sociable, nursing a soda water and slice of lime, they ate with a funny furtiveness, keeping their plates close and sheltering their meals with their hands.

"You know, you do look—better," Fletcher allowed, abandoning his muffin.

"I've lost fifteen pounds. It's only been a month. But Edison's lost *thirty-nine*. When you're that big, it drops off like nobody's business at the beginning."

"Gotta say, I never thought the guy had it in him."

"He's into it now. Or I should say, *we* are."

"In the olden days, when you said 'we' it referred to you and me."

"It still can," I said. "This is a time-limited, goal-oriented project, not a new normal."

"Is he clear on that?"

"Of course!"

"Christmas," said Fletcher. "It was depressing. I couldn't pull it off."

"Look, we talked about this. Holidays are centered around

meals. Even if you'd lifted my exile, Edison and I would have rained on the family parade. People feel weird eating around us. Besides, the holiday's relentless. I loved getting the kids presents, but otherwise it was a relief to skip it a year."

"It reminded me too much of right after splitting with Cleo. That bloodless, going-through-the-motions feeling." He added with effort, "I miss you."

I put a hand on his. "I miss you, too. I know I'm asking a lot, but this thing with Edison is working, and it's making me happy. I feel like I'm making a difference, a big difference, to at least one person—"

"But I'm one person, too. You make a difference to me."

"You don't need me in the same way. It's not forever. Just don't let your where's-my-woman macho side get the best of you."

"Here's the thing: I wanted to ask you—to *beg* you. Please come home. It sounds like your brother's on a roll, if you're telling me the truth. So why can't you be his 'personal trainer' from our house? Visit, phone, give him pep talks—whatever you're doing. This separation, it's no good. I don't want to get used to your being gone. You can play Mother Teresa if you have to, but from a couple of miles away."

From Fletcher, a proposal that involved Edison in our lives at all was a major compromise. And I was tempted. My bed at Prague Porches was big and cold. Our sibling duo provided the kind of emotional nutrition that lacked a vital mineral whose absence was cumulative; much longer and my hair would fall out or something. On the other hand, I was stricken by the picture of Edison sitting forlornly through meal-free evenings in that barren apartment all by himself.

Fletcher filled the silence. "I did say *beg*."

Men did not readily prostrate themselves, though I wondered why not; throwing yourself on another's mercy is so much more effective than hectoring and force. Fletcher had melted me so, huddling over the sad crumbles of a dry-looking muffin that he regretted ordering—in modern America, even a lousy muffin could incur a crippling social disadvantage—that I could not say flat-out no.

"Let me think about it," I said.

We caught up on kid stuff, and it was obvious that matters between him and Tanner were going seriously south. For years I'd acted as a buffer, managing food fights by preparing the children escape valves of mac and cheese. I curved their defiance into droll communal mockery with my Fletcher doll. To discourage my stepson's iffy ambitions, I told manipulative stories from my invidious childhood, whereas Fletcher went for imperatives: you *are* going to college. I'd seen it between Travis and Edison when my brother was seventeen, the exact age at which young men make the awesome discovery that they don't have to do what you say. Woe to any parent at war with a teenage boy: you lose.

"I've tried and tried to get him to visit me and Edison, and he blows me off," I said. "I almost get the impression that it's only solidarity over how dumb this dieting stunt of mine is that still keeps you two on-side."

"There may be some truth to that. He doesn't think you're coming back. He's practicing living without you. I guess I've been doing the same thing—without much luck. But it's not like Tanner doesn't care. The real problem is he does."

When we parted beside the bicycle it was too cold to linger, but while fastening his helmet Fletcher couldn't resist a final pronouncement that soured somewhat his artful beseeching inside.

"This living with your brother, Pandora, in your forties—it's a little weird. And it's regressive. Like you're going back to being thirteen, and your mother's just died, and your father ignores you, and you're clinging to big brother for a port in the storm. That was almost thirty years ago. I don't think this is healthy."

"To the contrary, the tables have turned. It's more like going back forty-four years—and I'm the firstborn. I'm the boss now. I say go for a walk, Edison goes for a walk. He drinks his four envelopes a day, and he hasn't cheated *once*. Maybe he's tired of being the 'big brother.' I think he likes being ordered around. As for our living together being 'unhealthy,' it can't possibly be less healthy than Edison a month ago."

"Honey, I hate to tell you this. But I've done some poking around online. Know how many people who lose more than thirty pounds keep it off five years later? *Five percent.* Even those poor bastards who get bariatric surgery and live on two tablespoons of tapioca. Who sometimes drop poundage in the hundreds. You realize how much, on average, they keep off over the long term?"

"I'm not sure I want to know."

"*Seven pounds.*"

"Why are you being so"—I reached for Edison's lingo, which was infectious—"so *dark* on this project?"

"I'm trying to protect you."

"You're trying to discourage me."

"I'm sorry, then. I didn't mean that. I only thought you should know the facts."

"Statistics aren't personal destiny, or you'd have had two-point-two kids."

"You're right," Fletcher backed off. "Of course you're right." Leaning down to kiss me, he knocked my forehead with his visor, and we laughed. "*Please* come home," he implored after we'd kissed with more success. "I won't interfere with your weight-loss tutorial. But I want you back in my bed."

As I scuttled to Prague Porches, I had to confess: it seemed a reasonable request.

W hen I walked in, Edison was feverishly wiping down our white laminated table with paper towels. "Hey, babe. Just doing a little house cleaning, dig? So how was coffee with the hub? Any news on the home front? Any idea when Cody's dropping by next? I downloaded a couple of tunes for her. She should really be introduced to Monk."

Finding surprising energy reserves during ketosis was one thing, acting jumpy and hyperactive quite another. A thick, spicy aroma mixed with the usual smog of tobacco, as if I were suffering hallucinations of the nose.

"Coffee was all right," I said warily. "You know, that table can't have anything but mint-tea rings. I don't see why you're working so hard."

"Gonna do anything, do it right. Got pretty slick at wiping down tables at Three Bars before they kicked me out." Despite this frenzy of cleanliness, he discarded the paper towels on the kitchen counter above the trash can. He washed his hands with the thoroughness of Macbeth, splashed his face, and scrubbed his mouth with a dishtowel.

"Edison," I said on a hunch, "how's your breath today?"

"Whoa, you don't wanna come near me! Afraid I been lax on the fluid intake. You know what that's like: dead rat. So what's on the program tonight? Scrabble? Seven-card stud? There's a

Jennifer Aniston rom-com on at eight-thirty, which isn't my bag, but I know you got a soft spot for that shit, and I could probably stand it."

If Edison was volunteering to watch Jennifer Aniston, something was fishy. I eased into the kitchen, where Edison blocked my way. "Excuse me," I said, reaching behind him to shove the paper towels through the trash-can flap. It met resistance. I pulled off the top, and the few things I'd thrown into a fresh liner that morning—empty BPSP pouches, a defunct box of laxatives, and the packaging from a couple of gloriously long books I'd ordered from Amazon—now bulged at the top of the pail. I lifted the liner out. Sure enough, another bag scrunched beneath it, angular with folded cardboard. That's when I pinpointed the smell: pepperoni, and garlic-butter stuffed crust.

"Edison, how could you."

"How could I what?"

I couldn't decide whether to shout or weep. "Tomorrow is our one-month anniversary. Why would you blow that? After *thirty-nine pounds*?"

"Got no idea what you're talking about." Edison was already rounding from innocent to hostile.

"Skip it," I said furiously. "You left the box. Why destroy a flawless winning streak for one crummy pizza?"

Edison folded his arms and narrowed his eyes to slits. "Well, whaddya think? *I got hungry.*"

"You're supposed to be hungry! After all we've sacrificed—was it worth it? For one greasy, sneaky gorge fest, that you probably shoved down in less time than it took to cover it up?"

"Yes, if you wanna know the truth! It was *great*. It was the best fucking pizza I ever ate!"

"I don't believe that. I think it was polluted with an after-taste of *stupidity*, and *self-hatred*, and BETRAYAL!"

"You mean betrayal of *you*. This was all *your* idea, and I'm supposed to get in lockstep with *your* program, and be a good lit-tle doobie all day long because sister says! Well, I may be fat, but I'm still a man, and if *I* want to order a pizza I'll order a pizza!"

"You have some nerve! You think this is how I *want* to be spending my life? Dissolving little envelopes of powder and think-ing up diversions to fill interminable evenings and babysitting my older brother? I may be slightly overweight—in fact, techni-cally I'm already down to the acceptable BMI for my height—but I didn't have to go on this gonzo diet! I could have cut back on carbs and skipped dessert like a normal person and accomplished the same thing on my own account, couldn't I? Most of all, I could have stayed home! Don't you think I miss my husband? Do you imagine I enjoy sleeping by myself every night, when I have a warm, handsome man waiting for me two neighborhoods over? Do you think I like having become an absentee mother, as if I no longer had custody and Fletcher and I were already divorced? I have put—EVERTHING—on the line for you, and you'll throw all that over for a pizza! I'm grievously offended! You're an ungrateful, selfish BABY and a total CREEP!"

I had been irritable, but thinking back I'm not sure I'd ever lost my temper with my brother. Thinking back, I hardly ever lost my temper with anybody.

"You left me alone," he said sulkily. "I had a crisis, and no-body was here to help me."

"I have to be able to leave you alone! If nothing else, I have a business to run. If I have to hold your hand twenty-four-seven just in case you're possessed by a killer zombie who wants a cheeseburger, this is never going to work!" I flopped into a recliner. The adrenaline was subsiding, and left me weak. "You know I was just bragging about you. Fletcher couldn't believe it. How much weight you'd lost. How faithful you've been. And now I come home to *this*. Fletcher's always said you didn't have it in you, and he was *right*."

"He claimed I wouldn't last a week. He wasn't right about that."

"What, so now you've proved you can make it past a week, never mind? The deal was you get back to *one-sixty-three*. And you remember what else I said at the outset, don't you?"

"What." He knew what.

"I said if you ever cheated the experiment was over and I was out of here. When you ordered that pizza, you can't have forgotten that little detail. So you either want to do this all by yourself, or you want to stay fat. Which is it?"

Edison looked down at his hands. The loss of thirty-nine pounds had reduced the fleshiness of his neck, but he retained the proportions of a little boy. "I didn't mean to throw the whole thing over. I had a lapse, that's all. I'll go back to the motherfucking shakes tomorrow. I promise."

"You promised before. Besides, you don't need me. You're obviously developing your own method: the Pizza Hut Diet. So go ahead. It doesn't take two to order the sausage and jalapeño."

"I do need you," he mumbled. "I can't do this by myself. I fucked up. I'm sorry."

"Are you assuming your minder is a gullible softie? Who doesn't mean what she says. It's my goo-goo-eyed little sister, after all. Who will always trot after big brother, whatever devilish, secretly attractive badness he gets up to."

"It's not like I didn't take you seriously, man. But, Christ, when you go to AA and confess you fell off the wagon, they don't kick you out. They don't say, you're obviously not a fucking saint, so we're washing our hands of your imperfect, mortal ass. It's more like: we're all sinners, and we'll support you one day at a time. Don't see why you can't tear a page from their playbook."

"I can't do this if I can't trust you. I don't want to come back here every day and have to search the garbage."

"It won't be like that, man. Come on, Panda Bear!" He kneeled by my recliner, assuming a suitor's position that he'd have difficulty getting up from. "Fix us some tea. Then we can watch that Jennifer Aniston flick."

As if Edison had spied on my tête-à-tête with Fletcher, he seemed to be making a hearty stab at *outbegging* my husband. Yet a smile played around Edison's hammed-up hangdog. He'd always been able to inveigle permission to go to a Roy Orbison concert from our mother when he was grounded, just as Caleb Fields had wrapped Mimi Barnes around his little finger, too; for all I knew, Edison had mastered the technique of wearing down women from watching *Joint Custody*. Besides, he knew that the prospect of having come this far only to throw in the towel made me sick.

"Think of it this way, babe," he wheedled. "It was like those sorry suicides who leave empty bottles of Percocet scattered around the bedroom. I didn't have to leave the box in the trash, did I? I could have taken it to the cans out back and committed the perfect crime. I wanted to get caught! It was, whaddya call it, a *cry for help*—!"

Though my brother gave every sign of having started to enjoy himself, suddenly his face blanched and shone with a light sweat. His expression of distress did not appear conjured for effect, though physical discomfiture would have made for a clever ploy. "Oh, man. I don't feel too good. Panda, you gotta help me up here. I gotta get to the head pronto."

By the time I'd helped pull him to a stand, Edison had unbuckled his belt. Jeans sliding, he shuffled in a double-quick waddle to the bathroom. Once he emerged ten minutes later, he had to lie down on the couch. I brought him a Diet Coke.

"You can't come off a monthlong liquid diet with a wolfed-down pepperoni pie."

"Yeah, well, duh," he groaned. "Satisfied now? I got my comeuppance. And I got a queasy feeling the punishment ain't quite through."

After Edison made two more trips to the john, we did end up watching *Friends with Money* that night, while he recovered lying down. After I'd taken my turn in the bathroom—which still reeked—he stopped me on the way to bed.

"Yo, Panda. We cool? I'm into it, man, like four shakes a day, end'a story. But I gotta have moral support. Somebody to hang with. And so far it's been, you know, kinda hip. The walks and shit. Trips to the mall, where I never thought I'd ever be shopping for a smaller belt. It's not like I take you for granted, kid. I know I'm taking you away from your family. But if you give me a break this one time, like, just cut me this little bit of slack, I *swear* it won't happen again."

I appreciated that he didn't try to slide back to business as usual without acknowledging my concession. "All right," I said. "But you've used up your only Get Out of Jail Free card. One more pizza box in that trash can and you're on your own, understand? Mother was a pushover. I'm not."

"Yes, ma'am!"

"And brush your teeth. You have rat breath from ten feet. Worse, rat with extra cheese."

I called Fletcher the next day. "It means the world to me that you want me to come home. Even if that entailed my still being Edison's coach. But I just—"

"You're not coming back."

"Somehow this whole hothouse setup . . . Keeping tabs from a distance wouldn't be the same. Having someone to report to and to celebrate his progress, at least for now having company on the program—it helps."

"You're honestly telling me that your lazy, two-faced brother has not eaten anything but those miserable protein shakes for a whole month. And you haven't caught him hitting the Twinkies and said, 'That's okay, sweetie, I'll overlook your stuffing your fat face as usual this one little time.'"

"That's right. I told you: if he ever cheats, it's over."

I hung up, dolorous. It wasn't only the lying. On the walk back from Java Joint, I'd allowed myself to seriously consider returning to Solomon Drive: I could make regular phone calls, stop by Prague Porches, meet my brother for walks. Besides, wasn't Edison in the groove now? Yet when I found that box in the trash can, it came home to me that an arm's-length involvement would never work. Perhaps that's the revelation for which the box had been planted in the first place.

chapter five

In reviewing Edison's tailspin in New York—which I'd related in detail to Oliver, in the hopes that pouring my brother's confidences into such a watertight vessel didn't make me a snitch—I failed to derive a simple answer to the chicken-and-egg question of whether he got depressed because he was fat or vice versa. His weight had narrowed his professional opportunities, which was depressing, which made him eat, which made him fatter. It narrowed his romantic and sexual opportunities, which was depressing, which made him eat, which made him fatter. Fat itself was depressing, which made him fatter. I could grudgingly see how when you're having such a hard time that you're forced to sell the primary tool of your occupation, and then your younger squirt of a sibling who you've never really imagined would amount to anything—who to the contrary you've regarded as your own private cheerleader—is suddenly thriving on a national scale, well, okay, that's hard to take.

Yet my-sister's-famous-while-I'm-nobody was one small

driver of a larger spiral into despondency. Edison had no real family of his own, and his career had hit the skids. He may have had friends, but in the last few years, by straining their goodwill, he'd lost more friends than he'd made. As I despaired to Oliver when we put our feet up in my office after hours, "The trouble is, he has nothing to look forward to."

"With one exception," said Oliver. "Which was all your idea. And if he ever does hit one-sixty-three, the only thing he still looks forward to evaporates."

"I know," I said, closing down my computer for the day. "When I first took this project on, I worried it was more than I could handle. But the real project turns out to be much, much bigger. I have to do nothing less than give my big brother a reason for living."

"You can't do that for anybody," said Oliver readily.

"I can nudge him in the right direction."

"What, get him excited about reviving his career? Talk up his résumé. Suggest he put out a solo CD. Goad him into boasting again—about all the headliners who've recognized his unparalleled talent." The delivery was poker-faced. Though Oliver had kept his grave reservations about my Prague Porches folly to himself, I'd known him intimately for fourteen years, and his diplomacy was wasted.

"Right," I said dryly. "Shore up the very vanity that triggered his if-I-can't-be-famous-then-fuck-it obesity in the first place. Reconstruct from the ground up the same egomaniac nobody could stand, including you."

"I never said I couldn't stand him," said Oliver innocently.

"Uh-huh. So getting him all jumped up over his career again isn't the solution. After all, achievement hasn't been the solution for me." I nodded at my messy office. "I mean, sure, it was nice to be able to give Fletcher space to make his furniture. I'd never be able to run a private rehab clinic without some extra cash. And for a while, yeah, Monotonous was a kick. But these dolls are sure to become old hat sooner or later, and when suddenly nobody will be seen dead with one I'll be relieved. For me, the big surprise has been that making a go of something professionally doesn't turn out to matter that much. It's not a reason for living."

"So what's the answer? *Love?*"

"In that case, he's shit out of luck. I'm not much of a match-maker."

"But, Pandora, what does the guy *do* all day?"

I shrugged. "Little shopping. YouTube. Lots of TV. When I come home, we talk."

"About what?"

"We do some soul searching," I said cautiously, not wanting Oliver to feel supplanted. "But nobody can dig deep all the time, and we've started to run out of stories. It's embarrassing, but the rest of the time we talk mostly about food."

Oliver laughed. "Like how?"

"You know, reminiscing about our favorite childhood dishes—my mother's 'Spanish Noodles,' with Kraft Parmesan and scads of greasy breadcrumbs. Which got soggier, Cocoa Puffs or Cocoa Krispies, and the color Fruit Loops turned the milk."

"Sounds stimulating."

"It is, believe it or not. The memories we trip are hallucino-genic. And you know I've been reading a lot, right? More than I have since college. I guess if I were more ambitious I'd be tack-ling *War and Peace*. Instead I've devoured Mark Bittman's *How to Cook Everything*—all thousand fifty-six pages. So when Edison's having trouble sleeping, I read him recipes. When I was small, he read me *The Little Red Hen*. Now I read him 'Fried Chicken Made Easy.'"

"Listen, why doesn't he get a plain old job? You're big on hard work. Nothing worse for the existential heebie-jeebies than time on your hands."

"Who's going to hire Edison?"

"You," said Oliver. "Put him to work here."

"Ha! I can't think of anything he'd want less."

"He didn't *want* to lose weight, and so far this bonkers diet has been the guy's only salvation. Problem is, it's temporary."

"I'll think about it. But I keep feeling the real answer is fiendishly subtle. Somehow he needs to learn to enjoy ordinary life." That said, I'd always resisted this expression. Nothing was ordinary about the seemingly-small-but-secretly-ample delights to which it alluded.

"What, like—the perfect color toast?" Oliver suggested mischievously. "The first sip of a tart little Sauvignon Blanc at the end of a very long day."

"Thanks. Yeah, I've scotched those thrills for now. But there has to be more to life than food and drink."

There *was* more, and I devoted myself to locating it: the dry, squeaky crunch of virgin snow when I refused to allow inclement weather to deter our walkabouts. The discovery that, despite a temperature of fifteen degrees Fahrenheit, trooping about after a blizzard raised a light sweat, and by the time we got home we were hot. Breaking out the box set of *Joint Custody* that I'd asked Cody to fetch from my study and rolling on the carpet in hilarity. Calling Travis and announcing that Edison had now lost sixty-nine pounds and taking wan satisfaction in the transparent insincerity of our father's encouragement.

Otherwise, I concluded Oliver was right: Edison could stand to appreciate the pleasures of unalloyed hard work, the kind at the end of which no one bursts into applause. Predictably, Edison resisted my becoming his taskmaster twice over. Yet once he gave Monotonous a reluctant try he was relieved to get out of the apartment, and the days went faster when he was busy. Assuming a woman's humility, he learned to sew. I also used him for recordings, his big booming voice perfect for blowhards for whom families had cooked up just deserts. The other employees came to like Edison, admiring his unerring dietary celibacy—no more pizza boxes had cropped up in our trash can—as he held forth with the passion of the convert about the evils of Cinnabons. Stitching miniature denim jackets, he'd festively recount his most extravagant binges of ribs and racks of lamb, tales especially popular before lunch.

By throwing himself into the soft, gooshy embrace of a meatball hero, in the process losing everything from his professional standing to his Miles collector's edition box set, and landing at last on the edge of a bathtub with his fly open while his own sister collected his turds like Easter eggs, my brother had emulated the alcoholic's notorious prerequisite to recovery: he'd hit bottom. Yet I don't think hitting bottom is therapeutic because you finally get to the point where things can't get any worse. Things can always get worse. It's more that you firebomb absolutely everything in sight that seems to keep you alive, only to wake the next morning perplexed, amazed, and maybe even furious that you're still here. Tinker around its edges, and both the curse and blessing of your own existence simply sits there. For Edison, that discovery had to have been accompanied by an intuition that all along "making a name for himself" when he already had one had been merely a little extra, a maraschino cherry atop something momentous. Not fat, *momentous.*

Nevertheless, one of the pleasures of "ordinary" life was music. Not appearing on posters or laying claim to big-name colleagues, but music, and for Edison that meant playing it. I'd a hunch he'd lost touch with the exhilaration of playing the piano for its own sake. So I rented one—an upright, whose very mediocre character I hoped would foster a casual attitude.

I'd arranged for Novacek to let the piano movers in that afternoon, so when we came home from Monotonous the instrument was sitting at a right angle to the scale. I was disappointed by Edison's reaction. He didn't look exultant. He looked worried.

"I don't know, babe," he said, surveying the piano from a safe distance. "I'm pretty rusty."

"It's a piece of junk. And I don't want you to 'practice.' Think of it as music therapy. You must have *liked* playing the piano once. So I don't want you to bone up your skills, and get all frustrated that your dexterity has deteriorated, or plot to make a smashing return to the stage in New York. I've always thought you were pretty good, but being good isn't the point. I don't honestly know, Edison, if you'll ever be an internationally renowned jazz pianist again." I tried to say this kindly. "I think it's important for you to be able to live with the possibility that you won't be. But no one can take music itself away from you, or the joy of playing it."

He approached the keyboard with trepidation. He struck a chord with one hand, something minor and a little complicated, letting its anguish resonate for some time.

He didn't want an audience, not even his sister. Edison Appaloosa not wanting an audience was a first, and not necessarily a bad thing. "We're out of cranberry-orange tea," I said. "I'll run to Hy-Vee, and you two can get acquainted."

To begin with, he'd only touch the piano when I was out, and I invented more errands to give him privacy. But after about ten days, I returned from another laconic, pulling-teeth coffee at Java Joint with Tanner, who would at least meet me on neutral territory. Edison was in the middle of "Bridge Over Troubled Water." "Please don't stop," I implored. And he didn't.

Word to the wise: anyone on an all-liquid diet should play an instrument, and I regretted playing nothing myself. The piano was more involving than television, and Edison would hit the keyboard after work the way he used to hit the pantry. My brother's musing, reflective riffs filled our apartment with life, compensating for the groceries that never slammed on the counter, the silverware that never clattered on the table, the baking pies that never spiced the air. His playing grew progressively lighter, trippier, more assured, but I almost didn't want to say so, because I'd claimed up front that being good was not the goal.

Since I wasn't encouraging him to sharpen his keyboard skills in order to plunge back into the Manhattan fray but only to keep us entertained, over time Edison relaxed his grip on the niche that had defined him, broadening gaily into ragtime, top-forty oldies like Elton John's "Tiny Dancer," standards like David Bowie's "Starman," and medleys of Queen, R.E.M., and Billy Joel. He took requests, and produced slant, improvised versions of the softie stuff I grew up on: Crosby, Stills, and Nash; James Taylor; Carole King. He played show tunes! Songs from *Chess* or

Sweeney Todd. My growing affinity for jazz was genuine enough, but I can't tell you the relief of getting a break.

Cody started coming by for lessons, though with her uncle's newly catholic approach to music the education worked both ways, she introducing him to Lyle Lovett as he had introduced her to Thelonious Monk. The piano tutorials gave her visits a welcome structure; it had always been socially thin, only being able to serve her diet soda. Even so, evenings cleansed of meal-time distractions had a bare-bones starkness, but also an intensity that I now look back on with nostalgia. Eradicating the froufrou of hospitality stripped away the chitchat, too—about weather and new shoes. As hostages thrown together with a slop bucket must also have learned, it's amazing how quickly you get down to emotional brass tacks with absolutely nothing to do but talk.

Cody became more forthcoming about her worries over choosing a career and the grisly host of eating disorders amid her classmates. She shared her humiliation at being forced to take a class in "Social Skills" because of being unacceptably withdrawn. "It's retarded," she said. "Six other rejects and a teacher who thinks she's cool because she has butterfly tattoos on her ankles. We have to fill out a chart every morning on 'How I Feel Today.' Then Miss Hannigan—sorry; *Nancy*—stands in front of the class and yells, 'I love you!' while shaking her fist and scowling. So we're meant to, like, have this revelation about how sometimes what people say and their 'nonverbal cues' don't agree. Well, if you have to 'learn' that, you should be taken out and shot. Now everybody knows I've been stuck with these losers, and I'll never live it down. What's wrong with being 'withdrawn'? Big deal, sometimes I don't have anything to say, so I don't say it. Unlike most people."

In times past, that "most people" might have seemed a dig at her uncle, but Edison no longer inclined toward monologues about jazz. He shared more details about his failed marriage and a few other crash-and-burn romances. He finally confessed to a particular low point of his compulsive eating the year before: being forced to file off the metal bracelet I'd given him as a fare-well present when he left for New York at seventeen, because the wire was biting his bulging wrist. When her uncle got maudlin over his estranged son, Cody pulled him up short: Just how hard had he really tried to arrange visitation rights? He admitted that to begin with he'd kept putting it off, anxious that Sigrid had poisoned the boy's head with lies about his dad (worse, with the truth). Then in the last few years, by which time Carson was old enough to make up his own mind, Edison had been too ashamed of his size to arrange a rendezvous: "Maybe the cat's always fanta-sized about finally getting to know his dad, going on hiking trips, or deep-sea fishing. How keen is the kid gonna be when he finds out the old man is close to four hundred pounds? I couldn't deal with it, man. Opening the door to my only son and watching his face fall."

I more than anyone appreciated that Edison's weight loss was gradual, since together we faced the sentinel beside the pic-ture window every morning at nine a.m.—recording the ver-dicts with a fine black roller-ball on a monthly calendar hang-ing alongside. The reduction wasn't, oddly, systematic; he would stall for a couple of days in dismay, only to drop three pounds at once. Yet the process was gruelingly sluggish, and as my brother came off the steep slope of his first few weeks his progress slowed further. After losing thirty-nine pounds the first month, Edison couldn't help but have calculated that he would therefore drop all 223 pounds in half a year. Wrong. Fat itself requires calories to maintain, so you burn less energy as you get thinner. "It's an algorithm," I'd explained. But Edison had never been good at math.

Despite the paint-drying languor of the exercise, my experience of finally recognizing the brother I grew up with was bizarrely sudden.

One late Saturday afternoon in March, I'd made another trip to Hy-Vee for toilet paper and tea. Edison had stayed behind to play the piano, at which he was seated when I walked in. Cutting a warmer, springier slant through the blinds, sun shafted across Edison's head, flashing on cheeks whose high bones were once the defining structure of his face. In concert with the wild, irradiated hair, those hillocks rising over concave hollows had helped to explain why so many of my junior high girlfriends were eager to drop by our house in Tujunga Hills—in the hopes that my loping, too-cool-for-school older brother with his low-slung jeans and collar open to the sternum would nod hello in the hall.

Ever since this imposter of a brother had hulked into Cedar Rapids Airport, Edison's cheekbones had been buried like stones in plums. While I had of course taught myself to recognize my own sibling again, in truth I had not been recognizing the brother I knew in childhood. I had instead trained myself to recognize a completely different person who by sheer coincidence went by the same offbeat name.

Yet in that moment, lusty spring sunlight unearthed his cheekbones like the treasures of an archaeological dig. The flesh below them sank in shadow, while the curdle of concentration in my brother's forehead finally formed sharp creases rather than rippled blobs. And I saw him. I saw Edison, the Edison I remembered. It was as if the man with whom I had in reality cohabited for months now had only just been restored to me after many years of having gone to ground. Unable to contain myself, I exclaimed nonsensically, "It's you, I see you!"

Edison looked up quizzically from a chord in one of Cody's favorites, the Roches' "Quitting Time." "Cool," he said uncertainly. "Glad I'm still three-dimensional."

I came up behind him and hugged. Firmer shoulders stirred earlier memories of being carted on his back, swung easily to the couch. Never had I dreamed that the brother I grew up with would get fat. I'd persistently failed to get my head around why that seemed so important. I'd tried to latch on to the health implications of obesity, but I knew better; I hadn't embarked on this project purely to ward off diabetes. I wanted my big brother back.

"I'm so proud of you," I said.

"Least I can be famous for something. Though from the shows I seen on TV, babe, I got wicked competition even in the I-used-to-be-a-load game."

"You are now in the top tier of what has become the national sport."

"Not through to the finals yet." Any suggestion that it was smooth sailing from here on in, that he could coast, or even cheat a bit, was anathema. Every day was hard; there was no such thing as "only" having to lose 124 more pounds.

"You've read the literature," I ventured. "So you know they strongly recommend that you come off the diet after three months—"

"No."

"Just for a week. Eating very carefully and healthfully—"

"*NO.*"

"But then you can go right back to it!"

"What part of 'no' did you not understand?"

"That's become an awful cliché."

"Imagine my giving a shit."

Having myself labeled his tendencies "extreme," I'd delayed raising the issue of the prescribed breather until two weeks past the deadline, because I knew what he'd say. Unclear on the risks of violating the program's rules, I'd not bothered to research them because I was certain to face a brick wall regardless. If Edison had an "addictive personality," he was now addicted to Upchuck.

chapter six

Oliver Allbless was my tech guru. When my computer spat error messages or I needed to password my router, I called Oliver. I'd first hired him to help with prep early in the Breadbasket days, when he'd needed some extra cash while earning his engineering degree at the University of Iowa. Somewhere in there we went out for about six months, and when I concluded that my feelings for him were a little too round, too muffled—too mild and edgeless, without some crucial sharpness, tension, or resistance that I later found in surplus with Fletcher—he accepted the rejection with the same natural equanimity that had probably fostered my edgeless feelings in the first place. We'd been friends ever since. As the technological demands of modern life continued to accelerate, for a while I'd started to feel guilty that I called him too often just to sort out yet another crisis with my printer. I didn't want him to feel used, even if Oliver liked being of practical value. When I put him on retainer at Baby Monotonous, at least he got something out of being on call, though he'd protested that he'd have advised me on updating pull-string doll technology for nothing. If Oliver was still sweet on me—the gangling, endearingly awkward telecom employee had never married—I was accustomed to it, and so was he. It was remotely possible that I was the love of his life, though for his sake I hoped not.

When Baby Monotonous took off, Oliver was far more excited than I was. Regarding my subsequent project, my best friend was still reserved. Obliging about being used himself, he was sensitive to any suggestion that Edison might be taking advantage of my good nature. After I'd explained the parameters of our regimen, Oliver had spent hours researching Big Presents in Small Packages, making sure there were no horror stories lurking online. I was married, firmly so, and I'd planted no reasonable expectation that this would change, so his assumption of the role of guardian angel in my life sprang from a selflessness so pure that it passed my understanding. The sole concern he'd allowed himself to express once I assumed residence in Prague Porches was that the arrangement might alienate Fletcher.

We were having trouble with string retraction in a batch of digital mechanisms—we'd had a few returns, which was a first—and I'd asked Oliver to stop by to diagnose the problem. As he took a malfunctioning doll apart, he kept peering up at me, and his screwdriver would freeze for a second. Before he left he asked, "Got time for a drink, or whatever you call an excuse to talk on that kooky diet?"

"Maybe, but let me check with Edison."

"You have to get permission from your *brother*?"

"We usually ride home together," I said coolly. Now that the weather had warmed, I'd had Cody bring my bicycle by, and I'd bought a mountain bike so Edison and I could commute in tandem.

"No prob," said my brother as he completed the stitching on a miniature Macintosh. "I'll hold off on 'dinner' till you get home."

I wheeled the bike beside Oliver to a nearby diner, where I reflexively ordered a soda water with lime. Though he'd avoided eating around me for coming up on four months, this time Oliver ordered a triple-decker BLT with fries. "Here," he offered, holding out a quarter of his sandwich. "Have some."

I recoiled. "You know I can't do that."

"Why not?"

"I never cheat. It's been quite a discovery—that it's easier to be perfect than only a little bad. I'm starting to see the attraction of monasteries. It's less of a strain to be a full-fledged saint than a small-fry sinner."

"Eating isn't a sin. It's what mammals do to survive."

"Apparently it's unnecessary," I said lightly. "Another discovery."

Oliver put down the sandwich gravely. "What do you weigh?"

I busied myself pouring artificial sweetener into my soda water. The ceaseless nickel flavor leaking from my gums got on my nerves, and I'd try anything to mask it. "You're never supposed to ask women that."

"All right, let's start with this: How much did you weigh to begin with?"

"To my horror, I'd hit one-sixty-eight, and that was after four days of starvation. Hilariously, I'm still keeping it secret from Fletcher how bad it had gotten, when it wouldn't have been a secret at all because he could *see* it—"

"And how much have you lost?" he cut me off.

Oliver's impatience surprised me. Teasing out the finer dynamics of my marriage was a mainstay of our friendship. "That's a trick question," I said. But he knew I wouldn't be able to resist the opportunity to brag. "Fifty-two pounds, if you must know. Closer to fifty-four, with what I dropped before I marshaled the nerve to—"

"When was the last time you weighed this little?"

I said quietly, "When I was fifteen."

"This has *got* to *stop*."

"Well, I realize that pretty soon—"

"Stop *now*. I read that Big Presents website. It's been four months, and you were supposed to come off the envelopes for at least a week after three. Did you?"

"I couldn't get Edison to take a break. He's afraid—"

"Even Edison has to return to the land of the eating eventually, and then he's got to learn how to have normal-size portions and quit. You said being 'perfect' is easier than sinning. But that's one disturbed version of perfection you've got, Pandora. Perfect is eating what you need, no more, and no *less*, either."

"That's easy for you to say. Not everybody has your metabolism." Oliver was one of those rarities who ate whatever he felt like, yet whose elongated dimensions hadn't varied noticeably since he was eighteen. The only thing the even keel cost him was any comprehension of everyone else.

"Your concentration sucks. When I tried to explain what was going wrong with the retraction mechanisms, I could tell you weren't taking anything in. I doubt you could recapitulate what I told you if your life depended on it."

Declining to take his little test, I wrapped my coat more tightly around me. The gesture was defensive, though I was also cold.

"That's another thing." He pointed at the down jacket that I would usually have retired with the advent of spring. "I'm sure you don't realize it, but it's *hot* in here. Overheated—just like Baby Monotonous. You've jacked up the thermostat. It's in the forties outside, and your employees are coming to work in short sleeves."

"Big deal, I get chilly."

"You look small in every sense. Timid as well as skinny. Your hair is flat and dry. Your clothes hang off you as if they're hooked on a hat rack. Your face looks older by five years. Your skin is gray—you have the complexion of a sidewalk. And you're weak. Just going up the few steps to this diner, you had to grip the railing and pull."

The way he described me didn't jibe with my experience of my newly buoyant, featherweight body in the slightest. I felt as if any day now I'd be able to fly. He wasn't being fair, and he was trying to take something from me. To rob me of something priceless and private and mine.

Oliver threw up his hands. "You've always been so level-headed! Now you've turned into a nut! It's this starvation thing. You're not thinking straight anymore. And *because* you're not thinking straight, you don't *know* you're not thinking straight. You told me at the outset that, of course, of course, you'd have to return to real food way before your brother did. Now you've forgotten all about that. You just said you've discovered eating is 'unnecessary,' and maybe you said that as a joke, but it's not a joke. You believe it."

"I was planning to come off the envelopes when Edison and I were both supposed to eat solid food at the three-month mark." I tried to sound moderate and self-possessed, although these were qualities that in the past I'd never needed to feign. "But when he refused . . . the natural juncture was lost."

"When you miss the turnoff for New Holland on the interstate, you reverse direction at the next exit; you don't keep driving until you reach California. You've turned into, I don't know, a junkie. You actually look strung out."

"Edison's the junkie," I said quickly. "I'm not the type."

"All right, prove it, then." He snagged our passing waitress. "Miss! My friend would like . . . a bowl of soup. Tomato soup."

"Don't!" I panicked. "I can't!"

"Bring the soup," he contradicted brutally, and this pushiness was wildly unlike him. Oliver was a retiring, genial, smart man whom I enjoyed bouncing ideas off of because he always agreed with me. "Now, *why* can't you?"

"I'm not ready," I stalled.

"You're past ready. You've gone off the goddamned deep end."

I was powerfully resistant to this depiction. Edison had the "addictive personality." Edison was the one with the problems. I was plain: white rice. Surely my very dullness inoculated me against getting too weird or doing anything dumb. I didn't have the flair for an eating disorder.

The soup arrived. The waitress looked between us and, not wanting to get involved, placed it mid-table. Oliver shoved it before me. The smell made me giddy. I was accustomed to swooning at aromas, but not to this proximity of contraband, which triggered such anxiety that my heart raced. I looked down. The pinkish soup was canned, and probably full of sugar. It was appetizing and disgusting at the same time. I poked the croutons to the sides with my spoon, like sending ships to port. Even sitting in front of this muck seemed like perfidy.

"You know I don't even get to eat in my dreams?" I said meekly. "I dream about food all the time. But it's always taken away, or I look at it with my lips pressed. In fact, I have a recurrent nightmare in which I'm sitting at a table and I put a bite of something in my mouth and start to chew. In the dream, I've simply forgotten, been absentminded, let my guard down. I always catch myself before I swallow and spit it out."

"What you're describing is mentally ill. Now put some soup on the spoon."

I folded my arms. "After we've talked about it so much, I'm surprised you don't appreciate the profundity of the pledge between me and Edison. Eating behind his back would be treachery. Of the worst order."

"Destroying your health is betraying yourself. For now, Edison doesn't have to know."

"But—there's no ceremony!" For I had dwelt on such a moment for months. I knew there were rules about how to come off a liquid diet—rules that, as Oliver knew, this soup adhered to—but within those limits I had contrived a variety of sumptuous dishes with which I might finally break my fast, like a cool vichyssoise spiked with mint and a squeeze of lemon. A thimbleful of sprightly white wine, poured in an elegant glass purchased for the occasion. I didn't even *like* canned tomato soup.

"We're not in church," said Oliver. "Ever since we sat down you've been listing back and forth as if you're about to black out. What you're doing is medically dangerous. If you don't finish that soup, I swear I will haul you to the hospital."

I pooled the puree in the spoon, lifted it to eye level, and stared it down like hemlock. Those nightmares rushed into my head, the ones from which I had often woken in a cold sweat, lest I swallow even a phantom of *solid food*. This single mouthful frightened me. And maybe that's what did the trick.

It frightened me that it frightened me.

I finished the soup.

On return to Prague Porches that night, I prattled when all I really wanted to do was dive for the bathroom to brush my teeth. I feared Edison would hear the scrubbing sound, and I wouldn't usually wash up before our nightly Upchucks. So I bolted mine in the kitchen, hopeful that the malt flavoring would mask the soup. Since I hadn't been able to resist the pleasingly half-soggy, half-crisp croutons bobbing on the edge of my bowl, I had officially crossed the line and imbibed solid food.

I didn't only feel traitorous. I felt exiled, ejected from Eden, an eternally pristine garden where Eve is forever unsullied by eating the apple because she doesn't eat anything. From the first book of the Bible, food correlates with evil, and I felt contaminated. Demoted to one more schlub who has to decide whether to have a second cookie, I wasn't special anymore, and here I was the one who'd chided Edison for his dependence on feeling elect. I had destroyed a perfect record, and were I ever again to exceed my personal best in starvation I'd be obliged to start back on Day One—reliving that first awful, gnawing twenty-four hours of choosing furniture when all I'd really wanted to buy was a sandwich.

Desolate, I begged off Scrabble and went to bed early, claiming I was tired, though in truth I was battling nausea. Once I lay down, I scrutinized a sensation I'd not felt for so long that at first I hadn't recognized it. I wasn't about to throw up. I was hungry.

What I remember most about return to solids was disappointment. I'd built up proper meals into such bliss that once I started eating again I found food bewilderingly commonplace. Lo, I'd been eating all my life, and I knew what it was like. I'd been looking forward to it the way you were meant to look forward to falling in love or having your first child. But a chicken breast was a chicken breast. It didn't take long to polish off, and whether it was dressed up with a little pesto or Thai curry sauce was neither here nor there. No meal no matter how nicely prepared would resolve what to do with your life on either side of chow.

More shockingly still, this ho-hum experience extended to being thin, which I had elevated to the rebirth and transformation that all the Jesus people in Iowa promoted through prayer. Oh, once my energy returned I relished the lightness, being able to sprint for the car before the meter ran out and not get out of breath. And, sure, at first it had been exciting to watch the lumps that had attached to me like bloodsucking parasites gradually loosen their grip and melt away to whatever cave they'd crawled from. But during the years I'd put on weight I'd trained myself to turn a blind eye to these expansions; only when I lost the weight had I truly noticed it in the first place.

After a couple of months of Upchuck I'd bravely installed a full-length mirror in my bedroom, and ever since getting down to 130 again I'd stopped glancing in the opposite direction when I passed it by. Once I could bear to confront the image, I had faced down that mirror naked with embarrassing frequency.

Thus an evening before bed after I'd been back to food a day or two, I closed my bedroom door to appraise the organism.

It was a relief to no longer feel ashamed, and that was probably the most intense emotion my new body stirred: a not-emotion. But I was in my early forties and looked it, fat or trim. Now that I'd taken the diet too far, I enjoyed the "leeway" that I'd envied in Breadbasket photographs—but "leeway" translated into tiny breasts that sagged and striated with wrinkles around the nipples. When I took a deep breath, ribs extruded in parallel tracks above my bosom, but as achievements go this one didn't do much for me. Aesthetically, I could see the merits of hip bones that looked as if a scoop of ice cream had been curled from each one, but the extra skin that withered on the underside of my upper arms and the inside of my thighs was hardly fetching. While I was a reasonably symmetrical creature, I was never going to be a knockout, for I hadn't been a knockout even during those few center-cut years when women turn heads. The single aspect of my reduced circumference that I did find pleasing was simply the sense that, physically, I was myself. A few months before, a proportion of my body had seemed to belong to someone else. Yet even this satisfaction was mild. A slender figure therefore joined career success in its so-whatness. Did anything at all in life deliver a proper payoff?

On the heels of this revelation, I feared for Edison. The anticlimax of losing fifty-four pounds was disconcerting; the anticlimax of losing 223 pounds could prove soul-destroying. For once I'd overshot my own target, what hit me over the head was the host of other problems that being a little slimmer didn't dent. Over the phone, Fletcher and I had sometimes grown so distant that we weren't even antagonistic. It was odd to miss his hostility, but without it we were losing that crucial tension for lack of which I had stopped going out with Oliver. Only months from graduation, Tanner had become a chronic truant, and if he failed his courses he'd have to go to summer school or repeat the semester next year. I was growing actively bored with my company, but if I folded or sold it I had no idea what I'd do next. And Edison . . . Well, my brother never made any reference to his life on the other side of this weight-loss project. How cataclysmically would all the balls he'd left in the air in New York come crashing down once he'd met his goal and discovered that being 163 didn't really solve anything?

M istrustful, and thus insistent on overseeing my rehabilitation one-on-one, Oliver stopped by Monotonous at the end of every workday that following week. Edison found this curious enough that he pressed me on whether Oliver and I had become an item. I was taken aback by the acid that laced my brother's accusation. If he'd been protective of Fletcher, fair enough, but I knew better. Fletcher had been merciless when my brother was our houseguest, and in the months since Edison had gotten in many a vengeful crack about "Feltch" (sans the *t*, slang for a sexual practice I'd rather not describe; rhyming with *belch*, *squelch*, and *welch*, the new nickname exuded meanness and vulgarity). In theory, my cuckolding his brother-in-law should have made Edison's day.

I lied that I was consulting Oliver about how we might redesign the mechanism to use flash drives, thus allowing customers to replace recordings grown tiresome with new sets of phrases (not a bad idea at that). Yet it was comical, what I was hiding: not a steamy, illicit romance, but a steamy, illicit supper.

Oliver and I went back to the same diner every evening. I'd had some explosive diarrhea, but otherwise returned to solid food without mishap. I carried a toothbrush, and ducked in the restroom to clean my teeth before heading what had started to feel, confusingly, like home. There I shared a protein shake with Edison, which served as cover and provided additional nutrition I could use.

Only days before, I'd looked forward to those concoctions so! Yet now I turned my head when downing mine lest Edison see me gag. Formerly passionate about flavors of herbal teas, I stashed the infusions arrayed on the counter in a cabinet, just so I didn't have to lay eyes on the ghastly boxes. Of course, sudden revulsion for these tokens of self-torture was rational: pursued much further, that punishing drill might have killed me. But real food also upset me, and quite apart from the fact that I was hiding it from my brother. After subsisting on four stingy envelopes daily, I no longer profoundly believed, as Oliver noted, that I required solid sustenance to live. Even if I gamely bought into the premise, food had become arbitrary, and scary. My first reaction on sitting down to a meal was panic.

I wasn't alone in this hysteria. You could see the same frenzy all over the Internet: diatribes about sugar, clever tips about using tiny plates or drinking lots of water, profiles on celebrities who claim to have "eighty meals a day," the charts listing the glycemic index of parsnips and potatoes. You could see it in the accelerating demand for extra-wide caskets, roller coasters reinforced with I-beams, and elevators redesigned to carry twice the load. You could see it in burgeoning retail sales for "bountiful" apparel, in the return of the corset. You could see it in the market for airline seatbelt extenders, "Big John" toilet seats, 800-pound-rated shower chairs, and "LuvSeats" for *couples of size* to have sex. You could see it in popular websites like BigPeopleDating.com, but you could also see it in the prestige designation of size-zero jeans and in the host of Cody's classmates who'd been hospitalized for starving or throwing up. You couldn't help but wonder what earthly good was a microprocessor, a space telescope, or a particle accelerator, when we had mislaid the most animal of masteries. Why bother to discover the Higgs boson or solve the economics of hydrogen-powered cars? We no longer knew how to eat.

T he Sunday that began the second week of my furtive feasts, I was feeling remorseful about leaving my brother by himself. At supper with Oliver, I rushed through a spicy chicken cacciatore with all the neglect I'd sworn over salmon in December to eschew, and hastened to the restroom. I couldn't find my toothbrush and had no time to run to a drugstore; I'd promised Edison that I'd be back in time for *Mad Men*, to which, if only to spite Travis, we'd grown addicted. So I picked the green pepper from my teeth, rinsed my mouth, and hoped for the best.

At Prague Porches, I stirred our dinner shakes, averting my face to avoid the smell. Edison watched me from the piano bench with an unnerving stillness that drove me to flights of hyperactivity—turning on the TV though the program wouldn't air for ten minutes, plumping throw pillows, rehearsing the plot of the last episode, which we both remembered well. With five minutes to go, I was retrieving our Upchucks when Edison walked straight for me with the accuracy of an intercept missile. Leaning in to sniff, he announced, "Chorizo."

"In your dreams!"

He strode to our trash can and lifted the lid.

"What are you looking for?"

"A pizza box. Or something like it."

I hadn't been that careless. "Tea bags and Senokot foils. As usual."

"That's what tipped me off, man." Edison jabbed my chest. "You got the trots."

"I do not!"

"This isn't that big an apartment, babe. I can *hear* you. Ain't *nobody* gets the shits on this diet." Looming over me, he chided with that piercing parental disappointment, "Panda Bear, how could you."

"How could I what?"

"After all our sacrifice!" He gesticulated as he paced. "Tell me, was it worth it? For a crappy piece of sausage?"

The game was up. I hung my head and sobbed. "I'm sorry!"

"You're an ungrateful, selfish BABY," Edison bellowed, "and a total CREEP!"

"It wasn't my idea! Oliver made me!"

But Edison couldn't keep it up, and started to laugh—a huge, rich belly laugh that I hadn't heard in ages. "Sure bit that hook, line, and sinker! I'm just razzing you, kid. You don't gotta explain. Look, you look hot as the blazes. Real skinny and real cute. Of course you can't keep living on five-eighty a day. You'd fucking die, man! But why you been sneaking around? Jesus, it's been so obvious, I only been waiting for you to come clean."

"I've deserted you." I couldn't stop crying.

He was getting stronger; when Edison embraced me, at long last he lifted me off the floor. He rested me down gently, and ruffled my hair. "Look, I've dug the companionship. But it's time you got off the boat. Just don't eat in secret, right? Christ, it could be better than the Food Channel. I should at least get to watch."

I wiped my eyes. "That sounds pretty dirty."

"I'm not through. Got a hundred nineteen more big ones to drop. So here's what I propose: I'll cook for you. I'll make your breakfast, and pack your lunches, and every night make you a dinner that's absolutely killing."

"You could stand that?"

"I would *love* that, man. I could buy food, and cut it, and stir it, and smell it, and pinky-swear I wouldn't snitch. You were starting to look a little pale there, pal. Now hop to." He tossed me the remote. "Already missed five minutes, and I know you got a hard-on for Don Draper."

So thereafter Edison cooked. He cooked up a storm. We'd have Cody over, and Oliver over, and one night we finally coaxed Tanner over, during which Edison regaled him with tales of fleeing to the East Coast at seventeen—at which point I sensed my brother's long war to win his de facto nephew's favor was starting to succeed, since for the first time in years my stepson was palpably impressed: "No *shit*!" he'd interject, or, "You left with only *twenty bucks*?" The meals were light and nutritious, and I never once caught the cook slipping a morsel in his mouth when he thought no one was looking. Why, like my successful suitor of yore, to keep from dripping on the floor he now instinctively shook his wet hands *splat-splat* at the sink before reaching for a dishtowel. Edison found enormous pleasure in his new role as house chef, and not from caloric voyeurism alone. In depriving himself these many months, Edison was exploding with the need to satisfy *somebody*. Was it the aerobic exercise? He'd grown smaller of girth, but greater of heart.

chapter seven

This time, I had not been invited to Java Joint. I had been summoned.

We arrived at the same time. Discarding my jacket, I paused the smallest moment before sliding into the booth, my version of a show-off twirl. In the six weeks since Fletcher and I had last seen each other I'd dropped another twelve pounds before leveling off; this was Fletcher's first viewing of the finished product. What's more, my tastes in dress had grown racier, at least for me: tight black jeans, a low-cut aqua blouse. My new contours in the mirror having proved such a private letdown made this single serious payoff—my husband's admiration—only more important.

As he furtively checked me out, I caught a look in my husband's eye that I hadn't seen in a long time. Yet my figure both aroused and annoyed him. "New clothes, I see."

"The old ones don't fit."

"You're looking . . ."

I waited. I had earned this. It was my reward.

"You're looking a little fragile."

"*Thanks.*" I couldn't believe he could be so ungenerous. Obviously he wanted to be the thin one. The fit one. The perfect person, who required a fallible slob at his side for contrast.

Fletcher backed off any more criticism, but the compliments I had anticipated were not forthcoming. "Never mind for now. We have to talk about Tanner."

"All right. Shoot." I hated sounding so clipped, but he'd hurt my feelings.

"He's quit school."

"That's ridiculous. He's two months from graduating."

"It's deliberate. He thinks he's *exceptional*. As far as Tanner's concerned, he's getting out in the nick of time, just before he becomes a plain old high school graduate like everyone else."

"This country is awash in dropouts."

"I've said that. But he also wants to spite me, and in that sense the ploy is working to plan."

"What can I get you folks?"

Fletcher had learned not to order a muffin. "Green tea, decaffeinated, no sugar," said Fletcher, and I chimed in, "Make that two." A draw.

"There's more," said Fletcher. "Two days ago, while I was in the basement working on a rush commission, Tanner packed up and left. No note. His computer's gone, all his favorite T-shirts. He even left his cell behind so I couldn't contact or track him. None of his friends have heard from him. I've been so desperate, I even contacted *Cleo*. No intel, except I did find out she's become a born-again, believe it or not."

"Predictable," I said. "Another addiction. So where do you think he went?"

"Where else? *California*. Just like your fat-headed dad. Tanner flunked American History—along with everything else. So the only history he has absorbed is *your family's*. Before he left he even started calling himself 'Tanner Appaloosa.' *Feuerbach*, I've been informed, 'isn't commercial.' "

"Does he have any money?"

"He'll have cleaned out his meager savings account. And my wallet."

"I'm so sorry." But I wasn't close enough to this story. I was "so sorry," as if I were comforting a neighbor or employee.

"There's more than his diploma at stake here. I want a son who works. Who doesn't loll around waiting for an inheritance or some other manna from the sky. Who understands that life isn't just something you're given but something you make. But kids, they're told in school now that they're God's little angels, that they're wonderful just because they exist, and they buy it. So they walk out into the world and expect everyone to bow down. It's dangerous, Pandora. The 'I'm Mr. Wonderful' thing, it makes them stupid and it makes them prey." Fletcher was starting to choke up, but there was fury in there, too, and it was directed at me.

"We see completely eye-to-eye on our son, so I don't understand why you keep acting as if we're having an argument."

"He didn't just get this stuff from Facebook or *Keeping Up with the Kardashians* or his teachers. It's you, and your brother. You two make fun of Travis, but only as an opportunity to remind everybody: Our dad was a TV star. That's the inheritance that Tanner's waiting for, and it's worse than waiting for money. Though after those magazine covers about your company, he figures you'll throw him a wad sooner or later."

"I've never dangled any pot of gold at the end of his rainbow. I've never glorified growing up as an 'Appaloosa,' either. Don't I go by Halfdanarson? In fact, I've bent over backwards with those kids, explaining that any celebrity I either cadged or earned was no big deal, or even a downer."

"They don't believe you."

I saw his point. You could never convince powerless, obscure people—like children—that they were better off powerless and obscure. It sounded suspicious, like the ruling class shoring up its advantage. For years Travis had tried to convince us kids that we wouldn't like "slimy" avocados, because he wanted all the ripe ones for himself.

I said, "I'm not getting how you expect me to help here."

"I want my kids to turn out *solid*." Atypically, Fletcher wasn't interested in practicalities. "I don't want them thinking there's some cheap shortcut. I want the kind of kids nobody has any-more. Who bear down, who do their part, who don't expect a leg up or a handout. And now your brother has poured all this crap in their ears. About honoring your 'talent' and how he's whizzed around the world unburdened by anything so clay-footed as a high school diploma, much less a college one. Where do you think Tanner got the idea of dropping out? Your fat fuck of a brother quit school at seventeen, too."

"Edison makes a better role model for our kids right now than either one of us. He's not taking any 'shortcuts.' He didn't opt for stomach banding or liposuction. He's skipping one meal after another, for months, and that's exactly the kind of hard work and humility you're touting."

"That's a stretch. Do something unbelievably stupid like put on hundreds of pounds and then undo it. That's hardly a model of constructive behavior. Like carrying a load of bricks to one side of the yard and then carrying them back again."

"Cody, whether you like it or not, is bowled over."

"Cody has the flu, and doesn't have a mother to take care of her. Which I thought I'd gotten for her seven years ago, but apparently not. Instead, all I seem to have installed in our house— for a little while—was some deadbeat's *sister.*"

I drained my tea. This was pointless. We'd gone around this loop continually: You've betrayed us, your real loyalty should be to your family, why is your brother so important, I'm only doing this for a short while and I'll be back but Edison needs me. Why further groove a broken record?

So I promised I'd let him know if Tanner got in touch, and noted that without a word from the boy himself there was nothing we could do. This meeting failed to accomplish anything tangible, but Fletcher hadn't come to me for a clue to our wayward son's whereabouts. He'd dragged me to that coffee shop to have someone to blame. And on some level, I wasn't sure he was wrong.

W hen you're seventeen, it's not called 'running away,' " said Edison while washing lettuce. "It's called 'leaving home.' That's what the cops would tell you, too. Tan's not a missing person. He's a left person. With a dad like that, it's a wonder he didn't cut out years ago."

"He's a young seventeen, and Fletcher's right," I said. "As soon as he runs out of money, that kid is ripe for any passing deviant."

"He'll clue-up pronto. My money says in no time some

slightly older fox takes him under her wing and pays for everything."

"But he has no understanding of how hard—"

"*It's not your job*"—Edison poked a wet finger at my chest—"to be *pre-disappointed* for him, dig? You and Feltch go on and on about how big and terrible 'the world' is. Well, maybe so. But in that case, it's the world's job to be big and terrible, not yours. You guys keep drilling into the kid he's not going to make it, he doesn't have a prayer. He has to be 'realistic.' You think you're protecting him. But you're insulting him. Take my word for it, that's the way Tan sees it: you're keeping a foot on his neck."

"It is protecting him, to at least ensure he graduates from high school."

"What for? In Tanner's terms? Besides, you may be all maternal on the guy's ass, and maybe you do think you have his interests at heart, but Feltch, man—Feltch just wants those kids to do what he says. He's an unforgiving authoritarian hard-ass, and it beats me what you ever saw in the guy."

I was less alarmed by Edison's characterization than by his final choice of verb tense. "Fletcher Feuerbach is honest, loyal, diligent, and, whether you personally can see it, kind."

"Kind! About time you noticed Tanner and Cody aren't the only ones that cat wants to control."

"He hasn't controlled me. He didn't want me to move in with you, and I did."

"Has he made it easy? Has he been *supportive*? Of a project you warned me yourself would be the hardest gig of our lives?"

I didn't bother to answer.

"All right, then." Edison brought a cleaver down on a chicken leg. "Case closed."

E hhh-di-SUN!" Cody gave my brother a high five. She'd dropped the "Uncle" for months, preferring the chantlike emphasis with which impatient crowds demand the appearance of rock stars. She propped her once-neglected bike against our own in the hall, since it had become evident, once Edison and I started cycling too, that her father hadn't personally annexed this efficient form of transport. She was looking a little peaked, and I recognized the mopy, lethargic symptoms as an ailment I'd come down with at the same age.

"If anyone asks"—she clumped her backpack on the kitchen pass-through—"I wasn't here. I told Dad I was working on a paper with Hazel and eating with her folks."

"You shouldn't lie," I said.

"Mom, it's not worth it. Dad gets so bent out of shape when he knows I'm coming here. He calls it 'the clubhouse.' He goes all quiet and moves around all jerky and stiff . . ." She did a demonstration, a cross between Charlie Chaplin and Frankenstein's monster, and we laughed.

"You could always invite your dad to come, too," I said.

"The only way Dad's coming to Prague Porches is with a gallon of gas and a match. Like, head for the exits, man." His daughter's recent penchant for *man* and *jive* and *crib* must have driven Fletcher insane. "And now with Tanner gone it's worse. Dad makes me feel like a traitor. And I hate leaving him by himself. With that gucky brown rice and broccoli so undercooked it's like chewing on a tree. It's totally depressing."

"Yo, it ain't your fault the cat can't cook," said Edison, tail-ing ten green beans at a stroke. We were having cod fillets with an olive, caper, and eggplant tapenade, one of my brother's specialties. I'd no idea how he did it without tasting anything.

Cody bombed into a recliner. "I can't tell you the relief of plopping in a chair that isn't some sort of *artwork*. Dad's stuff isn't, like, totally uncomfortable or anything, but soon as you sit in one of those things he starts staring all beady-eyed and shit, making sure you don't put a wet glass on the arm or scuff your shoes on the wood. So just sitting there I get an anxiety attack. Half the time I can't stand it and just sit on the floor, dig?"

"Tell me about it," said Edison, pulling a charred whole eggplant from the oven.

"He finally fixed the Boomerang, you know," said Cody.

"Let's hear it for superglue," said Edison.

"Not exactly," said Cody. "But I don't know why he bothered. I guess the chair darkened over the years, so the new wood isn't the same color. He keeps running his hand over the rail and scowling, or picking at some little joint where the pieces don't meet absolutely, one hundred percent, exactamundo flush."

"You know your dad's a perfectionist," I said, setting the table. What I'd missed most during my Upchuck days wasn't food but the event of food, all the surrounding activities like putting groceries in cupboards and folding napkins. I now adored setting the table.

"Supposedly that's a compliment," said Cody. "But what's so great about being a perfectionist? You're never happy. You do all this work, and then the stuff you've made just pisses you off." Since her regular lessons with Edison, Cody had grown more blasé, tougher-seeming, but she hadn't changed that much, and caught herself. "Anyway, the main thing is the Boomerang's okay, right, Edison? It's back. You didn't, like, mess it up. Or, you know, whoever messed it up—didn't."

This was a perfect opportunity for Edison to admit responsibility once and for all, but Cody wasn't the only one who hadn't changed that much.

"The times you have told your dad you're coming here," I said, "what have you told him when you came back? About what it was like?"

She looked away. "I don't know. I guess I say it's depressing."

"Which is exactly the way you described what it's like at home."

"Well, I don't think it *is* depressing. Here, I mean. You know I have a pretty cool time. My improvisation's getting better, and we play Fictionary when Oliver's over—"

"Do you tell your dad when Oliver's come over?"

"Um," she said glumly. "Generally, no, I guess I don't."

"And do you tell your dad that we play Boggle, and Monopoly, and go for walks? About dividing up the parts and reading aloud Tennessee Williams plays, and practicing our hicky Southern accents? Or how we built that snowman out back in February—the really massive one that we made to look like Edison before he went on his diet, using some of his old clothes that no longer fit? That was hilarious."

Edison shouted from the kitchen, "Even in Iowa, thought we was gonna run out of snow!"

"Of course I don't!" said Cody impatiently. "I tell him we just sit around and watch TV. That's what he wants to hear, so that's what he's going to hear, know what I'm sayin'?"

"Yes, I know what you're *sayin',*" I said. "But you shouldn't have to cover up having a good time here, and you shouldn't think you have to tell us that your dad is miserable, either. It's not fair to you."

"Who said anything about fair? I'm just trying to get by. Nuts, it's just like that stupid program Grampa was in. Those kids never told the truth—to either one of their parents. Which is, anyway, like, big surprise, since kids don't tell the truth to their parents even when they're together."

"Fletcher and I *are* together," I corrected sharply.

"Yeah, right."

As we sat down to eat, I recounted an early episode of "that stupid program" in which Caleb, Maple, and Teensy all collude to portray their mother's life as desolate to their father, and their father's life as desolate to their mother, while in truth both divorced parents are living the life of Riley. Driven by mutual pity, the parents meet up and compare notes, although only after conducting a comical conversation in which each utterly misapprehends the other's state of mind.

Edison waited table, wearing a chef's apron whose tie could now reach all the way around his back and then knot in the front—a feat he had only achieved the previous week. The fish was garnished with rosemary sprigs, our whole-wheat couscous dotted with roasted hazelnuts and slivers of dried apricot.

"So, do you miss your brother?" I asked Cody. It was what no one had asked me back in the day.

"Yeah," she said warily.

"And . . . have you been in contact?"

She tried to get by with a shrug.

"The kid's not going to rat out her own brother," said Edison, having a seat with his Upchuck and a straw; chocolate malt, I determined.

"I'm not asking her to rat. It would be comforting to know if Tanner's all right."

"I got a hunch," she said, "he's all right."

"When Edison absconded to New York at the same age," I said, "I was under a lot of pressure to tell our father where he'd gone."

"Though Travis didn't want to track me down out of *concern*," said Edison. "He wanted confirmation I'd landed face-down in a puddle. Feltch isn't any different, either."

"And did you tell?" Cody asked me.

I considered fibbing. If Cody blabbed, my locating Tanner's hideout would win me a few grudging points with Fletcher. "I said I'd no idea where he was and he hadn't told me anything before leaving and he hadn't contacted me, either."

"I have no idea where Tanner is," Cody recited, "he didn't tell me anything, and he hasn't contacted me, either."

"Whoa, that's the kind of little sister I can dig!" said Edison.

"Yes, we're all alike," I said. "We cover for you, we lie for you, we take the heat for you. We clean up your messes and mollify our parents for you. We never fail to come across with undying adoration whether or not you deserve it, and we can't take our own lives nearly as seriously as we do yours. We snuffle up the crumbs from your table on the rare occasions you notice we're alive."

Edison gestured at our dinner. "But, hey, not bad crumbs!" My characterization pleased him.

The landline rang. I picked up.

"Panda-monium! Your brother still laying off the Fritos?"

"He hasn't looked at a Frito in five months," I said. "You could hardly call him chubby. He looks great, his spirits are high, and he exercises every day. He practices the piano nonstop, and he's got his chops back." I hadn't changed, either. I was still the founding patron of the Edison Appaloosa Defense Fund.

"Isn't that swell," said Travis, as usual overwhelmed with joy on hearing glad tidings of his only son. "But answer me this: a sad-sack, henpecked high school chemistry teacher riddled with cancer suddenly becomes a big-time drug dealer. How plausible is a premise like *that*? This 'Walter White' bozo is a timid, scaredy-cat loser, and I don't buy it. That shit won't see a second season."

I'd no idea what he was talking about. "To what do we owe the honor of this call? If you picked up the phone every time you were incensed by the TV listings, we'd hear from you every day."

"I've tripped across one of your belongings, which you *mis-placed*," said Travis, hamming it up. "Seems a little careless. I taught you to pick up your toys."

With Edison in the room, I was braver with my father. "That's a pretty crappy way of referring to your own grandson."

"*Step*-grandson." Everyone in my family availed themselves of this distancing prefix only when it suited them.

"So he's staying with you?"

"The boy threw himself on the mercy of my hospitality, and I wasn't going to toss him on the street, was I? Although I gotta say, for a homeless waif that's one cocky kid. Don't know what sort of fashionable parenting thing you got going, but he sure thinks right well of himself. One big *Please, sir, can I have some more*."

"I bet you took second helpings too, at his age. Is he all right?"

"Still has his fingers and toes. Kid wants to apprentice him-self, learn the tricks of the media trade. Trouble is, mentors with credits the scale of mine can pull in sky's-the-limit fees, and my new houseguest expects a family discount."

I could see it: when Tanner first washed up on Travis's doorstep—a handsome young man conveniently pre-plied with Appaloosa lore—my father was flattered, which is why he'd kept the young man's whereabouts to himself for the last week. Miraculously, God had at last bequeathed to this underappreciated icon of groundbreaking television a proper flesh-and-blood fan. Unfortunately, the new live-in acolyte being a teenage male meant that he did not shop, pick up after himself, spring for the take-out bill, or launder his own clothes, although, a bit of an operator and enjoying access to no other free crash pad in California, Tanner was doubtless shoveling a measure of obsequious shit in his grandfather's direction in lieu of rent.

Talking to my father usually drove me to catatonia, but for once I was thinking on my feet. "Then make him sing for his supper. You've always wanted to write that memoir. Get him to sort out your papers. Find and assemble all your old fan mail—I *know* you didn't throw any of it away. Get the scripts in order—since he claims he wants to write them. Tanner could polish up your website, add more hyperlinks."

"You may have an idea there . . ." The prospect of deriving any inspiration from his dull, undistinguished middle child was far-fetched. "But even if I do sic the kid on those boxes in the basement, I'm racking up expenses here. Up till now, the only beneficiaries of your stepson's arrival have been Taco Bell and In-N-Out Burger. Now, I'm auctioning a trove of props on eBay, top-of-the-line memorabilia from *JC*, but so far collectors are low-balling me something scandalous." (I surmised: he hadn't sold a thing.) "Damn, if this economy is so soft that priceless items like

Caleb Fields's sheet music aren't getting snapped up for top dollar, I'd be worrying about that doll-baby outfit of yours—"

"I'll send a check," I interrupted. "For one favor in return: put my son on the phone." If the long ensuing silence weren't enough, Tanner's surly "Yeah?" cleared up any ambiguity: he'd been forced to talk to me. "Listen," I said. "I want you to really apply yourself out there. Grampa may be a little out of the loop, but he knows a fair bit about TV from the inside. He could teach you plenty. So don't waste your time sleeping late and cruising the streets for glimpses of Tom Hanks. If you're serious about this career, then act serious. Learn the ropes. Meet his contacts. Do what Grampa asks you to, okay? He needs a crackerjack researcher for his memoir, which will involve getting his files in order, maybe interviewing the producers and other actors about their memories of *Joint Custody*. Think of it as an internship. And interns work real hard, and long hours, for no money. You're paid in experience. You copy?"

"Uh—yeah, sure." He sounded dazed. "Like, that's what I had in mind anyway, whaddya think? . . . Still, what about Dad?"

"His first instinct will be to hop in his truck to drag you back to New Holland. I'll do what I can to hold him off. After all, you'd just pick up and leave again, wouldn't you?"

"Better believe it." This much was said with conviction.

"We both love you; we both understand it's your life, to do with what you wish; and we both want you to be happy. We also want you to be successful at whatever you choose to do, even if you find that hard to believe right now. I'm mostly relieved that you're safe. Remember you can always call here, if you have any questions or if you just feel like catching up. If you decide California's not up your alley after all, there's no embarrassment in coming home. But you're not going to do that, are you?"

"Hell, no."

"That's the spirit. Now, give Grampa a hug for me, and get to work."

When I returned to my cold fish, both Edison and Cody were staring at me in disbelief. "You didn't try to talk him into coming back," said Cody.

"Nope," I said.

"You didn't give him a hard time about how all-fired important it is that he finishes high school," she said. "None of that 'but you're joining the slave class,' like Oliver said."

"Nope," I said brightly. "Though that's obviously what he expected." I piled tapenade on a bite of cod. "Oh, Edison, get this: Travis has put Caleb Fields's sheet music on *eBay*."

"Which that jive motherfucker Sinclair Vanpelt couldn't even read," said Edison.

"Here's what kills me," I said. "After you left for New York, Travis converted your old room to a home theater, remember?"

"And why would Travis want a home theater?" Edison quizzed Cody.

She didn't miss a beat. "For watching reruns of *Joint Custody*."

"To the head of the class," said Edison.

"So he crammed all *your* stuff in the trash," I said. "Including the sheet music—of a *real* person who's his *son* and could actually *play* the piano. The music of a fake son with fake talent he stores for thirty years. God, Edison, no wonder you're screwed up."

"*Au contraire*, babe, under the circumstances I'm fucking well-adjusted."

I picked a hazelnut from the couscous. "At least you're off

the hook, Cody. Grampa *told*. All intergenerational relationships are inherently traitorous."

She thought about it. "Doesn't that mean I can't trust you, either?"

"Yup."

"So why *didn't* you badger Tan to come home?" Edison puzzled. "I thought the kid was a 'young seventeen.' Not ready for prime time."

"You're the one warned me off of being 'pre-disappointed' for my children," I said. "Besides, think about it: if Tanner starts digging in that basement, he's going to exhume scripts that were barely up to the mark at the time and in hindsight are appalling. Any fan mail from the old days will be from eleven-year-old girls and written in crayon. And Tanner's bound to trip over the residue of a dozen failed business ventures that postdate the show—like that goofy playhouse prototype that was supposed to re-create Emory Fields's eco-friendly bungalow, which Travis never got anybody to market. Then there's the videos and DVDs of all those awful three a.m. ads on Nick at Nite—for $9.99 electromagnetic dusters, 'pop stoppers' for aluminum cans, and 'granny grabbers' for when you're too old and fat to pull up your own socks, with two free high-shelf grips thrown in, *but only if you order now*! Meanwhile, he'll have to listen to Travis fume by the hour about how much he hates William Shatner. Talk about the ultimate in 'cautionary tale'! No offense to your brother, Cody—but Tanner and Travis deserve each other."

chapter eight

I was leery of another joust at Java Joint, so for a marital re-union at the beginning of June I suggested a bike ride instead. That way Fletcher could deliver those patronizing pointers about bike repair, even if the sight of him tottering around pigeon-toed in clip-in cycling shoes wasn't very sexy. I apologized up front that I'd be slow, hoping to head off any suggestion of competition.

So what possessed me? Was I really that stupid?

It was that eternal rock-and-a-hard-place, I suppose. The rain had been relentless all spring, and I hated leaving my brother alone on what was forecast to be, for the first time in weeks, a sunny, temperate Sunday. Protective of our hideaway and a little bereft when out of his jazz element, he never brought anyone home; his diet was antisocial. By then, too, Edison was approaching his six-month anniversary of Upchuck, and that had to be much too long to live daily on four envelopes of powder. Between exercise and no longer dragging his own deadweight like a cadaver, he'd seemed robust in early spring, but the renewed strength had ebbed. He'd grown shorter of breath. At the piano, his hands had developed a tremor. His concentration was so poor that at work he sometimes stitched seams with the finished side of the fabric facing out. When we cycled to Baby Monotonous, I had to tap my brakes to keep from getting ahead. So maybe I was hoping to demonstrate how any continuation of this debilitating all-liquid diet was out of the question. Oh, and doubtless I was also influenced by the usual sappy, middle-child, Maple Fields prime directive: why can't we all get along?

In sum, idiotically, I asked Edison if he wanted to come on the bike ride, too. He jumped at the chance—oiling our chains, pumping our tires, and teeming off to Hy-Vee to buy ingredients for a picnic. Had I forewarned Fletcher that I'd have my brother in tow, my husband might have said no, in which case I'd have to *un*invite Edison, a worse outcome than never having asked him in the first place . . . At least simply showing up with you-know-who was a fait accompli.

That morning, Edison weighed in at 228.7—only two-tenths of a pound less than the day before. He'd enough experience with uneven progress to deal with these small, temporary disappointments. But this time he blew up. "Fuck this, man! I am not digging this, man, not one bit!"

I pointed at the family photo from my birthday, taped beside the scale to provide an image of his baseline. "The difference is staggering. Stop sweating the little daily crap."

Getting ready, Edison changed three times. At last he emerged in khaki cargo shorts, a rayon short-sleeve, and blazing-white Nikes, all topped off with razzle-dazzle shades. I saw him daily in a ratty kimono stolen years ago from a Tokyo hotel, so he was not dressing up for me.

"You're going for a bike ride," I said, "not getting married. Pack up the panniers, or we'll be late."

Sure enough, Fletcher was propped against the fence when we rolled up.

Fletcher hadn't seen Edison Appaloosa since our giddy farewell on Solomon Drive—when we'd merrily gunned off on our unlikely quest as if planning to conquer the South Pole in windbreakers and straw hats. I'd provided my husband regular updates on my brother's shrinkage, but numbers are abstract, and he probably thought I exaggerated. At 228, Edison was a substantial guy, but at cafés no one scrambled for an extra-wide chair. In modern American terms, he was handsome—which suddenly struck me as unfortunate.

Edison extended a hand over his handlebars. "Yo, long time."

Fletcher shook perfunctorily. "So it's a threesome, is it?"

"Such a nice day," I said. "I thought we could all use some fresh air."

Fletcher shot me a look. "What kind of mileage you have in mind?"

"I don't know . . . twenty?" I said.

"I do twenty in less than an hour. I thought you wanted to make a day of it."

"We're not in your league," I said. "Twenty-five to thirty, then? At the turnaround point, we can break for lunch. Edison packed us a picnic."

"Swell," Fletcher snarled. "Ready, then? Anyone need to pee?"

He pushed off while I was taking a slug of water, and once I caught up I was huffing. While the pace was surely slower than his solo speed, I had to bear down to stay within hailing distance of his back tire. This hyperventilating slog contrasted with the whimsical putter I'd pictured beforehand: pedaling lazily three abreast, trading anecdotes. We'd take breaks, watching ducks, skipping stones, catching some rays . . . But Fletcher was on a *ride*, and when Fletcher went on a *ride* he didn't stop.

Fletcher's narrow back tire drew further in front. By the time I shouted, "Hey! Wait up!" I doubt he heard me. That's when I looked over my shoulder, and Edison was nowhere in sight. I turned around. I found him with his bike propped against a tree about two miles back, smoking.

He squinted down the path. "So where's Feltch?"

"Somewhere over the rainbow," I said.

"What's he got to prove? Besides being a dick? I knew that already."

"Oh, he might have waited for just me. Another guy . . . He has to show off. You still up for this?"

"Sure. Long as you're ready to hang."

"I promise," I said, "I'll *hang*."

We saddled up, proceeding side by side. "I sat down with a calculator the other day," I said, steering idly down the middle white line, "and crunched that monthly weight-loss tally of yours. I know you've memorized it, too: 'thirty-nine, thirty-three, twenty-six, nineteen, sixteen.'"

"Sixteen *point four*."

"But this month you'll barely make fourteen. The drop-off can't only be explained by your burning less energy because you're lighter. Your metabolism is slowing to a crawl. Ostensibly you burn fifteen calories for every pound you weigh. But I can only get those outputs by cranking that number down, to fourteen, thirteen, twelve . . . Right now you've plateaued around ten."

"Body thinks it's starving," said Edison.

"It's figured out that five hundred and eighty calories in little envelopes is all it's going to get. We'll have to shake the organism up. So start getting your head around a return to solid food."

"Upchucks may not work well as they used to, but they're still working, babe."

"It's not safe," I said mildly.

This was merely laying the groundwork for the coming showdown, and our tones were pleasant. We ranged to other matters: like how Edison was convinced that Oliver was "totally hung up" on me—a conviction he relished—and my admission that if my best friend were ever to marry I'd be indecently jealous. How Edison pictured Tanner coming up from Travis's basement something like that kid in Sweeney Todd emerging from the innards of Mrs. Lovett's pie-baking factory, his hair turned fright-white. I laughed. This was the convivial, freewheeling wend along the river that I'd hoped for, with the small exception of the personnel.

"If we ever see Fletcher again," I advised, "don't bring up the prodigal son. I may think Travis is the best possible inoculation against a life of California dreamin', but as far as Fletcher's concerned Tanner's been abducted by aliens. I've talked him out of kidnapping the boy back, but it's touchy."

The path veered from the river, and it is not true that Iowa is completely flat. Climbing a killer hill, we got off and walked. Which mustn't have made us look intrepid to Fletcher, who was inscribing tight circles at the crest.

"I was going to ask what took you so long," said Fletcher, "but now it's obvious."

"We're not in a hurry," I said casually. "Think you could

unhook from those pedals? This is a pretty spot, and I could use a rest."

Fletcher turned one foot smartly and dismounted. No embrace, no peck on the cheek. He hadn't touched me all day.

"So what's the mileage, man?" Edison's eyes glinted. "Must have gone at least forty."

"My cyclometer says seventeen," said Fletcher disdainfully. Edison knew perfectly well we hadn't gone forty miles.

I unfurled a bedspread under a tree while Edison smoked. The cigarette would have excited Fletcher's disgust, but my husband couldn't fault the content of our plastic containers: shrimp dressed with low-fat yogurt, lemon juice, and chives. Cherry tomatoes with mint and only a drizzle of oil that Edison had slow-baked on low heat. Seaweed salad, with hijiki and sesame seeds. For dessert, seasonal blueberries bursting with antioxidants. Our groaning board adhered to the letter to Fletcher's own dietary catechism, in response to which my husband tore off vengeful bites of his apricot jerky. Edison railed about Fletcher being a tyrant. But sometimes the most enraging thing you can do with tyrants is to comply.

"I'm not especially hungry," said Fletcher.

"What a shock," said Edison.

"Well, I'm starved," I intervened, weighing down napkins with paper plates. "Oh, and Edison, Upchuck now comes in a *new flavor*! Cherry-chocolate. Like Cherry Garcia." Edison accepted the thermos, swirling the shake like fine wine. "Hold it! I remembered your favorite glass." I unwrapped the faceted, soda fountain–style glass, and polished it with the dishtowel.

"You packed a *glass* for a bike trip," said Fletcher, standing on the sidelines.

Edison poured a measure and toasted. "Presentation, dig?"

He slipped a CD into our portable player, and Fletcher's face twitched. My husband wouldn't have heard jazz for half a year now, but he didn't seem to have missed it.

"Don't tell me," I said, averting my face from the CD cover. " . . . Sonny?"

"Yeah, but that's too easy," said Edison. "Who's on drums?"

I frowned. "Philly Joe? No, wait! Max Roach."

"Not bad, kid. Now what tune's Sonny riffing on?" Helping me out, Edison hummed the notes at the beginning of each four-bar phrase.

" 'Sweet Georgia Brown'!"

"Could have fooled me," said Fletcher.

"No gal made has got a shade," I sang over the music, *"on SWEET Georgia Brown!"* Honestly, I wasn't trying to make trouble. I was trying to perpetrate at least the illusion of a carefree, jovial jaunt with two of my favorite people. For Christ's sake, it was a picnic.

"Why do you people never play the song?" said Fletcher. "It's like you're above songs."

"Us people?" said Edison. "We're above and below the song, man. It's a dance. A courtship. A romance."

"No, it's like you're too good for the tune, any tune. Like you don't believe in the whole idea of a tune. And then you wonder why nobody normal listens to your stuff anymore. What kind of a musician doesn't believe in songs?"

"Why don't you make plain old chairs?" Edison shot back.

"You should explain to him," I said. "About how record companies used to pressure jazz musicians to play little enough of the original melody so the companies didn't have to pay royalties . . ."

Tightening his front brakes, Fletcher wasn't listening.

I felt geometrically awkward. Edison had plunked at my side, his back against a tree. Fletcher continued to stand, holding his bike. I considered clambering up to give him a hug, but the gesture would seem artificial. Even when you're married, you can't, physically, do whatever you think would help matters at any given moment. It has to be possible; you have to find a route in. It wasn't possible.

Fletcher gazed longingly at the food, but he'd staked out his position—he wasn't hungry—and now he was stuck with it, refusing the tastes I held out on a plastic fork. I felt self-conscious as the only one eating, but my pretense of a hearty appetite was part of the theater. I was going to force this expedition to be jolly if it killed me.

"You trying to tell me you made that whole spread," Fletcher charged my brother, "and you never sampled, like, a cherry tomato?"

"That would violate our loyalty oath," I said. *"I pledge aversion to the flab—"*

"Of the derided waists of America," Edison picked up.

"And to the repulsion for which is stands—"

"One nation, underweight," we recited together, *"practically invisible, with misery and smugness for all."* Edison and I gave each other the high five.

Fletcher stood tolerantly for this performance, but didn't crack a smile. "So you never licked the olive oil off your fingers."

"I'd no more put oily fingers in my mouth than stick them in a live socket." Edison stretched out. "Cooking, I can tell if the shrimp is done with a squeeze. But the idea of eating one is revolting. This whole fasting trip, it's been motherfucking deep. I finally dig why Gandhi quit eating."

"From fat man to philosopher," said Fletcher, leaning skeptically on his crossbar. "Wonder why Socrates and all those guys bothered. Instead of agonizing over the meaning of life, all they had to do was skip lunch."

"Well, sometimes you're a little fuzzy," I said, "but others, you focus like a laser. We've read dozens of books, some in one sitting. There's a purity . . . Even a high . . ."

"So," said Fletcher, deadpan, "starved yourselves into seeing the face of God."

"I never said anything about *God*," I said.

"It's just, sure, maybe it's satisfying to drop a few pounds." Fletcher wouldn't let it go. "But I don't know about claiming that a fad diet has anything to do with *wisdom*."

I wasn't letting it go, either. I wasn't sure what, but my husband seemed driven to take something from us—something hard-won, something we'd really sacrificed for, maybe as simple a matter as a little *credit*. "Most religions do associate revelation and fasting," I said. "When Jesus spent forty days in the desert, he didn't pack a sandwich."

"Hunger is my shepherd, I shall not want," Edison intoned, reclining. *"It maketh me lie down with long novels. It leadeth me to drink still water—"*

"Skipping lunch restoreth my soul," I picked up gamely, grateful for the little bit of Sunday school we were dragged to before our mother gave up. *"It leadeth me in the paths of righteousness for the avoidance of type 2 diabetes' sake."*

"Yea, though I walk through the valley of the shadow of Doritos," said Edison, *"I shall fear no weight gain—"*

"For my Upchuck art with me. My laxatives and my artificially sweetened herbal tea, they comfort me."

Edison frowned. "Some shit about a table . . . ?"

"Thou preparest a table before me," I supplied.

"Which is my enemy!"

"Thou annointest my fingers with olive oil, though I shan't lick them," I said. *"My cup runneth over with cherry-chocolate-flavored protein powder and essential enzymes."*

"Surely goodness and mercy shall follow me all the days of my life," we recited together. *"And I shall dwell in the house of . . ."*

"Starvation?"

"Privation?"

It was a cute solution, but in retrospect I wish I'd come up with another idea: I cried victoriously, "Prague Porches!"

"And I shall dwell in the house of Prague Porches," we resumed in unison, *"forever!"*

We rolled on the bedspread laughing. Giddy over having a good time rather than merely pretending to, I took too long to notice that, not only was Fletcher not laughing with us, he'd turned white.

At first I figured that he was irked by our having appropriated his making fun of us, in effect hijacking his joke. But it was worse than that, more grammatically profound. It wasn't the joke; it was the *us*. And it was the wrong *us*.

"You want to stay at your little clubhouse *forever?*" Fletcher swung a leg across his bike and clipped hard into a pedal. "Be my guest."

Now when I sprang up from the bedspread, there was nothing artificial about it. "Come on, we didn't mean anything!" I reached for Fletcher's shoulder. "The *Lord*, Prague *Porches*—it just sounded good!"

"Yeah, it obviously sounds good to you. I'm sure you'll be very happy together."

"Don't be ridiculous, sweetie, we were just horsing around! We do that all the time!" But no matter what I thought to say, it was *we* this and *we* that, and there was no inclusion of my husband in that pronoun.

"I warned you from the beginning about this cockamamie scheme." Hands braced on his handlebars, Fletcher employed that hypercontrolled, level delivery that chilled my blood. "You walk out on a man and his family for six months—a *year* is what you prepared me for, once you'd done your sums. Well, that has consequences. I told you: feelings change. Not because of what someone decides to feel. Because of cause and effect. Like a hammer on a board. You remember?"

"Yes, I remember." I was panicking. This was moving too fast. It was just a bike ride, a picnic, and later I could apologize that maybe bringing Edison along hadn't been a brilliant idea. We could talk it all out, and I could explain how, given the role of peacemaker that I'd not only been born into but that had been double-imprinted by Maple Fields, I compulsively kept cajoling my husband and my only brother to strike a truce . . .

"You feel close to me?" Fletcher asked point-blank.

If he'd asked whether I loved him, I'd have said of course right away, which is probably why that's not what he asked.

"Because you sure don't act like it." My hesitation had been answer enough.

"Obviously, when we haven't spent much time together—"

"You chose not to spend time with me. You chose to spend a year—a whole year—with your brother instead of me. You know, once you're in your forties, and we're talking good years, still in good health, still energetic? *There aren't that many years.*"

"It's not that much longer, and you can see, look at Edison, how much better he looks, it's working—"

"If I disappeared on you for a solid year, I'd be out on my ear for keeps."

"That would depend on what you left for."

"Crap. Leaving is leaving. You've demonstrated in no uncertain terms who's most important to you. Generally"—he glanced at Edison—"I don't like to air dirty laundry with an audience. It's private, it's our business. But I don't think you have any comprehension of 'our business' anymore. So I might as well say this stuff in front of you both, if only so you don't scurry back and report everything I said almost word for word but slightly wrong so that I seem a little more ridiculous and a little more the villain. You think I don't know how *siblings* work? I'm not that dumb."

"Honey, hardly, we should really talk this out when we're alone—"

"*I want a divorce.*" Even when issuing that ultimatum about Edison's having to be out of the house by the day of his plane reservation, Fletcher had never used that word.

"This isn't fair," I whispered. "I've only been trying—"

"Trying to have it both ways. You can't. Sometimes you have to choose. You chose. Live with it. Oh, and for the record: they're my kids, and they stay with me."

"Tell that to Tanner," Edison cried from the bedspread, and I wished he'd please stay out of this. I wished, too, he'd not lit another cigarette, as if the better to enjoy the show.

Fletcher swiveled. "While we're at it, Travis tells me a certain formerly fat fuck is talking on the phone all the time to my son. Lay off the *fatherly* advice. You've poured enough bullshit into that boy's head already."

"He talks to us," said Edison, "because he refuses to talk to *you*, man. So maybe you should consider, like, why that might be."

"Sweetheart, this is crazy," I said. "Really calling it quits, it's too important to decide so impulsively—"

"I wouldn't call it impulsive. Today just confirmed what I already knew. Like I said, I'm not that dumb."

Fletcher pushed off, accelerating further down the bike path—for a *real* ride, unencumbered by slowpokes. I collected our picnic containers in silence, for suddenly all the chummy sibling camaraderie had fallen away, and when I told Edison to turn off the damn music I felt a trace of real acrimony, dislike for *all that jazz* and my brother, too. As with fiscal assets, there had to be such a thing as emotional net worth, and Edison's account had just plunged into the red.

chapter nine

The homeward slog did feel like forty miles, since it once
more started to pour. After a long, hot shower, I left my
soaked, mud-spattered clothes in a heap on the bathroom floor.
I unpacked the remains of our picnic and threw out the leftovers
with rancorous abandon, whether or not the seaweed would have
kept.

That night, and for days thereafter, I was taciturn and morose; Edison left me to my sulk. He was waiting for me to get
over it, as if a nearly eight-year marriage and the adoption of two
children were on a par with the junior high crushes he'd watched
implode in a torrent of tears as a world-weary high school track
star. Meanwhile, I left Fletcher pleading phone messages. I sent
beseeching emails and texts, eliciting not a single reply. It was
murder to stop myself from using Cody as a go-between.

Edison lobbed a few unpersuasive assurances that Fletcher
and I would patch things up after my husband got over his snit,
but I knew Fletcher—a man of few strong moves, who when he

packed up his kids and walked out on Cleo had never looked back. Besides, my brother failed to suppress a burbling cheerfulness about this turn of the wheel, and he didn't *want* to be persuasive.

Yet for me, all that had once been thick had gone runny, the way a reheated cornstarch custard can break its emulsion and water. Edison as an addition to my family was one thing, as the whole of my family quite another. I grant there's a comforting steadiness to the sibling tie; except for the odd blowup like the one over the pizza box in January, Edison and I had thrummed along with the mild ebb and surge of crickets. But I missed the more orchestral crescendos and glissandos of marriage, and had never imagined myself getting old with my brother. I knew there were such couples, at whose loyalty others marveled, but mostly people felt sorry for grown live-in siblings, who had settled for something lesser and slightly wrong. Without any inbuilt conclusion to our dodgy cohabitation, this weight-loss project dribbled to the horizon, no longer finite and climactic, but ceaseless and a chore. The fact that it never stopped raining made me feel trapped in a giant pathetic fallacy—as if I were starring in a heavy-handed film noir.

Having been working myself up to a showdown over solid food, following that fatal bike ride I wasn't in the mood. On the six-month anniversary of Edison's having taken the BPSP pledge—and I now refused to reference their envelopes as "Upchuck," our in-house lingo too pally—I skipped all the prefatory jollying I'd been contriving for weeks and cut callously to the chase.

"No more liquid diet," I announced on our return from Monotonous—my business now aptly named, since the tedium of manufacturing *doll babies* was suddenly rubbing me the wrong way as radically as my overnight roommate-for-life. We'd taken the car; I wasn't biking in this weather. "Time to eat."

"I'm nowhere near one-sixty-three," said Edison, as I'd known he would.

"You already skipped the week of real food in the middle. The literature is unequivocal. Six months max." My tone was retributive, as if I planned to force gray, lumpy gruel down his throat with a plunger.

"Just a couple more months, then," Edison parlayed.

"Not one more day. You will start with soup, including soft, digestible starch like overcooked potato, along with fruit juices and vegetable purees."

He bunched in his recliner and folded his arms. "Sounds fuckin' awful."

"I don't care." I'd originally contemplated making him the cool, bright vichyssoise that I'd pictured for my own fast breaking, but now I couldn't be bothered and strode to the kitchen to open a can of commercial cream of chicken. I wasn't a bit concerned with whether he liked it.

I slopped orange juice into a glass and banged the soup bowl on the table. I felt sadistic. It was a new feeling, one I could come to like. "You will now consume eight hundred and ten calories per day for the next month."

"This is nuts," he objected. "We can't just—"

"I know. *But there's no ceremony.* Well, I've got news for you: after all this build-up, food is a big drag. It doesn't take much time. It's not interesting. It never was interesting. So eat your stupid soup, drink your stupid juice, and then we've still got to find a stupid movie we can stand to watch on TV."

"I don't want any."

"Too bad. Just because you've ruined my marriage doesn't mean I'm stuck in this apartment regardless. Deal's the same as ever: do what I say, or I'm outta here."

His voice went small. "I'm scared."

"So? If you had any sense, you were scared the first time you played the piano in front of a live audience. You can at least face down cream of chicken."

Edison eased warily from the recliner, eyeing his sister from a distance as if assessing a pet exposed to rabies.

"Hurry up, it's getting cold."

Edison settled at the table, his chair pushed back from the bowl. "I told you, man: I don't want it. And I don't *wanna* want it."

"*I do not give a shit.*" I swear, it was all I could do to keep from hitting him, or hurling the soup in his face. "You think the last six months were the hard part? Well, think again. Eating nothing is easy. Eating something but not very much is an ever-loving bitch. You're right, you're not finished, not at your target weight. But guess what. You're never going to be finished. You think this is about getting to one-sixty-three, and then you can relax. Big surprise, *bro*. You can never relax. You have to learn to eat all over again. And the bad news? Once you've messed up as badly as you did, and made food into this personal pitfall, and then this giant source of anxiety, going through all the obsessive hullabaloo with little envelopes, well . . . Eating is never going to be the same again. It's always going to make you nervous, and it's never going to be much fun. You've ruined that. Got it? So the *next* six months, they're going to be *even harder.*"

Pitching his soup as challenge rather than indulgence was

canny. Edison edged his chair closer to the table and leaned over to sniff. He glowered. "Smells terrible."

"*Eat it.*" I had a future as a prison guard.

He loaded a spoonful. It pooled there, congealing. How impatient Oliver must have felt with me, the first time at our diner. Under my hard glare, Edison took a sip.

"There," I said viciously. "Thanks to a few shreds of chicken and specks of melted potato, you've lost your virginity. Back to Go. You're mortal again. Just a regular guy, gotta drop sixty-five pounds—nothing special, dull as dishwater."

Edison finished the spoonful and looked wretched.

"How's it taste?" The question was malicious.

"Like . . ." He scuppered the spoon and wafted his hands. "Like who-cares."

"Told you," I said victoriously. "Now, since your sister will pour the rest of it through a funnel into your nose if she has to, you might as well finish the bowl." I marched to the kitchen to prepare my own stupid little chicken breast, stupid little pile of stupid little rice, and stupid little salad.

"This is depressing, man," came from the dining table.

"Tough."

A little later: "That wasn't fair, man. What you said before. About ruining everything."

"It's true," I said. "You have ruined food, probably forever. That's what happens when you put on hundreds of pounds of self-pity for no reason."

"No. That crack about your marriage. I don't see why Feltch's issuing you a pink slip is all my fault."

I couldn't control myself. "Fact: if you hadn't popped up as a basket case on my doorstep, I would at this very minute be sitting down to dinner with my husband and stepdaughter, exchanging the stories of our day. No big fat Edison, no divorce."

"I never intended to break you guys up, did I? And I tried to be cool with the cat. Feltch was the one kept picking fights with *me*."

"You've gotten what you wanted. Little sister, on call, slipper-fetching, unencumbered by any of the inconvenient relationships that *grown-ups* have. Now we can be brother and sister, living together happily ever after, the sort people whisper about and wonder if there isn't something strange going on. Just exactly how I wanted my life to turn out. But what does my life matter, if big brother has finally lost some weight."

A wisp of a memory visited of how horrible I had been to Solstice, convincing her at four after a few strands came out in the comb that every bit of her hair was going to fall out and she'd better get used to wearing hats, when in truth I was angry my mother was dead, and taking it out on a weaker party wasn't going to change that.

"Look, I'm sorry, man." Edison had started to blubber. Perhaps he was fragile after the crushing disappointment of that soup and his humiliating demotion to humdrum dieter in a spoonful. Besides, never underestimate the effects of starvation on the brain. He'd cried a few days earlier because he couldn't claw the packing tape off an Amazon shipment. "I shouldn't have let you do this, man. Not when Feltch wasn't cool with it. I shoulda gone off somewhere, on my own like a monk or something, and only showed my face again when I wasn't a fucking embarrassment."

Okay, I couldn't keep up the brutality, though as it slipped away I knew I would miss it. I shuffled out, slid my plate on the table, and squeezed my brother's hand.

"It's not really your fault," I said glumly. "This whole thing was my idea. Fletcher warned me up front. I didn't take him seriously enough. I'm only blaming you because you're here. Brothers and sisters get to treat each other like shit. It must be, like, in the Constitution. A *human right*. And in the end we're still brother and sister because *you* can't tell me you want a divorce. We're stuck with each other. That's what's bad about us, but that's what's good, too. Maybe it helps me to have someone to yell at."

"Yell your fuckin' heart out, then." I hadn't bothered to provide him a napkin, so Edison blew his nose in his shirttail. "If it makes you feel better."

"Even the other day. The bike ride. I knew we were being too chummy. Leaving Fletcher out. I knew that would make him mad. But I still hung with you. Because it was easier. We have a thing now. Fletcher's harder for me to reach. I shouldn't have asked you along in the first place. But I was anxious about spending the day with him. I thought I asked you to come because you could use the day out. But I obviously asked you for my own sake. To feel safe."

"I make you feel safe?"

"Yeah." I took a flavorless bite and chewed. "And Fletcher could tell. That I was sort of clinging to you. That was the last straw, I figure." I pushed my plate away.

"I ain't the only one gotta eat, babe." He pushed it back. He closed my hand around my fork.

Sourly, I stabbed a lettuce leaf. "Sorry about the soup. Could have done better, for your first meal."

"Wouldn't have made any difference. It's just, you can't help but fantasize . . ."

"I tried to describe the big letdown in April, but I could tell you didn't believe me."

"So what's the moral of the story? Everything sucks?"

"Not everything. Food sucks. But, you know. Us, here. Sometimes. It hasn't all totally completely sucked."

"Put that on my gravestone," said Edison. "*It hasn't all totally completely sucked.*"

"That's more than most people could claim."

"You regret it, though?" asked Edison. "Do it all over again, you put me on that plane?"

I thought about it. I didn't want to give him a cheap answer. "Nah," I concluded. "I'd do it again, I guess. Something might have gone off the rails with Fletcher, even without Prague Porches. Maybe there's something deeper wrong. At least . . ." I choked up a little. "At least I'm not all by myself."

Being directly emotional with my brother always felt awkward. I think siblings are supposed to take each other for granted. Which has a bad reputation, but the world out there is precarious, as I'd recently discovered, and it's a joy and a relief to take someone, anyone, for granted.

Many of my neighbors would find this inexplicable, but I may not be the only one who looks back on the rest of that month with a backhanded nostalgia. Personally, I was desperate for distraction, and grateful to be pulled out of myself—to do good works on a larger canvas than my brother's belly. They don't call these things "disasters" for nothing, of course, and the reconstruction is still not completed to this day. But I was moved by how utterly Edison threw himself into the community effort. The brother who arrived nine months earlier would have put his feet up and watched the spectacle gleefully on TV.

New Holland is on raised ground, though multiple base-
ments filled with water. I was sorry that my status as persona non
grata meant I couldn't give Cody and Fletcher a hand with moving his backlog of furniture in the basement to the ground floor;
the table saw was too heavy for them to manage, and I gather my
estranged husband's most treasured tool of his trade was ruined.
At Prague Porches, we were on the second floor, so we didn't have
to worry about Edison's upright—which freed us to volunteer
our services in Cedar Rapids. Once we'd secured our stock on
upper shelves, I closed Monotonous until further notice, so that
my employees could pull on rubber boots and lend a hand. It was
the worst flood in Iowa on record, on a scale the state shouldn't
expect more than once every five hundred years.

For the first time, I discovered one line of work more fatigu-
ing than a catering business: sandbagging. To deplete different
sets of muscles, I mixed up the tasks—shoveling, passing bags
down the line, and stacking pallets, though the job of keeping
the sacks open while someone else shoveled we tried to reserve
for kids, since whole families cropped up in droves. (Cody joined
us on a couple of afternoons, but of course it was an issue, and
most of the time she lent a hand nearer to New Holland with her
father. Her primary job was to ascertain where we were working
so that Fletcher could work somewhere else.) For five solid days,
round the clock, thousands of volunteers from the area—and a
handful of Katrina survivors who drove up from Louisiana with
vats of Cajun chicken and a slightly knowing been-there-done-
that attitude that got on a few people's nerves—piled line upon
line of sandbags along the Cedar River and at the entrances of
businesses downtown. We relayed stacks around the Cedar Rapids Public Library while another set of volunteers packed books

into cartons to shift them to the second story, and fortified the ground floor of Mercy Medical Center to protect the generators in the hospital's basement.

Edison and I were grateful to have gotten in on the effort early, because in short order the big problem was an excessive response to KCRG's call for volunteers, and the station soon had to beg good Samaritans to stay away. The locals who'd braved hell and high water to lend a hand only to be told they weren't needed were the only folks I saw acting grumpy—as if they were being cheated, and I suppose in a way they were. For there's nothing like a catastrophe for bringing out warm good humor in people, and the spirit of heave-ho hilarity was contagious. I remember remarking to Edison, "You know, you sure wouldn't have been much use here at three-eighty-six," and he said, "Yo, six months ago I'da *been* one of the sandbags, kid."

My brother was a comfort to workers who'd been relocated to Prairie High and were trying to take their minds off all the chattel they'd lost back in their evacuated neighborhoods. Most had rescued photographs and a change of clothes, but the furniture, electronics, and whole wardrobes were write-offs, and it was common for a sturdy, stoic volunteer to freeze briefly in a sandbag relay, shoulders slumping with a heavy sigh: "Oh, no, that quilt from my great-grandmother." Worst of all, since the river was fingering into areas that weren't previously on the flood plain, most of these exiles had no flood insurance.

"That's rough," Edison would say. "A while back, I lost everything I owned myself, save a few threads didn't fit anymore and an ancient computer. You wouldn't think it, but it's cleansing. Makes you lighter, man. Like, you wouldn't believe all the shit you can live without. It weighs you down"—he'd heft another bag along the line like a visual aid—"and not just by making you drag it from place to place. The shit makes you be the kinda person who has that shit. Suddenly you can be somebody who has totally different shit. Or no shit. Suddenly you can be anybody. It lets you go."

This was a situation that brought out the best of the Midwest, and while a few codgers made self-deprecatory jokes about bad backs, I never heard anyone really complain—even at the start, when it was still raining. Never mind the steady pummel from the sky, the real problem was getting soaked from sweat. Yet even once the sun came out, the Cedar River continued to rise.

The first couple of days, Edison had weighed out smoked turkey for his stinting packed lunch, but by the third day we'd run out of sandwich meat, and at the end of our shift a thankful local business drove in pizza pies. My brother was horrified. I said, "I am your coach, and you've just expended fifteen hundred calories in sand. Eat the pizza. And that's an order." It was thin-crust, while he generally preferred the chewier New York style, but Edison said later that—unlike the verboten one in January—it was truly the best pizza he'd ever had.

The flood protection effort was a social enterprise, so perhaps it was to be expected that over that pizza Edison asked his bag-filling partner—a younger woman I'd be tempted to call a "girl"—back to our apartment for "a cup of coffee." It was a long drive for coffee, so I should have known the real agenda, but ever since Edison's weight gain I'm ashamed to say I hadn't thought of him as remotely sexual. So I made something of a fool out of myself, hanging about the living room with the two of them well after the coffee no one wanted had cooled. Exhausted from the day's labors, I was waiting impatiently for her to ask for a ride home, until I realized that they were waiting with considerably more impatience for *me* to go. Embarrassed, I went to bed.

I woke stiff and in the first really bad mood since the welcome distraction of civic-mindedness began. The girl—Angie or something—was still here, and the fact that she'd come in our car so of course she was still here didn't quell my irritation. She emerged from Edison's bedroom with that languorous sense of territorial entitlement that intimate congress grants total strangers, however temporarily. Slender with lustrous enough chestnut hair, she still didn't seem that attractive to me, and I'd an intuition "Angie" had volunteered in Cedar Rapids to begin with merely for bragging rights. That morning, she kept draping herself around Edison's shoulders while he played the piano and I made coffee at a time of day people actually wanted to drink it. After gushing over my brother's playing, she ran down a series of women's-glossy dieting tips, when Edison's intake was my department, thank you, and I found it a tad inappropriate that, having known this woman for less than a day, he had already spilled his guts about his history as a walking Lifetime documentary. He could have been a little more private.

That evening, I felt sheepish that I hadn't been friendlier, though this mild remorse was facilitated by the fact that Edison had refrained from bringing her back a second night. He evidenced some of the old swagger of his randy adolescence, and I was pleased to see it. "Shit, man," he said, stretching beside the scale whose high tolerance he no longer required, "haven't let anyone see me in the buff in ages. Can you believe it? She thought I was hot stuff."

"You are," I said bashfully. "Barring a certain few years, you always were."

Looking back, considering how much the encounter boosted his confidence, I should have encouraged him to keep seeing the girl, and I don't quite understand why I was so relieved at the time that he didn't follow up.

On June 13th, the Red Cross and National Guard decided we'd done what we could and it was time to clear out. Our dismissal was crushing. We didn't want to give up, and if we were honest with ourselves we were having a wonderful time. Edison and I watched the river crest on local news back home, luxuriating in having electricity—unlike most of the residents we'd been forced to abandon. On news-helicopter footage, rooftops looked like lily pads. Later they estimated that the flood covered thirteen hundred city blocks. The mid-river island on which the Cedar Rapids City Hall sat was completely submerged, and the roof of the library we'd worked so hard to save barely rose from the gray, murky sea. Street signs poked an inch above the water, as if identifying roadways in Atlantis.

Nobody involved in that mobilization likes to admit it, but most of our sandbagging didn't do any good.

I have a bittersweet memory of that summer. As the weeks went by, with nothing but stone silence emanating from Solomon Drive, it came home to me in a series of agonizing increments that Fletcher was serious—the most painful our anniversary in July, which my husband wouldn't even acknowledge with a text. I wasn't taking a break from my home life to coach my brother's weight loss; I was separated, and lived in daily dread of a bailiff at my door serving formal divorce papers. At least Cody continued to treat me like her mother, making dogged visits and accompanying us to the movies. Though I discouraged her from playing up her father's pining in my absence—"I've seen this series, sweetheart," I abjured, "even the reruns"—she played the go-between anyway. She thought she was sly, but there's only so subtle a fourteen-year-old gets.

Commonly, in summertime Iowa comes into its own—the air musty with overturned earth, the corn rising by the day to tower by the roadsides, sweeping with alternating patches of bluer soy fields to the horizon. I associated this time of year with the happiest periods of my childhood, when Edison and I were ritually packed off to visit our paternal grandparents for a solid month. (So indelibly had Iowa in July been imprinted on my mind that my first experience of an Iowan winter was a shock. Before I moved here, I envisioned the Midwest as eternally hot, thick, and green.) My brother's memories of those stays weren't as bucolic as mine; he'd resented being put to work during his vacation, and when he got older he stayed behind in L.A. to haunt jazz clubs and practice his piano. But I loved giving the Grumps a hand on the farm. Having relished physical labor from an early age, I gladly fed their few hogs, mucked out the barn, and harvested flat beans in the beating sun.

Yet that summer defied the season's halcyon stereotype, and a desolate countryside mirrored the muddy sensation that daily sludged the pit of my stomach. Dismal tracts of our devastated local corn crop were taunting reminders that my life, too, was now a washout: lo, I was no longer a woman who, after a long, lonely young adulthood, had at last found herself a reliable, quietly passionate man with two animated, ready-made children—a woman who finally had a life—but a divorcée in waiting, entering middle age with my older brother for a helpmate. The rows of dead sticks that stubbled slick black fields painted a landscape of stunted promise, blighted hopes. Everywhere I looked I saw pointless destruction and ravaged domestic comity, the curbsides stacked with mottled couches and water-logged freezers, the region's sanitation workers overburdened by all-too-tangible emblems of loss, resignation, and grief. Roadside vistas that June and July—the tarmac itself often cracked and caked, the gutters strewn with mashed litter and the mangled detritus of lawn furniture, windshield wipers, and jungle gyms, all uniformly muted by a putrid, diarrheal silt—reflected back at me the brown, sodden interior of my own head.

In the very season of my discontent, the spoilage of my own Iowan idyll, Edison was cleaving to the land of our father's with a new ferocity. The retreating floodwaters left a mournfulness in their wake that he inhaled like the aroma of fertile soil—for if mournfulness has a smell, it's loamy, with that hint of corruption, like cow manure. The sorrow in the air supplied my brother a density, a seatedness, a gravity and depth that contentment alone cannot provide.

Why, he'd dropped altogether all those cracks about our no-wheresville state and the crackers who dangled silver "bull's balls" under the license plates of their jacked-up dually pickups, with GO HAWKEYES plastered on the bumpers. My brother wasn't so far gone that he'd caught the local mania for U of I's football team, but he'd started to delight in the easy pace of life here—the expanse, the serenity, and the space. He seldom mentioned New York, much less referenced any intention to return there. He used to fret at the quiet, but now savored the subtle surge of crickets, a rooster crow, the *eh-eh-eh* of goats. Rather than roll his eyes while checkout clerks at Hy-Vee chatted amiably about the popularity of a special on butter, he'd shoot the breeze with the bagger himself, still amazed that no one in the line behind us ever acted impatient. He no longer plied the grocery boys with a five-spot for loading our bags in the trunk, knowing they'd be insulted; a bit of buoyant banter en route to the car was all the payment they required. He was starting to see the point of people who talked to each other, even when there wasn't always much to say, and he commiserated with displaced or financially devastated neighbors in a spirit that conveyed the flood hadn't happened to *them* but to *us*. I no longer detected in him any hint of contempt or restlessness in this big, blank place, and I heard him more than once on the phone to Tanner *defending* my stepson's home state, whose charms were rarely apparent to the young people who were born here. Honestly, I began to suspect that, as far as Iowa was concerned, Edison was a convert.

With more energy on proper food—come July, I upped his daily intake to 1,200 calories—he grew more adventurous, checking out the Iowa City Jazz Festival and driving into the university town on weekends to sit in on jam sessions at The Mill. I often went with him, and was struck by how absolutely he declined to name-drop. When I'd tagged along to his gigs in New York, he'd schmoozed with the audience between sets, always managing to insinuate the fact that he was Travis Appaloosa's son. These days, when he introduced himself he routinely stuck his hand out announcing his first name alone. He never mentioned the "heavy cats" he'd played with, either. He arrived like any old guy who happened to play the piano in his spare time, and as a consequence he knocked their socks off.

My brother contended with his ongoing terror of comestibles by becoming obsessively scientific. After consulting the poster of calorie values now magneted to the fridge, he weighed every tomato to the exact ounce on a digital scale. He worked out the total energy in his ingredients on a calculator, and I never caught him rounding down. Indeed, the kitchen was littered with pads, their pages striated with columns of figures. I was tempted to urge him to relax a bit—an extra half carrot would hardly be the end of the world—but he didn't trust himself one hair off the straight and narrow, and if all this lunatic weighing and sawing away little lumps of veal helped him feel self-possessed, fine.

Albeit on a slower schedule, the solid-food stage of this project continued to produce steady progress. In Month Seven, Edison lost twelve pounds, only two fewer than the previous one, when he'd still been on protein shakes. It's true that the final weigh-in of Month Eight was a particular low point, for which he blamed me, railing that he should never have commenced that 1,200-calorie daily intake. *I* said that most people would be pleased as punch to have lost eight pounds in a month, and at 209 he was looking better than ever. (I know this numerical stuff seems dry, but you can't imagine how emotional these confrontations with the scale were; for Edison, the drop from twelve to eight pounds in a month was devastating.) At least subsequent totals demonstrated that I'd been right: he had to eat more to burn more, and his metabolism was ramping up.

Though our refrigerator was full of produce from roadside farm stands, I was doleful about missing out on our garden on Solomon Drive, and found myself calculating from afar how big the zucchini were growing, when the green peppers would come on, whether the sweet-pea vines had peaked. I continued to fruitlessly scan my inbox for fletcher.feuerbach@gmail.com, and to retrieve the last of my cell-phone messages with a heavy heart.

Running errands in New Holland, I was tortured by familiar glimpses, only to discover that the cyclist was Korean. On one occasion I really did spot Fletcher; stricken, I about-faced. The dizzying effect of the adrenaline whited out any useful intelligence: what he was up to, whether he looked cheerful or glum.

Alas, the dispositional disjunction between Edison and me was a revelation: apparently no matter how satisfied a loved one, how proximate his pleasure, how drastic the contrast between his present joy and the dejection of his recent past, or how abstractly gratified you may feel by having played a substantial role in his restoration, no one else's happiness can quite stand in for your own. Battling a pernicious dolor, I often felt as if I were observing my brother from a great distance when he was only in the next room.

Yet better to watch a boisterous, diligent, considerate brother from a remove than a despondent, suicidally fat one from close up. After we were mugged by yet another unsolicited care package from Solstice—containing a wind-up donkey, a tiny framed picture of the Dalai Lama, and a fancy enameled ballpoint that didn't write—he conducted a couple of long calls with his younger sister whose slight tedium was worth it; embraced by her legendary sibling, she stopped regarding the two of us as being holed up against her. Since I'd put him on salary at Baby Monotonous, he no longer hit me up for spending money, and lived within his means. Initially reluctant to work for his sister and so resentful of my company's success that he'd had the gall to blame that cover story in *New York* for triggering his compulsive eating, my brother was now campaigning to become the general manager at our plant, freeing me up for more creative exploration of new products. While during our original furnishing of

Prague Porches Edison had hung back sullenly and smoked, he'd started browsing online for a grander dining table now that we propped something more amusing on the laminated one than herbal tea—though I was interested that he never suggested we move to a better apartment or proper house; maybe he was afraid that moving together would open the door to the possibility that we could also move apart.

Somehow, miraculously, and I am not sure how this happened, Edison Appaloosa had adjusted to the idea of a normal life. That may sound a modest achievement, but for anyone in our family it was monumental. In the limitless temporal pasture one wanders on an all-liquid diet, perhaps he had reviewed his own career highlights—like accompanying Harry Connick in an impromptu jam session—only to conclude, as I had regarding mine, that these were not the highlights of his larger life. However he did it, the glad embrace of a quietly productive, low-profile existence requires far more spiritual maturity than the insatiable pursuit of headlines, and in this sense my big brother was finally growing up.

Yet a conversation with Oliver in August stands out in my memory. We'd had a difficult time finding a date to get together one-on-one without my excluding Edison so emphatically that it might have been hurtful; my brother was forever filling our free time with jaunts to the IMAX, the Science Museum, and pick-your-own raspberry farms. At last when Cody asked to spend a long day at the Iowa State Fair in Des Moines alone with her uncle—Edison was so touched that his eyes welled—I invited my old friend to dinner.

Oliver hadn't been by for a few weeks, and surveyed our apartment with uneasy appreciation. "Wow, this is beginning to look—settled."

Although to begin with the place had had that impersonal cookie-cutter quality of a model apartment, now framed black-and-whites of Edison's icons lined the walls—Bud Powell, Art Tatum, Herbie Nichols, and Earl Hines. The barn-plank dining table had arrived by then, with funky, rough-hewn chairs. The rooms were warmed with touches—a kooky umbrella stand, an antique milk crate bulging with back copies of *Jazz Times*, begonias on the kitchen pass-through. The round face of our big red scale was topped with a yard-sale Stetson, lending our sentinel a cowboy strut, while the Pandora doll leered drunkenly atop the piano. A photo montage improved on the lone birthday shot of my brother at 386: Edison and me at Monotonous; Edison and me sandbagging; our most recent addition, Edison entering his weight on the calendar the first morning he dropped below "two large." Seeing our lair with Oliver's eyes, I realized it wasn't a rehab clinic anymore. It was a home.

"I've been surprised to discover Edison's domestic side," I said. "I always thought of him as the sort who never has milk in the fridge. But after losing everything to that storage company, maybe he's ready to anchor himself with stuff again."

"He's ready to anchor himself with something," said Oliver warily. He ambled over to my double and pulled the string: *Oh, no, not ANOTHER photo shoot!*

"There's nothing like having your nose rubbed in your fake humility to keep you humble for real." I poured us cautious glasses of white wine. "It's good for Edison, being *settled*. I'd never have believed it, but he may stay in Iowa for keeps."

"I don't find that surprising. *You* live in Iowa."

"So? My living here didn't influence his residence for twenty years."

"No . . ." Oliver took a seat at the table. "Is he seeing any-body?"

"Not that I know of, and I'm sure he'd tell me. He hasn't brought anyone over since that one-night stand during the flood. It's as if he was making sure the equipment was still in order, like getting your car inspected once a year. Maybe he's not ready."

"Why should he ever be ready? What could he find in some strange woman that he doesn't have now?"

"Sex, obviously. Our relationship isn't that kinky."

"It's pretty kinky."

I busied myself in the kitchen. I'd been looking forward to our tête-à-tête, but this conversation was setting me on edge.

"After all, a little sister makes the perfect wife, in a way," Oliver continued. "Undemanding. A known quantity—intimate, but not in any way that's scary. Adoring. Permanently second fiddle, since don't imagine a little bossing around about his diet trumps hardwired birth order. You've provided him a de facto family with Cody, and isn't he still funneling advice to your step-son over the phone?"

I trimmed the fat off our pork loins. Now that Fletcher had used the D-word, I'd half expected Oliver to make a move on me again. A respectful period of time had passed, too, but he hadn't—as if I were still married, but not to Fletcher.

"Yes, he is," I said lightly. "I hate to admit it, but Edison is the only one who takes Tanner's screenwriting ambitions se-riously. He's a big proponent of preposterous dreams, since he pursued one himself."

"My point is, your brother's got everything he needs. Maybe not sex, but I bet when you've been that heavy for years you're used to living without. A girlfriend would blow all that. He'd have to take his chances with someone he hasn't known since she was zero years old, who isn't structurally subservient, and who feels free to break it off."

"Remember, officially this arrangement of ours is only for one year."

"It'll have been a year in three months. When was the last time you told Edison that in early December he's got to find another apartment?"

"I didn't say that."

"So this living together thing—it *is* permanent."

"I didn't say that either."

"No. You haven't said much."

I brought our salad to the table and sat squarely across from Oliver. "Do you *like* Edison?" Strangely, I'd never before asked him this point-blank.

Oliver considered. "I'm *sympathetic* with Edison," he determined. He was scrupulous about emotions, careful to be as precisely truthful about his feelings as he would be about external facts. It was one of the things I loved about him: he never chose the first bland word at his disposal out of laziness, in this case "yes."

"I can see 'sympathy' as of a year ago," I said, "but not now."

"Especially now."

"Why? I've never seen him happier in his life."

"Exactly."

This conversation was upsetting me; I wasn't sure why.

"He still hasn't learned to eat like a normal person, has he?" Oliver continued. "He's still measuring every morsel to the tenth of an ounce."

"That's right. He's closing in, but he hasn't reached his target. This isn't changing the subject?"

"It isn't changing the subject. And he still won't go out to eat?"

"He doesn't trust restaurants, even when they post calorie counts."

"And you said he was addicted to heroin for a while, too."

"Another *non* non sequitur? He claims he wasn't addicted. He only tried it."

"This whole project. With you. It's everything he lives for. It's the latest heroin. But you can't be on a crash diet forever. The only thing left for him to do when your project is through is to gain the weight right back."

"You sound just like Fletcher! Edison could instead move on to doing something more *interesting* than either eating or not-eating, and I don't know why everyone is so goddamn cynical!"

"Calm down. I said I was sympathetic. But all the measuring, and notating, and weighing in. This setup, this pretend-open-ended playing house with you. He's delicate. He is not in control of himself. He's only in control of the control. Once the controls are lifted, he's in control of nothing."

"Right over my head."

Oliver tried again. "Exercising control is not the same thing as being in control. It's the opposite. When you're really in hand, there's only doing what you want. There aren't two of you."

Still opaque to me, and mercifully we moved on.

Cleaning up after Oliver went home, I reflected that, if a little sister made an ideal wife, I was less convinced that an older brother made an ideal husband. I despaired of the very companionability that Edison treasured, an absence of friction that I associated with bad sex. Yet one of Oliver's points was well taken: my brother did indeed give every indication that he expected our arrangement to continue indefinitely. He wondered aloud if "we" should consider buying a new car, weighed in on whether I should accept interview requests from local publications like the *Des Moines Register* as if he aspired to be my personal manager as well as my production plant's, and had recently proposed a cross-country bike trip through the Midwest once he was well established on a full-calorie maintenance diet the following summer. He took it as a given that we would shop together, ride to work together, dine together, and hit jazz clubs in Iowa City together. These hand-in-hand presumptions were sweet, but an anxiety had started to build in me that, contrary to Fletcher's prediction that Edison was destined to "break my heart," I was more apt to break my brother's.

chapter ten

Those last three months I observed Edison's tunnel vision with conflicted admiration and disquiet. In his determination to fulfill his purpose by our one-year anniversary, my brother had eerily duplicated my husband, as if I were karmically fated to live with Mr. Perfect. Biking to work, he was the one who urged me to hurry up. He'd started jogging as well, keen to retrieve some semblance of his track-star adolescence. He was so focused on the end point at which he would clock in at exactly 163 that he never alluded to any occasion that might proceed it, not even Christmas.

What did he think was going to happen—he'd turn into a butterfly? Ascend to sit at the right hand of God the Father? Where would he channel all that obsessive energy when we'd achieved our goal? I hadn't wanted to give ground at the time, but Fletcher had been right at our disastrous picnic: weight loss made for a pretty shabby religion, if only because for faithful adherents it had a sell-by date; you could only continue to worship at the altar of comestible restraint if you chronically failed your vows. I kept remembering what it had been like to overshoot my own destination. Downsizing hadn't made me happy. Rather, I'd felt lost, and bored, and robbed, as well as frightened and flummoxed by something as mundane as regular meals. Looking back, too, what had been most soul destroying was getting a grip: taking a step back in the privacy of my room, facing the mirror squarely, and confronting the fact that being a little thinner was trivial. On a host of levels, from health to self-respect, I supposed it was important that Edison would no longer draw cruel remarks at baggage claim from people who'd resented having been seated next to him. But it didn't matter a jot if he weighed 163 or 164, and I worried that this discovery could plunge him into darkness. I wondered why people ever tried to accomplish anything when attainment of every sort was inbuilt with a forlorn *Well, so—what's next?*

"You do realize that the *really* hard part is *after* you've attained your objective," I warned in mid-November while Edison was toweling down after a run.

He guffawed. "You're such a trip. What, a year ago, losing this weight was gonna be 'the hardest thing I'd ever done.' Got that right. But then solid food was 'the really hard part,' and now being a normal-size person is 'the really hard part.' Man, talk about a moving target. No matter what I do, the 'really hard part' is still glooming down the road. You gotta lighten up, babe. As a coach, you might figure out a better motivating strategy than unrelenting dread."

"All right. Let's plan something to look forward to, then. We should have a party. To celebrate. A Coming of Size party."

"Now you're talkin'."

We consulted the calendar. In Month Eleven, he'd dropped 10.2 pounds. If he upped his burn to twelve pounds with additional exercise, Edison should be sliding into home plate on our one-year anniversary to the day. "Don't you want to give yourself a little leeway?" I proposed.

"Panda Bear, before I arrived in your lap, I'd allowed myself a whole lifetime's worth of *leeway*. December sixth is the ticket. We got three weeks and change, just about the right lead time to send out invites. Speaking of which—you figure your ex-in-waiting is an honorable cat?"

"I don't know how *honorable* it is to jettison your wife just because she's loyal to her own brother." I'd grown a little bitter. "But until last June I'd have said yes, supremely honorable. That's why his big-baby flouncing off was such a shock."

"Then you gotta invite Feltch. He owes me, man: one whole chocolate cake, downed in a sitting."

"You remember that."

"I remember that jive, condescending wager every day."

" . . . I can't promise he'll come through. Circumstances have changed."

"What ain't changed is he insulted me, man. All that shit when the fucking chair broke, about not being able to find my dick. About how I'm some homeless loser leeching off my sister, just 'pretending' to be a respected jazz musician. Then when we left, how I'd never be able to do it, how my will was 'flabby.' Fuck him. I want to see him eat crow. I want to see him eat humble cake."

So benign had Edison's demeanor grown of late that his acidity took me aback. Somewhere in there was still the wounded pride that had gotten him into this mess, and had also gotten him out. But however I feared the prospect of Fletcher refusing or accepting the invitation in equal measure, I owed it to Edison to extend one. It was his achievement, his party, his guest list.

T he single enduring satisfaction of my own diet had been self-recognition: the image in my mirror bore some relation to me, replacing a swollen imposter who had doubled as both caricature and rebuke. For me, Edison's transformation over our year together had been marked by a sequence of recognitions, most dramatically that afternoon in March, when the sun's shaft through the window unearthed his cheekbones at last.

His final weeks of tapering issued in a threshold shift more dramatic still. The loss of that last handful of pounds scooped oysters of flesh from his cheeks, chiseled his chin and nose, and dissolved the little overhang above his belt. Consequently, that wild keyboard smile consumed a larger proportion of his face, seeming larger, brighter, more dangerous. Geometrically, he retrieved the rhythms of his teenage years—his hips low slung, his thighs sinewy from running, his shoulders sharp. I knew he was dismayed by the excess skin that creped his torso, so that he wouldn't leave his bedroom without a shirt, and I'd hinted that maybe we could have the slack taken up surgically if it continued to bother him. And he couldn't do anything about the fact that his spine had compressed; he was permanently a couple of inches shorter. Be that as it may, during that final month he even moved differently, with the loping, double-jointed looseness with which he had sauntered the halls of Verdugo Hills High whistling "Summertime." As December 6th drew close, my brother turned heads in the street again, and not because he was fat.

So far I've played down the pleasures of narrowing my own mortal coil on the horizontal axis, not wanting to seem a petty slave to women's glossies. But once again burning with wide-eyed admiration for my brother, well—that didn't feel petty. Maybe it is impossible to inhabit your own achievements, because you get attached to the quest itself, its drive, its addictive amphetamine buzz and powering sense of purpose, so that any mission's fulfillment feels like a loss, all that energy and direction replaced with a stillness within whose halo strivers rapidly grow restless. Yet it may be possible to glory in the achievements of people you love—in the fact that my brother's beauty, always perceptible to me in some measure, was once more made manifest for everyone to see.

He says he'll come." Closing our door behind her, Cody couldn't contain her excitement. This time I'd had to use her as an interlocutor, since I'd had no confirmation that Fletcher read my emails or listened to my phone messages. And I'd promised my brother. "He wasn't going to," she said, "but I reminded him of that bet. You know, he's a stickler."

"Yes, he's always adhered to the letter of the law," I agreed, already jittery, though the party was days away.

"Yeah, but if the cat's 'a stickler,'" Edison noted, "I can't weigh in two-hundredths of an ounce over one-sixty-three or no cake."

"Well, you can't gain weight from reading," I said. "Because we have to find a recipe—as evil as possible."

That evening we pored over the cookbooks I'd accumulated while living on protein powder, finally settling on "Chocolate

Dump Cake," which I quite liked the sound of. The name had an assaulting heaviness, a thunking quality, the *kaboom* of a colossal confection that would land on your lawn from the back of a truck. The following night, Edison brought home two rectangular baking pans so big that they'd barely fit in the oven.

"Aren't you going overboard?" I said. "You can't expect Fletcher to consume an iced, two-layer sheet cake all by himself."

"He said 'a' cake. Didn't say how big, man. Now who's the stickler?"

"But you'll make him sick! Pukingly, violently sick!"

Edison laughed. "Look. We can't have all these folks over, serve a motherfucking gorgeous chocolate cake, and only let one guest have any. So, do I mean to horrify the living fuck out of him? Sure. But once he's stuffed his fatuous face with a shit-eating piece, it'll be open season."

G iven that Edison had lived in Iowa for just over a year, I was surprised by how many people were eager to help him celebrate having successfully photocopied himself at 42 percent. All my employees said they wouldn't miss our party for the world. Regulars at the Mill, a covey of students begged for invitations; they lionized my brother for his keyboard skills, with no idea he'd ever played at the Village Vanguard. A handful of acceptances came from functionaries with whom Edison would never have been on personal terms in other parts of the country: our landlord, a bank teller, a grocery bagger, a waitress at Java Joint, the guy at Barnes & Noble who special-ordered jazz magazines. Dr. Corcoran jumped at the chance to fête one of his rare success stories.

In planning the menu for our party, Edison eschewed the fried and the sweet—with the singular exception of the Chocolate Dump Cake, whose execution demanded a tippling tower of butter packets, two dozen eggs, and so much baking chocolate that he was obliged to clean out more than one supermarket. Yet that first week in December he never let shopping or chopping get in the way of his daily run, whose length he'd increased to an alarming ten miles. Once he'd weighed in at 168, too, he'd spurned the scale each morning, and for two weeks the calendar went blank. Drama is hard to come by in this game, and he wanted his first weigh-in at or below his target to serve as the theatrical centerpiece of our occasion. Considering the stakes, and the big brown gooey gauntlet Edison was planning to throw down before his bête noire, I admired his gambler's nerve.

The day before, he wasn't taking any chances. He upped his mileage to twelve (which was ridiculous—he limped back so tired that my brother the motormouth couldn't talk), and that night took a double dosage of senna that kept him in the bathroom half an hour the next morning. After one cup of black coffee, he refused to eat or drink all day, though he was on his feet from the get-go, and I knew firsthand how much physical work was entailed in catering a party for thirty-five. Alas, all this self-denial doubled his consumption of cigarettes, about which I'd started to nag—but Edison said, "Look, babe. Something's gotta give. One heroic transformation at a time, dig?" Oh, he'd never quit. My brother believed that paragons were "creepy," and only those unfiltered Camels now separated him from Fletcher Feuerbach.

I'd taken the day off from work to clean up, lay in drinks, arrange the rental china, and occasionally crack open a window to let out all that smoke. Unsure how one decorates for a Coming of

Size party, I wrapped a festive tie around the neck of the scale and tucked a feather in its Stetson. I placed a brace of leftover BPSP envelopes in the clutches of the Pandora doll atop the piano. On the one living room wall that wasn't covered in jazz icons, I tacked the voluminous pair of jeans we'd used on our snowman in February. Above them, I draped the shapeless cardigan in which Edison had habitually shambled on Solomon Drive. Then I rooted out my camera.

"Cheese!"

When Edison looked up from slicing mushrooms, I captured some of the old hunger, and not for french fries. His grin flashed with that voracity of times past, an appetite for life that mine could never equal. While the expectancy in his eyes must have regarded the party to begin in a few hours, this was also the face of the jazzman who had flown to Brazil, the south of France, Japan, who had stayed up until five a.m. tirelessly bashing keyboards in Manhattan jam sessions. Golden afternoon light softening the lines born of regret, obscurity, and disgrace, that photograph could almost be mistaken for a head shot taken in his room in Tujunga Hills, chin raised from his backpack as he prepared at seventeen for his seminal journey to New York City. Though I taped the printed-out eight-by-ten above the scarecrow of colossal clothes, the photo was so moving that the comedy I'd intended was lost.

With the cooking dispatched, Edison's computer preprogrammed with a tailor-made playlist—thick with inside jokes, like *Fats* Waller's "Ain't Misbehavin'" and *Fats* Domino's "I'm Livin' Right"—we dressed, our garments laid on our beds with all the solemnity with which one garbs the dead. In preparation for his ritual weigh-in, Edison had selected light fabrics—black slacks too thin for the season and a slithery cream short-sleeve striped in musical scores. I wore a matching cream-collared black dress, a present from Edison for my forty-second birthday the previous month that was shorter and more revealing than I'd ever have dared to wear the year before. We made a handsome couple.

Fortunately, we had nearly an hour, just us two, before the guests were due at eight. I needed to get my mind right before Fletcher arrived, and I wanted to give Edison his Official Trim Person present in private.

Edison hefted the package. "Whoa!"

"I know it weighs a lot, and you don't have to wear it when you take your turn on the scale. But you're going to be chilly in that flimsy outfit, with all those people opening the door. And"—I smiled—"I want to see you in it."

What he lifted from the wrapping had taken hours of online research to locate. "Man! This is enough to get me to believe in life after death! What did you do, track down some bargain-hunting hoarder at Box My Pad?"

"It's taken me a while to figure out where and when, but sometimes the application of a little money delivers."

As if donning the robes of a religious office, Edison whispered his arms through the lining, settled his shoulders into the cape, and raised the collar at the hugger-mugger tilt it had always assumed in New York. "Fuck me." He smoothed his hands down the front and nestled them deep in the pockets, striding gingerly to the mirror in his bedroom. "I swear, Panda Bear, it's the same fucking coat."

"It's Italian. Given the price tag, the leather must have come from Kobe beef. But let me tell you, it was worth it. You look fantastic. You look like yourself."

"*Was* it worth it? I don't mean just the coat."

"I have done one good thing. Maybe that's what I want on *my* gravestone."

Edison embraced me with fig-soft leather, and for a moment it did seem like his reincarnated trench coat: it had the same smell. I don't know how long we might have remained that way if the doorbell hadn't rung.

"Sorry I'm early." Cody bustled in with a wrapped box, a sheaf of music under the other arm. "But I walked over, in case you need some help. Besides, I wanted to go over this riff I've been working up for the refrain of 'The Boxer.' You know, all those *lie-la-lies* sound kinda dorky, but the intervals have possibilities." She dragged off her running shoes, and pulled a pair of dazzling high heels from her pack.

"You're going to play tonight?" I asked. Pre-Edison, Cody would never have performed for a crowd.

"Of course! And Edison and I have been working up a duet. What else?" She slipped into the heels. "'He Ain't Heavy, He's My Brother'!" She gave Edison a high five and stepped back. "Hey, you look fucking sharp, man! Hip threads! And that coat is the shit!"

"Don't look so bad yourself, sister."

I thought the slinky, rhinestone-decked cocktail dress a little grown-up for her, but then, I would. At least she still enjoyed a girlish impatience, insisting her uncle open his present right away: a fat, numbered, limited-edition Miles box set of twelve LPs, including a bio, photos, liner notes, and soft, heavy sleeves. Edison was delighted. If the underappreciated castoff she'd been so excited about tripping across at a yard sale wasn't the same as the set he'd lost to that self-storage joint, he didn't let on.

"You'd better not have snuck any Mars bars, man," she announced, sliding onto the piano bench. "'Cause I can't wait to see my dad's face plastered with fudge icing. Poor guy's been on this *raw food* jag lately, and all I ever see him eat is carrots. Finally got him to admit his jaw aches."

Now, over the years I've been forced to conclude that most celebrations don't work. The more carefully planned a signal occasion, the more likely it will trickle by on a pale tide of dilute well-meaningness. Christmases, birthdays, award ceremonies, and weddings are swallowed by planning and preparation on the one side and cleaning up on the other, and almost never seem to have actually happened. Speeches, applause, gift openings, presentations of plaques—somehow all these desperate gestures make the tribute fall only flatter, serve only to emphasize that an event has mysteriously failed to *occur*. I'm not sure what the problem is, besides a species-wide incapacity to seize the day, or a universal inability to anticipate that standing around with a drink in your hand is never going to be that great.

Yet once in a rare while the stars align, and a company convened for a purpose will be fully present. If we neatly lop off the very end of that evening—and let's do—Edison Appaloosa's Coming of Size party was one of those nights. I can't remember any other gathering that pulsed so with pleasure on another's behalf. For let's not forget that our guests did not congregate in a vacuum, but in a particular place at a precise point in time, and in the American state of Iowa early in the twenty-first century there was nothing folks admired more than dropping 223 pounds in a single year. It was one of those rare social circumstances in which guests greeted their host at the door with, "Hey, you look terrific!" and meant it.

Most people arrived with food—lasagnas, Carlotta's famous enchiladas, until we were running out of room on the barn-board table—and nearly everyone brought presents. Oliver, a handsome thirty-four-inch black belt pointedly lacking extra notches. Dr. Corcoran, a "World's Best Patient" coffee mug. Novacek, alas, a book of two-for-one Pizza Hut coupons, on the premise that his scrawny tenant could now afford to splash out on garlic-butter stuffed crust. One of our bank tellers, who had herself tried every diet under the sun to little avail, produced a garish velour tracksuit that Edison wouldn't be caught dead in, but he appreciated the nod toward his restored athleticism. Edison's little fan club of students from Iowa City had discovered my brother's discography online, and showed up with not only a top-shelf single malt, but copies of Edison's own CDs that they wanted him to sign.

We waited until after nine to bestow his present from the employees at Baby Monotonous. I was determined not to be distracted by the fact that Fletcher had still not shown up.

"Look, man, I could see where I was headed." Edison was holding court with the students beside the scale. "And it don't matter if you do yourself in with smack, booze, or hot dogs. Coroner did the autopsy thought Bird was sixty years old, man. Poor fucker was thirty-four."

I clapped. "Listen up!" Cody finished off "Mrs. Robinson" with a flourish as the crowd cleared a space. "I'm sorry for this to be so predictable"—I handed over the box—"but we worried that if you *didn't* get one, you'd be heartbroken."

Edison recognized the carton's proportions; he'd packed enough of them himself. "What else? Edison Appaloosa," he said before lifting the lid, "talking shit."

I'd given my workers a heads up about the trench coat—which Edison had kept on all evening—and they'd sewn a miniature in sumptuous black leather, with the same raised collar and tie belt. A cigarette was stitched between two fingers, in acknowledgment that expecting him to drop his last bad habit was a bridge too far. I was especially pleased with the hair, which knurled in dark-blond curlicues as if the doll had been electrocuted, and on our slimmest model looked cool and rock-star, just as on Edison's slender frame his real hair no longer imparted that Little Lord Fauntleroy quality of the spoiled toddler. He pulled the ring:

I was a *heavy cat*!

I've played with some *heavy cats*!

This Iowa trip is *deep*, you know what I'm sayin'?

Metheny is jive, man.

Wynton is jive, man.

Jarrett is such a douche. Bley is where it's at.

Steely Dan ain't *nothin'* without Wayne Shorter.

Where's your ear, Panda Bear, that couldn't be Ornette, it's *tenor* sax!

Trouble is I never played with *Miles*, man.

Jazz *education* about *followin'* the rules, *jazz* about *breakin'* 'em, *DIG*?

I lived on four envelopes of powder per day for six months.

Beat that, motherfucker.

These cornfields are the shit!

Oliver had had a ball with the too-hip-by-half recording, but I'd had a disconcertingly difficult time writing the script. Though I'd thrown in the lines about the *heavy cats* and Miles as a nod to the boastful and sometimes bitter brother who was wheeled into Cedar Rapids Airport the year before, Edison Take 2 neither habitually trotted out celebrity colleagues, nor incessantly bewailed that if he'd only managed to associate himself with his field's ultimate icon he'd be a star. He no longer carped about not having been born black. While the Edison doll I'd have crafted a year before would have sneered at Iowan hicks, he'd recently remarked at the fittingness of referring to the Midwest as America's "heartland" with a straight face. At Solomon Drive, he'd been a slob; at Prague Porches, craving busywork, he'd become a neatnik. Curtailing his verbal incontinence had introduced my brother to the big wide world of listening to someone else. After our late-night confessional dialogues, he was far less prone to broadcast a numbing barrage about Charles Mingus or Chick Corea as a substitute for saying what he felt. I was at a loss to explain it, but he'd dropped a great deal more than weight, as a consequence of which my revamped brother was a challenge to parody. But if his double was only so witty, it was only so insulting, too, and Edison loved it.

The doorbell rang again, and my pulse womped. Everyone else was here.

I'd spent an atrocious proportion of the previous six months muttering indignant diatribes to my estranged husband, and when Cody let fly something cutting about her dad I lapped it up. I was furious with him, walking away when all I was trying to do was help my own brother, and I could get pretty unattractively self-righteous on this point. I'd even worried that when he

showed up I'd lose my temper and ruin the evening with a shout-
ing match. We'd never staged scenes in public in the past, but I
was bursting with a sense of injustice, and maybe it wasn't only
Edison who had changed.

So it was a shock to open the door and melt. I'd forgotten
how handsome he was—maybe not to every woman's taste, but
I found his Pinocchio pointiness appealing. He'd dressed in a
nice shirt and slacks—respectfully, for Edison's big night. His
expression was anxious, his stance awkward. He wasn't looking
for a fight.

"Hey," he said.

"Hey," I said. We smiled.

"I brought a friend," he said, and for one horrible instant
before he stepped aside I thought he was about to introduce another woman.

"Tanner! You're back!" I hugged my stepson, burnished with
a California tan, and looking more grown-up, yet also chastened.
"Is this for keeps, or just a visit?"

"For keeps, long as Dad'll have me."

"What happened in L.A.?"

"Oh, Pando. How long you got?"

"Not long enough for now. Go say hello to your uncle.
Get yourself something to eat—there's loads. Since you're eighteen, and under parental supervision"—I glanced at Fletcher for
permission—"you might as well have a drink."

"Christ, is that *Edison*?" Tanner last saw his uncle a hundred
pounds heavier.

"Essence of Edison." Once Tanner left to clap my brother on
the back, I lingered in the foyer. "Thanks for coming."

"I said I would."

"You always do what you say you'll do."

"Yes, though—that can be a problem." He touched my elbow. "You look beautiful."

"Thanks." I wondered why he couldn't have extended the compliment when it would have meant so much to me at Java Joint back in April.

"I haven't nixed the whole idea," Tanner was telling Edison. "But I couldn't stand the idea of ending up like that. God, he never shut up about all this boring crap he did ages ago. Really started getting to me. Like, don't take this wrong, but your dad is sad. I don't mean depressed, even if he should be. I mean *sad*. And those actors from *JC*? Sinclair? Tiffany? *Loooooo-sers*."

"He's agreed to finish high school," said Fletcher. "You were right."

"My, I don't hear that very often."

"You might be hearing it a lot more often from now on."

"That'll be a change. That is, hearing anything."

"Your brother looks fantastic. You've worked a miracle."

"It's not my accomplishment," I demurred, though just then it did feel like my accomplishment. I'd never been good at drawing or painting; Edison Redux was my lone work of art.

Lacking a glass—all night, I'd yet to see him imbibe a thing—my brother rapped the scale for quiet. "Yo, since I see our doubting Thomas has made his appearance, it's time for our little soirée's *piece of resistance*. You folks ready, man? *Dig this*." He shrugged out of his heavy coat, and handed it to me. He slipped off his shoes as well before stepping up to the stern arbiter of his whole last year. The needle swung up, down, up again, and settled: just over 161.

The room erupted. I have never attended a single sporting

event, church service, concert, musical, or election victory rally that duplicated the same explosion of spontaneous joy. I don't want to sound sacrilegious, but on a throne from Walmart my brother exuded a messianic promise for everyone in that room. What he'd done wasn't only about becoming more attractive or less prone to diabetes. He'd proved it possible to reverse the most nefarious of misfortunes: those that you've authored yourself.

Edison raised his hand for the cheers to die down. "Listen, man. It's been a long year. But it's also been one of the best years. Maybe *the* best. I've got down with this Iowa thing. Like the doll says, '*These cornfields are the shit!*' But otherwise . . ." If he'd rehearsed the speech in his head, he was getting emotional, and the prepared phrases had fled. "I'd never've been able to do this by myself, man. It's fucking lonely when you can't go out to eat with cats or even meet for a drink. You got no idea how time drags without food! And we all have those moments of weakness, know what I'm sayin'? I needed company, and moral support, and even somebody to figure out how to fucking *do* this, when losing two hundred twenty-three big ones—"

"Two-twenty-*five*!" shouted Cody.

"Well, you can imagine at the beginning it seemed motherfucking impossible. And then when I got on a roll, I also needed somebody to force me to get real. Since there was a point, I swear, I wasn't puttin' another bite in my mouth for the rest of my life, and without a gun to my head and a bowl of soup I might have died. See, most of all I needed somebody who believed in me more than I believed in myself. Who loved me more than I loved myself. Who was willing to put more on the line than I'd ever put on the line for anybody else. So I want you all to raise a glass, man."

Oliver poured Edison a glass of wine, which, post-weigh-in, he accepted.

"To my sister, Pandora."

"To Pandora!" our guests shouted raucously back, draining glasses in a gulp.

Edison pulled me up with him on the scale. I glanced behind us at the dial: together we totaled over a hundred pounds less than my brother had once weighed by himself. He put an arm around me and smiled wickedly at my husband.

"Now, as some of you folks know, Fletch here was *skeptical* that his wife's, quote, 'lardbucket' of a brother had it in him to go the distance. The resolve of this, quote, 'broke, homeless, self-indulgent food junkie' was sure to collapse, because if you put Edison Appaloosa in a room with a plate of french fries, quote, 'the spuds win every time.' This cat was so sure he had my number—which at that time was three-eighty-six—that he promised to eat a whole chocolate cake in a sitting if I ever hit one-sixty-three. So now my pal here ain't just gonna eat it; he's gonna *fletcherize* the bastard. Cody—you wanna do the honors?"

"I don't think I can carry it by myself."

"Tanner, give the girl a hand."

My stepchildren returned from the kitchen carrying the cutting board, and everyone started to laugh.

"Edison, you sadistic joker," cried Oliver. "That's not vindication, it's homicide!"

The Chocolate Dump Cake was the size of a small suitcase. The kids' grip on the board looked precarious, so I hustled off the scale to clear space on the table. Edison had gone to town on the decoration, bordering the top with a keyboard motif of white chocolate and Tootsie Rolls, in the center of which spangled a big

163 in M&Ms whose last digit Cody was hastily rearranging into a *1*, giving her uncle credit for every ounce. In one gooey brown corner Edison had propped a little porcelain crow; a small magazine cutout of a pie that, half submerged in fudge icing, looked suitably humble; and nine tiles from our Scrabble set spelling out Y-O-U-R W-O-R-D-S. It was this section he carved for Fletcher's slice. My husband looked sufficiently rattled by being the center of attention that I doubt he solved the rebus puzzles. Yet he accepted the plate gamely, and though he hated public speaking he realized some reciprocal ceremony was required.

"First off, I notice some of you folks brought gifts," said Fletcher, reaching for a package in his sports jacket. "So—here."

Edison unwrapped the rectangle suspiciously, but when he pulled back the paper he held the box aloft like a scalp. "DVDs of *The Thin Man*!"

"I admit, I underestimated this guy," Fletcher continued, desperate to relinquish the limelight. "So if this stuff makes me sick, well"—he raised a forkful as others had raised their glasses—"I deserve it."

The party cheered Fletcher's first oversize bite, which left the very fecal smears of icing around his mouth that my brother had envisaged with such pleasure.

"Now, all you cats better help Fletch out," Edison announced. "Grab a plate, and that concludes our formal festivities for tonight's show!"

"You going to be able to finish that one piece?" I asked quietly.

"Watch me." Fletcher fished a Scrabble tile from his mouth and sucked off the icing. "Under the circumstances, I guess he's letting me off lightly. And don't tell him—but it's pretty damn good."

As the guests lined up, Edison cut me the sliver he knew I'd prefer. Turning the fork handle in my direction seemed both tender and proprietary.

"I can't eat that and hold your coat," I said. "Should I put it with the others in your bedroom?"

"Nah. Lemme put it back on." He glanced at Fletcher as I held the arms open. "I swear, Panda Bear must have gone all the way to Italy to find this thing."

After smoothing the cape and raising his collar, I whispered, "Congratulations" with a kiss on the cheek.

"I meant all I said, babe," said Edison, brushing a lock of hair up my forehead. "Never coulda done it without you. Wouldn'ta meant nothin' without you, either." His hand carried down and rested on my bare shoulder. I didn't mind my brother being affectionate, and the *cats* in New York had always been pally, with lots of back-clapping and hand-slapping. So it wasn't the physicality that made me uncomfortable, but the tinge of claiming. I wasn't sure that he'd have brushed that lock of hair or squeezed my shoulder in quite that manner if Fletcher hadn't been watching.

"You've cooked all day and haven't eaten a thing. Let me fix you a plate of some real food." My assembly of a square of lasagna and a pool of ratatouille from the buffet beside us probably read to Fletcher as more collusive tending between thick-as-thieves siblings, but really it was a ruse to get out from under that hand.

"You guys sure fixed this place up," Fletcher said behind me.

"Yeah, we're thinking of getting a big Turkish rug for this room," said Edison. "Warm the pad up a little. Though Panda and I are considering a long bike trip next summer, like, following the Mississippi all the way down to the delta and back? You know anybody might want to apartment sit, lemme know."

"If I meet anyone looking for a room," said Fletcher, "I'll send them your way."

"Truth is, I think my sister needs more than a vacation. She's getting antsy at Monotonous. We've talked about her handing over the day-to-day management to me. So she can blue-sky a little, dig? Maybe start something new."

"I'm surprised. You're not going back to New York?"

"No plans to just yet. Not unless Pandora gets it into her head to head to the city, and she's pretty committed to this Iowa scene. Me, I'm cool with it. All those fields, the light . . . Somethin' *spiritual* going down here, know what I'm sayin'?"

"I know what you're *sayin'*," said Fletcher.

I offered Edison his plate.

"Whoa! You tryin' to reverse all our hard work?"

"I'm trying to keep you from fainting."

"Pandora," said Fletcher. "Is there somewhere we could talk in private?"

"Well . . . sure, I suppose."

Edison looked wary. "You be nice to her. This is as much my sister's party as it is mine."

"I'll be nice to her," said Fletcher, though I wondered if that wasn't what Edison was afraid of.

Taking my cake and wine, I led Fletcher to my bedroom with apprehension. Since his arrival I'd seized on his every casual remark that might indicate we had a future. But this was a man who'd announced in no uncertain terms that he wanted a divorce. He'd only come tonight because of an old, rash, silly wager, not because of me. I was loath to relive that rejection while collecting dirty plates, ending this of all evenings in tears.

I put the refreshments on my bedside table, where Fletcher

also slid his killer square of *humble cake*. Closing the door felt oddly outré, though technically we were still married. I perched on the edge of the bed. Fletcher pulled up a chair opposite.

"Are you really going to keep living with your brother? Bike the Mississippi, go into business together?"

"I don't know. I don't have any plans at the moment."

"Your brother sure does."

"I've been very focused on the completion of this undertaking. On which I officially signed off only twenty minutes ago."

"Well, whatever you decide to do . . ." Fletcher kneaded his hands and looked at the floor. "I wanted to say I'm sorry."

I waited. Fletcher may have been a man of few words, but this cryptic apology was insufficient. "Sorry for what?"

"You've been in a bubble with him. I haven't been able to get in. All the in-jokes about *Joint Custody*. A whole hunk of your life I don't have access to . . ."

"Everyone has a childhood."

"I didn't. Not like yours. What you're always saying, and you're right: I don't know what it's like to have a sibling. Far as I can tell, it's like all the good stuff of a marriage and none of the crap."

"Oh, there's plenty of crap. And some of the good stuff is missing."

"But you've seemed so happy here—despite what Cody says, since I can see right through her. Even happier—than with me."

"That's because I've had a project. A sense of purpose." Strains of Edison and Cody's piano duet of "He Ain't Heavy, He's My Brother" filtered through the door.

"Don't you have a sense of purpose with me?"

"Can we get this straight? What are you saying?"

"He's a new man. Not only the weight. He actually seems—a *little* less annoying. I thought you were being selfish. But it was the opposite of selfish. I should never have punished you for your own generosity."

It's a rare business when any woman gets exactly what she wants to hear from a man, but a grudge was nagging. "Back in April, when we met at Java Joint. Why were you so withholding, when I'd stinted with those crummy envelopes for months? Why couldn't you at least bring yourself to say, 'Looking good!'?"

"Because you weren't looking good," he said readily.

"*Great.*"

"You were too thin! You looked pale and weak and you scared me half to death. Honest to God, I almost said something admiring, more than once, and stopped myself. I was afraid any compliment might have encouraged you to get even thinner."

"I thought . . . you were miffed because you couldn't feel superior to me anymore."

"Superior! You've started a runaway successful company from nothing. You know my carpentry runs at a loss. It isn't even called a business when it doesn't make money. It's a hobby—ask the IRS. As for the cycling, and trying to get a grip on what I eat—well, I've lost my hair, haven't I? I've got kind of a weird face, and you're the only woman who's ever thought I was good-looking. I've been trying to be good enough for you. Slow the rot."

"The nutritional fascism has been a big power trip, with me and the kids both, and you know it. Still, why have you always poured cold water over this whole thing with Edison, when by your own lights it should have been an effort you applauded?"

"Maybe I was a little unnerved by your beating me at my

own game. Along with beating me at everything else. Fitness, a healthy lifestyle—it's all I've got."

"Oh, it is not. Your furniture is gorgeous."

"Then why do I stockpile most of it?"

"We should probably work harder to get you into some of those big shows on the East Coast."

"So do you mean . . . ?"

"Let's not get ahead of ourselves. Again, you are saying *what*?"

"Want me to spell it out?"

I nodded, although I appreciated that his evasiveness was not springing from presumption or pride, but anxiety. The trouble with direct questions is that they solicit direct answers, one of which could always be "no."

He reached for my hand, and the difference between this touch and Edison's, the extra charge, was a shock. "I asked you once before, but you weren't finished, and I understand that now. Please come home."

"What's changed? Is it Tanner?"

"Partly. He's my only son. I thought your family had ruined him."

"You should have more faith in both of us."

"But I guess the main thing that's changed . . . Well, the year. The whole interminable year you said you'd be gone." He raised his eyebrows. "It's over."

We weren't discovered in flagrante delicto, but merely kissing fully clothed. Even if we had been nakedly entwined, it was my bedroom, and I was lying with my legal husband, which doesn't rank as a transgression anywhere I know.

"Excuse me," said Edison coldly. "Corcoran and Novacek are leaving, and I thought you might want to say goodbye." He closed the door with a sharp report of reproach.

When we emerged well over an hour later—you can imagine we had a lot to talk about, including how weird that intrusion had been—I was surprised to open the door to an uncanny quiet. Most of the guests must have cleared off, though it was just past eleven p.m. The gathering had been so jubilant; I couldn't imagine what had driven them home. Though Edison's computer wouldn't have run through its packed playlist, the speakers were silent.

Anxious to conceal from Edison that Fletcher had reneged on dispatching the whole of his lenient portion of cake, I crept with our plates to the kitchen, where the dishwasher was already churning. Cody and Oliver were rinsing and stacking the remaining china—cautiously resting plates so they didn't rattle, like harried parents who'd barely managed to put a baby to sleep. Wrapped leftovers still sat on the counter, and as I jigsaw-puzzled them into the fridge Cody shot me a look I couldn't decipher.

"I can't imagine how Edison will get through all this food," I said. Softly spoken, my remark rang jarringly loud, and I was left with the odd impression that this had been the wrong thing to say.

"Done what I can do, so I'm heading off," said Oliver. "And, listen, tomorrow?" He, too, gave me a look, brimming with a mysterious sympathy. *"Call me."*

Intending to give Tanner a hand with collecting the last glasses, I walked into the living room—where Fletcher was standing stock-still, lips parted, as if mesmerized by the gruesome climax of a horror movie.

One foot on the piano bench, Edison was tipping a chair back beside our new dining table, on which only the cake remained. His right hand was gucked with icing and clinging crumbs to the third knuckle, and he'd smeared butter-cream fudge onto the sleeve of the leather trench coat. The cream shirt with its tracery of musical scores was marred down the front with chocolate stains. He wore an airy, bemused expression, and had timed his next claw into the cake with my exit from the kitchen.

Perhaps owing to the nature of the occasion, our guests had cut sparing pieces, and two-thirds of the monster was leftover. Or had been leftover, since I could discern the original blade-sharp borders, into which a rough gouge crudely intruded. The missing chunk itself the size normally baked for birthdays, the cake looked mauled.

"Whaddya think, Feltch? Think *I* can finish it?" My brother grinned; his teeth were blacked in the interstices with chocolate, which made them look decayed. The smears around his mouth were brown, not red of course, but still reminded me of a coyote's bloodied snout when stuck into cow. Edison swigged from the bottle of whiskey and wiped a dribble with his sleeve.

"Stop it," I said.

"Seems to me I don't take orders from you no more," said Edison, his voice slurred from icing or scotch or a great deal of both. "Ain't your year of indentured servitude officially *finito*? 'Sides. I earned a little indulgence, didn't I?" He reached to pull the string of his present from my employees, now flopped beside the platter as if having binged itself unconscious, and the doll spouted, "I lived on four envelopes of powder per day for six months. Beat that, motherfucker."

"That doesn't look like *a little* indulgence. Now, cut it out.

It's not going to work. Not this time. Cody? Tanner? Are you ready to go?" I put on my coat.

"Where are *you* going?" said Edison. "When you're already home?"

"I'm going home-home." I took Fletcher's hand.

"This just a sleepover, or a desertion?"

Fletcher said, "Look, your sister just gave you a solid year of her life—"

"And now the bell's rung. Time! I get it." Edison picked an M&M off the icing, now garnished with cigarette ash.

"This is blackmail," I said, and nodded at the kids. "Come on."

Cody hung back. "Maybe Edison needs company right now."

"Company is exactly what your uncle doesn't need, sweetie. Believe me."

Removing my brother's real family entire at a stroke, Fletcher and I walked out with the kids trailing, as Cody shot her uncle the kind of backward glance that in the Bible would have turned her to salt.

III: Out

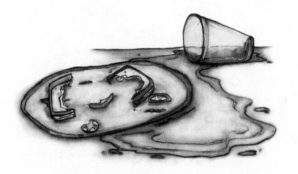

I didn't abandon my brother, but I found our visits painful, and spaced them widely to spare myself. The rapidity with which he gained back every pound seemed biologically unfeasible, and Edison grew impatient with my proclivity for bursting into tears. He assumed a droll blitheness during the proceeding months, an infuriating whimsy. He relished afflicting his sister, for whom he would stage theatrical binges on whole cherry pies or gallons of Rocky Road. For that airiness he'd assumed while mauling the Chocolate Dump Cake did not abate, and he soon acted as if our onerous endeavor at Prague Porches had simply been a lark, at which he now looked back with a wheezy *hee-hee-hee*. Cody was more faithful about stopping by an apartment whose rent, for reasons opaque to me, I was still paying. Her nature is forgiving, though even my stepdaughter returned from these missions disconsolate. In an apartment that could increasingly be described as a rat hole, he was growing into a shut-in, having given up the bike but no longer enjoying access to my car.

358 · lionel shriver

I never saw him in that leather trench coat again. After a couple of months, it would no longer have fit.

I did read him the riot act more than once before the situation got too far out of hand, but he was impervious to my displeasure, on which if anything he feasted. As the months wore on and his dimensions continued to swell, we went back to the say-no-evil policy of his arrival in New Holland, when any mention of the elephant in the room had seemed impolite.

About two years into Edison's backslide, I did make one last-ditch effort to get my brother to feel invested in himself again. Through Slack Muncie I tracked down the ex-wife Sigrid, who reluctantly put me in touch with her son Carson, now nineteen and playing the trumpet at the same Brooklyn dives in which Edison had performed before decamping to Iowa. As I expected, Carson was curious about his dad, and accepted the ticket to Cedar Rapids that I offered him over the phone.

I wasn't about to mug my brother at his door with his long-lost son, so we asked this lovely young man to stay at our house. I lured Edison from his lair, arranging to meet at the outside tables of an upper-level restaurant in Westdale Mall, whose armless chairs wouldn't present too tight a squeeze. My nephew and I arrived a few minutes early, and I spotted Edison rising from the escalator. He shambled toward our table, but the moment he recognized the boy—perhaps he'd followed his son's budding musical career online—he froze. His face turned red as a stoplight. With more alacrity than you'd think a man that size could marshal, he turned heel. Carson followed my gaze, and must have glimpsed the back of a big man in yard-wide jeans. Called to a loyalty still more primal than the one I owed this near-stranger nephew, I said nothing. We waited forty-five more minutes, nursing Cokes, until I said I guess he isn't coming, I'm sorry. Carson was disappointed. And my, did I get it in the neck from Edison the next day. "Do I want my son to see me like this, man? What were you thinking?" Somewhere in there still lurked the old sense of pride.

Which is why I was relieved when Travis died immediately thereafter: thank God I had thought to email our father the photograph I snapped of Edison on the cusp of his Coming of Size party. Eager, luminous, and lean, that image would have been the last portrait of his firstborn with which Travis had been left, making a death that hit Edison unexpectedly hard a trace easier to accept. In single moments we appear our deep, true selves, and I was lucky to have captured then, as I'd told Tanner that night, "essence of Edison," which I've had framed and continue to contemplate, always with a complicated falling sensation, on the wall of my study.

Whether my product became passé or was the victim of a vertiginous economic downturn wasn't clear, but orders at Baby Monotonous did indeed dry up, and this was one project whose reversal left me dry-eyed. I was sorry to let my employees go, but if I hadn't closed up shop promptly I'd have lost my family's savings. Besides, the company had been founded on a good joke that had worn thin. Our pull-string dolls had too often evidenced a mean streak that didn't suit me, and when I sold off the sewing machines and shut the warehouse for good I felt lighter and cleaner.

At least I didn't have to fire Edison, who never returned to work after that party. Instead, after he'd eaten through his savings, he got a job . . .

N o, I said he'd become "a virtual shut-in," didn't I? So maybe he started working from home doing . . .

O r strike that. He was able to live off the windfall from . . .

N o, an inheritance would be risible. Travis contrived to leave this earth as we all should: house refinanced, credit cards maxed.

Come to think of it, why on earth would Edison stay in Iowa? Why would any New York jazz musician have moved to Iowa in the first place? How would a chronically self-deceiving hedonist like my brother ever lose 225 pounds in a single year?

I 'm sorry, but I can't keep this up. It's all a lie. Or nearly.

T his much is true: Tanner did in fact go through a protracted and largely awful informal internship with his
step-grandfather. He did come back to Iowa and finish high
school, though after graduation he followed up on an old contact from Edison, and he's now a runner for HBO. I really have
learned not to be "pre-disappointed" for my children, no matter
how seemingly unattainable their hopes, and that really is advice I got from Edison somewhere along the line. I *have* folded
Baby Monotonous—though I now miss the very solicitations to
do this and that interview that I'd come to find so irksome; that
is, I miss finding them irksome. (Maybe it's more satisfying to
fend off the world's attentions and howl at the heavens that you
long to be left in peace than to be left in peace. Which is to say:

you can't win.) Travis really did suffer a fatal stroke. But in truth, Cody is still painfully shy, and would never be coaxed into playing the piano for a whole party of adults. Under her uncle's brief tutelage she did learn to improvise a little, but in short order she ceased altogether to stray from the notes on the page.

The rest is a story I tell myself, and not a convincing one. Maybe my imagination finally failed in that flailing of ellipses because for my hip, downtown brother to have buried himself anonymously in the middle of the country is fanciful, especially after he'd already buried himself in himself, hiding between the perimeters of his own enormity as I have hidden between coasts. He was never a disciplined man, and chances are that a prolonged crash diet with little envelopes would have proved beyond him. For me to suppose that he might have made such a sacrifice if only to please me is to exaggerate my importance to him and to grossly inflate my influence (always tiny). In other words, I flatter myself. As for that character transformation I celebrated, maybe it was just a device for explaining what about my brother bugged me, what I would have changed if I could have, which I couldn't. All that girlhood admiration was genuine enough, but admiration keeps its object at bay. When you look up to someone, you turn a blind eye to more complex or disheartening information that takes him down a peg but also turns him into a real person. In consequence, I never knew my brother very well. I remained in awe of the man from a distance. Close up, he was often trying, and I preferred his company in small doses.

Rest assured that, right up until my wistful visit to our guestroom on Solomon Drive while Edison was packing, this tale is earnestly recounted. Bloated literally beyond recognition, my brother did visit my family for two very long months, although I never urged him onto any industrial-grade scale, and his then weighing "386" is merely a wild guess. He and Fletcher did not get along. That night before his flight back to LaGuardia, I was indeed seized by an impulse to propose something rash— perhaps a sequestering of just us two, so that I could coach him to lose weight and come to some better understanding of why he'd gained it in the first place. Yet I bit my tongue. I knew Fletcher would find the idea absurd, and wouldn't take kindly to a desertion. My marriage was just young enough that I didn't want to test it, and I told myself as well that I had adopted two children, who had to come first. The truth was less noble: Live still longer and even more intensively with my difficult brother, assume the rank of four-star general in the Confectioner's Sugar Wars? I just didn't want to.

So rather than unfurl my grand accord and offer to rent us our own apartment, I wandered downstairs and checked the laundry, discovering that pair of jeans that I pretended we used on our snowman and later deployed as tongue-in-cheek décor at an apocryphal "Coming of Size" party. I brought them upstairs so Edison could pack them, dreading the prospect of coming upon this flag of his metamorphosis once he was gone. I drove him to the airport the following afternoon, in plenty of time to catch his plane. On my return home, the empty, broken-down maroon recliner at the head of the table was so upsetting that I had Fletcher cart it to the dump with his pickup the very next day.

After that, I kept in sporadic touch with Edison through email and telephone. Since neither medium forced me to confront the spectacle he had become, this communication required little. I bought him health insurance, which was frankly in my interest. I sent him money from time to time. I wish I'd sent more.

In the months proceeding Edison's departure I did make a soldierly effort at losing some weight myself, since that nonsense about my having dropped fifty-four pounds in sibling solidarity was just as outlandish as Edison's equally fictitious deflation. I did eventually starve off about fifteen "big ones," not through any all-liquid diet but the conventional stinting portions. It was a tedious period for the whole household, and the results left me indifferent. Experiencing the same mutinous reaction to my mortification of the flesh as I had to his own puritanism, at last Fletcher grew less militant about food. With the miraculous resurrection of manicotti, Cody and even Tanner on his return from L.A. made fewer excuses to skip the family meal.

Nowadays, we're all bored to death with fretting over what one should and shouldn't eat, and through the arbitrary choices of largely apathetic diners we've maintained a varied and not especially terrible diet. Granted, when Cody came home last Christmas after her first semester at Reed our beanpole had grown stocky, but that's common at an age of late-night brownie-bonding, and I haven't said anything. I've regained a handful of that lost poundage myself, and I don't care. I remain a solid twenty pounds overweight, and plan to stay that way. I gladly trade a svelte figure for the capacity to think about something else. If I am not the most attractive woman in this part of Iowa, I am also not a pill.

After Edison's marathon visit to New Holland, I next saw my brother in L.A. for Travis's memorial two years later. I'd sent him a business-class ticket, in the hopes that a more luxurious seat and flight attendants who would feign being nice to him would make up for the fact that by then he found flying logistically treacherous. Fletcher, Cody, and I flew ahead and met him at the airport in a capacious limo. We were elaborately patient with the slowness of his gait, and all went to a great deal of trouble to ensure that he did not feel he was any trouble. He didn't exasperate me anymore, not even Fletcher. Instead he inspired a crippling tenderness. He'd gotten bigger, you see. By then suffering from emphysema, he pulled an oxygen tank behind him everywhere he went like a dog, and only removed the air hose from his nose to light another cigarette.

We all met Solstice for dinner that night, and she was such a mess that I had to ask our waiter for extra napkins so she could blow her nose. Edison and I had always imagined that Solstice grew up in a different family, having missed out on Travis's heyday as a TV star, but with two siblings who'd shunned her in order to feel closer to one another and a mother who died when she was three, she'd pretty much grown up with *no* family. When she wouldn't hear a word against our father, I discovered what a gaping hole the man left behind: without Travis to hack on, Edison and I had shockingly little to talk about.

We held the reception in our father's favorite Mexican restaurant, which rented its back room for private parties. Tanner took time out from hustling for an entry-level job in television to pay his respects; after all, Rosita's was a twenty-minute drive from his grungy apartment share. Even the surviving cast of *Joint Custody* made an appearance. Edison's and my ridicule of these icons-cum-nemeses had been more fun behind their backs. The actors we'd despised had been children, and there was nothing to be gained from mocking middle-aged has-beens whom we barely recognized. A testimony to the success of antiretrovirals,

Sinclair Vanpelt still had a hand in television, and was talking up a pilot that didn't sound promising: a gay take on *The Odd Couple*, when the original series had been about a virtual-gay relationship already. Sinclair emblemized that sort who receives just enough B-list recognition to keep bashing his head against the wall. Then mobilizing what would prove an unsuccessful bid for the Senate, Floy Newport was predictably warm; having been a child actor had foreshortened into a quaint curiosity of her bio. Refurbished by Narcotics Anonymous, Tiffany Kite had become a fundraiser for battered-women's shelters. I wondered if personal experience had attracted her to the cause, or whether she simply wanted people to make that assumption, the better to play the drama queen.

Maybe this phenomenon was more noticeable in California: while milling under the bright piñatas that dangled from the ceiling, I was struck by how people who hadn't seen each other in years were literally *sizing each other up*, this mental weigh-in a ridiculous shorthand estimation of how we were faring in other spheres. Sinclair looked drawn and scrawny, but the slimming effect of AIDS didn't inspire much envy. Like me, Floy had put on just enough padding to make her seem down-to-earth, which may have been to her electoral advantage. Tiffany was skeletal, and exuded that prim, neurotic brittleness that drove me to a second quesadilla. Naturally, Edison dwarfed anyone else's thriving gut into a throw pillow. In the mourners' defense, the jalapeño-spiked air of Rosita's back room went thick with compassion. Travis's friends and former associates all made a point of talking to Edison, though they appeared to have a dreadful time looking him in the eye.

Impelled to shield Edison from their pity, Cody and I were

solicitous, finding him a suitable chair when he got tired, or grabbing him an extra crab burrito from a passing platter. I acted as interlocutor with strangers, explaining that we were Travis's children, my introductions of my brother the widely recorded New York jazz pianist defiantly unapologetic. Whether from the stress of the previous couple of years or our father's death, he was subdued. I missed his bluster. I wanted to hear about the tours and the CDs and the gigs and the high-flying colleagues, even if he had to make them up.

Nevertheless, in my alternative-reality fairy tale, why did I conclude with a fall from grace initiated by that Chocolate Dump Cake (a real recipe that I tried once, found too heavy and sickly sweet, and never baked again), rather than fashion a proper happily-ever-after ending? You know, newly lithe brother lives on 2 percent milk forever more, runs marathons, falls in love, maybe even sires a couple of children who aren't borrowed from his sister, continues to play the piano as an avid amateur while contentedly pursuing a modest calling to pay the bills—he could be a seed salesman, why not?—and joins numerous civic organizations in his adoptive state . . .

Surely it's obvious. I was letting myself off the hook. *See? However extravagant, your intercession wouldn't have worked anyway. It never works, does it? Had you put your time and even marriage on the line, and had he improbably cared enough to please you, Edison would still have lost weight for the wrong reasons, and what do you want to bet he'd have gained it all back?* Of course, there are plenty of heroic exceptions to those gargantuas who lose hundreds of pounds and then on average gain back all but seven, and I never attempted to discover if my brother might be among them.

A year ago, Edison Appaloosa died from the complications of congestive heart failure. It wasn't clear-cut that his death was the direct result of his weight. Strictly speaking, what killed him was one of those hospital infections. But then, the overtaxing of a body weakens the immune system, and the heart failure itself was unquestionably occasioned by a circulatory system strangled by excess tissue.

My brother had been in and out of the hospital several times by then, and his doctor at St. Luke's hadn't portrayed the situation as life threatening before Edison took a turn for the worse. I was rushing to arrange an immediate flight to New York when I received Slack Muncie's call, assuring me sadly that I could now take my time. I gave St. Luke's permission to proceed with cremation; renowned for work with obese patients, the facility possessed the large-capacity incinerator that Edison required. I didn't urge them to wait until I could view the body because I wanted to preserve as best I could the image of my brother as I had known him for most of my life.

I caught the flight anyway, and Slack insisted on meeting my plane, though he had to take the subway and then a bus. He invited me to stay at his apartment in Williamsburg. Once I got a look at the place, I was adamant about booking into a hotel in order not to crowd him, but I could finally appreciate the generosity of Edison's most steadfast comrade. The lanky saxophonist had put my brother up for years in a cramped one-bedroom, where Edison had slept semireclining in the living room's La-Z-Boy. Slack had laid out my brother's tiny stash of chattel, in case I wanted keepsakes: that once-white, early-generation Mac now grayed by ashy fingerprints. The great shapeless black cardigan, scattered with hard holes from cigarette burns. A bottle of my brother's favorite barbecue sauce. A box of CDs on which Edison had played that he'd never been able to sell. A fat rubber-banded stack of envelopes comprising correspondence with the IRS, which had been hounding him apparently, and a spiral notebook full of lists of income and expenses going back a decade: cash fees from door gigs of $22, $13.50; a debit of $42 for a taxi. I wept at the waste.

It was Slack who filled me in about how Edison had grown desperate enough to go by "Caleb Fields" for a time. How his dabbling in heroin had made Sigrid walk out with his unborn son. How aping Travis by acting the prima donna had earned him a toxic reputation. How Edison was forced to sell the Schimmel only to subsequently "eat the piano." How his band's fee was docked because he'd gorged on the buffet at a wedding gig. How he lost nearly all his possessions when he fell behind on the rent for self-storage. How his friends got together and found him that little hideaway above Three Bars in Four-Four, only for Edison to blow it by pilfering from the kitchen after hours. I might have inferred something of the sort once my brother admitted that his tour of Spain and Portugal was fabricated, but I'd shied from construing from that one lie all the heartache that might lurk behind it, and I'd had no idea.

Instead of driving Edison to the airport that afternoon in late November, should I have offered to shunt him off to an ad hoc rehab at Prague Porches, a real development a couple of miles from here? I'm never certain. In any event, this parallel universe has grown hauntingly alive to me since Edison's death at the untimely age of forty-nine: dissecting tiny triangles of shrimp tail at the Last Supper. Dancing at our Ketosis Party. Railing and then relenting after uncovering the pizza box. Renting Edison a piano and hearing him adventure into *West Side Story* and Lyle Lovett. Seeing those cheekbones rise again into the sunlight for the first time. Biking and hiking and sandbagging together, reciting our fractured oaths, *I pledge aversion to the flab of the derided waists of America*, with all the attendant hilarity, until he steps onto a scale before a host of witnesses who've grown to love him and weighs in at a triumphant 161.

Of course, I never arranged to fly Edison's son to Iowa— although the boy did meet his father shortly before Travis's stroke. On his own initiative, Carson located his dad at Three Bars in Four-Four, where Edison was known to still congregate with his friends. My brother called me that very night—waking us up, though I didn't mind. He was exhilarated, sincerely for once, not generating the usual billows of optimism as a smoke-screen, hoping to nurture a relationship with his only child at last. But Carson never got in touch again, and the contact de-tails he'd provided his father in the club that night turned out to be bogus. I assumed the kid was shell-shocked. Edison in that expanded form wouldn't have offered up the image of the ideal dad.

To my surprise, Carson introduced himself at Edison's im-pressively well-populated memorial at Three Bars. Tall, under-fed, and sharing the bright knurl of his father's hair at that age, he delivered condolences in great earnest. I had hopes the boy's attendance was meant to help compensate for breaking his fa-ther's heart—as, I reminded myself, Edison must have repeatedly broken his son's. Effectively fatherless for most of his life, Carson had far more to forgive than his dad's dimensions. Thanking the young man profusely for coming, I was prepared to enfold him into our family, until Cody—hardly a cynic—pulled me aside. "I talked to that little worm for twenty minutes," she whispered. "All he wanted to know was what make of car you drive, do we have a swimming pool, and did your company ever make the Fortune 500. He gives me the creeps."

Smashingly handsome at twenty-two, yet having shed the narcissism that marred him in high school, Tanner sidled beside his sister. "You're not going to believe this. That guy? My *stepcousin*? I watched him slip three bottles of wine into his backpack. I mean, let him have them. But really. Pretty low rent."

Sure enough, after a series of passionate, touchingly inarticulate testimonials by my brother's fellow musicians, Carson impaired my enjoyment of the proceeding jam session with fulsome fawning over Baby Monotonous—the very yakking-over-the-music that Edison had often decried. By the time Fletcher rescued me, the boy was supposing that I might like to establish a "grant program" in his father's honor, providing stipends for aspiring jazz musicians.

I'd presumed that at nineteen the boy had tracked down his father for the usual reasons: to understand his origins, to fill the maw in his childhood. Now I had to wonder if the young man had merely been nosing around for resources, which Edison conspicuously lacked. To be fair, his father must have meant something to Carson, unless a penchant for jazz is genetic. And given Edison's neglect, maybe a son's callous opportunism was one more misfortune that my brother had actively courted.

His paternal shortcomings aside, during this last year I've listened to Edison's CDs with the concentration I might have applied when they were freshly recorded. I've come to believe that my brother was a fine musician. What a travesty, were he mostly remembered for being fat.

Had you told me when I was younger that my brother would get that heavy I'd have been incredulous. Yet taking a step back, I wonder if the story isn't pretty simple. Edison's life started out exciting and ascendant, and then it went into a spiral and he got discouraged. He reached for the one gratification at ready hand, on an assumption he had nothing to lose that became self-fulfilling. That's a sad story, but it isn't mysterious. As for the larger social issue that my brother unintentionally embodied, in the end I can contribute only one small thought. I keep referring back to Baby Monotonous—the baffling lassitude of affluence, the sheer boredom of garnering a surfeit of the very worldly attention of which Edison felt so cheated. The word "disappointment" doesn't begin to cover it. However gnawing a deficiency, satiety is worse. So here is the thought: We are meant to be hungry.

It is impossible to gauge what you owe people. Anyone of course, but especially the blood relation, for as soon as you begin to calculate the amount you're obliged to give—as soon as you begin to keep track, to parcel the benevolence out—you're done for. *In for a penny, in for a pound.* I could not have said, "I will help you lose weight for three months, but not for four." Once I assumed the role of my brother's keeper there would have been no limit, don't you see? And who's to say whether such an escapade wouldn't have ruined my marriage, leaving me as half of a sexless, barren sibling couple in an arid development owned by an overweight Czech? Even under the dubious assumption that my decadent big brother would have found the fortitude to diet to successful effect, who's to say whether in the long run he wouldn't have gained the weight right back? In preference to tackling the byzantine emotional mathematics of my exact responsibility for my brother, it was simpler to adjudge that I bore none. But nothing in this life is free. Having dodged paying the piper while Edison was still alive, I pay now instead. I pay every day.

About the Author

L ionel Shriver's novels include *The New Republic*, the National Book Award finalist *So Much for That*, the *New York Times* bestseller *The Post-Birthday World*, and the international bestseller *We Need to Talk About Kevin*, which won the 2005 Orange Prize and was adapted into a feature film starring Tilda Swinton. Earlier books include *Double Fault*, *A Perfectly Good Family*, and *Checker and the Derailleurs*. Her novels have been translated into twenty-eight different languages. Her journalism has appeared in the *Guardian*, the *New York Times*, the *Wall Street Journal*, and many other publications. She lives in London and Brooklyn, New York.